Resurrecting Rain

Resurrecting Rain

by

Patricia Averbach

Golden Antelope Press
715 E. McPherson
Kirksville, Missouri 63501
2020

ISBN: 978-1-936135-82-0 (1-936135-82-5)

Library of Congress Control Number: 2019951571

Published by:
Golden Antelope Press
715 E. McPherson
Kirksville, Missouri 63501

Available at:
Golden Antelope Press
715 E. McPherson
Kirksville, Missouri, 63501
Phone: (660) 665-0273
http://www.goldenantelope.com
Email: ndelmoni@gmail.com

In Memory of my Sister
Jane Abrams

The stars come out. We're out
of ourselves, but collected. We point
to the new moon, its discipline and slender joy.
—Rumi

And God said to the moon Levanah,"Renew yourself!"
—From *Kiddush Levanah*, traditional Jewish
blessing of the new moon

Part I

Part One

Chapter One

Deena wasn't a drinker, but she unearthed a bottle of vodka from under the sink and a bottle of cranberry juice from the back of the refrigerator. By the time Martin got home from work she was well into her third Crantini. Wednesday was his early night, so it was still light outside when he walked through the back door. Deena was sitting at the breakfast bar they'd installed when they thought that they were rich. Her glass left a pale pink ring on the granite counter.

"This came today. I guess we'd better start looking for an apartment." She took another long swig of her Crantini and held up the final notice from the sheriff's department. She felt as though she were looking at her husband through the wrong end of a telescope. He appeared small and light years away. His eyes were red rimmed and puffy, his skin hung on his large frame like a suit too big for his bones. He was only forty-five, but he had the washed out, done-in look of someone already defeated by life.

Martin took off his coat and hung it in the entry, ignoring the paper dangling from her hand. She stood up, waving it in front of him. "Take it. Read the fine print." She wasn't going to let him look away from the mess that he'd created.

He took the notice, glanced at it briefly, then set it on the counter. "Where's Elliot?" He filled a glass with tap water and stood holding it without drinking.

3

"He's still at the pool. We'll have to tell him when he gets home. I think he'll be OK, but I don't know about Lauren. She's such a drama queen." Deena collapsed back onto the stool and put her head down on the granite, allowing the cool stone to soothe her hot cheeks and overwrought emotions. What was the matter with her? They weren't going to be out on the street. They'd just move into a perfectly decent apartment. God knows, she'd lived in worse, a lot worse.

Martin seemed to read her thoughts. "It's not the end of the world. No one's being marched off to a death camp. We'll get through this."

If her head hadn't been swimming in grief and confusion and vodka maybe she'd have said something consoling, something brave and insightful, but she didn't have it in her at the moment. She felt his hands on her shoulders and stood up abruptly, moving away so she couldn't see the expression on his face. She wanted to hold onto her anger awhile longer and couldn't risk seeing the pain in her husband's eyes. She'd just wind up forgiving him again. "I'd better pick Elliot up. Swim practice is over at six o'clock."

"You've been drinking, I'll go get him." Martin reached over and took a quick swig of her Crantini and made a face. "What is this?"

"Hemlock." Deena opened the refrigerator and pulled out a package of ground meat and some corn tortillas. Tacos were Elliot's favorite; maybe they'd soften the blow. "We'll have to find something in Shaker Heights. There's no way we're making him change schools his senior year."

Elliot arrived home with his hair still wet and smelling of chlorine. He sat at the table, numb and slack mouthed, staring at his plate, his big hands helpless in his lap as Martin tried to conjure consolation from the things that they could keep, things that wouldn't be lost on the auction block. "Your mother and I still have our jobs." Martin's voice sounded strangled; Deena could see the cords bulging in his neck. This was costing him, but he deserved it. "We'll get a nice apartment and you'll graduate with your class, you can still compete with the swim team. Your mom and I would have sold the house when you went off to college anyway." This was a lie. She and Martin had planned to spend the rest of their natural lives in the snug colonial, mortgage free, hiking through the small park down the street and puttering in the garden.

"I don't understand. If you're making all this money, how can we be bankrupt? It doesn't make sense." Elliot was his father's son: logical, deliberate, and responsible to a fault, but he was only seventeen. Deena watched as he struggled to wrap his mind around the mess that was their new reality. High risk real estate speculation wasn't part of his vocabulary; it was a violation of everything he'd been taught, everything he knew about his parents. Deena wanted to defend herself, to say, *it wasn't me. I warned him. I told him not to. He signed those papers without my permission,* but she held her tongue while Martin floundered, searching for the right words. Finally, all he could say was, "I'm sorry. I did the math. I crunched the numbers. It looked like a sure thing."

"What are you talking about? This is crazy. Who gambles away a whole house? I can't deal with this right now." As he shot up from the table, Deena was, as always, amazed by his height, six feet two inches of beautiful, raw, gangly adolescence.

Martin looked as though he'd been struck in the face. He tried to shout, but his voice came out a thin, high pitched whine, "Don't you ever talk to us like that." Deena waited for the rest of the speech. *We're your parents and you're to treat us with respect,* but Martin didn't say another word.

Elliot knocked over his chair as he backed up, set it right without slowing down and headed for the door. "Sorry, I didn't mean that, but I need some time to think. I'll be at Sasha's."

Deena blinked back tears. "Elliott, please we only meant..."

The door slammed and she and Martin were alone in the kitchen. As furious as she was at Martin, Deena was glad Elliot had been spared the sight of his father pleading with her to sign the papers. That argument had been so out of character, so unexpected, that Deena had been blindsided. Her careful, conservative husband, a man terrified of letting time run out on a parking meter, had decided to play at high stakes real estate. A pharmacist who measured everything to the milliliter, he'd ultimately gone behind her back to guarantee a construction loan with the equity in their house and all their savings. The funny thing was, Martin didn't even care about the money.

When Danny first came to them with a business proposition, he said he was giving them the opportunity of a lifetime. Florida real estate was booming and developers couldn't build fast enough to keep up with demand. At the beginning, it was simply a matter of Martin trying to close an old wound from adolescence. His cousin had been a big shot in high school, a star athlete, popular with the girls while Martin had always been on the outside looking in. There'd been a brief period in college when Martin outshone his cousin, making the Dean's list and winning biking marathons, but then Danny married into a Cleveland building dynasty and went into high end real estate leaving Martin in the dust. So, when Danny offered Martin an equity position in River Parc Mall, he mortgaged the house and their life savings, delighted that his cousin had finally dealt him in. Neither of them had been savvy enough to realize that becoming equity partners in River Parc Mall meant they were also buying its debt. That awful realization came later.

Deena wrapped a sheet of foil over Elliot's uneaten dinner. The muscles in her shoulders were so tight that her head was beginning to throb. "That didn't go too well."

"No," Martin's voice was as hollow as his eyes.

"Well, what did you expect? We just ripped the kid's house out from under him."

"I said I'm sorry. I'm sorry, I'm sorry, I'm sorry. What do you want me to do, put a gun to my head?"

"No, don't do that." Deena softened at the sight of the large man hugging himself and rocking back and forth in the kitchen chair. She put her arms around his shoulders. "It's not all your fault. Danny put you up to it."

"How about if I shoot Danny. Would that make you feel better?"

"Maybe." She kissed him on top of his head. " How about just setting fire to his yacht? How many years would we get for that?"

"Don't bother, the yacht's gone. His father-in-law repossessed all his toys."

Deena shook her head. "Don't worry about Danny; his wife may have him on a short leash but he's still sitting pretty in a big house in Moreland Hills. I guarantee he's not worrying about you."

"You're too hard on Danny. Honestly, he thought he was helping us out. How could he predict that both our main tenants would go bankrupt?"

"It was his business to know, due diligence or whatever. Losing both your main tenants to bankruptcy isn't just bad luck it's incompetence or criminal negligence or...I don't know what. But he should have seen it coming. He should have protected us."

"No, it's my fault. I should have protected us." Martin turned to look out the window where twilight was already obliterating the maple and the forsythia hedge. "I should have listened to you."

Deena sat back down and looked across the table. The man who'd once been her rock, the source of everything good and orderly and predictable in her life had become a puddle of remorse. "Do you want some salad?" She held out the wooden bowl as a sort of green peace offering.

Martin stabbed a cherry tomato and stared at it glistening at the end of his fork. "It's a nightmare. Everyone involved in the deal got burned."

Deena glanced around the kitchen with a sense of nostalgia for everything they'd have to leave behind. "What did Allen tell you? How much has to go and what do we get to keep?"

"You know attorneys, they always give you the worst case scenario, but it looks bad. What really hurts is that we're being punished for being so damned responsible and paying things off. If we didn't have so much equity in the house and cars we could probably keep them." He raked his fingers through his thinning hair. "This should never have happened. The deal was fail-safe, guaranteed. There was no way we could lose."

"Well, we lost, now what do we get to keep?" Their house was being sold at auction in one month and she didn't have time for a pity party. They had to make plans, and they had to move fast.

"We can keep most of the furniture and personal stuff. Theoretically, you should turn over your jewelry but Allen says to just keep it. Your wedding ring is exempt and the other stuff isn't that valuable. We can keep your car, but the Honda goes."

"How will you get to work? You have to have a car." Deena looked up in alarm, the impact of their situation hitting her full in the gut. "What about our savings? What about the kids' college fund?"

Martin looked at her with eyes that floated out of focus beneath a pool of tears. She watched him try to speak, then simply swallow and shake his head. So that was that. She couldn't think straight; all she could feel was the cold fear that they'd wind up living in a derelict house with no plumbing and broken windows. After a lifetime of doing everything possible to escape, she was being sucked back into her mother's world. Maybe she'd been marked from birth for a life of poverty and chaos. Maybe it was hubris to think she could elude her fate.

Deena visualized her mother squinting at her, sizing her up then shaking her head in disgust. In memory, Rain, as Leah Marcus had renamed herself, was still the rebellious hippie of her youth. She stood barefoot, arms akimbo, her blond curls alive in the spring wind blowing off the Sangre de Cristo Mountains. "Well, Miss Harmony, you finally got what you had coming." Deena cringed beneath the imagined rebuke. "What did you expect, trading your family for a bunch of junk? Hope you remember how to cover your windows with old newspaper when it gets cold this winter."

Deena got up and staggered to the powder room they'd updated when they still had money, and threw up in the environmentally conscious, low-flow, gravity assisted toilet.

As predicted, Lauren freaked. She wanted to drop out of school and come home the minute she heard there was no money for next year's tuition. It took all of Deena's strength to convince her to stay in Boston and finish the semester.

"What's the point?" Lauren whined while Deena clenched her teeth. "Why torture myself studying for finals? It's not like I'm going to graduate."

"You're going to graduate." Deena had been firm. She'd been reasonable. She hadn't screamed back,*you spoiled little twerp. What about us? Can't you think of anyone but yourself?* Instead, she'd said, "You might not be going back to Brandeis, but you'll go somewhere and those credits will transfer. So help me God, if you leave early and throw away a whole semester I won't let you in the house. I'll lock the door. Do you hear me?"

Lauren was crying. She was twenty years old, but still a baby. "OK, I'll finish the semester, but I'm not coming home. I don't even have a home." Deena heard a strangled sob, then, "Oh, my God, are you and Daddy going to be homeless?"

Deena closed her eyes and inhaled deeply. Why couldn't

Lauren have taken after her father? The entire maternal side of the family was nuts. Without ever setting eyes on her grandmother, Lauren managed to channel her every gesture, mannerism, and vocal intonation. The only difference was that Lauren was boy-crazy and her grandmother was a lesbian.

There was a long pause as Deena exhaled slowly to the count of ten. Lowering her voice as though she were talking to an injured child she tried again. "We're not going to be homeless. We've found a nice apartment on Van Aken Boulevard. Your dad and I still have our jobs. Elliot will graduate with his class. We're going to be OK. It's not the end of the world."

"Good, I was scared you were going to wind up living under a bridge or something." There was a pause while Lauren sniffled and blew her nose. "But, honestly, I'm not moving back home. I'll help you pack, but then I'm going back to Boston. I'm twenty years old and I can live wherever I want."

Deena's heart clenched with the old, familiar fear that Lauren would disappear from her life the same way she'd run away from her own mother. Losing Lauren was her nightmare, the feared retribution for her own defection. Lauren was her darling, her best friend. Until Lauren left for college they'd shared the same wardrobe, attended the same yoga classes, cried at the same movies. Losing her would be unthinkable. "We'll be done packing before you're done with finals, but it will be great to see you. As for staying in Boston, you're a big girl; you can live wherever you want as long as you can pay the rent. I just want you to know that there's still a place for you with us."

"Thanks, I really mean it, but I've had a better offer. I'm just going to pick up a few things then move back here."

"Where are you moving?"

"That's all I'm saying for now. I'll see you in three weeks, as soon as I'm done with my exams."

"What better offer?"

"Bye Mom. Tell Elliot I said Hi."

"What better offer?" but there was no one on the line.

The day appraisers from the Sheriff's office walked through her home, violating her most private spaces, inventorying and tagging items that resonated with her family's history, their daily rituals, their very DNA, had left Deena shattered. She'd opened the door to admit the two very polite and efficient women, pointed out the pieces she'd be keeping, then quietly slipped into her bedroom closet, buried her head in an old tweed suit, and bawled her eyes out.

Most of the good stuff, the appliances, the oriental rugs, and the oil painting over the sofa were being auctioned off. Her grandmother's Waterford and sterling would go on the block along with the Rosenthal china, but not the silver menorah or the candlesticks that had arrived from Belarus with her grandparents in 1938. Those were hidden away in a bundle of blankets beneath the bed, silent and still, like hidden Jews concealed from Nazis pounding on the door.

Deena had used a week of her vacation to pack up what they'd take and to discard the rest. It was the most exhausting and soul wrenching work she'd ever done. How could they have accumulated so much stuff? Every drawer and closet bulged with outdated insurance records, manuals for appliances they no longer owned, flashlights without batteries, pens without ink, coats the kids had long outgrown and a sequined dress she hadn't worn since college. There were pots without lids and lids without pots, endless computer cords, a trove of ancient floppy disks and a lifetime of books. Deena picked up *The Handmaid's Tale* by Margaret Atwood and started to open the cover, but stopped herself and tossed it into a box being donated to the library.

When had she become the Countess of clutter, the Duchess of debris, the Raja of rubbish? The...she looked around and realized it was true. Why had she accumulated all this junk? What was it for? Then with a sudden painful clarity she knew the answer. This crap was what she'd gotten in exchange for her mother and New Moon. She'd traded them for the house, the clothes, the gadgets, the makeup, the matching dishes and fondue pots she was tossing in the trash or leaving for the sheriff. *Well Mom*, she thought to herself, *it looks like you got the last laugh after all.*

Martin wandered through the house in a daze as if he'd been dropped from another planet. He was clearly slipping into a depression, but Deena was too exhausted and angry to haul him out. He needed detailed instructions to purchase strapping tape and bubble wrap, couldn't find his hammer in the tool chest or butter in the refrigerator. A simple request to assemble a few boxes was met with confused dismay as though he'd been asked to fold them into origami swans.

At least Elliot pitched in on the week-ends. He drove back and forth to Goodwill with load after load of things not good enough for the sheriff's sale, but too good for the growing mountain of trash bags looming behind the house. What did it mean to own things anyway? Something she remembered her mother saying, came back to her. *Do you know who's rich? A person who's happy with what he has, that's who.*

For someone who was so organized and meticulous Deena had amassed quite a collection of worthless paper. It was mostly trash, but something forced her to give each sheet a cursory glance and a quick trial before its summary execution. Old to-do lists, expired warranties, recipes clipped from magazines: toss, toss, toss. Then a red folder emerged from a bureau drawer, a relic from her childhood. It held report cards, term papers, the program to her high school prom and brochures from several universities. Deena riffled through its pages, deciding to let it go after one last nostalgic look. As she buried the folder in a large trash bag two sheets slipped out and landed on the floor. She recognized them at once. Had those incriminating pages been lurking in her dresser all these years? Thankful that no one else was in the room, she smoothed the two pieces of paper across her lap and began to read.

Garfield University

Application for Undergraduate Admission

October 18, 1987

Personal Essay: An Experience That Changed My Life

I was born on the New Moon Commune just out-side of Santa Fe in the summer of 1970. My Mother named me Harmony—just Harmony, one word, like Madonna or Prince, the same way she'd named her-self, Rain. I would have been Harmony Marcus if my mother hadn't jettisoned her last name along with her four poster bed, her color TV, and her college fund. My father was some guy hitchhiking to Berkeley who had gone his merry way before my mom knew she was a lesbian. Everyone called him Dante, but that's prob-ably not his real name. I don't know his real name and neither does my mother.

My mom's partner, Casey, had inherited the house and some land when her parents were killed in a car ac-cident the summer she turned fifteen. She lived with her aunt in Albuquerque for a while, but she got preg-nant and didn't want to raise her baby in a city so she left for Santa Fe and moved back into the farmhouse where she'd grown up. Her son Paz was a baby when she met my mother and a big guy named Buddha at a Grateful Dead concert. They all moved in together and named the place New Moon Commune.

New Moon started out as a normal three bedroom farmhouse with a garage, a tool shed and a chicken coop, but when I was small there was often no elec-tricity or gas because no one paid the bills. We got

> *water from a hand pump in the yard and flushed the*
> *toilet with water from a bucket. A woodstove kept the*
> *kitchen warm in winter, but the bedrooms got so cold*
> *we could write our names in the frost.*
>
> *Casey's son, Paz, and I were the only two kids in*
> *permanent residence if you didn't count the Rios clan*
> *next door. There were others who came and went. The*
> *New Mooner with frizzy blonde hair sticking out from*
> *under an old cowboy hat was my mother who never,*
> *not for a single minute, behaved like the mothers you*
> *read about in books. Casey came closer, but you*
> *couldn't exactly take either one of them to a mother-*
> *daughter tea. I'd go to Daffodil Days by myself each*
> *spring and lie to my teachers about my mom being*
> *sick. It was awful going alone, but it was better than*
> *letting the other kids see what my life was really like.*
>
> *My Mom and Casey are probably still there. I was go-*
> *ing to say that I might still be there too if circumstances*
> *had been different, but that's a lie. I would have left*
> *one way or another. I would have tunneled my way*
> *out of there with a teaspoon.*

Deena couldn't read another word. She folded the papers
in half and looked away. Old memories blurred her eyes as
she remembered those early years. She'd shown the essay to
Bubbe, her grandmother, not sure how she'd react. Bubbe
had handed it back as though it was *treif*, something unclean.
"Your mother's dead. She's dead to both of us. Throw this
away. Write about something else." So Deena had written a
different essay and buried her past along with the old papers.
But why hadn't she thrown them away? Anyone, Martin or
her kids, could have found them and discovered that the whole
story she'd invented about her childhood was a lie. The lie had
started with Bubbe, but that was over thirty years ago. Deena
felt a hollow ache at the center of her being. Nothing she'd

said or done had been completely honest since the day she'd left New Moon. She'd yearned for her mother with an orphan's longing, yet she hadn't called or written and her mother had not written her. With a flash of anger, Deena knew that if Lauren had moved away she'd have followed her to the gates of hell. But her own mother, her universal love and peace hippie mother, had simply let her move to Cleveland.

Why hadn't she ever told the truth? How had her life become so twisted? She tore the papers into narrow strips, and then ripped the strips into tiny squares, before burying them all at the bottom of a bag bound for the recycle bin.

Her mood swings were manic but her hands kept moving. She went at the task of dismantling her life like the librarian that she was: organize, classify, shelve, toss, donate, pack, until the final drawer was emptied and the last room swept out. That moment was the worst. She collapsed half way up the stairs and surveyed the bare room through the wrought iron banister. It was the home of a family that had failed, that was forced to vacate the premises under a court order. There was no evidence that she'd created a neat, orderly home, that she'd been responsible, law abiding and paid her bills on time. Or, at least, she'd paid them on time until Martin's one financial fling had cost them everything they owned.

Descending the last few stairs, she walked over to the large bay window and pressed her head against the glass. Fernway Road was lined with maples, honey locusts, and a few remaining elms. A golden aura hung over the old slate roofs as the afternoon sun dipped toward Horseshoe Lake a few blocks to the northwest. Iris and peonies bloomed behind tidy viburnum and boxwood hedges. A scattering of sparrows hopped across the lawn. A pair of crows pecked at something in the grass then looked up, staring back at her through the window with shrewd, discerning eyes.

The houses were architectural gems, smaller versions of the great mansions that stood along Eton and South Park

Boulevard. Most were nearly a century old, but they'd aged
well. A few needed paint or a bit of tuck pointing, but over-
all the neighborhood remained gracious and welcoming. The
original owners, the old guard Protestants of British ancestry,
had given way to a diverse mix of religions and ethnicities.
Children named Sasha, Kumar, Huan, and Jamal ran back and
forth between the yards while their parents chatted compan-
ionably across the drives and hedges.

There'd been cookouts, coffee klatches, summer evenings
spent chatting on front stoops, and yet there were no close
friends. Something always held her back. Why hadn't she
opened up to her neighbors, laughing, gossiping, and sharing
stories? Blushing, she knew the answer. The sense of alien-
ation she'd carried from her youth still haunted her. Even
now, a marriage and two grown children later, she still felt
like an outsider. Growing up on a hippie commune had made
her a freak, an alien at school. When other kids had talked
about TV shows or computer games she'd withdrawn and become silent. When they'd shown off their boom boxes, permed
hair and fancy sneakers, she'd made herself invisible. She'd
learned to keep her distance and to distrust people who might
have become friends. Even now, normal people still seemed
vaguely dangerous. They asked questions, made assumptions
and forced her to tell lies. It was hard enough keeping the
truth from Martin and her children, deceiving the rest of the
world was just too great an effort.

She took off the bandana tied around her hair and used
it to wipe her eyes. How was it possible to lose so much so
quickly? Is this how it starts, she wondered. Is this how people lose their grip on their carefully constructed lives? She felt
vulnerable and naked, like a turtle without its shell. The old
ache returned and she knew it wasn't just the loss of her house.
It was the longing for a home and family that had always felt
just beyond her reach. "Oh Harmony," she whispered to herself, "What have you done now?"

Chapter Two

Deena had never lived in an apartment and it was hard to adjust to the cramped space, the dimly lit hallways, the cooking smells, and the shared laundry. Their furniture was too large for the small rooms and she kept bumping her shins on the coffee table. The kitchen cupboards were so narrow she had to store large pots in the oven. Worst of all, there was no outdoor space, not even a balcony where she could get a breath of fresh air or plant a flower. Of course, the apartment was a palace compared to New Moon, the derelict commune of her youth, but at least New Moon had offered the luxury of space and unbroken natural vistas.

Elliot set up his computer in his new room, put his trophies on the bookshelf and then disappeared. Well, he didn't actually disappear. He was conscientious about letting Deena know where he was: at swim practice, the library, studying with Sasha, or at the mall, but he was never home. There was something pale and distant about him on those rare evenings when he deigned to join them at the dinner table. Was he losing weight? At least he did his homework and was keeping up his grade point average.

Lauren was another matter entirely. Two days after the moving van emptied what was left of their possessions into the rundown apartment that was now their home, Lauren arrived with a dubious-looking group of friends. They followed her from room to room as she opened cupboards and closets and checked out the view of brick walls and the tangle of wires. Inspection complete, she turned to Deena and said, "It's not what you're used to, but, I guess it's OK."

Before Deena could reply that Lauren might be surprised by what she was used to, a short, pugnacious-looking boy with bottle tops embedded in his earlobes butted in, "Maybe losing your house was a good thing. We all have to learn to live with less. It's hard to change old habits, but who wants to be a slave to their possessions, right? Think of this as the first step toward your liberation from capitalism."

Where had Lauren found these scruffy looking kids with their purple hair, their piercings and elaborate body art? Were they the rebellious, over-privileged kids of wealthy parents or vagrants off the street? She couldn't tell. More to the point, where were they going? Which one had made her daughter the "better offer"?

Lauren shrugged apologetically. "We're all trying to learn to live with less, but I'm sorry about the house. I really am."

Deena and Martin watched dumbfounded as Lauren threw a few things into a large backpack while the kid with the bottle cap ears hovered beside her as though she might need his protection.

"Well that's it." Lauren turned and gave them each a hug. "I'm afraid I've got to get going."

"You can't be going already. We haven't seen you since Passover."

"Sorry, I'll lose my ride if I don't leave now, but I'll be in touch, promise."

"Wait. Where are you going? We don't have your new address."

"I'll be in Boston. You have my cell."

"How will I know where to forward your mail? I need to know where you're going. I'm your mother." Deena could feel panic welling in her chest. It was irrational but real, the old fear of losing her children that always haunted her.

"Don't worry, I'll be fine." Then, just before she followed the last grubby kid onto the elevator, Lauren turned and kissed Deena on the cheek. As the doors closed, Deena touched her face, so grateful for the kiss that tears blossomed in her eyes.

Martin got up every morning the same as ever and dressed in the dim pre-dawn light of early autumn. His normal disinterest in clothes had become so extreme that he'd wear the same shirt for weeks unless Deena grabbed it while he slept and threw it in the hamper. Without a car, he left an hour early to take the rapid transit and then a bus to the drugstore where he'd worked for eighteen years. Deena prayed that he didn't stumble around at work as mindless and distracted as he did at home. What if he gave someone the wrong prescription? What if he lost his job? She wondered if his coworkers had any idea why he'd become so silent, so preoccupied, so peculiar. He'd gained twenty-two pounds but refused to buy new clothes. His shirts gapped beneath his lab coat and he'd stopped tucking them in to conceal the fact that his pants were unbuttoned at the waist. What had become of the young athlete that she'd married, the long distance biker who'd dreamed of crossing the country on the titanium frame bike his parents had bought him as a graduation present? Life happened, that's what. He'd sold that bike not long after they were married to raise money for a second car.

At first, Deena tried to maintain the illusion of normality: cooking dinner, setting the table, trying to engage in the pleasant banter about work or current events that used to fill their evenings, but she'd given up by mid August. Now, she just handed her husband a plate and let him eat on the sofa by the flickering light of the TV while she ate by herself in the kitchen. Most nights Martin fell asleep on the couch then staggered into bed long after Deena had turned out the light. They hadn't eaten at a restaurant in months. They hadn't gone to a concert or a movie since March. They hadn't had sex since, when? Deena couldn't remember the last time that Martin had rolled toward her in the night, passionate, aroused, whispering sweet endearments in her ear. She knew it had been too long. That was another thing she missed.

There had been one night in late June, a few weeks after they'd moved into the new apartment, when she'd decided enough was enough, and set out to seduce her own husband. On a Friday night when Elliot was out of town at a swim meet, she'd prepared a candlelight supper, changed into a low cut blouse and put on Martin's favorite Christina Aguilera album. He'd sat across from her at the table, dutifully making his way through the lobster bisque, the honey bourbon salmon, asparagus risotto, and limoncello mousse. He'd helped her clear the dishes, then taken her in his arms and whispered, "Thanks Honey, dinner was great but I promised Danny I'd stop by to watch the game tonight." Then he'd kissed her on the cheek, blown out the candles, and driven away while Deena cleaned the kitchen, finished off the pinot grigio and tossed Christina Aquilera in the trash.

The library was Deena's saving grace. It remained calm, cool, and orderly, buzzing with the muted hum of students doing research, writing papers, flirting in the cafe, and nodding to the silent beat of music streaming through their earbuds. Work was heaven. Every time a student approached her, flummoxed by the task of finding material for a thesis or a dissertation, Deena felt the thrill of the chase. She loved tracking down obscure books, out of print periodicals, pointing students in new and unexpected directions. Her fellow librarians were a cheerful, competent group, untroubled by the internal politics that disrupted other campus faculties. She was grateful to move about her day impervious to pity or to censure, glad that no one knew her secrets, glad she hadn't engaged in hallway gossip or afterhours confessions over beer. Not even her lunchroom pals knew that she'd lost her house to bankruptcy; that her daughter had moved away without a forwarding address, that her son spent less and less time at home, or that her husband could barely look her in the eye.

Lauren hadn't called or answered her phone in weeks and Deena was terrified that her nightmares had come true, that her daughter had cut them from her life, reinventing herself as an unencumbered orphan. Then, on the morning of September 14th, Deena's phone began to croak its odd froggy ring tone. She fished it out of her purse while keeping one eye on the road.

"Happy birthday, Mom. Did you get my card?"

Deena's mood brightened at once. Maybe the world hadn't come to an end after all. "Hi, Sweetie, it's so good to hear your voice. Is everything OK?" She began scanning the street for a place to park.

"I'm fine. Did you get the birthday card I sent?"

"No, not yet, but talking to you is the best birthday present ever. I was getting worried. We haven't heard from you in ages." Deena pulled into the parking lot of a small strip mall.

"Sorry about that. I lost my phone, but I found a used one on eBay so everything's good now. So, is Dad taking you out for dinner or what?"

"We haven't decided what we're doing yet," Deena lied. She knew exactly what they were doing, watching television and eating left-over lasagna. Maybe she'd treat herself to a cupcake for lunch. "How are things in Boston? Did you get that job at Halibuts?"

"Yep, I'm working three afternoons and three evenings. The tips are great and the manager's OK, except I have to wear this stupid hat that looks like a fish. Oh, and I'm taking acting lessons at the community center and I might audition for a play."

"That's fantastic, but what's with the interest in theater? The last time we talked you were all about video games and computer graphics."

"Maybe I'll do both. Anyway, right now I'm taking acting."

It sounds like things are going well. So, are you ready
to give me your new address? That would be a wonderful
birthday present."

"Mom, stop worrying. It doesn't matter where I'm staying,
just have a happy birthday and let me know when you get my
card. It's really funny, OK?"

"OK, Sweetie, thanks for calling. I love you."

"Love you too. Bye."

Deena was grateful for the call, and Lauren sounded happy,
but something still wasn't right. Why the secrecy? What did
that child have going on that she didn't want anyone to know?

She didn't know whether Martin worried about Lauren or
not. In fact, she wasn't sure how much got through to him
at all. Questions were answered with a grunt or a nod and
conversation was beyond him. He was absent, a zombie going
through the motions of a life. His back ached, his stomach
burned, he lived on antacids and muscle relaxers. He ate crazy
things at crazy hours and watched way too much TV. Deena
knew that he was sinking and she tried to pull him out of it.
She teased and cajoled. She flirted and lied. She even assured
him through gritted teeth that the bankruptcy wasn't all his
fault, but she couldn't budge him out of his funk. The man was
too far gone. Finally, she'd had enough. "You're depressed
and you're going to see a doctor." Martin had protested, but
Deena was insistent. "I made an appointment for you to see
Dr. Rabinsky."

"What's the point? He'll just drug me up with Prozac or
some other SSRI, that's all they do," Martin had whined.

"Well, you need to be drugged up with something. You're
a mess."

"There's Xanax in the medicine cabinet from when I had
my wisdom teeth removed. Maybe I'll try that."

"No, you're going to see a shrink. Your appointment's at
two o'clock Thursday afternoon. I'll go with you if you want."

Her formerly strong, sensible husband averted his eyes like a guilty child and said, "I don't want to go."

"Why the hell not? You're falling apart."

"Because it feels like you're sending me to the principal's office to get yelled at. I'm not a child. I can deal with this myself, OK?" He didn't go and she didn't bring the subject up again.

Housekeeping took less time in the new apartment, there were fewer rooms and less clutter, but laundry seemed to take forever. At first, she was annoyed at having to ferry clothes up and down in the elevator to the cinder block laundry room in the basement, but she eventually came to like the warm, dank room and the soothing white noise of the machinery. Instead of making multiple trips, she'd settle into one of the plastic chairs that lined the walls, pull out a good book, and read undisturbed until it was time to transfer a load from one machine to another. Occasionally, someone else would intrude, throwing in a load of wash or grabbing something from a dryer, but she could usually feign such deep concentration in her book that they'd leave without engaging her in conversation.

Then, one day in mid October, a man walked into the laundry room with a hamper full of dirty clothes and a small volume tucked under his arm. He threw a pile of sheets and towels into one washer and everything else into the other; then he took a chair and started to read. Annoyed, but curious, Deena peered over her copy of *Fatelessness* by Imre Kertesz, and discovered that the man sitting across from her was reading the same book. Furthermore, like hers, his book bore the stamp of the Alfred Seibel Library. She looked back down at the page she'd been reading but couldn't find her place. She stole another peek. He was probably in his late fifties, tall and thin, with salt and pepper hair, a neat goatee and wire rimmed glasses. His long legs, stretched out in front of him, practically touched the opposite wall of the narrow room. There was something about him, something different, what was it? The answer came to her. He was Russian or European, definitely foreign. It was the cardigan over the button down shirt with the sleeves artfully rolled up that gave him away. She noted a small stud in his left ear. She went back to her book satisfied that she had him sorted out and cataloged, but there was something else. She couldn't concentrate. It was the book; it was so strange that they were reading the same book.

Her dryer dinged and she stood up. The man looked up and smiled at her. She smiled back and then winced, alarmed at the prospect of folding her shapeless cotton panties and utilitarian brassieres in front of this attractive man. The machine had been set on air dry so her delicates were still damp, but she bunched them up, shielding them from view, as she threw them on top of her neatly folded shirts and jeans.

He pointed to the book she'd left on her chair. "Look, we're reading the same book." He held up his copy. "Are you a fan of Kertesz?" He had an accent, Deena grinned, pleased that she'd guessed right.

"Are we?" Deena feigned surprise. "I've just started reading mine, so it's too soon to tell." That was enough. Courtesy didn't require another word, but to her surprise she kept on talking. "Actually, I generally avoid Holocaust material. My grandmother's family was wiped out by Hitler so, to be honest, the subject scares me to death, but Kertesz won a Nobel Prize so I thought…"

"I am so sorry."

"Oh, my grandmother was already in this country. She didn't go through the war herself." Deena paused, reflecting on the rigid, humorless woman who had taken her in as a teenager. "But I think it damaged her anyway. She lost two sisters, a brother, her parents, her whole village. It made her kind of weird, kind of rigid and judgmental." Why was she telling him this? Deena never discussed her family with anyone.

"Losing your family like that would change anyone. Have you read *Dossier K*? A lot of people think *Fatelessness* is a memoir, but it's not. If you want to know how the war changed Kertesz you have to read *Dossier K*."

"Maybe I'll read it if I survive this one." Her arms were full of warm laundry, but she managed to lift the slight volume from the chair.

"Look," he said, pointing to the spine of her novel. "Our books are both from the university library. Are you a student there or maybe a professor?"

"I work at the library. I'm head of the Arts and Humanities Collection."

"Really? You're a librarian at the Alfred Seibel Library?" His face lit up. "This is amazing. I will be giving a talk there this afternoon at three o'clock."

"Then you must be one of our visiting scholars. What's your topic?"

"Street photography in Hungary. You might enjoy the presentation. There will be a lot of interesting images."

"Sounds intriguing, but I probably won't have time." She balanced the basket on one hip and headed toward the exit. "Enjoy the book."

"This isn't a book most people enjoy. It's very dark, very provocative. I read it in Hungary when I was at university. I'm reading it now to see how it sounds in English."

Deena paused to consider. "You're right, a lot of things don't translate. If we meet again, you'll have to tell me what you found."

"Then I will hope we meet again." He smiled and bowed gallantly from the waist. Deena looked away, mortified that she was wearing one of Elliot's Star Trek T-shirts over a pair of frayed cut offs. Would it be too weird to tell him that the Star Trek shirt wasn't really hers?

"Well, nice meeting you. Good luck with your lecture." Deena turned and fled, tongue tied and embarrassed. She was almost halfway down the hall when she felt a hand on her shoulder. Startled, she turned to see the fastidiously groomed Hungarian standing behind her.

"Excuse me, but you dropped these." He placed a pair of baggy cotton underpants, gray and fraying at the waist, in her laundry basket.

Appalled, Deena barely managed to blurt out, "Thank you," as she scurried toward the elevator.

Dumping the warm laundry on the bed, she began carefully folding the sheets and towels. Sun shone through the cheap vinyl mini-blinds covering the windows, and she could see a clear expanse of blue sky above the apartment building across the street. Checking her watch, she saw that it was only one o'clock. Martin was working until eight and Elliot was studying with Sasha and wouldn't be home for supper. In the old days, when the kids were small, they'd spend Sundays at the movies or the park, but now Deena was alone. The day was too nice to waste. Maybe she should go to the library and learn something about Hungarian street photography. Why not? It would be nice to just sit in the audience for once without the stress of making sure that everything was running smoothly. Even if the subject didn't particularly interest her, it didn't matter. She needed to get out of the house. So, she brushed her hair, put on some lipstick, and went to work on her day off.

The library was quiet on Sundays, but there were always students milling around the lobby and lined up at the service desks. Deena stopped to study a bulletin board and locate the flier for the Sunday lecture series. Today's talk was titled, "The New Face of Social Realism: Street Photography in Eastern Europe." She'd have preferred a talk on literature or the environment, but photography might be interesting. At least there'd be some good slides.

As she took one of the chairs in the small second floor lecture hall, Deena noted how few people were in attendance.

It was probably the weather, in Cleveland it was always the weather. A lot of people didn't come because they wanted to spend the last nice days of fall planting tulips or riding their bicycles. But then, once the weather got bad, they wouldn't come because it was too wet, or too cold, or too snowy. Too bad, she knew how much effort went into these events. Deena settled into her chair and began reading the program she'd been handed at the door.

Dr. Andor Farkas, *visiting professor of photography at Cleveland Institute of Art, is best known for curating the exhibition, "Images of the Greater Revolution: Hungary 1944-1991" which opened at The Hungarian University of Fine Arts in June, 2006. Jan Niewald of KulturSPIEGEL called the exhibit, "a riveting visual history of the changing face of Hungary under Soviet occupation." Dr. Farkas is a recipient of the prestigious Moholy-Nagy Prize (2004) and a fellow of Budapest's Georgi Szabos Council for Contemporary Art.* The small black and white photo that accompanied the text was blurred, but the image was familiar. Someone turned out the lights and a tall, distinguished gentleman with a well manicured goatee took his place behind the podium.

He was still dressed in the cardigan and jeans he'd been wearing to do laundry, but something, the beard and glasses, or maybe his accent, exuded an aura of authority. His talk was informative and engaging, his photos stunning. Deena was impressed. How old was this Dr. Farkas? The silver in his hair might have fooled her. On reflection, he might be only fifty, maybe even a few years younger. Every student in his class probably had a crush on him. As soon as the lights came she gathered up her sweater and headed toward the door.

"Excuse me, one minute please." Deena turned to see Dr. Farkas signaling for her to wait. He pushed passed a small group waiting to speak to him and hurried toward her. "I saw you sitting in the audience, so, I was wondering, is this another coincidence or are you stalking me?"

Deena was taken aback. She started to say, *but you invited me*, until she saw the grin spreading across his face. It was a joke. She surprised herself by answering in kind, "Do women often stalk you? Do you have a problem with that?"

"I would not have a problem if you stalked me." He smiled again and Deena felt her ears grow hot.

"I enjoyed your talk very much," she said, trying to bring the conversation back to solid ground. "You're an excellent speaker. I'd never heard of street photography before."

"Thank you, a compliment from the head of the library's humanities department means a great deal to me. Perhaps we could talk some more over coffee. There is a small cafe downstairs on the first floor. Do you have time for a coffee?"

Deena paused, glancing up at the large clock on the wall. *Martin wouldn't be home for hours and Elliot was eating at Sasha's.* "Sure, I have time for a quick cup of coffee. Why not?"

"Excellent! Please, wait just a few minutes while I talk to some of my students. I promise, I'll join you as fast as I can."

"I'll wait for you downstairs." Deena smiled and left Dr. Farkas surrounded by a small group of admirers all vying for his attention.

Stopping in the ladies' room before heading to the cafe, Deena paused to smooth down her hair and freshen her lipstick. *Was that famous photographer flirting with me?* The thought was so improbable. She was a middle aged librarian with grown children. She ran a comb through her hair; it was the same ashy brown bob she'd worn since high school. Maybe she should color it or add some layers. *Stop that*, she chided herself. *What in the world's the matter with you?* She blotted her lipstick on a paper towel and headed for the cafe.

Deena bought herself a cup of coffee and a biscotti wrapped in cellophane then sat down at a small table and pulled out her iPhone hoping for an email from Lauren. It made Deena crazy not knowing where her daughter lived, but Lauren was of age. She was lucky Lauren called at all. That was more than she'd done for her own mother. By the time she'd answered two work related emails, read an online book review, and sent several dubious solicitations to her spam folder it was almost five o'clock without a Hungarian in sight. She brushed the biscotti crumbs into her empty cup, tossed it into the trash, put on her sweater, and called it a day. *Probably just as well,* she told herself. *What were you expecting anyway?*

Elliot was staying out later and later. He claimed to be at swim practice, at the library, or studying with friends, but Deena was worried. He'd leave at seven-thirty in the morning and not reappear until ten at night. He always called with some excuse so she wouldn't worry, but where was he really? Cell phones made it too easy for teenagers to get away with murder. Elliot was no party animal. He wasn't holed up in some basement, getting drunk or buzzed out on Ecstasy — the way she feared his sister might. But where was he?

Deena tried to engage Martin in a discussion about their son, but Elliot was the one thing he wasn't worried about. "What's the problem? He's a kid. Kids hang out with their buddies."

Maybe Martin was right. Elliot's grades were good and he was captain of the swim team. If something was wrong, his coach would be on his case. Why look for trouble? But still, her instincts told her something wasn't quite Kosher.

The answer came four days later when she stopped at a pricey boutique grocery on her way home from work. It was unusual for Deena to go shopping in the middle of the week, and more unusual to shop at Fresh Market, but she was in a hurry and only needed a couple of items. She grabbed a bunch of organic broccoli, raced to the fish counter where she threw a pound of salmon into her cart, she added a pint of sour cream and a container of Ben and Jerry's ice-cream, then swung down the next aisle toward the register. There was Elliot, standing straight ahead of her, looking as though she'd caught him with his hand in the till. Actually, his hand was in the till; he was standing behind the register ringing up groceries.

"Elliot, what an unexpected surprise." Deena was equally embarrassed, although she didn't know why she should be. "Why didn't you tell us you had a job? Why all the mystery?"

"Can we talk later? I'm busy now." He scanned a package of tofu, then put a bag of tomatoes on the scale. His movements were efficient and experienced; apparently he'd been doing this for some time. The woman ahead of Deena paid for her groceries and moved on. Elliot scanned and bagged the items from Deena's cart, almost as though he didn't know her.

"Elliot, why the secrecy? There's nothing wrong with getting a job."

"That'll be twenty-two dollars and forty-three cents."

"Elliot?"

"Later, Mom." He smiled apologetically as he counted out her change, "and next time buy the Chunky Monkey." Deena leaned across the counter and gave him a quick peck on the cheek before she left.

What is with that kid? Deena shook her head in bewilderment as she pulled out of the parking lot. *Why didn't he want us to know he had a job?* Then it came to her. It was five-thirty on Tuesday afternoon and Elliot should have been at swim practice. He'd dropped off the team and hadn't even told them.

The silhouette of a well dressed man fell from a skyscraper, gradually descending past billboards selling fashion, liquor, fast cars and seductive women as Deena heard Elliot's key in the lock. She clicked off the television and turned to her husband who was mining the carton of Cherry Garcia for slivers of chocolate. He looked up, startled, "Why'd you do that? I thought *Mad Men* was your favorite show."

"Elliot's home. Remember what I told you. Get your head out of the ice-cream and help me figure out what's going on with your son."

Martin dutifully pulled himself off the couch and returned the ice-cream to the freezer. He'd already changed into the sweat pants and T-shirt he wore to bed. The pants sagged as he headed toward the kitchen revealing the white half moon of his butt. Deena closed her eyes and took a deep cleansing breath. She'd deal with Martin later; right now her job was to get Elliot back on track.

"Hey Sweetie, welcome home. Come talk to us." Deena sipped at the matcha tea that she drank after dinner to calm her nerves.

The tall, lanky figure of her son appeared looking tired and a bit stooped. He'd clearly put in a long day. "Mom, could we talk later? I have homework."

"It can wait a few minutes. I want to hear about this new job of yours." Were those circles under his eyes? Had he been losing weight? She stood up and put her arm around Elliot's shoulders. "Have you had supper? There's leftover salmon and rice. Do you want me to fix you a plate?"

He shrugged her off, "I got a sandwich from the deli department. Can't we do this another time?"

"No, your mother's worried about you and she wants to talk now." Martin reappeared sounding parental and authoritative, making Deena homesick for the man he used to be. "How about telling us what's going on." But that was it, the moment didn't last. Martin sank back onto the couch and turned to Deena for guidance.

Deena began on a conciliatory note, "Your father and I are both happy that you've got a part-time job, and Fresh Market's very lucky to have you." She sat back down and took another sip of her tea. "What we don't understand is why you've been keeping it a secret. Did you think that we'd be angry for some reason?"

"I don't know." Elliot shifted from one foot to the other. "Maybe."

"Why would we be angry about a part-time job at a grocery store?"

"Because it's not actually part-time." He looked directly at his mother for a fraction of a second, then dropped his gaze to the floor. "I'm working a forty-hour week." He may have been staring at the carpet, but there was something like defiance in his voice.

No wonder he looked so tired. "Forty hours? When do you have time for school?"

"You don't have to look so worried. I've got everything under control. I go to school from eight to three like always, then I work from four to nine on weekdays. Saturdays and Sundays I work from one in the afternoon until closing. No problem."

"But what about your homework? What about your swimming?" Deena felt a little dizzy.

"I do my homework when I get home and, well, I don't swim anymore. I dropped off the team."

So, she'd been right. But why would he give up the thing he loved most in the world? Her heart lurched and little alarms went off. "Elliot, you're the captain; their star swimmer. The team was counting on you."

"They'll be fine. Joe Haffey took over as captain. Everything's OK. Can I go do my homework now?"

"But why? Why are you killing yourself like this? You love swimming. I don't understand." She turned toward her husband for support, but found him picking at a hangnail. "Martin, pay attention. Elliot's dropped off the swim team and he didn't even tell us."

"Look, it's no big deal," Elliot shrugged. "I knew you'd get bent out of shape about the swimming, but I wanted to make some real money. What's wrong with that?"

"You don't need to make that kind of money. Your mother and I are still working. It's not like we're..." Martin's voice trailed off, because, of course, they *were* broke, and Elliot knew it. "We're still working," Martin repeated.

"I thought you were applying for a swimming scholarship. What happened to that? A scholarship would be worth more than you'll ever make at a grocery store." Deena stood up again. She wanted to pace, swing her arms, make large, dramatic gestures, but the damn room was too small.

"Mom, did you know that there are exactly nine division one men's swim scholarships in the entire country? Did you know that? That's why I dropped off the team. I mean, what were my chances? Like none, and let's face it, your money's gone. I'm on my own."

"We're still working." Martin said again, although his voice had lost all its conviction.

"How much are you making?" Deena wanted to know what Elliot was getting in exchange for giving up the great passion of his life.

"$584.00 every two weeks, that's $475 take home. If I work through the summer I'll have enough to cover a year's worth of tuition and fees at Cleveland State."

Deena nodded, trying not to let tears give away her broken heart. Maybe Elliot was right. With the bankruptcy on their record, they wouldn't qualify for a loan, and the money they put aside each month wouldn't cover everything. And what about Lauren? What if she decided to go back to school? There just wasn't enough to pay her tuition as well. "OK, but I wish you'd talked to us first. We would have fought to keep you on the team. I wanted to watch you set a new record for the 100 meter fly."

"Sorry, can I go now?"

"Sure, don't stay up too late."

Elliot retrieved his book bag from the front hall and disappeared into his room. Deena waited for the door to slam shut before turning to Martin. "We don't deserve that boy."

Martin nodded, "He's a good kid."

"Well, more unexpected consequences." Deena sat across

from Martin on the chintz wing chair that belonged beside the fireplace in their old house, their real house. It was one of a pair she'd inherited from her grandmother, but the apartment wasn't big enough for both of them so she'd had to let its partner go. "Danny sells you a stupid piece of real estate and now your son has to drop off the swim team to put himself through college. Is there any corner of our lives that man hasn't ruined?"

"It's not Danny's fault. We've been through this. He feels terrible." Deena stared at her husband's gut pouring over the waistband of his sweatpants. The bigger he got, the smaller he seemed to become. "If he feels so terrible why did he leave you holding the bag?"

"Don't be stupid. He lost a bundle on the deal."

"Maybe, but I didn't see his signature on that loan. He wasn't the one who owed the bank more than he'd ever make in a lifetime after that development went bust."

Martin raked his fingers through his hair. "Danny would have signed for the loan if he hadn't already been stretched so thin. You know that. We've been through this a million times. Let it go already. Things happen.

She wanted to stop. She knew she was hurting him, but the news that Elliot had dropped off the swim team had pushed her over the edge. "How can I let it go when my daughter dropped out of college because we can't pay her tuition, and my son, who's still in high school, is working a full-time job because he thinks his parents can't support him and maybe he's right."

"Deena, please, are you trying to kill me? I wish I'd never heard of River Parc but it's over. You're ripping my heart out."

Deena clapped her hand over her mouth, ashamed she'd gone so far. She got up to sit beside Martin on the sofa and took his big hand in hers. "I'm sorry. You're twice the man that Danny is, but you let him lead you around by the nose. He might not have known that his anchor tenants were going bankrupt, but he knew the risk we were taking when we signed that loan. That's all I'm saying. He should never have asked us to take that risk, and we should have had the guts to tell him to go to hell."

"He thought he was giving us a great opportunity. We thought it was our big chance. He didn't mean to hurt us."

"Maybe, but he didn't do anything to protect us either, did he? Did he?"

Martin didn't say another word. He sat with his eyes closed and his head thrown back against the sofa cushion. Deena waited a moment, and then, when it was clear she wasn't getting a response, she simply got up and left. As she padded down the hallway toward the bedroom she could hear the television click back on, and then the smarmy voice of some jerk hawking replacement windows.

Chapter Three

The next day Deena arrived at her office so distracted and out of sorts that she'd hung up her coat and turned on her computer before she noticed the pot of yellow chrysanthemums on her desk. It was a large pot full of showy blossoms. A card fixed to a little green plastic stake read, "To Ms. Deena Berman, Director of Arts and Humanities." She tore open the small envelope and read, "To a lovely librarian, with my sincere apologies. I beg your forgiveness. Andor, suite #703N." Then there was a telephone number. She turned the note over in her hand. There wasn't any more, just "I beg your forgiveness," and a phone number.

Does he think I'm going to call him? What would I say? The flowers gave off a spicy, autumnal scent. The florist's tag read, *Chrysanthemum Gold Country, Perennial, Hardy to Zone 5.* She would have planted them in the narrow bed that ran along the drive if she still lived in her old house. They would have been happy there. Now, she had nowhere to plant them. They'd go in the trash when the blooms were gone.

Deena picked up the pot and tucked it away behind her desk where no one would see it and went back to her computer. Ten minutes later she realized that she'd come to the end of a long article without any idea of what she'd read. While her eyes had been scanning page after page of text about library security, her mind had been lost in a daydream involving a remorseful professor with an exotic accent and European manners. *Idiot!* She chided herself. *Get a grip. Chuck the damn flowers in the trash.* But she didn't. She took them home, discreetly concealed beneath her coat, and gave them a place of honor on the dining room table.

Martin didn't notice the chrysanthemums when he got home. He took off his coat, asked when dinner would be ready, then collapsed into his usual spot on the sofa. Deena stared at him, remembering the old days when he used to bring her flowers. He'd been so smart and funny, and he knew so much about the Civil War and politics. Now all those facts and stories were locked away somewhere she couldn't reach. Simple conversation seemed too much for him. Even when his parents called from Scottsdale, Arizona, he'd just mumble a few pleasantries, then hand the phone to Deena. She missed her husband terribly, but it seemed that he was gone.

She bent over the yellow blooms, inhaling their pungent scent. The flowers were lovely and they certainly warmed the room. Maybe she *should* call Professor Farkas and thank him for his gift. Deena retrieved the small enclosure card from the pocket of her blazer and reread it, *Andor Farkas, Unit 703N.* So, he lived in the north wing that had its own elevator and a separate entrance. No wonder she hadn't run into him again, and there was his phone number. She really should call; it would be rude not to acknowledge a gift. She glanced back at Martin who was engrossed in the evening news. Taking her cell phone off its charger, she went into the bedroom and shut the door.

"Dr. Farkas? This is Deena Berman."

"The library lady, I am so happy you called. I am so ashamed. I wanted to explain but I didn't know your name, I didn't know your phone number, I didn't know anything except you are director of Arts and Humanities at Seibel Library. That's how I found you."

"Yes, well, I'm just calling to thank you for the flowers. You really didn't have to do that, but well, thank you. They're very pretty." Deena couldn't think of anything more intelligent to say. She was no good at these things. "Well, thank you again and well, good-bye."

"No, no don't hang up. I want to explain to you how sorry I am for last Sunday. Victor Morano, you know him? He curates twentieth century prints for the museum. He surprised me by showing up and he had so many questions and so many people for me to meet that it was late by the time I could leave. I ran down the stairs as fast as I could, but you were gone like Cinderella and I didn't know where to find you.

"No, not like Cinderella." Deena smiled into the phone. What an image. "It just got late and I couldn't wait any longer. I have a family. I had to make dinner for my husband."

"Of course, I understand. The fault is mine, but I would love to talk to you some more about Imre Kertesz. He's not a popular author, especially not in your country, but you were reading him. That makes you interesting to me."

Was this guy kidding? Lots of people read Kertesz. He'd won a Nobel Prize for God's sake, and yet there was a part of her that felt flattered that he found her interesting. Well, there was no harm in discussing a book. That's what she did for a living. "Actually, I just finished *Fatelessness*. It was moving, but I can't say that I liked it. The disconnect between all the gruesome Holocaust stuff and the dispassionate tone of the narrator was disturbing. It was almost like he was making excuses for the Nazis."

"Exactly, you understand exactly. The boy tries to believe that things make sense, that there is some justice or purpose. How else could he survive?"

"But it didn't make sense; it was all completely insane."

"Of course, precisely. Will you allow me to buy you dinner? It will be my apology and we can talk some more."

"No!" Deena's response was so sudden and emphatic that

she felt embarrassed, afraid that she'd offended the man, so she back peddled a bit. "Not dinner, but we could meet for coffee at the library. Do you want to give that another try? I usually get off work at five o'clock."

"Can we meet tomorrow? I don't teach on Tuesday afternoons and I promise that I will not disappoint you again."

Deena was intrigued, but wary. *Why in the world was this Dr. Farkas so hot to talk to her? But, why not?* What could it hurt? "OK, then, tomorrow at five. I'll look forward to seeing you." She was alarmed to discover that her heart was pounding double time as she clicked off the phone.

The room remained dark even after Deena switched on the overhead light the next morning. One of the bulbs had burned out and the other, an anemic 60 watter, was no match for the opaque gray clouds that obliterated any hint of sun. Rain pounded relentlessly against the window and pinged against the aluminum gutters. She didn't need more light to know that Martin's side of the bed was empty, a common occurrence these days. Slipping into a bra and panties Deena began rummaging through the closet for something nice to wear. She selected a slimming pair of black wool pants, but couldn't decide on a sweater. Why were her clothes all so shapeless and bulky? Tip-toeing across the hall, Deena looked through Lauren's closet and found the aqua cashmere she'd given her for Chanukah the year she'd became Goth or Punk or something that definitely didn't include aqua cashmere. Deena bit off the tag and pulled it over her head. It clung to her breasts and hugged her waist in a way that made her feel self-conscious. She was probably too old to wear anything so revealing, but it was stupid to let such an expensive sweater go to waste.

Deena applied her usual lipstick then added an extra gloss of pink blush. She tried to fluff up her short, utilitarian hair, but it wasn't designed to do anything frivolous and continued to lay flat and uncompromising against her face. She stepped into the black flats she always wore to work, then immediately discarded them for a pair of open toed shoes with wedge heels. *Oh, for God's sake,* she chided herself. *You're not going on a date.* She took off the heels and put the flats back on, then went to make sure Elliot was up and getting ready for school.

His bedroom door was ajar and the rumpled bed was empty when she peeked inside. Deena could hear him puttering in the kitchen. Good, everything was on schedule. She was about to head into the living room to check on Martin when she noticed the screen on Elliot's computer. In letters too large to miss she read: JOIN THE NAVY- A GLOBAL FORCE FOR GOOD. She stared at the computer for a full minute before closing the door and going to look for her husband.

Martin was still asleep on the couch wearing the clothes he'd worn to work the previous day. This was becoming a regular thing. He'd doze off watching TV after dinner then sleep right through the night. He couldn't seem to stay awake. Deena shook his shoulder. "Hey, wake up. It's after seven."

His eyes opened a slit and he struggled to sit up. As she boiled water for her matcha in the kitchen, she heard him lumbering toward the bathroom. He needed to see a doctor. He was sleeping way too much and seemed lost in a fog even when he was supposedly awake.

"Bye Mom," She heard the front door slam as Elliot left for school. The sound of his voice, confident and manly, a pitch lower than it had been the year before, resonated in her ears. There was no way she was letting him enlist. The family had lost too much already.

"Did you make coffee? I could really use a cup." Martin appeared in the kitchen, still bleary eyed, but clean and shaved.

"I think Elliot made a pot."

Apart from the fact that he was still wearing the clothes he'd slept in all night, Martin seemed pretty normal. They were so polite with each other these days. Neither of them mentioned that Martin had spent another night sleeping on the couch. He poured himself a mug of coffee. "Do you want some?"

"No thanks, I've started drinking matcha in the morning."

"Good, it makes more sense to drink your matcha early in the day. It has a lot of caffeine."

Deena bristled, had she asked for a pharmaceutical consultation? "Well, it calms my nerves and it doesn't seem to keep me up." Martin hadn't said anything offensive. Why was she so irritated with him? She poured a tablespoon of hot water into her cup, added a tablespoon of matcha powder then stirred them into a paste before adding more hot water and whisking the concoction into a foamy broth.

Martin grabbed a box of powdered donuts from the counter and sat down at the table. She watched as he broke one in two and dunked it in his cup. It dripped on the table, narrowly missing his shirt.

It was nearly eight and she had to leave for work, but she couldn't ignore the queasy feeling in her gut. She took a sip of the matcha then asked, "Has Elliot said anything to you about the Navy?"

"No, why would we talk about the Navy?"

"I'm afraid he might be thinking about enlisting."

Martin blinked and stared at her, clearly startled by the idea. "He's not enlisting. He's going to college. What in the world would make you say a thing like that?"

"He's been looking at the Navy recruitment website. It was open on his computer. Maybe you should talk to him, make sure he's not planning to do something stupid."

"Wouldn't he let us know if he was going to do a thing like that? Anyway, he's only seventeen. He can't enlist without our signature." Martin was patting at coffee that had sloshed onto the table with a paper napkin.

"He's almost eighteen, in another couple months he won't need our signature for anything. He sure didn't consult us before dropping off the swim team. I think he's written us off as a pair of hapless geezers."

"Maybe he's doing research for a school assignment."

"Get real, Martin. This could be serious. Enlisting is like signing up for a life of involuntary servitude."

"Enlisting would be voluntary."

"This isn't funny. This is our son's life we're talking about."

"OK, I'll talk to him; but don't go jumping to conclusions. If he was looking at a juggling website would you think he was planning to run off and join the circus?"

Why was her husband so obtuse? Couldn't he smell danger? "Martin, just talk to him, OK? I've got to run, but I'm counting on you."

"Yes ma'am," he saluted, leaving a trace of white sugar in his hair. "Have a nice day. I'll make sure Elliot doesn't ship out before you get back." He reached into the box and pulled out another donut, studied it a moment, then shoved nearly the whole thing into his mouth.

Deena stared at her husband chewing open mouthed, powdered sugar covering his chin and dotting his rumpled shirt, before taking a last sip of her matcha, then running back into the bedroom to switch into the open toed shoes with the wedge heels.

The library was already buzzing by the time Deena took her place behind the information desk a couple minutes after eight. If they had more staff, they'd keep the library open 24/7 like an all night diner, but of course, the library couldn't afford that level of staffing. In fact, following recent budget cuts, the director had instituted a hiring freeze that had everyone stretched thin. Deena's department was down two positions, Acquisitions was down one, and Administration was down three. She was lucky to have a job at all.

Deena opened the computer. In addition to her regular duties, she was now on call whenever a sick clerk created a critical vacancy. Today, that meant that she was information central, a human switchboard connecting students and faculty with library services and staff. Even before her computer booted up, a small line of students, all anxious and desperate, all looking as though they hadn't slept for days, began competing for her attention. Deena looked at the worried young faces and smiled a patient, benevolent smile. Her day had begun. A pale undergrad wearing blood red lipstick and layers of eyeliner and mascara smiled back at her with a ghoulish grin. Vampires were evident all over campus this year.

"Excuse me, but I need to see a copy of this book." The Morticia look-alike shoved a piece of notebook paper across the desk. It read: *The Art of Midwifery Improv'd, Instructions Requisite to Make a Compleat Midwife. Illustrated with 38 Cuts Curiously Engraven on Copper Plates. Hendrik van Deventer, Published by London: Printed for E. Curll, etc., 1716.*

Deena scowled at the paper then did a quick computer search. "This book isn't available for general circulation. You're going to have to see Taylor Smythe in Special Collections, and you'll probably need a letter from your professor. Mr. Smythe's in Archives on the lower level. Do you need a map?" She handed the notepaper back across the desk.

"Oh, for God's sake. It's just a book. Is this a library or the Gestapo?" A small white hand with black enamel nails snatched back the paper and the student marched off in disgust. It was going to be one of those days.

She was exhausted by five o'clock and the bathroom mirror tactlessly informed her that the fatigue showed on her face. She reapplied her lipstick, slapped her cheeks to bring out some color and combed her fingers through her hair. *OK, let's see what this guy wants,* she muttered as she made her way across the central lobby towards the Studyo 54 Cafe.

Andor was sitting at one of the small tables working on his laptop. He was wearing a tweedy professorial sort of sport coat over jeans and a black T-shirt. Long salt and pepper curls fell across his face as he bent over the small keyboard. There was no denying it, the man was movie star handsome. What could he possibly want with her?

Deena slipped into the chair across from Andor who looked up, startled. He slammed his computer shut then turned to her with a smile that warmed her all the way down. "There you are. I've been waiting here for an hour so I couldn't miss you. It's so nice to see you again." He stood up and held out his hand. There was something so formal, so foreign and yet so charming in his manner. Deena offered her hand in return, half expecting him to kiss it like a count in a Tolstoy novel, but he only held it a moment longer than a friendly handshake would require. "May I get you a coffee or maybe a cappuccino?"

While Andor was getting coffee, Deena glanced around the room to see if any of her co-workers were watching. What if they were? She was entitled to drink coffee with a member of the faculty. In fact, Dr. Richter, the library's director, encouraged librarians to interact with faculty and students. Deena realized that she was crossing and uncrossing her legs and fidgeting with her hair like a school girl. Planting her feet firmly on the floor, she folded her hands on the table and forced her face to assume what she hoped was a pleasant, but neutral expression.

"I didn't know if you like milk or sugar so I brought these." Andor dumped a small pile of creamers and an assortment of sweeteners on the table.

"Oh, I just take it black, but thank you." She took a sip through the vent in the paper lid. *They were here to discuss a book. Talk about the book.* "So, you're a fan of Imre Kertesz. I'm afraid my Kertesz credentials are pretty thin. I've only read *Fatelessness* and the bio of Kertesz on Wikipedia."

"Yes, but it was such a coincidence that we were reading him at the same time. I thought maybe it was fate. I should get to know this woman." He smiled, waiting for her to admire his little joke.

Deena didn't roll her eyes but she couldn't suppress a low laugh. "I don't know about that. Anyway, you'd probably be disappointed. I'm not even sure I like Kertesz. His book is so unsettling on so many levels."

"That is what makes him a great writer, no?" Andor held Deena's gaze and waited for her response as though it held weight, as though it mattered.

"But don't you find his ideas disturbing? Is he implying that the victims of the Holocaust were somehow complicit in their fate?"

"But he doesn't believe in fate. He calls his book *Sorstalanság, Fatelessness*."

"That's what I mean. If we aren't governed by fate, then we have free will, right? Our lives are the result of the choices that we make. I can buy the idea of free will for some things, like not sticking to a diet or making a bad investment, but not the holocaust. Some things are beyond our control."

"So, you *are* a fatalist. You believe in destiny. Perhaps it really isn't a coincidence that we are reading the same book." Andor smiled at her, teasing. Or was he?

"When it comes to the holocaust, I believe in evil." Deena was surprised by her sudden unpremeditated response. The words had just spewed out of her. "Maybe that sounds medieval, but a large part of my family was murdered in the holocaust. I don't know another word for it."

"Of course, I forgot. It's not something to make jokes about. So, you're Jewish?"

Deena took a long breath, started to explain that her mother was Jewish but that she had no idea who her father was, stopped herself, exhaled, and simply said, "Yes."

"Were they Hungarian?"

"No, they were from Belarus, some little town. My grandmother didn't like to talk about it. She'd just say between Minsk and Pinsk, like it was a joke."

An attractive blonde with improbably long eyelashes and an eastern European accent suddenly appeared beside their table. "Andor, there you are. I knew I'd find you drinking coffee somewhere." She leaned over and gave him a kiss on the cheek. Deena could make out the uneven line where her eyelashes were stuck on with glue.

Andor stiffened, obviously embarrassed. "This is Krystina Pyszka. She manages the Hermes Gallery on Euclid Avenue. Krystina, this is Deena Berman." Deena smiled at Krystina who batted her eyelashes in her general direction. "Mrs. Berman is head of the humanities department here at the library. She's the lady I told you about. The one who lives in my apartment building."

They were talking about me? Deena was startled.

Krystina's eyes widened. "Oh, of course, and you work right here at the library? Isn't that wonderful?" A broad smile brightened her face as she leaned into Andor, whispered in his ear, and giggled coyly.

Well, whatever he wants from me it's obviously not female attention. He seems to have that covered. Deena picked up one of the small creamers, peeled back the top and poured it into her coffee while Krystina and Andor carried on a conversation in Hungarian as though she were invisible. She peeled back a second creamer, then a third and a fourth and a fifth. What had possessed her? Well, this was her reward, sitting here feeling old and foolish, a third wheel on someone else's date. For God's sake, he'd introduced her as *Mrs.* Berman. Stirring the lukewarm liquid with unwarranted concentration, she watched it go from black to beige to white.

"It was nice meeting you, but I've got to run." Krystina was already on her feet, tucking a sleek black purse under her arm. It had a designer logo that probably indicated that it was very expensive to people who recognized designer logos.

Deena nodded back at Krystina, hoping she didn't look as discombobulated as she felt. Krystina hurried away, her four inch heels clicking toward the door where she stopped and turned back toward Andor. "Friday at four, don't forget."

"Friday at four." Andor waved good-bye and Krystina

clicked her way out into the corridor.

"My goodness, is it six o'clock already? I've got to be going." Deena shot up as soon as Krystina was out of sight. "It was nice chatting with you. Thanks for the coffee, and the chrysanthemums." She tossed the cold coffee into the trash, "and it was lovely meeting your friend. She seems very nice." Deena headed for the door without waiting for a reply.

Andor rose from his seat, rushing to catch up with her. "I didn't invite Krystina. I didn't expect her to show up and disturb our conversation. There are still so many questions I want to ask you. Perhaps we could meet again in a few days?"

"I don't think so; like I said, I don't know much about Kertesz, but it was nice talking with you."

Andor put his hand on Deena's arm. "All my questions would not be about Kertesz. Please, let me buy you more than coffee. I know a good Hungarian restaurant that makes wonderful paprikash with dumplings and they bake their own dobos torte."

"Thank you, but I don't think so."

"Have you ever had Hungarian wine? We call it bull's blood. It makes Hungarian men strong like bulls." He smiled at her hopefully.

This was too much, Deena was utterly confused. She turned and looked at Andor. "What is this about? Why are you so interested in talking with me?"

"What is so difficult to understand? I'm new in this city and I'm lonely. You are a beautiful woman who reads books by Hungarian authors. Why wouldn't I want to know you?"

"You can't be too lonely. That young lady seemed very friendly."

"I understand what you are thinking, but you're wrong. Krystina flirts with me because she wants me to do a show at her gallery. She thinks no one can resist her. Maybe I'll do her show, maybe not, I don't know, but she's not my friend."

Deena stared at the hand still resting on her arm. It was a

sensitive hand covered with fine dark hairs that grew thicker above the wrist until they disappeared beneath the sleeve of his sweater. She pivoted toward the door jerking her arm away, "Andor, I'm not sure what you're thinking, but I need to go home now and make supper for my family."

"I was thinking we could be friends." Andor stepped back, bowing slightly from the waist. "Enjoy your supper and thank you for meeting me for coffee."

Deena had been lying when she told Andor that she had to get home to cook dinner for her family. In reality, neither Elliot nor Martin would be home before ten. Usually, she was delighted to walk into an empty apartment, make a cup of tea, stream her favorite oldies, check her email, and catch up on the day's news, but not this evening. The apartment felt cold and empty and she was jumpy and unsettled. Instead of putting on the kettle, she pulled out her phone.

"Hi Martin, would you like me to pick you up tonight? No, no problem. Sure, I'll be there at eight. Have you eaten? How about if I pick up some Chinese. OK, see you in a couple hours." As soon as she clicked off the call to Martin, she dialed her daughter's number.

Lauren answered immediately sounding pleasant and up-beat. "Hi Mom, what's up?"

Deena smiled as soon as she heard her daughter's voice. "Oh, not much really. I was just thinking about you, wondering how things were going."

"Everything's OK, actually better than OK. I've got some big news."

Could this be her daughter not sounding peevish or defensive? Deena couldn't remember the last time Lauren had sounded so happy. "Well, don't keep me in suspense. What is it?"

"I auditioned for *Dancing at Lughnasa* and I made call backs. Can you believe it? It's just a community theater, but they always bring in equity actors for the lead roles and you won't believe this, Jason Casey is going to play Michael."

"That's fantastic." Deena had no idea who Jason Carey was.

"Honestly, I think I have a real shot at this. Do you want to hear my Irish accent? The director thought I was born in Dublin."

Deena smiled into the phone, this was the Lauren she remembered: upbeat, creative, chatty and a bit scattered. "Tell me more about Jason Casey. I'm afraid the name doesn't ring a bell."

"He's been the star of *Kilkee* goin' on tree years now. Jason plays Oran, the Oyrish vampoyre who's mad in love wit Gael Cassidy. If ye saw him, I'm sure ye would know who he is straightaway."

"Unlikely," Deena chortled. Lauren's Irish accent wasn't half bad. Then, rather than humiliate herself by revealing a total ignorance of TV vampires, she asked, "When will you know if you got the part?"

"I probably won't get it, I mean I'm going up against two girls who studied acting in New York, but still, even making callbacks is incredible."

"I'm so proud of you. Good luck or break a leg or whatever you're supposed to say. Wouldn't that be something, seeing my daughter on stage with a famous actor." Deena calculated each word when talking with Lauren these days, and she was pretty sure that she'd stayed on safe ground, that she hadn't said anything to set her daughter off. She was wrong.

"Mom, please, don't even think about coming. I shouldn't have said anything. I was just so excited that the news spilled out, but it wasn't an invitation. I need you to stay out of my space. I don't want you or Dad anywhere near Boston right now. I'm sorry. It's nothing personal."

Deena detected panic in her daughter's voice. "Lauren, what's this about? Is it because we lost the house and had to move?"

"No, of course not. I mean, I feel terrible that you lost all that money, but I love you guys. Please don't think I'm mad about the house."

There was a long pause while Deena waited for more, but there was no more, just a long silence. Finally, Deena said, "OK then, what is it? What's going on?"

"Honestly, everything's OK."

"Lauren?"

"That's all I'm saying. Anyway I have to go, I'm meeting someone for dinner, and don't worry. Everything's OK."

"Wait a minute!" Deena shouted into the phone as though she were calling after someone receding into the distance.

"What?" Lauren sounded annoyed, but she was still there.

"I wanted to ask you something about Elliot. Has he ever said anything to you about joining the Navy?"

"The Navy? Are you crazy? Why would you ask me a thing like that?"

"It's probably nothing. Moms just worry about their kids. You know I'm worried about you too, Lauren."

"I told you to stop worrying. Both your kids are OK, OK?"

"OK." Once they'd hung up, Deena finished her tea, grabbed a handful of pita chips and stood nibbling them in the doorway to Elliot's bedroom. It was so neat, so ship shape, she thought to herself. Elliot's computer screen had gone dark, but she could still see the flag, the Navy recruitment slogan, and the image of earnest young men in blue and white uniforms in her mind's eye. Neither Martin nor Lauren could imagine Elliot enlisting in the Navy, but Deena could. Sensible, predictable kids sometimes did crazy things that were completely out of character. God knows, she had. Her mouth went dry and a pita chip stuck in her throat as she remembered throwing a duffle bag onto a bus and leaving New Moon without even saying good-bye.

The following day should have been utterly routine and uneventful, but it wasn't. Deena forgot a staff meeting, lost her key to the faculty bathroom, and misfiled a professor's research notes sending the poor man into a meltdown. She was worried about Elliot and she kept thinking about Andor. She imagined him perusing the stacks and sipping cappuccino in the café although, in reality, he was as absent as if he'd never moved to Cleveland. *Well, that's a relief,* she told herself as she tracked down books from distant libraries and compiled bibliographies for desperate graduate students. *It's not as though I don't have enough problems already.*

They spent the Jewish High Holidays with Danny and his family, as usual, but everyone was tense and out of sorts. Deena had once been good friends with Danny's wife, but now their conversations were strained and awkward and they hadn't exchanged a word since Yom Kippur. Now, it was late October and the new semester was two months old. Deena's closet should have transitioned from cottons and linens to woolens and tweeds, but the weather remained unseasonably warm, reaching into the mid 70s most afternoons. There was something about sunny days in late autumn that made Deena restless. The feeling was visceral, a gnawing low in her gut that made her inexplicably nostalgic for something she couldn't name.

Heidi, her yoga instructor, said her second chakra was blocked and that she should visualize orange and practice the Cobra and Dancer's Poses. Although Deena's yoga practice was sporadic and undisciplined, visualizing orange was easy with all the trees ablaze and every store front full of pumpkins.

She normally ate her lunch in the windowless staff lounge, but now she couldn't stay indoors. She bought gyros or falafel from a Middle Eastern deli and strolled around Wade Park where she shared them with the ducks in the lagoon. Two weeks later the temperature plummeted into the forties, but the sky remained blue and a few yellow leaves still clung to the ornamental trees that ringed the park. Deena zipped up her quilted jacket and decided to lunch *al fresco* one last time before the lagoon turned to ice and the entire city was buried under snow. She finished her sandwich and tossed the wrapping into a trash barrel, but it was still early so she climbed up the marble steps leading to the art museum. There might be just enough time to take a quick look at the Japanese prints she'd been reading about.

The Thinker, the great muscular nude by Rodin, sat at the top of the stairs outside the main entrance to the museum. Its lower legs and pedestal had been blown away by hooligans in the 70s as some sort of anti-war statement. Now the bronze figure sat bent over its ruined legs, its head resting on a massive hand, seeming to ponder a world in which such things could happen. Deena paused, as she always did, to give him a commiserating look.

"When I was a boy, we used to say he is trying to think where he left his clothes." The deep voice had a familiar Hungarian accent.

"Oh, my goodness, you startled me." Deena turned to see Andor straddling an old mountain bike. He wasn't wearing a coat, but a blue scarf was draped artfully around his neck. It exactly matched the color of his eyes. "Aren't you cold? My hands are starting to freeze."

"Riding the bike keeps me warm." There was an awkward silence broken by the honking of a flock of large birds passing overhead. "Lucky ducks, they're flying south. That's where I'd like to spend the winter."

"Those aren't ducks, they're Canadian Geese," Deena corrected. "But you're right. By February we'll all want to fly south." Deena put her hands in her coat pockets and found a crumpled tissue that she used to dab her nose.

"It's the same in Budapest. I'm used to the cold. Still, I dream of palm trees in January."

"We all dream of palm trees in January." Deena stared out at the lagoon, imagining it frozen over. "My husband's parents live in Arizona, in a retirement community near Scottsdale, but we won't be visiting them this year so no palm trees in

January for me."

"My next job is in Florida. I'll be teaching photography at a school in Sarasota this spring."

"Do you always move around like that, teaching at different schools each semester?"

"I like to travel so why not? I used to think I'd get a tenure track position one day, but it seems I'll always be a rolling rock."

It took a moment for Deena to translate. He meant a rolling stone. She smiled, but didn't correct his English. "Don't you ever want to settle down, have a real home?"

"I have a house near the town where I grew up. It has plum trees and a view of Lake Balaton from the upper windows. Unfortunately, I can only visit there a few months every year, but once the mortgage is paid off I'll retire. I'll sit on my own porch drinking plum wine, reading old novels and taking photographs of ducks."

"Sounds nice, but you're not that old. Retirement is still a long way off."

"Retirement starts the minute I make the last payment on my house. Until then, I keep moving from one university to the next. My contract with Garfield University is over in March, then I fly to Florida to start the new job. I understand it will still be cold in Cleveland when I leave."

"You understand right." Deena looked at her watch. She wouldn't have time for the exhibit now. "Well, it was nice seeing you again, but I need to get back to work."

"Good-bye then." Andor hopped back on his bike and wheeled off along the narrow path to the street where he pivoted in a large circle and pedaled back toward Deena. "Do you remember Krystina Pyszka, the woman who owns the art gallery?"

Deena nodded. She absolutely remembered the woman.

"She is hanging a show of my photographs at the end of the month. Would you and your husband come to the opening as my guests? It will be a nice party with food and music."

"Thank you, I'll see if we're free."

"Excellent, I'll make sure you get an invitation."

Deena waved as he pedaled away, then turned back toward the library feeling strangely warmer than when she'd left.

Chapter Four

Since when did she dress up to do laundry? Seriously, what was she trying to do? Impress a man with her ability to rinse and spin, load and fold? But all the while she was chiding herself, she was changing into a black T-shirt with a plunging V-neck, skinny jeans and long dangling earrings she hadn't worn in years. She added a gloss of pink lipstick, then headed to the basement with a basket full of dirty clothes.

The sound of washers churning was audible as soon as she stepped out of the elevator. What would she say to Andor if he were there? *Just be natural and do your laundry. Talk about work or Kertesz. No, don't talk about Kertesz, that's too emotional, and don't talk about anything personal. In fact, don't talk, just sit and read your book.* But she'd forgotten her book upstairs.

As soon as she turned the corner, she saw a man crouched in front of a dryer loading sheets and towels into a white plastic hamper. She couldn't see his face, but she was sure Andor wouldn't be wearing pajama bottoms and a Browns sweatshirt. *Well good*, she thought to herself, *Seeing Andor again would have just been awkward.*

Stopping in the mail room on her way back upstairs she found her box filled with nothing but solicitations and advertising circulars. She chucked them into the recycle bin and was starting back upstairs when she saw a neatly wrapped package with her name hand printed on the front. Curious, she tore it open to find a copy of *Dossier K* by Imre Kertesz and a flyer promoting *The Street Photography of Andor Farkas, a special exhibit at Hermes Gallery November 18th through December 12th. Patrons preview party November 17th by invitation only.* Scrawled across a reproduction of one of Andor's photographs were the words, *I hope you will come, Best Regards, Andor.*

It was only six o'clock, but the streets had been dark for an hour. The windows in the apartment building across the street were little squares of light that blinked on and off as the unknown occupants came home from work, changed their clothes, and started supper. Martin had just hung up his winter coat and was heading toward the couch when Deena intercepted him. "We got an invitation to a gallery opening today. Do you want to go?"

"I don't know. I'm not really into that stuff." Martin completed his bee line toward the sofa.

"It's not paintings, it's photography. I think you'd like it."

"Maybe, at the moment I'm more worried about this invitation." He pulled a threefold brochure out of his pocket and handed it to Deena.

Below a photo of a battleship she read, *Navy a Global Force for Good.* The brochure began to tremble in her hand. "Where did you find this?"

"In the kitchen. It was sticking out of one of Elliot's textbooks."

"Martin, we've got to talk to him. We need to know what's going on."

The sofa cushions sighed as Martin shifted his weight. For once he was looking Deena straight in the eyes, obviously concerned. "I think you're right. He's up to something."

"I knew something was wrong. He should be knee deep in college catalogs by now. He should be meeting with his guidance counselor, filling out applications, obsessing about his GPA, but he won't even sign up for the college boards. I'm

getting to the bottom of this if I have to beat it out of him."
Deena was pacing, so far as anyone could pace in the small
living room.

"Good luck. When I asked about his plans for next year he
clammed up like he was protecting nuclear codes. I couldn't
get a thing out of him." Martin took off his shoes and put his
feet up on the coffee table. "Elliot never used to be like this."

"No, he's changed since we lost the house." Deena looked
at her husband who looked back at her. Neither of them said
it, but the truth was they'd all changed. Nothing was the same.

Deena was in the kitchen sautéing mushrooms when she
heard the voice of Judy Woodruff and the *PBS Newshour* coming from the living room. Syrian Defense Forces, supported
by American airstrikes, had liberated Raqqa, one of the final strongholds of the Islamic terrorists. The city had been
bombed to rubble and a thousand civilian causalities reported,
but ISIS had been driven back. Deena's spatula froze above a
pan of mushrooms sizzling in olive oil. Was this good news?
It meant the defeat of the evil fanatics that had terrorized Iraq
and Syria for years, but at what expense? Without even looking at the television she could see the burned out buildings
and warrens of crumbling concrete that had become familiar
images on the nightly news. How many civilians were trapped
beneath those buildings? How many soldiers had been lost?
What if Elliot really did enlist? What if ISIS or the Taliban
turned their primitive, incomprehensible violence against her
son, her beautiful boy, who'd never known anything but safe
suburban streets, good schools, and first world comforts? She
felt as though tanks covered in layers of sand were rolling
through her kitchen, aiming at her heart.

By the time she heard Elliot's key in the lock Deena had
worked herself into a panic. Her dinner sat uneaten on the
kitchen counter and she was picking at her cuticles, an old
habit she thought she'd outgrown years ago. She stared rue-
fully at Martin who was lost in a television series about Rus-

sian spies pretending to be a normal American family. How could he watch so much TV? He used to read books, listen to music, ride his bike. She stepped between Martin and the TV, deliberately cutting off his field of vision.

"Hey, would you mind? You're blocking the picture."

Deena didn't budge. "Elliot's home, you said we'd talk to him when he got home."

"OK, the show will be over in ten minutes."

Deena turned around and punched the power button. "It's over now."

Martin blinked, "Sheez, you could have waited a couple minutes."

Deena wasn't interested in a television drama when there was a real life crisis in the next room. "Elliot's in his bedroom, let's go talk to him. We need to present a united front, so you'd better back me up."

"Whoa, slow down. How can I back you when we don't know what's happening? How about hearing him out before we impose a sentence."

"Please Martin, I'm really scared."

"OK, Sweetheart, calm down. Don't panic. Let's hear what he has to say." Martin pulled himself out of the sofa and followed her down the hall.

Elliot lay stretched out on his bed, typing into his phone. He put it down when he saw both his parents standing in the doorway. "Hey, what's up? Did something happen?"

"I don't know. I guess we were hoping you could tell us." Deena walked over to Elliot's desk and sat down in his swivel chair. "It's almost Thanksgiving and you haven't even looked at a college catalogue. First, you practically kill yourself trying to earn your own tuition and then poof, you're not even applying anywhere. What's going on?"

Martin sat down on the foot of Elliot's bed and smiled at his son. "Yeah, what's going in that head of yours?"

"Dad, I told you, I don't want to discuss it yet. I'm still doing research. Anyway, the deadline for Cleveland State isn't until July. It's not like I'm applying to competitive private schools. If I apply to Cleveland State I'll get in. So please, just chill. Everything's under control."

Deena tried to appear calm. "Elliot, you can still try for one of those top schools. With your grades and athletic skill you'd stand a good chance at a scholarship. Also, you know that we'll help with your tuition. We lost our savings, but your father and I are still working. We're still making decent money. Have you even talked to your guidance counselor? She'd tell you the same thing."

"I have talked to her, and she said those schools give way more loans than scholarships. Kids graduate from Columbia and NYU a hundred thousand dollars in debt."

Martin was holding Elliot's foot and rolling it back and forth, an affectionate gesture he'd begun when Elliot was a baby. "OK, so what's the plan? Why the big secret? Your mother's going to lose her mind if you don't tell her what's going on."

"I'll tell you both really soon. It's nothing awful. I just want to make my own decision without other people's advice. We'll talk as soon as I've finished my research."

"Research on what? What have you got cooking that you're not telling us about?" Deena stood up suddenly and faced her son. "Oh hell, let's stop playing games. Your father found this." She thrust the brochure at him. "Just tell us, Elliot, are you enlisting in the Navy?"

Elliot swung his long legs over the side of the bed. Soft brown curls were visible through the open neck of the button down shirt he wore to work. It didn't matter to Deena that her baby had a hairy chest or that he towered over her and needed a shave. She was prepared to throw herself between him and the entire United States Navy.

"OK, Mom, I didn't want to talk about it yet, but yes, the

Navy is one of the things I'm thinking about."

Deena 's knees went wobbly forcing her to sit back down. *My mother would die if she knew her grandson might enlist.* She remembered the old anti war chants that remained embedded in New Moon tradition long after the war was over. *Hell no, we won't go* and *Draft beer not men.* At one time New Moon had been a haven for draft dodgers and now her own son... There was a ringing in her ears and for a moment she was afraid that she might actually black out.

Martin acted as though the idea of his son dodging bombs and bullets was perfectly normal. He didn't even flinch. "So, what has your research revealed so far?

"It seems like the Navy might be a good deal. They pay for college when you get out and there's other stuff, like they pay you almost $1,500 a month salary and I wouldn't have to pay for room or board or medical insurance so I could probably save most of it, and I'd probably get to travel."

"Oh yeah, you'd get to travel. I understand Afghanistan is lovely this time of year." Deena could hardly breathe. Her heart was hammering inside her chest like a machine gun.

"Come on Deena, let's hear him out. This is his life and his decision."

"Are you crazy?"

Elliot sighed and threw himself back onto the bed. "This is exactly why I didn't want to talk about it. I haven't even made a decision yet. It's just something I'm thinking about. Could you leave now? I'm really tired."

"No, we can't leave. This is too important. You're putting your whole future at risk, your whole life. You might get killed." Deena was on her feet, but she wasn't going anywhere. She wasn't going to budge until Elliot assured her that he would never, ever enlist, that joining the Navy was a crazy idea, and that he'd put it completely out of his head.

She felt a firm hand on her back as Martin walked her toward the door. "Come on, we can talk about it later. Let the boy rest now. He's had a long day."

"This is how you back me up?" she hissed as he led her down the hall. "I thought we were going to present a united front, or don't you care if your son gets shot by terrorists?" Deena was frightened and she wanted Martin to make things right. That was his job. He was Elliot's father.

"Of course I care. I just said we'd talk when we're not so tired." Martin had steered her toward their bedroom where they stood arguing in lowered voices so that Elliot wouldn't hear them. There was no privacy in the stupid apartment. It was a fucking fishbowl.

"Are you out of your mind? If he enlists, the Navy owns him. They can send him anywhere. They can make him do anything. They'll put a gun in his hand and tell him to shoot people. Do you want Elliot shooting people?"

"Well, someone's got to defend the country. It's his life and his decision. He's almost eighteen years old and mature for his age."

"Exactly, he's not even eighteen years old. He's a child. He belongs in school."

"Let him figure it out, Deena. Maybe the Navy's not such a bad idea."

Deena stared at Martin in disbelief. "Traitor," she hissed as she gathered up a pillow and blanket and threw them at her husband. "Why don't you leave now. I think the TV misses you."

Martin stood facing her with the bedding in his arms. He looked blindsided, as though he hadn't expected her to be so angry. He started to say something, then seemed to change his mind, and backed out of the room. Deena locked the door behind him.

Deena lay alone in the king size bed that filled the small bedroom while IEDs exploded in her head. Her son in the military? The thought made her dizzy. Deena visualized the words written in large bubble letters on the psychedelic poster that had hung in the front hall of New Moon as long as she'd lived there. *Make Love Not War*. If New Moon had a mantra, a guiding principle, that was it. Stripes of light undulated on the ceiling as air from the furnace billowed the curtains. It was after midnight and she'd been in bed for an hour, but her mind was wide awake. It kept taking her back to the dilapidated farmhouse on the outskirts of Santa Fe where she'd spent her childhood. The place had always been her dirty secret, something shameful to hide from people in the normal world. As a child, she'd invented elaborate lies to conceal the fact that she lived in a house without electricity or running water and that their toilet was hardly more than a retrofitted chamber pot. It had been bad enough being poor, bad enough having a mother who couldn't afford school supplies or tennis shoes, but why had she been so...so...what?

An image of her mother flashed across Deena's inner eye. Rain was standing bare chested at the water pump, her bare feet caked with mud. She was wearing nothing but a Mexican serape wrapped around her waist and a cowboy hat tilted forward against the sun above a tangle of frizzy blonde curls. Her heavy breasts bounced emphatically as she worked the pump. Why had her mother been like *that*?

Deena turned over to check the clock. Its illuminated dial said 12:47. She sank back into her pillow and closed her eyes. It had been thirty years since she'd fled the chaos and squalor of New Moon. She tried not to think about those early years. She certainly never talked about them. Why was her mind taking her back there now? The story she told her kids was that she'd been born in a small town in New Mexico where her parents taught on a Navajo reservation. Her father had died of asthma when she was just a baby, but she and her mother had continued to live outside Santa Fe until she was fourteen when she'd been sent back east to attend high school. Sadly, her mother had been killed in a terrible car accident shortly after Deena arrived in Ohio. Fortunately, she'd had a loving grandmother who'd provided her with a wonderful home and education so everything had turned out just fine. It was a sappy story, thin on details, but they'd bought it. In fact, they'd been more interested in stories about the Navajo kids than about their grandparents and Deena truthfully shared what she remembered about life on the nearby reservation. Was she protecting them or protecting herself from the taint of the unwashed hippies who had raised her? Or was it just too complicated to untangle all the lies after a lifetime of deceit?

The taint of unwashed hippies? Had New Moon really been that bad? Deena did an inventory of old memories: filthy sheets, washing outdoors with cold water from the pump in the summer, not washing much at all in the winter, their neighbor, Mrs. Rios, arriving with baskets of tamales when she knew they had no food. Yes, there was a time when it had been that bad but, in fairness, things had improved a lot by the time she was a teenager. In fact, there'd been some really good times after her mom and Casey found jobs and started paying the bills. Unexpectedly, she found herself overcome with nostalgia for a place that she despised.

She remembered days in late November when the aspens had lost their leaves and their silver branches reached up into a clear blue sky. They'd all hike out to an old pecan orchard with bags and boxes and Navajo baskets. She and Paz would shimmy up the branches and shake nuts down onto blankets spread beneath the trees while her mother, Casey and the Rios clan gathered them up like squirrels.

There were other things too, things she hadn't thought about in years, like when they cooked up pots of red beans and rice, cornbread and stuffed peppers and ate around the table like a regular family. And there were the times her mother took her to the library and Miss Novak filled her arms with books, the times they went camping and the times they went swimming in the city pool.

And there was the music. She could still see Buddha with

his full beard and burly body sitting on the back steps playing his guitar. He could played everything: folk, pop, country and riffs he made up himself. He wasn't around that much, his job as a professional musician kept him on road, but he always came back to New Moon and he always brought good times with him. Everyone would sprawl on the grass listening and he'd say, "Come on Rain, don't be shy." Then Deena's mother would join in with an amazing warm contralto that swooped and bopped and trilled like something on the radio. They'd keep singing and playing until Buddha finally stopped to fish his stash out of his guitar case and light up. That was the signal that the show was over and everyone would wander back to whatever they'd been doing. Her mom and Buddha were good though, really good, not that it mattered in the end. Deena's mental screen went black. There were memories too painful to relive. She clenched her eyes shut in the dark bedroom trying not to see her mother's ashen face as she received the news that Buddha had OD'd in a McDonald's men's room just outside of Albuquerque.

That had been the final straw. She'd tolerated the privations and eccentricities of New Moon for fourteen years, but now her whole system rebelled against the place. She fled to Cleveland where Bubbe's neat suburban home provided the solace of wall to wall carpeting, a floral bedspread and her own TV, but those luxuries came at a price. She never saw anyone from New Moon again, not her mother, not Casey, not even Paz who'd been her best friend, practically her brother. Buddha's death hadn't been their fault. They didn't know he did hard drugs when he was on the road, but it didn't matter. She left them for the normal life she'd always craved, not knowing she was leaving them for good. What had gone so wrong? Other teenagers ran away, other families suffered grief and trauma, but most found their way back to one another. Not hers. Even after Bubbe died Deena never sent any of them so much as a postcard and not one of them had ever written her.

Deena bought a little black dress to wear to Andor's opening at the Hermes Gallery and she stuffed Martin into the suit he'd worn to Elliot's bar mitzvah. Of course, he didn't want to go, but she'd insisted. Now, looking around the gallery, she felt foolish for coming. What did she know about gallery openings? Her notions were all based on stories in *The New Yorker*. Apparently real openings, at least in Cleveland, were a tad less glamorous. Most of the men wore jeans and sweaters. The few who arrived in suits looked like lawyers stopping by on their way home from work. A few women wore silk blouses, or interesting jewelry, but no one else was wearing an actual cocktail dress and high heels. No one, that is, except Krystina Pyszka, who was running the show on four inch heels with effortless aplomb.

Krystina had assumed a proprietary attitude toward Andor, shepherding him from one potential buyer to another. She flirted and flattered her way around the room, finding an excuse to make physical contact with nearly everyone as she greeted them. She straightened a tie here, patted a back there, leaned into a shoulder to share a laugh with someone else. Deena stood in the corner sipping Merlot from a plastic wine glass, eavesdropping with new respect. Krystina knew everyone by name and remembered minute details of their collections and previous acquisitions. The woman might be pushy, insensitive and presumptuous, but she knew her business.

Andor, for his part, looked both pleased and embarrassed by all the attention. There was something very appealing about his awkwardness. He should have been accustomed to these sorts of events, but instead of being the extroverted glad-hander she'd expected, Andor seemed cowed by Krystina who led him by the hand from one group to another.

Andor gave Deena an apologetic smile as Krystina dragged

him past her toward an elderly couple studying a photograph of an urchin asleep on a city sidewalk. Deena smiled back then pretended to be engrossed in a large format work titled *Liberty Bridge at Night*. Even with her back turned she could hear Krystina gushing, "Henry, I'm so glad you're here. There's something special I have to show you. No one else will appreciate it the way you will."

A young musician, probably a student, was standing on an improvised riser valiantly playing the flute over the animated din that all but drowned her out. Deena was about to move closer to the musician when she spotted Martin coming toward her carrying a paper plate piled high with crackers, hummus and small cubes of cheese. He held it out toward her. "Try the cheddar, it's really good."

Deena took a piece of cheese from his plate. "So, what do you think of the photographs? Did you see anything you liked?"

"Yeah, but we're not taking anything home. Did you see the prices?"

"Do you want me to introduce you to the photographer? He's over there talking with that white haired couple and the lady in the red blouse."

"I don't know. He looks busy, maybe later if he's not talking to anyone else." Martin was always shy at these sorts of events, but Deena was feeling bold.

"Come on. You'll like him. He's travelled all over the world. Anyway, he lives in our building. You should say hello."

"Could we just listen to the music for a few more minutes?" Deena, realizing that Martin was feeling awkward and out of his depth, followed him to the front of the gallery where strains of something by Bach were clearly audible. They were standing side by side sipping their wine and smiling at the musician when Andor appeared, momentarily free of his keeper.

"Deena, I'm so glad you decided to come. It's so nice to see a familiar face. And this is your husband?" Andor beamed at them both.

"Yes, this is my husband, Martin. Martin, this is Andor Farkas, the amazing photographer who's produced all this work." Deena beamed back. The occasion demanded a lot of smiling.

Martin handed Deena his empty cheese plate so he could shake hands with the artist. "I don't know much about photography, but these are fantastic. You must have a really good camera."

"I do." Andor looked slightly amused. "My photos aren't digital. They're shot with film and hand developed like in the old days. Maybe it's a bit retro, but I like it better."

"Really? Why's that?" Martin perked up, forgetting his shyness. Anything techie caught his interest.

"Film has better spatial resolution and dynamic range. There's always a compromise, of course. Digital is easier to manipulate and actually has greater depth of field, but you could never do this with a digital camera." He gestured to a small photograph of a young woman standing by a bus stop. "She's lovely isn't she? She reminds me of this lady." He nodded toward Deena. "Maybe one day I will take a photograph of your lovely wife, with your permission, of course."

Martin blinked and turned to take a better look at Deena just as Krystina turned up with a bearded man in cowboy boots and a bolero tie. "Andor, this is Reno Cartridge, the man I was telling you about." She turned toward Deena. "Why, I believe we've met. You're the lady from the library, aren't you?" She turned and whispered something to the aging cowboy who smiled and gave Deena an appraising look. Before Deena could respond, Krystina cut her off. "I'm sorry, but I'm going to have to steal Andor for a minute. He and Reno have some important business to discuss." As Krystina herded Andor and Reno to her private office she turned back toward Deena. "It's so nice seeing you again. Thanks for coming."

By ten o'clock the musician was packing up her flute and the noisy throng was beginning to thin. What had she expected? She didn't know, but she felt let down and out of sorts.

"I think the photographer likes you." Martin made a pitiful attempt at a Hungarian accent. "Maybe vun day I vill take a photograph of your lufly wife."

"Yeah, right. Did you see that scarf he was wearing? Kind of affected, don't you think?"

"I thought he was OK. If that woman hadn't dragged him away, I was going to ask him to recommend a good camera for a beginner."

"She acted like she owned him. If he's interested in anyone, I'd bet it's her."

"Well, he can have her. I thought she looked kind of dangerous, like she might keep a stiletto stashed in her stilettos."

"You're right," Deena laughed, delighted that Martin shared her antipathy for the woman. They finished the wine in their little plastic cups, then she took his arm and they left for home.

Winter was definitely getting closer. As Deena scraped frost from the windshield of her ten year old Taurus, she yearned for the attached two car garage that had protected their cars and her frozen fingers for so many years. She and Martin had sworn to economize, but maybe they could afford a little extra for an indoor parking space.

As she pulled out onto the street she was glad to see that the roads were clear. With luck, snow would hold off for another month. The blues and greens of summer, the oranges, reds, and yellows of the fall had disappeared. Patches of olive dotted the browned out lawns reminding her of army camouflage.

Deena was groggy and in a nasty mood as she slid her electronic key through the slot at the employees' entrance and headed toward the coat room. If she could just manage a cup of coffee without speaking to a soul, she might be able to face the day. But, of course, that was too much to ask.

"Deena, there you are. I was hoping to catch you. We need to talk." Otto Richter was smiling his most ingratiating smile, revealing an uneven row of yellow teeth. Deena had worked for him long enough to know that if he was smiling, something was wrong.

"I was just going to grab a cup of coffee. Can we talk in the lounge?"

"Get your coffee and bring it to my office. We can chat in there." Otto was as monochromatic as a Cleveland winter, nothing but gray and white — apart from those yellow teeth that made Deena think of dog piss in the snow. Gray hair was combed neatly above the collar of the gray suit he unfailingly wore with a clean white shirt. His complexion matched his suit, gray creased with a pinstripe of fine lines. Thick white eyebrows jumped like startled dust bunnies when he spoke. He was not, by nature, a smiler, but he was competent and intelligent and he'd brought the library to national prominence during the thirty-four years he'd served as its director.

Deena returned, mug in hand, hesitating at the door to Dr. Richter's office. He waved her toward one of the black Barcelona chairs that sat across from the mission table he used as a desk. For a library office there were surprisingly few books, just a pile of review copies stacked on a credenza behind the table, and nothing at all except a computer monitor and a telephone on the desk itself. However, unlike its occupant, the room was awash in color. There were framed Kandinsky prints on the walls and a red Persian rug that covered most of the floor. A replica Calder mobile hung in front of a large window that looked out on a quiet side yard. Position definitely had its privileges.

"Sit down, this should only take a moment." Otto's tone was jovial, making Deena wary. "I don't see nearly enough of you, but the reports are excellent. We're very pleased with the work you've been doing. Dr. Friedlander, in particular, mentioned you. I think you'll find your name listed among the acknowledgements in his new book."

"It was an interesting project. I was happy to help." Deena's defenses began to crumble. Maybe she was being offered a promotion, or better yet, a raise.

"Well, you've certainly become a valuable member of our team, which brings us to the matter at hand. As I'm sure you know, every department has had to deal with recent budget cuts and, of course, the library is no exception."

This was definitely not the prelude to a raise. He was letting her go. She'd heard positions were being cut. Could they live on unemployment until she found another job? Forget the indoor parking space. They'd be hard pressed to pay the rent, and where would they get the money to help Elliot with his tuition? Deena's head was spinning and she couldn't focus. Otto Richter continued talking, and she continued smiling and nodding, but her own inner voices had drowned him out. Then his mouth stopped moving and he was looking at her with anticipation. Apparently, he expected her to say something. She stared back, nonplussed.

He mistook her silence for indecision. "I know that I've thrown this at you without any warning, but we'll need your decision by the end of the day. Someone has to assume responsibility for Archives and Special Collections as soon as possible."

He was putting her in charge of Special Collections? When was the last time she'd ventured into those locked, humidity controlled stacks where the library stored its oldest and rarest books? That was Taylor Smythe's domain. But it was a job. She wasn't being fired. "Of course," Deena blinked half blind with confusion and relief. "Absolutely, I can manage Special Collections, but who's going to cover Humanities?"

Otto's eyebrows leapt and quivered near the top of his forehead. "I thought I'd made that clear. You'll be managing both departments. I understand you'll be stretched a bit thin, but we wouldn't have asked Taylor to leave if we could afford to keep you both." There was an awkward pause as Otto searched for the right words. "Unfortunately, Taylor left rather abruptly yesterday afternoon, so he won't be able to show you the ropes. However, Alice knows the system and she'll be there to help if you have any questions. I'm sure you know Alice Krol. She's been the Archives clerk for years."

"When would you want me to start?" Deena managed to keep smiling through her clenched teeth. How the Hell was she supposed to manage two departments? It was crazy, but she felt a guilty thrill play down her spine. She still had a job and Taylor didn't.

"Actually, why don't you go down to Archives and talk to Alice this morning. I'm sure you'll do a fine job. I knew we could count on you." He shook her hand, his eyebrows jumping with pleasure that she'd agreed to take on the extra work, "Congratulations."

Alice wasn't at her usual station behind the glass wall that protected the Special Collections desk. A pimply faced sophomore sat in her chair engrossed in his phone. He didn't even look up even when Deena leaned against the counter directly in front of him. Exasperated, she rapped on the desk with her knuckles. "Excuse me, do you know where Miss Krol is? I need to talk with her."

The kid glanced up, clearly annoyed. "She's in the stacks, but you can't go down there." He went back to typing something with his thumbs.

"Allow me to introduce myself." Deena fixed him with the evil eye she reserved for unruly children and particularly pig headed husbands. "I'm Deena Berman, I'll be replacing Mr. Smythe as head of this department. Now, where can I find Miss Krol?"

To his credit, the young man sat up and looked at Deena, although without the deference she'd been hoping for. Leaning forward, he addressed her in a low, conspiratorial tone.

"Well then, I guess you can go down there if you want, but I wouldn't if I were you."

The oldest books in the library were housed in the newest, most high tech wing of the building. Deena fumbled through her purse for the scrap of paper containing the security code Otto had given her. She shook her head as she typed 5551216, the library's phone number, into the keypad on the wall. You wouldn't need to be Sherlock Holmes to crack that code. There was a click, and she pushed open the heavy metal door. Inside, long shelves of books were visible through the dim infrared light. At the end of an aisle on the far side of the room she could hear a woman sobbing.

Chapter Five

"Hey Sweetie, guess what?" Lauren's address remained a mystery, but Deena called her daughter several times a week as though she were just away at college. "The director of the library called me into his office this morning and put me in charge of Archives and Special Collections."

"Awesome! That's totally epic." Deena smiled, Lauren sounded so ... Lauren.

"Well, it's not really that awesome since they expect me to do my old job too. Apparently, the plan is to save money by having half as many people work twice as hard."

"Wow, that sucks. Are they at least giving you more money?"

"Nope. But they're letting me keep my job, and at the moment I'm pretty grateful for that." Deena was ironing while she talked and using a headset to keep her hands free. "Do you still want that striped shirt with the button down pockets? I just found it at the bottom of the ironing basket."

"God no, give it away. So, what does an Archive and Special Collections librarian do anyway?"

Deena tossed the shirt back into the ironing basket. "Mostly, just protect the material because it's all so valuable and one of a kind: first editions, original prints, historical documents, that sort of thing."

"Really? What's stuff like that worth?"

"I don't know, but I guess I'd better find out if I'm going to manage the collection. Some of it must be worth a bundle because they run the department like Fort Knox." Deena paused, put down the iron and sat on the edge of her bed. "Lauren, I wasn't kidding about being grateful to still have a job. It turns out that it was just dumb luck that I wasn't laid off today."

"What do you mean? I thought you just got a promotion."

"Yeah, some promotion. It turns out the only reason I got the job was because Taylor Smythe wouldn't take mine. Do you remember Dr. Richter, the head of the library?"

"Sure."

"Well, he gave me this whole spiel about how he was giving me extra responsibility because he had so much confidence in me, that he just knew I could manage two departments, that he could count on me to be a team player, yadda, yadda. Then he sends me down to talk to Alice, the department clerk, because she's supposed to train me. By the way, the woman hates my guts for taking Taylor's job. Anyway, she told me that Dr. Richter offered Taylor my job yesterday."

"Wow, that's harsh."

"Yeah, the only reason I've still got a job at all is because Taylor got insulted and walked out. I guess you can do that when you're sixty-two and independently wealthy. Anyway, Taylor told Richter that his department was already under-staffed and there was no way he was managing an additional department. Then he went back to his office, said good-bye to Alice, gathered up his stuff and walked out. You've got to hand it to the guy. He's got guts. I found Alice in the stacks crying her eyes out this morning. I thought she might actually take a swipe at me she was so mad. She said if I had an ounce of integrity I'd walk out too. But I can't do that. I need the job."

"What did Dad say?"

"I haven't told him yet. I'm waiting until he gets home from work, but I just had to tell someone."

"I bet he'll tell you to quit."

"I'm not quitting. I'll do the best I can and Richter will just have to understand if a few things fall between the cracks." Neither of them said anything for a long time. She shouldn't have dumped this on Lauren. Now her daughter was going to worry about her. She put the iron down and went fishing in the laundry basket. "Hey, I just found your favorite yoga pants. If you give me your address I'll mail them to you."

"Nice try, Mom. Put them in my room and I'll pick them up when I come home."

"You're coming home?" Deena's heart skipped a beat.

"Well, I'll come home eventually. I can't make any plans until I know whether I got that part I auditioned for. It's down to me and one other girl."

"When will you know?"

"They said just a few more days. Wouldn't it be too fantastic? Send me good energy, Mom. Tell the universe that part is mine."

"Absolutely, I'll email the universe as soon as I've finished the laundry." Deena did her best to sound enthusiastic, but she was actually calculating how much sooner Lauren might come home if she didn't get the part.

The next day was overcast and cold just like every other day that week. Deena was walking across campus toward the student union with her head bent into the wind and her hands deep in her pockets when she heard her name called out in a familiar Hungarian accent.

"Deena, Deena, stop, please." She waited while Andor, red cheeked and out of breath, caught up with her. "I've been wanting to thank you for coming to my opening. It was so good to see you there."

"We had a wonderful time and it looked like you sold quite a few photographs."

"Not so many, but a show like that really helps when you're trying to live on an adjunct's salary. Did your husband like the exhibit?"

"He did. In fact, you inspired him. He wants you to recommend a good camera for a beginner."

"Excellent, I would be happy to tell him about cameras. Have you eaten yet?"

"I was just heading over to the student union to grab a quick sandwich."

"No, don't eat a sandwich. Let me take you to a good Hungarian restaurant. It's very close. We can walk."

"Thank you, but I have to be back at work in less than an hour."

"It's five minutes away. You'll be back in plenty of time." Andor took her arm and led her around the corner and up a flight of stairs into a small restaurant she'd passed a thousand times without noticing.

It was only lunch, not supper, but Deena's eyes flitted frenetically around the room on the lookout for anyone who might pause to sniff the air and smell a fresh tidbit for office gossip. But why would they? She met male colleagues for lunch all the time. There was absolutely nothing unusual about conferring with a professor over lunch.

The menu was printed on the back of an illustrated map of Hungary that Deena studied intently so she wouldn't have to make eye contact with the attractive Hungarian sitting across from her. An endless loop of traditional gypsy dances competed with a television mounted above the bar. Disposable white paper covered the tables, but beautiful, hand embroidered tablecloths decorated the walls. A small vase of red carnations sat beside the salt and pepper shakers. Deena reached out to touch one of the ruffled flowers and was surprised to find that it was real.

"You don't need a menu. I'll order for you. We'll have paprikash with chicken livers. It's delicious here, just like my mother makes." Andor's voice was kind but insistent.

"Oh, I couldn't eat that much for lunch. Maybe just salad,

or the mushroom soup." Deena thought she'd sounded quite definite, but he confiscated her menu and signaled for the waitress.

"You will love this dish. Enjoy a good meal now, then don't eat so much for supper." Andor was beaming, obviously delighted to be sharing lunch with her.

Ten minutes later the waitress placed overflowing plates of chicken livers in gravy and tender yellow spaetzle in front of them. Deena eyed her plate with suspicion. She picked up her knife and fork and cut into the tender meat. It was pink inside and very soft. She hadn't eaten a chicken liver in years. A moment later she remembered why.

The first tentative bite turned to bile in her mouth as she was transported back to her grandmother's dining room where she was a bewildered teenager sitting shiva for her mother. It was January of 1984 and she'd been in Cleveland only a few weeks. In the days after her arrival there had been a flurry of calls and letters between Deena's mother and Bubbe that had gone badly. Although Deena never knew the details, she knew that her mother had refused to come back to Cleveland, even with her daughter held as bait. A final phone punctuated by screams and ultimatums ended with Bubbe ripping the phone from the wall and tearfully tearing the fabric of her blouse before staggering to her bedroom.

The next morning Bubbe had emerged, grim faced and red eyed. She'd sat down at the kitchen table with her small, green leather address book and called everyone she knew to inform them that her daughter was dead. Deena understood that this was a symbolic death, that her mother was still alive somewhere in the world, but from that day forth she was dead to them. Why hadn't she protested? Why had she played along with that mean charade? Had she been that hungry for a safe, clean home in the suburbs? No, it was more than that. She'd wanted her mother to reappear, to rise from the undead and drag her back to Santa Fe, but she never came. That was the sadness. That was the source of her anger. She'd been the one to run away, but in her heart she'd always felt abandoned by her mother.

Overnight, she'd become an orphan. Friends and neighbors arrived by the carload. Her grandmother's small brick bungalow filled with strangers who smothered her with kisses as they wiped their eyes. Deena was never sure if those well-meaning people understood that this was merely a show orchestrated by her grandmother or if they believed that her mother was truly dead. She remembered a rabbi, a real *rebbe* from the old country, in a black hat and long black coat, leading the prayer for the dead and lighting a memorial candle that burned for a week. What had her grandmother told him? The dining table was covered with small gifts of food: Russian tea biscuits, mandelbrot, herring and gefilte fish. Deena was seated at a small table with her grandmother and fed hard boiled eggs and chopped liver that tasted like death.

"So, how do you like it?" Andor leaned across the table, filling her glass with red wine. Deena forced herself to swallow. "Oh, it's good. It's very good, but I have to be back at work in half an hour. Please no wine for me." Where were those friends and neighbors now? They'd all disappeared after Bubbe died.

"But you're the boss, you're in charge of a big department."

"Actually, I'm now in charge of two departments. My boss decided to save money by having one person do two jobs."

"So, what is this second department? Is it something interesting to you?"

"It might be interesting if I knew anything about it. They call it Archives and Special Collections. It's basically a vault where they keep all the really old and valuable stuff." Deena took another bite. She couldn't do it. She'd have to find an excuse for leaving her entire meal.

Andor perked up the moment he heard about her new position. He seemed to imagine it was some huge promotion.

"Next, maybe they will make you head of the whole library. Who will care if you're a little late?"

"Alice. She's my clerk, but she watches me like a hawk. There's nothing she'd like better than having a reason to report me to the director."

Andor was slathering a slice of bread with a thick coat of butter. "You should fire her. You don't need a clerk like this."

"I can't fire her. She's the only one who knows how the department works. I'm lucky she lets me into the stacks at all. Those books are her babies. You'd think she'd written them all herself."

"But she can't really keep you out. You must have the special key." Andor took a sip of wine and smiled at her. He had excellent teeth. "You could change the lock and keep her out, no?"

"There's no actual key; everything's electronic now, but changing the security code wouldn't help anyway. It wouldn't change the fact that I can't manage the department without her or that she can't stand the sight of me." Deena patted her lips with a napkin as Andor refilled her glass from the carafe of wine he'd ordered. "To be honest, I think she was in love with the previous director. They worked together for thirty years."

"How old is this Alice?"

"I don't know, late fifties, maybe sixty. She's never married. That department is her whole life."

"I'm sorry for her, but this is a common story. Did the old director have a wife?"

Deena shrugged, "Probably, I don't know. We never talk about our personal lives."

"Lucky you have the..." Andor stopped and made a great show of glancing around the room and leaning forward with a conspiratorial air before whispering, "secret code. Did you memorize the numbers then swallow the paper — or maybe it was written with disappearing ink?"

"God no, it's just a library phone number. We're not exactly the CIA. The challenge would be getting past Alice. She's
the dragon protecting the treasure. As long as she's on the job,
our books are safe."

"You make me laugh. It is such a pleasure to be with you."
Andor broke into a deep chuckle. It was the first time Deena
had heard him laugh. "Why aren't you eating? Don't you like
the livers?"

"No, they're wonderful, perfect, but my stomach is a bit
upset. I shouldn't have ordered a full meal."

"Do you think you could manage some *dobos torte*? I want
to keep you a little more time." He touched the watch on
Deena's wrist with one finger, then ran it down the back of
her hand where it lingered as he spoke. "A photographer is
trained to see things, and I see that you could use a friend.
Would it be such a bad thing if we occasionally share a meal,
drink some wine, maybe discuss a book we like? Don't tell me
I've guessed wrong. I know what I see."

Of course, he was right. Deena took another sip of wine to
disguise her trembling lips. How had this virtual stranger seen
something she'd hidden even from herself? She was lonely and
had been for a long time, but she was also married. Even the
sort of friendship he proposed would be a betrayal. Andor
stared back at her expectantly with an expression that had
gone out of fashion in the thirties. It belonged on the face
of the romantic lead in a black and white movie: confident,
amused, attentive. He rattled her, made her feel like a stupid
school girl.

"I'm sorry Andor. I have to get back to my office."

"But you'll think about what I said. Maybe you'll have
dinner with me one day next week."

"Thank you for lunch. It was nice seeing you again. No,
please don't get up. I have to leave right now or I'll be late."

"OK, run back to your office. But I'll call you in a few days
and then we'll talk again."

"I'm in love! Love, love, love, looooove." Lauren was beside herself, giddy with joy.

Deena smiled indulgently. She'd heard this song before. "So, who is he? Where did you meet him?"

"His name is Matthew Bacon and he's the stage manager for *Dancing at Lughnasa*, but he's not just some amateur. He graduated from Yale. I mean, can you believe he actually went to Yale? Then he went to New York and got his equity card and worked at La Mama and some other places. Now, he mostly works in television. That's how he knows Jason Casey. He's so good, Jason wouldn't even do the show unless we agreed to hire Matthew too."

"That's quite a resume. Just how old is this Matthew Bacon?" Sirens were going off in Deena's brain, but she kept her voice level and tried not to sound alarmed.

"I don't know how old he is. I mean he's older than the guys I usually date, but he can't be that old, I mean he's absolutely gorgeous."

"You're dating this man?"

"No, not exactly dating. He's in the middle of some ugly divorce and he can't date anyone right now. But I can tell he likes me. He sits next to me when the director gives us notes after rehearsals, and he calls me Mimi, isn't that cute?"

"Mimi? Why would he call you Mimi? That's kind of weird."

"I don't know." Lauren prickled, sounding defensive. "It's just a nickname."

"Listen Lauren, you're a big girl in a big city and I can't tell you how to live your life, but this guy is still married and I'm guessing he's way too old for you. There's something about this Bacon that isn't quite Kosher."

"He's only technically married. He hasn't lived with his wife in years. Honestly, Mom, if you met him you'd be crazy about him. He's amazing."

"My God Lauren, sometimes you remind me of my mother.

How do you know who he is or isn't living with? Don't be so naive. You can't believe everything men tell you. What do you really know about him?"

"Wait a minute, what do you mean, I remind you of your mother? Is that a good thing or a bad thing? What was Grandma like?"

Deena's hand involuntarily covered her mouth. She recovered quickly and tossed out a few innocuous facts that didn't give anything away. "My mother had a theatrical bent and she could really sing. I think you must have gotten your musical talent from her."

"She was an actress? I thought she was a school teacher in New Mexico."

"Oh, she was never on the stage, she just had, I don't know, an artistic temperament. Maybe that's what I was saying. She wasn't a conventional person."

There was a pause as Lauren absorbed this new information. "That's not how I pictured her. Tell me more."

Deena started to panic. Her years in New Mexico were a closed book. She was ashamed of New Moon, ashamed of leaving the way she did and ashamed of the lies she'd invented to cover her shame. Her mind churned through old memories seeking a response that would be truthful without revealing secrets. "Your grandmother looked a lot like you, or rather I guess you look like her." That was good. There was no reason Lauren shouldn't know what her grandmother looked like.

"Why don't we have any pictures of her? I don't think I've ever seen a photo of your parents."

"There's a box of stuff from Bubbe's house in my bedroom closet. There are a couple photos of her in there. I didn't think you were interested."

"Of course I'm interested. She was my grandmother and I never met her. Tell me more about her."

"I think she would have liked you. You probably would have gotten along with her better than I did."

"Really? Why's that?"

This conversation was veering in a direction Deena had spent a lifetime trying to avoid, but something propelled her forward. "Your grandmother was always open to new experiences, to trying new things, the way you are. I mean, she went off to New Mexico and you've gone off to Boston while I'm still here in Cleveland. And she never cared what anyone else thought. I guess that's a kind of courage."

"I'm sorry I never met her."

"Yeah," Deena said, "Me too." And it was the truth.

Something about Deena's conversation with Lauren resonated long after she'd hung up the phone. She'd given her daughter good advice. *Don't be so naive. You can't believe everything men tell you. What do you really know about him?* Yet, she found herself fantasizing more and more about a man she didn't really know. The more she tried to clear her mind and concentrate on things that really mattered, the more Andor intruded on her thoughts. His bemused blue eyes seemed to follow her wherever she went throughout the day. She imagined him standing behind her at her desk, walking beside her through the halls, waiting for her when she opened the door to her apartment. *Stop it!* she chided herself. *Stop thinking about that ridiculous man. You have a husband and children to think about.* But there he was, a constant presence lurking in the dark corners of her mind. One thing he'd told her was true for sure. She really was lonely.

"Martin, let's go out to dinner for a change. We haven't gone out in a long time." Deena was sitting across from her husband stirring her morning matcha.

He was reading the comics and didn't look up, but he grunted agreeably, "OK, when do you want to go?"

"How about tonight?"

"Can't, I'm closing tonight. I won't be home until ten."

"Well then, how about tomorrow?"

"That's Thursday, I'd miss *The Big Bang.*" Of course, there was no way he'd miss his favorite program.

"What about the week-end?"

"I don't know. Danny invited me over to watch the game on his new big screen TV Friday night. Actually, this week-end's not good. Saturday, I'm filling in for Walter at the store, and Sunday's the final episode of a two part mystery I've been watching. How about next week?"

"How about if I just bring in a pizza and we can eat in front of the TV."

"OK, great." He'd clearly missed the sarcasm in her voice. How much longer could she live with a man who was so oblivious, so absent? She was tired of fruitless efforts to get him out of the house, of trying to make him take an interest in something– like her for instance. She was only forty-eight. Wasn't she entitled to some joy and excitement in her life?

The library was so busy the Friday before midterms that she didn't notice Andor until he was standing in front of her desk. She looked up in surprise, "Dr. Farkas, I didn't expect to see you here." Deena looked around to see if anyone was watching. "Is there anything I can do for you?"

His blue eyes crinkled at the edges, "Is this the Special Collections Department where the library keeps its most rare and valuable possessions?"

"Yes, it is." Deena looked down at her desk calendar, afraid that her face would give her away.

"Excellent, because I would like to take out something rare and valuable."

My God, he's too much. Who talks like that? Deena's ears felt hot and she hoped they hadn't turned bright red. "For heaven's sake, Andor," she hissed. "I'm at work. You can't flirt like that in the library."

"You are right. So, I will meet you after work and flirt with you over supper."

Deena did a quick calculation. It was Friday and Martin

would be at Danny's watching the Browns lose another game. Why eat alone when she could have supper with a charming professor? Admittedly there was something smarmy about him, but she didn't care. She needed a night out. "There's a Greek place at the corner. We could meet there after work.

"Excellent. I'll look for you at six o'clock."

Deena watched Andor as he walked away. Her heart was beating double time. What was she doing? She loved Martin dearly, but he didn't even see her as a woman anymore. She was just someone who cooked, did laundry and made sure there was ice cream in the freezer. He wouldn't be hurt if the flirtation didn't go too far. She wouldn't be unfaithful, she'd simply enjoy the attention of a ridiculously handsome man, permit herself one last meaningless dalliance before she was too old. Andor will be gone in March, she reassured herself, Martin will never know and it will be as if I'd never met him.

The first dinner led to another and another. They continued to meet under the pretext that Deena was helping Andor organize a syllabus. This wasn't a service her department generally provided, but it gave Deena cover–at least in her own mind. She was helping a professor. Their meetings were vaguely within the scope of her employment. At first they met in restaurants then in his apartment. Even when she was sitting on Andor's sofa while he toyed with her hair and nibbled on her ear she continued to pretend the flirtation wasn't serious, until it was. The afternoon Andor pushed her back against the sofa cushions and kissed her on the mouth she kissed him back, closing her eyes without a murmur of protest as he unbuttoned her blouse, unsnapped her bra and carried her over a line she'd never meant to cross.

That night, lying beside Martin in the bed they'd shared for a quarter century, she was overcome with shame. What sort of woman was she? How could she have betrayed her husband, the man she loved? But even as her heart pounded with guilt and self loathing she was remembering Andor's body pressed to hers, the sweet words and caresses that had awakened something joyful and alive. She turned toward Martin and put her arms around his back hoping to erase the guilty memory, but even in sleep he eluded her, wrapping the blankets around himself and rolling out of reach.

It was too easy. Martin was never at home and Andor lived one long corridor and an elevator ride away. It wasn't long before she felt as much at home in Andor's apartment as in her own. He rubbed her back and sang her love songs in Hungarian. She cooked for him and learned to say *kerem, köszönöm, te szep* and *csókolj meg újra*, please, thank you, you're beautiful, and kiss me again. Oh, and they danced. Deena hadn't danced in twenty years, but now she danced to the cheesey beat of Cascada, Lasgo and September, and made love to the pulsing thrum of the vaguely psychedelic Hungarian rock band, Omega. She lightened her hair with a blonde rinse and began wearing more and more of her daughter's castoff clothes and the miracle, she told herself, was that Martin never even noticed. As long as he didn't know, why not enjoy her fling? Andor would be gone in a couple of months and then she'd have the rest of her life to be a faithful and dutiful wife.

The person who did take notice was Elliot who seemed pleased by her transformation. "You look great with your hair like that. Dad ought to take you out to eat or something."

"Thanks Honey." She tucked a lock of blonde hair behind her ear. Her hair was longer now. She might let it grow all the way to her shoulders. "Maybe we'll do that, but you know we've both been working crazy hours. There just aren't enough hours in the day. Of course, you know about that; we hardly see you anymore."

"It's not all work. I've started swimming again. The coach is letting me train with the team in the morning before school. I see my friends and stay in shape. Win-win." He gave his mother a second appraising look. "Have you been working out or something? You look really good."

Deena was momentarily rattled. Did she look that differ-ent? Would people start to wonder, start to guess? She shook her head as nonchalantly as she could. "No time. It must be the new hair color. I should have lightened it years ago."

"Well, you look really good for your age."

Deena fixed him with a mock scowl. "For my age? What are you saying, that I look good for an old lady?"

"No, you know what I mean. You look good for a mom."

Thank God, he didn't suspect. Deena let her face relax into a grin. "Well thanks, you look pretty good for a son." It was true. He looked amazing. How could he work a full-time job, maintain a stellar grade point average, and still look as though he'd spent all day at the gym? *That's youth for you,* she thought to herself. *Youth, plus incredible discipline and stamina.* She could hear him doing pushups in his room as he began his evening exercise routine.

Deena stood by the window in the living room of Andor's apartment with her head tilted slightly toward the camera. She was wearing a simple white sweater and no makeup per Andor's instructions. "OK, now look out the window with your back to me," Andor directed. It was late January, but on this particular Saturday morning the sun poured through the open blinds casting streaks of warm light across the floor. Andor danced around the room snapping shots from various angles while ordering her to lift her arm, turn to the left, or look away from the lens. Portraits were not really Andor's forte, but he seemed to be having fun. He stood on the sofa aiming his camera at the back of Deena's head. "Now, turn and look up at me. That's it. Beautiful. Imagine you're looking at one of your rare and beautiful books." Deena rolled her eyes. Martin would never say anything so cheesy.

"Got it." Andor stepped off the couch and detached the lens from his camera. His shirt was unbuttoned exposing the graying hair on his chest. "So, what book did you imagine? What is the most remarkable book in your collection?"

"Sorry to disappoint you, but I don't fantasize about old books."

"Really? I dream about famous photographs. I imagined librarians dreamed about beautiful books. There must be a book in the collection that intrigues you, something very rare and valuable?"

"Not really, not like that. Well, there are some art books locked inside a metal cabinet locked inside the locked stacks. Those must be worth a bundle but I certainly don't dream about them."

"But they are safe because Alice the Dragon is guarding the key."

"They don't even trust Alice with that key. Richter has one copy and I have the only other one. The system is like a set of Russian nesting dolls. A thief would have to steal the desk key from my purse, steal the cabinet key from my desk, break the electronic code, locate the cabinet and then make off with the treasure. It would be easier to get past a dragon."

"You're right. Who would go to so much trouble to steal old books?" Andor sat down on the sofa and began fitting the camera and accessories back into their case. "Let me play with the images before I show them to you, but I think you'll like them. Choose whatever you want and I'll give you the prints."

"I'd love the prints but how could I explain photographs taken in your apartment? Let's not rock the boat." Deena flopped down on the couch beside Andor. Neither of them wore shoes and their bare feet leaned into each other on the coffee table.

"Why would he care? You have your clothes on. If they were beautiful nudes I'd understand, but you won't let me photograph your body." This was a sore point between them. "Tell him we made the photos in my studio."

"You don't have a studio. Besides, he's not an idiot. He'd recognize the view through the window." Deena pointed to the distinctive trolley cables and the familiar apartment building across the street, the same scene visible from her own apartment.

"I'll Photoshop in a new background. Would you prefer the Swiss Alps or the Eifel Tower?" They'd begun a game of foot wrestling while they talked.

Deena drew away from Andor, putting her feet firmly on the floor. "It's not a joke, I have to be careful. This has been fun, but Martin's my husband. You're leaving soon and I need a life to go back to."

Andor stood up and started toward the kitchen. "Actually, I'll be leaving sooner than we thought. Do you want some tea?"

"What? When are you leaving?"

Andor answered without looking back. "March 1st, the school in Florida wants me a few weeks early for orientation."

February was particularly brutal, made even colder by the arctic expanse that separated Deena from her husband. With a double work load, Deena rarely got home from the library before seven while Martin had begun working six days a week, accepting all the over-time that he could get. On those rare occasions when they shared a day off Deena would make an effort to be pleasant. She'd cook elaborate dinners or try to coax him to the movies or outside for a walk. He'd eat the meals and talk about the kids, but never felt like going anywhere. None of the movies interested him and he certainly wasn't going for a walk in the bitter cold.

Deena was worried about Martin, but she wasn't lonely. She usually had lunch with Andor or met him for a glass of wine after work. He was the one who understood her fears for Elliot and never made her feel cowardly or manipulative for trying to undermine his plans to enlist. It was Andor who helped her select a floral arrangement for Lauren when *Dancing at Lughnasa* opened in Boston, and it was Andor who held her in a great bear hug while she sobbed on his shoulder after Alice sent a scurrilous letter to Otto Richter citing her for incompetence and lack of reverence for rare books.

It hadn't mattered that Richter assured her that he understood she was doing her best in a difficult situation and that he was grateful for the extra time she'd been devoting to the job. "You'll get the hang of it," he'd promised her. "Alice can be a little over protective, but she's a good soul. I'm sure you girls can work it out."

You girls can work it out? You girls? She'd left his office shaken and diminished. Alice hated her, but Deena couldn't manage without her and Richter knew it. If it came down to it, he'd keep a clerk with thirty years experience over a humanities librarian who knew nothing about curating a rare book collection. It had been days before Deena could look Alice in the eye and weeks before she'd found the courage to confront her.

Alice had been unrepentant "We have systems and procedures for a reason. You barely seem to comprehend the difference between an original William Blake printed from type with hand colored etchings from a Penguins Classic."

"Of course I know the difference. I'm not an idiot, but I've never worked with this sort of material before." Deena was putting on a brave face, but she was intimidated by her assistant's knowledge of the field. Acknowledging her inadequacies was a risk, but maybe she could still turn Alice into an ally. "You're going to have to help me. I need you to bring me up to speed on the collection. Let's start with the Blake as an example."

Alice had recently allowed her platinum blond hair to go gray, but she still wore heavy rouge and bright red lipstick. She smelled of something floral and cloying. Her red lips twisted into a smirk. "We have several nineteenth century volumes, a *Book of Urizen,* two reprints of *Songs of Innocence,* and a beautiful copy of *Poetical Sketches.* Of course, the jewel of the collection is an eighteenth century *Illustrations of the*

Book of Job. That book alone might bring a hundred thousand at auction. They were all gifts from the Montgomery Family Trust." Deena nodded sagely, as though she were conversant with the books and the Montgomerys.

Alice wasn't fooled. She shook her head at Deena's cluelessness. "Gerald Montgomery is a nationally recognized collector. He's a trustee of the American Bibliophilic Society. You should be having lunch with him, bringing him bottles of Scotch. That's part of the job."

"No it isn't." Deena was indignant. "That's a job for someone in Development. I don't know anything about schmoozing money out of donors."

"Not money, books. The development people don't know books, but you're supposed to. Gerald Montgomery's been collecting rare books for fifty years and Taylor spent the past ten making sure that he leaves them to this library."

"Oh." Deena was stunned. Courting donors wasn't in her repertoire. "What else does he have?"

"He has a lot. It's an important collection and wildly eclectic. It's worth millions." She looked Deena straight in the eye to make sure this information had sunk in. It had. "I know Taylor was dying to get his hands on an illuminated *Book of Hours* from the fifteenth century, and an astronomical treatise by Giovanni...." Alice paused, trying to recover the astronomer's last name. "Giovanni Somebody, a sixteenth century Italian."

"Richter never told me about any of this. He can't expect me to..."

"I doubt that he expects you to do anything except protect what we already have until someone with proper qualifications can be found to replace you."

"What?" Deena couldn't believe what she'd just heard. Alice was supposed to be her assistant, a mere clerk, albeit a clerk with more experience and expertise than Deena would ever muster. "What did you just say?"

"I'm sorry, really I am. I've said too much, but honestly you don't know what this job entails. Richter's made a mess of things and we're all paying for it."

Chapter Six

Andor ordered a bottle of Chianti at Palermo, a cozy tavern in Chesterland, a small town half an hour east of Shaker Heights. Deena was curled up beside him in a wooden booth, one hand resting on his knee beneath the table. Palermo was their favorite trysting spot since it was both charming and discreet. It felt like a magical space carved out of time where they were protected from the perils and responsibilities of the outside world. Of course that was an illusion. Some part of Deena must have known it even then.

Was it fate that intervened, bad luck, or simply her own bad judgment? If she'd refused to meet Andor that night, how would her life have changed? Later, Deena would look back at that evening as the tipping point, the moment that set her on a course she had never imagined. It was late afternoon, or maybe it was already early evening. The sun had already set so it was sometime after five. They sat by a large picture window watching snowflakes swirl in the beam of passing headlights as a real fire crackled in a large stone fireplace. The tavern smelled of wine and garlic, wet wool and burning pine. All the holidays were over: Christmas, New Years, Martin Luther King's birthday, even Valentine's Day. There was nothing to look forward to but long cold nights and endless snow until the spring. In two weeks Andor would be gone and Deena's marriage would return to its old routines. She'd go back to being a reliable wife and mother and no one would ever know she'd taken a short sabbatical from her real life.

Andor took her hand and pressed it to his lips. Deena pulled it back and shook her head. There were limits. She needed to maintain some credible deniability. He looked at her with such concern and affection that Deena felt a pang of loss, a premature nostalgia for the time they'd spent together. He'd been so kind to her, so tolerant. He'd just spent the last ten minutes listening patiently to her familiar litany of complaints about her assistant. "Why do you worry about that jealous bitch? Alice is a clerk, she's nothing. You have all the power, use it. Stand up for yourself. Dr. Richter thinks you're gold and that's the only thing that matters."

Deena smiled, unconvinced, but grateful. "Thank you, you've been a good friend. Who's going to keep up my spirits once you're gone?"

"Come with me. Give up everything for love. Why not? You could do it." He was toying with her. He knew there was no way she would jettison her life to follow him to Sarasota, but it was a game they played. "Why wait? We'll leave right now." He kissed her on the lips. "I'll get the car."

"Andor, don't," Deena laughed, giving him a quick kiss in return. "We're out in public."

"You're right." Andor feigned a change of heart as the waitress headed toward them with two steaming plates of pasta. "Let's wait until we've had our supper."

It was so cozy sitting knee to knee with this charming man, exchanging university gossip, flirting, and sipping wine. They discussed Andor's new job in Florida, European cinema and a recent rash of drive-by shootings while slurping forkfuls of fettuccini drenched in butter, cream and melted cheese. What they didn't discuss was Andor's life. She knew nothing about his childhood or his family and that was fine with Deena. The most personal thing she knew was that he owned a house in Hungary with a mortgage that he was desperate to pay off.

Dinner over and the bill paid, Andor helped Deena into her coat. She felt his hands linger on her shoulders and his lips nuzzling her neck. There was no question about it; she'd miss him when he was gone. Yet, at the same time there was something else, something ready to let him go and to move into spring without fear, guilt, or excess baggage.

They kissed goodbye in the unlit parking lot then left the restaurant in separate cars. Snow had buried her old Taurus while they'd been eating dinner and Deena drove hunched over the steering wheel, navigating through a porthole she'd cleared in the windshield. Mayfield Road was unplowed and treacherous. Normally, she'd have taken the highway home but there'd been an accident and the exit was blocked by two police cars and an ambulance. She wouldn't be home before nine at the speed she was going. There was no excuse for her behavior. At the very least, she should have called Martin with some lame alibi. He deserved that much. She was getting careless, careless and selfish. She'd have to watch herself. The thing with Andor had gotten out of hand.

Deena clutched the wheel trying to keep her car on the icy road. Andor's tail lights had merged into the flow of traffic and disappeared long ago, and she was now following a white SUV sporting a bumper sticker that read "God and Guns — Two Things You Can Believe In." Hitting the brakes when the SUV came to a sudden stop, Deena fishtailed to the left nearly colliding with a tow truck. Slowing to fifteen miles per hour, she finally turned onto Lee Road and inched her way toward Van Aken Boulevard. She was within a mile of her apartment and starting to breathe normally again when a patch of black ice sent her swerving off the road. When the car finally came to a stop Deena found herself on the lawn of St. Peter's Lutheran Church facing the wrong way. As shaken as she was, she managed a quick inventory and concluded that neither she nor the Taurus were in immediate need of repair. To her great relief, the engine started right up, but then the car wouldn't budge.

The tires simply spun, digging deeper and deeper grooves into the muddy, snow-sodden grass.

Deena switched off the engine and reached for her phone. "Martin, I'm sorry I'm late but I've been in an accident. No, I'm fine. It wasn't serious, but I'm stuck in a snowdrift in front of St. Peter's. That's sweet, but you don't have a car. There's really nothing you can do. Do we still belong to Triple A?"

A few minutes later she called again. "Just wanted to give you an update. Triple A says it can't keep up with all the calls coming in. It could be two hours before they get a truck out to me. No, don't worry, I have a full tank of gas so I'll be fine. See you in the morning. Bye." Deena clicked off the phone. She would never have chosen to spend two hours trapped in a snowbound car, but the accident had given her cover. Maybe skidding off the road was an act of good fortune. Accidents make people late. Martin hadn't even mentioned the time. It was going to be a long night, but she had a good heater and a radio. Deena turned on WCLV, closed her eyes, and sank into a violin concerto by Vivaldi.

Persistent tapping on the window brought her back to consciousness. Had the tow truck arrived already? She couldn't have been asleep two hours. Her eyes took a moment to focus and then she saw Martin's face beaming at her. He was bundled up like an Eskimo and carrying a shovel. Deena lowered the window and smiled back at him. "Martin, how in the world did you get here without a car?"

"I walked." He was clearly delighted with himself.

"In this blizzard?"

"Yep. Have shovel will travel."

Waves of conflicting emotions made Deena queasy. Part of her, a substantial part, was deeply moved by her husband's gallantry and devotion, but she also bristled, annoyed that he was being so nice, that he was oblivious to the vast chasm that had opened up between them, that he didn't understand that she didn't deserve his loyalty and attention.

She turned off the radio. "Are you OK? Do you want to sit in the car and warm up a minute?"

"Nope, let's get this baby back on the road." He began shoveling at the snow encasing her back tires.

Deena got out and stood next to him, hugging herself against the cold air as large wet snowflakes stuck in her hair and eyelashes. "Is there anything I can do? Do you need some help?" He was huffing great clouds of breath from the unaccustomed exertion. Why was Martin doing this? He'd pull a muscle or catch a cold.

"Yeah, hand me the floor mats, then get back inside. No point both of us freezing to death. Anyway, I'll need you to start her up in a minute."

Deena did as she was told, then waited until Martin gave the signal. With a bit more shoveling, a repositioning of mats, and a mighty push, the tires finally found enough traction to roll slowly off the lawn, over the curb and back onto the road.

Martin shook out the mats, threw them in the back, then climbed into the passenger seat. He was panting hard. Even in the dim streetlight Deena could see that his cheeks were bright red. There was a time when he'd been as fit as Elliot. He'd played varsity tennis and taken long cross country bike trips, but that was years ago. Now, Deena watched her husband try to catch his breath and hoped he wasn't going to have a heart attack. "You shouldn't have come out like this. It's way too cold and slippery. You could have fallen and broken something or gotten frostbite." Martin didn't say anything. He was holding his hands in front of the heater trying to defrost his frozen fingers. "But thanks, that was really nice of you. I thought I was hallucinating when I saw you out there with your shovel."

"No problem. You're my wife. We're supposed to look after each other." He patted her affectionately on the knee.

That did it. She'd thought she was so smart, so in control, but she'd been kidding herself as much as her husband. A tsunami of conflicting emotions crashed against the last of her defenses and spilled out in a deluge of tears.

"What's the matter? What happened?"

Deena couldn't see clearly and the car began to weave with the spasmodic heaving of her shoulders. One of her tires hit the curb. She felt it bounce and slide, but managed to stay in her own lane.

"Whoa, you'd better pull over. I'll take it from here." Martin put his hand on the wheel and guided them toward a plowed driveway. Deena brought the car to a stop and handed him the keys. He waited while she wiped her eyes and blew her nose before asking, "Now, what's all this about?"

"I don't know." Deena wasn't lying; she didn't know why she did anything anymore. "I guess I was more frightened than I realized. Thank you for saving me. I'm so sorry for everything. I don't know what I'd do without you."

"That's all right," Martin pulled her close and kissed the top of her head. "There's nothing to be sorry for. You didn't even ding the car."

Their gloved hands sat intertwined on the seat between them as they drove the rest of the way home. Neither of them said a word as they parked the car, rode the elevator up to the third floor, unlocked their door and hung up their coats. They stood facing each other in the small entry hall as awkward as teenagers on a first date. Deena was about to break the silence, to say something that might narrow the rift between them, but Elliot chose that moment to come barging through the door.

He didn't look at his parents as he tore past them toward the bathroom dripping blood from a gash on the back of his head. He slammed the door shut and locked it before Martin and Deena could catch up with him. All they could do was shout questions and advice from the hallway. "What happened? Do you need to go to the ER? Someone should look at that. Were you in an accident? What's going on?"

They could hear their son opening and shutting the medicine cabinet and rummaging through drawers. "I'm alright. Go away and leave me alone."

Martin began jiggling the doorknob and pounding on the door. "Don't make me break this down. What the hell happened? Open up this minute."

"I'm OK. I just don't want to talk. Back off, will you? Ouch!"

Deena became more alarmed. "What's happening? Are you in pain?"

"Oh, for God's sake," Elliot's voice had a hard edge she'd never heard before. "Could you get off my case and let me take care of this?"

Martin and Deena looked at one another, bewildered. Backing off wasn't their style, but Elliot was eighteen. This was new territory. Were respectful parents supposed to let their almost adult children bleed quietly in private? Martin dropped his arms to his side, a gesture of defeat. "OK, but we'd sure like to know what happened when you're ready to talk."

"Yeah, sure. Now leave me alone."

Deena turned all her fear and anxiety toward Martin. "That's it? Your son's just had a serious injury, maybe a concussion, and you're just going to walk away? Don't you care?"

"He's an adult, Deena. There's nothing we can do."

"I can get a screwdriver and take that door down. That's what I can do." Deena was being irrational and she knew it, but she wasn't having a rational night.

"No, you can't. Don't be crazy. We'll have to wait until he's ready to talk to us."

"Did you just call me crazy?" And like that, whatever *rapprochement* had been possible a few minutes earlier was gone. Deena stomped into the kitchen to make herself a cup of tea. Martin slumped back into the living room and switched on the TV, and Elliot remained locked in the bathroom behind an impregnable door.

"I don't know how to talk to him anymore." Deena had stayed after her yoga class to put away the mats and foam blocks. If her instructor didn't have another class for a while she'd sometimes chat or give Deena a little private instruction during the break.

Heidi smiled sympathetically as she headed toward the back office. "Husbands are like that. No one knows how to talk to them."

Deena felt a shock of panic. Heidi was getting away and she was desperate to talk to someone. There was a time when she would have confided in Danny's wife, Shirley, but since the River Parc fiasco they barely spoke. Heidi wasn't a real friend, but she took an interest in her students and was a sympathetic listener. It was rude and against the rules, but she followed Heidi into the private off-limits space where instructors retreated between classes. "It's not my husband. I gave up talking to him ages ago. It's my son. He won't even look at me anymore. I don't know what's going on, but it's making me crazy."

Heidi was a good soul. Without a word of reproach, she poured two cups of green tea from a small Japanese pot on her file cabinet and handed one to Deena. "Elliot? I thought he was your perfect kid." She gestured with her chin toward a futon by the window.

Deena lowered herself into the seat with a sigh of relief. Heidi knew things, she was like a guru in spandex. Talking with her would put things in perspective. "That's just it. We've never had a problem with him. He's been a dream child: good grades, athletic, well behaved, lots of friends. He practically glowed in the dark, and then a couple weeks ago something happened. I think he got into a fight with someone. Whatever it was, he's done a one eighty and now I hardly know him."

"Weird, I can't picture Elliot in a fight. He's always been

so easygoing, but he's a teenage boy. They're all hormones, completely *tamasic*. I wouldn't take it personally."

"Well, it sure feels personal. He stomps around the apartment slamming doors and refusing to talk. He's never been like this before, never." Deena's tea was sloshing in her cup and she realized that her hands were shaking. She set it on the floor.

Heidi came and sat beside her on the futon. "You poor thing. You're completely out of balance. Honestly, sometimes I'm glad I never had children. Let's try a little acupressure to open up your Sen lines." She began kneading Deena's neck and shoulders and Deena could feel her Sen lines, or *something*, open up. Heidi continued talking as she worked. "Elliot's just going through a stage. Some boys are impossible from the minute their voices start to change. Count your blessings. He'll snap out of it. It's probably about some girl. *Cherchez la femme*. That's what they say, isn't it?"

"Mm hm." Deena wasn't going to argue. She let Heidi ease the kinks and knots out of her upper back and buoy her spirits with reassuring words.

"Speaking of *la femme*, how's your daughter doing? Lauren, right? Is she still in Boston?"

"Who knows?"

Heidi paused, resting her hands on Deena's shoulders. "What do you mean?"

"I'm being stupid. She has to be in Boston. She's in a play there. I've seen the website promoting the show and she's listed in the cast. But she won't give me her address. It's this big mystery."

"That's odd." Heidi resumed kneading the tense muscles in Deena's neck.

"It's more than odd. She sounds perfectly normal when she calls, but then she freezes up if I ask where she's living. Why would she do that?"

"Honestly? She's probably living with some guy and she's

afraid to tell you."

"That's what Martin thinks, but she never talks about a boyfriend. I just have a feeling that there's more to it."

"Well, that's my best guess." Heidi stood up and stretched, then immediately bent backwards into a full upwards facing bow before gracefully raising her legs over her head, lowering them behind herself, then uncoiling into a standing position. "Now, no meat this week. You have to calm your system. I want you on a clean *sattvic* diet: yogurt, melon, cheese, beans, sweet potatoes, kale and regular practice. Yoga is medicine. I promise, you'll feel much better by next Saturday."

"Thank you. I feel better already. The massage was amazing."

"My pleasure. I've got to get ready for my next class now, but don't forget what I told you, and don't forget to breathe."

Late February was transitioning into March and the days were noticeably longer. Pots of daffodils and primroses greeted Deena at the grocery and, like the rest of the city, she was looking forward to spring. Passover was still a month away, but it was time to start tearing her cupboards apart, discarding anything leavened or made of grain. Why were these ancient habits so hard to break? Even in Santa Fe her mother had led a sort of improvised Seder, long on civil rights and short on tradition, but still a Seder. And her mother had always bought matzo so all the New Mooners, Jewish or not, could taste the bread of affliction. More and more, Deena found herself remembering those years in New Mexico. *Why now*, she wondered, but there were too many pressing demands requiring immediate attention to waste time sorting out old memories.

Deena followed Heidi's advice and she was feeling stronger and more like her old self. Andor was leaving at the end of the week, the days were getting longer, and life would soon return to normal. As exciting as the brief affair had been, the intrigue and guilt had worn her down. She'd miss Andor, but she already thought of him in the past tense. She was more than ready to kiss the man good-bye.

Andor wouldn't tell her where they were going on their last night together. He'd only warned her to wear something warm. It would be a short night since Martin would be home by eight, but there was time for a quick dinner and Andor's surprise. She'd expected candle light and white tablecloths for their last meal together, but instead Andor took her to a food truck on Wade Oval where they dined on burgers and fries before renting skates and trying their skill at the outdoor rink that miraculously appeared each winter. Loudspeakers blared a Strauss waltz and small white lights danced on wires that swayed with the wind as she teetered out on the ice. The cold and the novelty of skating at night were exhilarating. She and Andor couldn't hold hands or skate with their arms around one another's waists like the other couples, the rink was a block from the library and much too public for such a risk, but they chatted and flirted and laughed themselves silly as Deena took one graceless pratfall after another.

For the few moments she spent gliding in great, wobbly circles in the dark, Deena felt young. The years slipped away, her troubled marriage and unfathomable children receded from consciousness, and she was twenty years old and skating toward a future she couldn't imagine. Once, twice, three times around and she finally found her rhythm. Her skates began to move in long, smooth strides as she picked up speed and left Andor far behind.

Later, after they'd returned their skates and become slow, plodding adults once again, Andor pulled her into a dark stairwell as they headed toward the parking lot and gave her a last, lingering kiss. "You're sure you won't come to Sarasota with me?"

"Sorry, I need to stay in Cleveland to work on my triple Lutz, but thanks for asking." It was their old game. They both knew Deena wasn't going anywhere, but it softened the pain of saying good-bye.

"I'll miss you, Library Lady. You're a very interesting woman. Let me know if you change your mind."

"Absolutely," Deena gave him one last kiss then started walking toward her car feeling lighter and less encumbered than she had in months.

With Andor gone, Deena expected her life to resume its old normalcy, but it didn't, because her easygoing, reliable, affectionate son wouldn't look her in the eye. As Deena pushed her shopping cart through Heinens, a spirited dialogue played out inside her head. *Why is he always so angry and morose? What's this all about?* She picked up a melon, sniffed it and put it back. *He's probably furious at me for trying to keep him out of the Navy, but that's only normal. What mother wouldn't want to protect her son? Of course he is eighteen. It is his choice.* A half gallon of milk and a pint of sour cream went into the basket. *Maybe I should apologize.*

Maybe I should be more supportive and honor his decision. But what if they send him to a war zone and he gets wounded or worse? Two boxes of frozen peas, a jar of marinara sauce, and a pound of ground beef found her still arguing both sides of the question like a Talmudic scholar.

The military's an honorable profession. It takes courage and discipline. She fished a fistful of coupons from her purse and headed for the checkout line. *All right then, I'll apologize as soon as he gets home.* She paid for her groceries and headed to the parking lot resolved to smooth over the rift with her son.

It was one of Martin's early nights and they'd eaten a hot meal in the dining room for the first time in ages. After washing the dinner dishes and tidying up, she sat in the kitchen fiddling with a crossword puzzle, watching the clock, and sipping a cup of tea. Martin was spread out on the sofa reading the newspaper. At nine-fifteen she heard Elliot's key in the lock.

"Hi Sweetie, welcome home." Deena cringed at the forced

cheer she could hear in her own voice. *Be normal,* she told herself. *It's just Elliot.* "I'm in the kitchen, why don't you join me. I baked some brownies." Ten long seconds went by without an answer. She wasn't going to let him disappear into his room without talking to her again. Deena raced to the front entrance where her son was hanging up his coat. "You're back earlier than usual. How about some brownies?"

"Thanks, but I'm not hungry." He slammed the closet door without looking at her and headed down the hall.

"They're still warm...." Deena's voice trailed off as Elliot went into his bedroom and closed the door behind him. This couldn't go on. She rapped on his door and waited. Nothing. She rapped louder.

"I said I'm not hungry." There was anger in his voice that carried an undertone of violence.

"Elliot, this is ridiculous. We have to talk. Please, I need to know why you're so angry with me. If it's about the Navy, I'm sorry for standing in your way. If that's really what you want, you have my blessing."

"I'm eighteen now. I don't need your blessing."

"Well then, what is it? What's been eating at you these last few weeks?"

"Ask Sasha."

"Sasha? What are you talking about?" Deena really was confused. She'd never exchanged more than an occasional pleasantry with Sasha in her entire life.

"If I tell you that his family has dinner at Palermo every Tuesday night would that be a clue?"

It was more than a clue, it was the answer, all of it. Deena leaned her head against the wall and closed her eyes. Even in the dark, the room seemed to spin. She couldn't deal with this. It was too much. What could she possibly say that would save her now? She couldn't talk, she couldn't even swallow, but silence felt like a confession. She had to put this back together. She had to make it right. "I was at Palermo a couple weeks ago with a professor from the art department, but I didn't see Sasha."

"Yeah, well he and his parents saw you and they were so embarrassed that they left."

"Oh for Heaven's sake, I meet with professors all the time. It's part of my job. If it gets late, sometimes we'll go out for dinner. What was Sasha thinking?"

"He was thinking that it didn't look like a business meeting. He said you were all over the guy."

"Don't be ridiculous, I was not." *My God, was I? Was I out of my mind?* Deena tried to recreate the evening. How close *had* she been sitting to Andor? "Elliot, come out here and talk to me. I'm not having this conversation through a closed door."

The door opened and a tall, angry man stared down at her. Was this her son? Deena began to babble lies. "It's all a misunderstanding. It was a business meeting. Maybe I was sitting close to him. I don't remember."

"You want to see the pictures? Sasha took photos of you on his cell phone."

"Photos of what? What's in the pictures?" Deena could feel all avenues of escape closing in front of her.

"You want to see them? He has a nice shot of you kissing the bastard. Sasha will send them to you if you want. Maybe he'll post them to Facebook."

"How dare he take pictures of people without their permission, and then he has the nerve... I should...."

"Don't bother, I already punched him out. Problem was, he shoved me back and I went down on the ice. I got that gash on my head defending your honor."

"Oh my God."

"Hey, you two, keep it down. I'm trying to read in here," Martin shouted from the living room.

"Please Elliot, don't say anything. There's no reason to upset him. I'm begging you." Deena was in a blind panic, all pretense thrown to the wind.

"Why do you think I haven't said anything for two weeks? It's been killing me, but I didn't want to hurt Dad and ..." Elliot looked away with eyes full of tears ... "I didn't want you two to get divorced."

Martin appeared at the end of the hallway. "What's going on? Why would your mother and I get divorced?"

Deena felt a cold chill run through her body. Her eyes met Elliot's. Neither said a word.

"Why would we get divorced?" Martin repeated, looking directly at Deena. "Is there something I should know?"

"No, we were just talking. Everything's OK." Elliot turned bright red. He was a terrible liar.

"Something's going on. Would someone be straight with me? What's happening?"

"Sasha saw me out to dinner with one of the professors and he got the wrong idea. It was just a misunderstanding." Deena struggled to make her voice sound normal.

"That's it? Deena could see Martin wasn't buying it. He looked at Elliot. "Seriously, is that it?"

Elliot shook his head, "No."

"How bad is it? What don't you want me to know?"

When no one answered, he said, "Elliot, go to your room. I think your mother and I have something to discuss."

The discussion gradually escalated to shouting, then accusations, confessions, apologies and tears. The battle continued late into the night, until the exhausted combatants, wounded and in pain, finally retreated behind closed doors. The muffled sobs of a man crying into his pillow were the only sounds that penetrated the cold expanse of hurt in which each of them drifted, frightened and alone.

Deena had never been much of a talker at work so maybe no one noticed her grim mood or the fact that she spent more and more time in the stacks by herself pretending to —*what?* She could hardly remember. Her mind was an endless feedback loop that did nothing but replay that awful night over and over again. Somehow she continued to assist students, purchase books, and attend staff meetings, but everything she did felt hollow and unreal. She'd have to snap out of it before things really began to slip. The student interns were already running roughshod over her and she was late with her budget for next year. If she didn't take herself in hand, she'd lose her job and that would be the end of her.

Alice was endlessly annoyed, and Deena knew she'd have to show some leadership if she wanted to be taken seriously as department head. In the meantime, everything she did, every decision she made, seemed to irritate her clerk. So, the fact that Alice was barreling toward her like a typhoon first thing on a Monday morning didn't strike Deena as particularly odd. She simply braced herself for the outrage *du jour* and hoped the phone would ring or a student would call her away before Alice got too far into her inventory of Deena's egregious failings. Unfortunately, no one came to save her and Alice was bug-eyed with rage.

"Call the police. No, call Richter first. I'll contact the RBMS to put them on notice in case something shows up on eBay or at one of the shows, and send out an AABA alert. Oh my God. I'm calling Taylor. He needs to know."

The word *police* made Deena snap to attention. This wasn't Alice's usual rant; something bad had happened, and it had happened on her watch.

"Wait a minute, slow down. What are you saying?"

"There's been a robbery. Who knows how much they took? We'll have to do an inventory immediately. For God's sake, call Richter this minute. Oh, never mind, I'll do it myself." She grabbed the receiver off Deena's large, old fashioned landline and began dialing.

Deena depressed the switch hook, disconnecting the call, and glared at Alice. This woman, this clerk, unapologetically treated Deena as though she were her idiot assistant, and Deena had been taking it, but not today. Deena walked around her desk so that she and Alice were face to face. "Miss Krol, I appreciate the gravity of the situation, but you work for me. First, tell me exactly what happened. Then I'll decide what action needs to be taken."

Alice was shaking and blinking back tears of rage, but she took a deep breath and kept her voice under control. "Someone broke into the book safe at the back of the secure stack. I found it ajar just now when I went to retrieve something for one of our students."

"OK, and do we know for sure that anything's missing?"

Alice gave Deena a look that would have stripped the gilt off the binding of an antiquarian book.

"We'll need to do a complete inventory, but I already know they made off with a French *Book of Hours*, the Blake and some early maritime maps.

"Go back into the stacks and do that inventory. I'll call Dr. Richter and let him notify the police."

"Good, then contact the Rare Books and Manuscripts Section of the Association of College and Research Libraries, and the Antiquarian Booksellers Association of America like I told you. They have systems for dealing with situations like this."

"Is there anything else?"

"Yes, tell Richter whoever got into that safe must have had a key."

Chapter Seven

"Mom, Elliot says you're having an affair with some professor. Please tell me he's a lying scumbag and I'll never speak to him again. Tell me you'd never do a thing like that." Lauren sounded scared. She knew it was true.

"Sweetie, it's not that simple." Deena was sitting in the kitchen staring at a cup of cold tea. Martin wasn't home. He hadn't been home for days. "Maybe I did get too close to one of the professors, but it was nothing serious. Anyway, he's already left town and ..."

"Oh, my God." Lauren hung up.

Deena redialed and Lauren finally answered on the fourth try. "How could you?" She was crying and hiccupping into the phone. "And you're the one who told me to stay away from Matthew because he's still married, and he's not even living with his wife. How could you do a thing like that? Don't you love Dad anymore? Don't you love us?"

Deena waited while Lauren wailed her outrage into the phone. What had she done, and for what? She despised herself and felt defenseless against her family's accusations. "Please Lauren, I'm so sorry. I didn't mean to hurt you or Dad or anyone. It was a terrible mistake."

"It sure was. Elliot says Dad's so depressed he's practically stopped eating. I was going to come home for Passover, but now what's the point?"

"Lauren, please let me explain. I've already apologized to your dad and begged his forgiveness, now I'm begging for yours."

"So, everything's OK between you and Dad now? He said, 'No problem, let's just forget about it'?"

"Of course not. Actually, he's moved in with Uncle Danny and Aunt Shirley for a while." Deena's voice sounded raspy and unnaturally low. "He won't even take my calls. I was hoping you could talk to him."

"Why? What would I say?"

"Tell him people make mistakes. Tell him that I love him and that I'm sorry. Tell him I want to work things out."

"I'll give him the message, but if you love him so much, why did you do it?"

Deena closed her eyes. Why *did* she do it? It was hard to explain even to herself. "Things weren't good between me and your dad after we lost the house. He practically stopped talking to me and then he started sleeping on the sofa. He didn't seem to care about me or anything else. Anyway, I met this guy at work who made me feel young and pretty. It's stupid, but that's the truth. I was helping him with a research project and I honestly figured he'd leave town at the end of the semester, and no one would ever know. I never meant to hurt you."

There was a long pause during which Deena felt her life teeter in the balance. When Lauren finally spoke her voice was almost unrecognizable. "I'll talk to Dad, but I don't want to talk to you for a while. I'm too angry and upset."

Now it was Deena sobbing into the phone.

"Mom, are you OK?"

"No."

"Please, stop crying. I'll call in a few days after I've calmed down, but you've really messed things up. Everyone's falling apart."

"I know. I'd do anything to undo the last three months."

There was such a long pause that Deena thought they'd been disconnected, then Lauren said, "Three months? You were sleeping with this guy for three months? I thought it was like a one night stand. No wonder Dad's a mess. I'll call again when I'm thinking straight, but I'm going to need some time to process this."

Deena sat frozen, listening to the second hand ticking relentlessly around the dial of the kitchen clock, *guilty, guilty, guilty.* How long would it be before Lauren called again? How long had it been since she'd spoken to her own mother?

The daffodils had finally popped and Cedar Hill was awash in yellow. The sky was clear and cloudless while the thermometer flirted with seventy degrees. Oblivious, Deena still sagged under the weight of her winter coat. The world outside hardly registered. Nothing mattered but her empty apartment, her unanswered phone calls, and the list of missing books tacked to the cork board behind her desk.

In the final analysis, only twelve books were missing, but they were worth a fortune. A sophisticated thief had targeted art books containing original prints. The special investigator the police had brought in explained that the books would be broken down like stolen cars in a hack shop. Individual pages would be sliced out, framed and matted, then sold at inflated prices by unscrupulous galleries or over the internet.

The police had mounted a thorough investigation and everyone in the library had been questioned about security and procedures. Gerald Montgomery had gone livid when he'd discovered that the Blake had been stolen and was consulting a lawyer. Alice no longer spoke to Deena. Richter couldn't look her in the eye. Deena tried to carry on as usual, but of course, nothing was usual. Students and professors began to complain that she was distant, preoccupied and inattentive to their projects.

Andor had been gone over a month and Martin had been gone for two weeks when she found a sealed envelope in the office mail summoning her to Otto Richter's office. Interoffice communication was usually breezy and informal, but this one looked like a death notice. Her gut immediately seized with dread. The bad feeling got a lot worse when she knocked on the door to Richter's office and it was opened by Detective Zelinski. Robin Novak from Human Resources was sitting beside Richter behind the table he used for a desk. Nobody was smiling and Deena suddenly wished she had an attorney with her.

"Deena, please come in and take a seat. We have a serious matter to discuss." Deena sat down in one of the Barcelona chairs. It was ridiculously low to the floor and propelled her backwards into a reclining position when every nerve in her body said, *sit up. Stay alert. You're in danger.* She maneuvered herself to the edge of the seat where she sat stiff and pale waiting for whatever came next.

Dr. Richter stared down at her as though she was a defendant in the dock. Deena stared back and saw his famous eyebrows twitch. He looked older than she remembered. He cleared his throat and began, "Detective Zelinski brought us some disturbing news a couple days ago. It seems that the theft from your department was an inside job."

"No!" Deena almost leapt from her seat. "That's not possible. Alice and I are the only ones with access to the stacks and you can't be accusing either of us. I thought the police determined that someone snuck in after hours. That's what Detective Zelinski told us at the last briefing." She turned to the detective for confirmation.

"You've got that part right." Zelinski was standing by the door, his legs spaced far apart and his hands locked behind his back, looking uncomfortable and out of place. "But whoever snuck in here at night knew your code and had a key to the locked book safe."

"*My* code? It's not *my* code and I don't believe it was my key."

The detective went on in an uninflected monotone. "Security video shows a woman wearing a coat with a deep hood that hid her face accessing the library through the rear entrance at 2:42 AM the night of the theft."

"Are you accusing *me* of having something to do with stealing those books?" Of all the scenarios that had played out in Deena's head, this one had never crossed her mind. "It could have been anyone. It could have been Alice."

The Detective Zelinski ignored her. "We know that you've had severe financial problems. You lost your house and went through bankruptcy less than a year ago." He went on as if he were reading from a script.

"That's none of your business. What's that got to do with any of this?" Deena grabbed the arms of her chair to keep from shaking.

"Speaks to motive."

"I've never stolen anything in my life. Thieves know how to steal keys and figure out codes. That's what they do. That's their business."

Otto Richter cut in. "And it was your business to make sure that didn't happen. We don't have enough evidence to accuse anyone at this point, but we do know that, at the very least, you failed in your duty to protect the collection. You are leaving under a cloud of suspicion, fired for cause."

"That's not fair."

"Miss Novak will walk you back to your office to retrieve your personal belongings. Please leave your key and your ID badge on my desk before you go."

Deena was shattered. She couldn't think of a thing to say. Her legs would barely lift her from the chair. Robin Novak grasped her arm and led her to the door.

"Deena," Dr. Richter stopped her just as they were leaving. "This investigation is far from over. We *are* going to find the person who did this."

Deena may have nodded or she may have just stared.

Robin tightened her grip and led Deena back to her office for the last time.

Deena's final paycheck arrived at her home three days later, along with a letter from Human Resources explaining that since she'd been fired for cause she wouldn't qualify for unemployment benefits. A call to Human Resources revealed that, although there was money in her pension fund, she couldn't touch it before her 62nd birthday. She did a quick calculation on the back of the envelope. All the money in their emergency savings account wouldn't keep her afloat more than a couple of months. She'd have to call Martin. She needed help.

The problem was that Martin wasn't taking her calls. He hadn't spoken to her since the night Elliot had unraveled the lie she'd been living. It was horrific how swiftly that idle dalliance had turned her life inside out. Deena had always flattered herself that she was too smart, too responsible, and too disciplined to lose control of her life. Apparently, she'd been wrong. Martin had moved in with his cousin, who was probably blaming her for everything, including the River Parc fiasco. Ironically, she'd have to call Danny if she wanted to get through to her husband. The sound of his voice made her break out in a cold sweat, but she picked up the phone.

"Danny, this is Deena. I need to speak to Martin. It's very important."

"I know who it is, but Martin doesn't want to talk to you. He said to tell you he'll call when he's ready, or maybe his lawyer will call. He hasn't decided yet."

"Tell him I lost my job. We have to make some decisions now."

"No, Deena, you don't get it. You already made your decisions, now Martin's making his."

Danny had always been an idiot and a bully, but Deena had to get through him if she wanted to talk with her husband. She made her voice as sweet and remorseful as she could manage.

"I understand that Martin is hurt and angry and with good reason, but this can't wait. Let me explain the situation to you. I've always paid the rent out of my paycheck and Martin's always paid for pretty much everything else. But now, I don't have a job. I can't afford to keep paying the rent." *Why did she have to spell this out for him? Who had made him the gatekeeper?* "We'll get evicted if he doesn't help me. I really need to talk to him."

"Why don't you call the professor? Maybe he'll help you out."

Deena wanted to jump through the phone and throttle the jerk, but she kept her cool. "How about just giving Martin my message and letting him decide what to do. Could you do that, please? I'd really appreciate it."

"Yeah, I'll do that. But, you know, I don't think Martin cares about that apartment. He told me he never wants to see it again as long as he lives. Too many memories, you know? Anyway, he doesn't need it. He can stay here as long as he wants."

"Please, just give him the message."

"Of course, I don't expect he'll be here long. Some cute chick'll grab him up in no time, a sweet guy like that with a good job."

Deena hung up the phone. She'd done this to herself. Half dazed, she wandered into the living room and sank into the permanent indentation Martin had left in the sofa cushion. There was no one to talk to, no one to call. She missed her husband, she missed her job, she missed Lauren, and, she realized as she doubled over with an involuntary spasm of grief, she missed her mother.

A day later she fluffed her hair, applied lipstick and mascara, said a quick prayer, then drove downtown to the drugstore where Martin was at work. There was a new pharmacy tech behind the counter who assumed Deena was a customer and riddled her with questions before Martin heard her voice and came out of the stock room looking befuddled and confused.

"Deena, you shouldn't be here." He was wearing a shirt Deena didn't recognize and his hair was freshly cut. Apparently Danny was taking good care of him.

"Well, what *should* I do? You won't pick up the phone or respond to any of my messages."

"Please, not so loud." Martin looked around to see who might be listening. "Let's go outside. We can talk out back." He caught the tech's eye, which didn't take much effort, since she was watching them with unabashed curiosity. "Tanisha, I've got to take a quick break. I'll be back in ten if anyone needs me."

Once they were standing in the alley that ran between the drug store and the dry cleaner's next door, Deena had the fleeting hope that Martin would open his arms and let her weep out her remorse against the familiar comfort of his chest. No such luck. He stood stiffly at attention, a decorous six feet away. Deena studied him for clues, for some evidence that he might relent. "How are you holding up?" she asked. "You look like you could use some sleep."

He made a wry face. "I've been better."

"I'm sorry Martin. Believe me; I never wanted to hurt you. I never meant to destroy our marriage." She started to leak. Tears trickled down her face and she couldn't make them stop.

"You're not stupid Deena. You knew what you were doing and you did it anyway."

He reached across the divide separating them to hand her his handkerchief. "I didn't want to have this conversation now and I certainly didn't mean to have it here." He gestured toward the overflowing trash containers and cigarette butts that lined the alley. "But I wanted to say that maybe I should thank you. You always were the one with guts. Our marriage wasn't making either of us happy and you had the courage to do something about it. You did it the wrong way, but maybe that was better than going on the way we were."

"No, don't say that. There's got to be a way to fix this. We can't just throw away twenty years and two kids. If you'd been unfaithful, I would have forgiven you."

Martin's eyebrows shot up. "Really? Sorry I don't live up to your lofty standards."

Deena winced. She'd never known Martin to be sarcastic. It wasn't like him. She wiped her eyes with her husband's handkerchief then blew her nose.

Martin's face softened, but he didn't move to comfort her. "I'm sorry, that was a cheap shot, but you broke my heart. I only invested in that stupid property for you. I wanted you to have everything you wanted."

"For me? What are you talking about? I warned you not to get involved with Danny."

"Yeah, but you also wanted a new car and a remodeled kitchen and private university for the kids. I'm a pharmacist, Deena. Pharmacists don't make that kind of money."

Deena stared at him in disbelief. She'd had it all wrong. He had done it for the money. "Do you really think those things matter to me?"

"Yeah, I do. Look, I knew you were high maintenance when I married you. It just got harder to keep up over time."

Shock was visible on Deena's face. "I'm not high mainte-nance. I'm the opposite of high maintenance. I get my hair cut every two months and that's it. How is that high mainte-nance?"

"Maybe that's the wrong term, but you know what I mean. You've always wanted a big house, new furniture, summer camps for the kids. I'm not blaming you. That's the American dream and I wanted you to be happy, but that life doesn't come cheap."

It had not occurred to Deena that Martin didn't share her respect for upward mobility. He'd done it for her. The thought was chastening.

"This whole thing has changed me, or it is changing me. I don't know." He hugged himself and made odd little rocking motions that reminded her of the old Jews *davening* at her grandmother's *shul*. "I'm not thinking straight right now. That's why I couldn't talk to you. Do you understand? I need to get my own house in order before I do anything else."

Deena nodded. She understood. "But what about the apartment? I can't keep paying the rent now that I'm not working."

"We don't need a big, three bedroom apartment anymore. Lauren's in Boston and Elliot will be off to boot camp in a couple weeks. I'm going to rent a one bedroom closer to work. Maybe you should think about doing the same thing."

"You're not coming home?" Deena had assumed Martin would come back after licking his wounds and satisfying himself that she'd suffered enough.

"We can't just go back to the way we were. Would you even want to?" He was serious. Her life was actually over. He went on, as though he'd rehearsed his lines. "There's no point in getting involved with lawyers, there's nothing left to fight over. The bankruptcy took care of that." The faintest glimmer of a smile, a reminder of the old, familiar Martin, crossed his face.

"But I lost my job." Deena was numb, in an altered state of consciousness where she could barely speak.

"Unemployment compensation should tide you over until you find a new position."

Deena started to say, *But I'm not getting unemployment and how do I find a new job when my previous employer thinks I'm a thief?* But then she looked at Martin and saw the raw pain in his bloodshot eyes. She'd done that. He was falling apart and it was her fault. And he was right; there was no money to fight over. He'd need whatever he earned to set up a new apartment and to pay his own rent. What more did she want from him? *He'd done it for her.*

His voice seemed to come from somewhere a long way off. Deena tried to focus, to make sense of words that arrived broken and distorted through the static of her anxiety. "You can keep most of the furniture, the car, the dishes, all that stuff, but I'd like the stereo, a bed and one good chair. Things are going to be tight for both of us, but I'll do what I can if you need help. Keep the money from our savings account. You'll need it to set up a new apartment."

"Don't worry about it. I'll be fine." She zipped up her purse. "Sorry to bother you at work. I guess I'll be going now."

"Bye Deena."

There was an awkward moment when they almost kissed, but didn't, then almost shook hands, but didn't. Finally, Deena gave him a small half-hearted wave, and said, "Bye, Martin." Then they went their separate ways.

The lease was up June first, and she couldn't sign a new one without a job. Deena turned on her computer and typed in *Craigslist Cleveland*. She had less than a month to find a new place, pack up, and move out. It was *deja vu* all over again. She put her head down on the keyboard and closed her eyes.

Elliot slammed through the front door an hour later with unusual exuberance, his arms full of bags from Eddie Bauer and Dick's Sporting Goods. Deena glanced at her watch; it was only three o'clock. "You're home early. I thought you worked on Wednesdays."

"Not today, I quit. I'm a free man – at least until June 12th."

Deena looked up and gave him a tentative smile. "It looks like you've been on quite a shopping spree. Do you need all that stuff for boot camp?"

"Nope, they make you show up for boot camp practically naked. You can't take much more than your wallet and a Bible."

"Then what's all this?" Deena did her best to project maternal interest that was loving without being judgmental, concerned without being intrusive. She had to get it just right or he'd be down the hall and sequestered behind a locked door before she could say, "I'm sorry, that's not what I meant."

Elliot hesitated, apparently unsure how much to tell her, but Deena could see that he was excited about something and desperate to talk. She waited patiently with what she hoped was an expectant, but undemanding expression on her face.

"I'm not just done with my job; I'm done with high school. They're mailing my diploma directly to the Armed Forces Processing Center so I've got over three weeks all to myself."

"That's wonderful. What are you planning to do with all that time?"

"I'm going camping. There's a place near Tucson — Saguaro National Park. The cactus are in bloom right now and it's supposed to be really pretty. Anyway, I've always wanted to see the desert."

"But what about prom and graduation?"

"I'd rather go camping. That's why I bought all this stuff."

"Well, that's great. In fact, it might be perfect because..." Deena hesitated. She didn't want Elliot to think that he was homeless, but they both had to be out of the apartment by the end of the month. "I talked to your dad earlier today, and we decided not to renew the lease on this apartment."

Elliot's head snapped around and he stared at her open mouthed. "You talked to Dad?"

"Yes, and we decided that with you and Lauren both gone we won't be needing such a big place, and you know I've been laid off from my job so money's a little tight."

"Where are you moving? Dad's renting an apartment at the top of Cedar Hill."

He'd already found a place? He'd taken an apartment without even discussing it with her? Deena swallowed and tried not to let Elliot see how devastated she felt by the news. "I don't know yet, but I'm sure I'll find something. It'll just be me so it won't be much. Of course I'd love an extra bedroom so you and Lauren could visit, but I'm not sure how far my money will stretch."

"How much do you have?" Elliot was exactly like his father, practical and direct.

"I was just trying to figure that out. We have an emergency savings account that should cover the first month's rent and security deposit. But there'll be moving expenses, and I guess I'll have to pay something to put some stuff in storage. But don't worry, if I get into trouble your dad said he'd help out."

Elliot looked glum and shook his head. "I wouldn't count on that. Dad couldn't cover his own moving expenses. Uncle Danny had to loan him the money. Look, I'll pack my own stuff so you don't have to do that, and I guess I can box up Lauren's things too."

"Thank you, that would be a huge help, I mean if you have the time. When are you leaving?"

"Don't worry about it. I'll make time."

Deena jumped up and threw her arms around Elliot's neck. He stiffened, not hugging her back. Deena dropped her arms and stepped away. "I'm sorry, I know you're still mad at me, but I just love you so much and I'm so proud of you and I'm so grateful that you're going to help."

"No problem." Elliot scooped up his bags and walked off toward his room.

Three days later Deena woke up to find that her son had slipped off without even kissing her goodbye. The contents of both his room and Lauren's were neatly boxed and labeled, and there was an envelope on the kitchen table containing twenty hundred dollar bills, two thousand dollars, a quarter of all the money he'd worked so hard for, a quarter of the money that had cost him his place on the swim team and all the fun of his senior year. That envelope was what finally knocked Deena off her feet.

The next few days disappeared into a miasma of doubt and depression. She wandered around in her nightgown wondering what to have for breakfast at four in the afternoon. Her hair hung limp and unkempt, and dishes piled up on the floor beside her bed. The worst thing was no one even knew she was falling apart. She'd always had Martin and the children for company and plenty of people to talk with at work. She'd never thought of herself as lonely, but now she was crushed by the realization that she had no real friends. There was no one to take her in or to offer compassion and advice. Martin still had his parents, even though they'd moved to Arizona, and he had his cousins, but she had no one. Her grandmother was dead and her mother was a distant memory. She had some cousins somewhere, but she'd lost contact with them after Bubbe died. She stared at the bottle of Xanax in the medicine cabinet and wondered how many pills were in the bottle.

It was Wednesday before she pulled herself together and got dressed. Five days of eating nothing but dry cereal and canned soup left her feeling like an invalid, but she finally roused herself to face the inevitable. Her body ached and her gut heaved as she swallowed two slices of buttered toast and a cup of tea. Time was running out, she had to lift her head up, stare at the damn computer screen and find a new apartment. There were plenty of places for rent in the neighborhood so finding something small and inexpensive couldn't be that difficult. It wasn't. What was difficult was finding a landlord willing to rent to a woman with no known source of income. After responding to scores of advertisements, viewing fourteen apartments and filling out a dozen rental applications she admitted defeat. On May 28th, she boxed up her belongings and put them in storage along with Elliot's and Lauren's things. She mailed the key to the storage unit to Martin along with the bill telling him to take whatever he wanted. She'd be on the road looking for a job. Then, with the clock ticking and her options closing before her, she picked up the phone and dialed the one person who might still be willing to help.

"Andor? This is Deena. I know we agreed to a clean break, but I'm in big trouble and need a place to stay."

Part II

Part Two

Chapter Eight

Two days alone in a car gives you a lot of time to think and Deena had a lot to think about. Mostly, she thought, *this is crazy. I'm going the wrong way.* It felt as though everyone she knew and loved was behind her, growing more distant the further she drove, only they weren't. Well, Martin was, but her kids weren't in Cleveland anymore, her grandmother was dead, and her mother... Deena had no idea where she might be. There was her nonexistent job and all the coworkers who hadn't said a word in her defense and all the friends she'd never made. Face it, she told herself, no one in Cleveland gives a damn about you. By the time it got dark and she pulled into a Comfort Inn, the earth had rotated 180 degrees to the east and her internal map had reoriented south.

The closer she got to Sarasota the more she thought about Andor. He had not been happy to hear from her. He'd never expected to speak to her again and that was the way they'd both wanted it. Despite the flirtatious banter about running off together, a complete split had been their unspoken deal from the start and she'd violated the contract. There'd been such a long silence on the other end of the line that she thought he might have hung up. She'd pleaded with the silence to let her stay for a just a few weeks, just until she found a job and could get a place of her own. She'd sleep on the couch, she'd pay half the rent. It had been humiliating, but in the end Andor had mustered some of his old charm and said, "Of course, how can I say no to an old friend, but it's a small apartment so I'm afraid you'll have to sleep in the living room."

She drove the entire twelve hundred miles in two days and arrived exhausted and despondent. There was no doorbell, but Andor must have heard her drive up because the door to his apartment swung open and there he was, watching her struggle up the stairs dragging her suitcase behind her. "Hi," Deena tried smiling, but didn't have the energy.

"How was your drive?" Andor was his usual dapper self, but grayer and more weathered than she remembered him.

She was probably no treat for sore eyes herself. Setting her suitcase down in the kitchen she looked around and realized they'd be sharing tight quarters. "Thanks for taking me in; between Martin leaving and losing my job I was desperate. I promise I'll keep out of your way and I won't be staying long."

"Do you want a beer?" Andor took a swig from a bottle of Heineken.

Deena shook her head. "Where should I put my things?"

He pointed to an end table beside the sofa. "You can put some things in there. Do you have much?"

The drawer in the small side table would barely hold her underwear. "I'll just leave most of my stuff in the trunk of my car."

"That would be a good idea. I'm gone a lot so you'll have the place to yourself most of the time, but when I'm home I need to work, so no TV or music while I'm reading or grading papers."

"Sure, no problem. I'm just glad you're letting me stay."

"How could I say no to such a lovely lady?" Andor tried to sound like his old, flirtatious self, but that time was past and his words fell flat. He changed his tone, sounding almost genuine, "I'm sorry if I'm partly to blame for your problems. I never thought these things would happen."

Really? What did you think would happen? Deena bit her lip and didn't say what she was thinking. She needed a place to stay, and besides, what had *she* thought would happen? She was more guilty than Andor. She was the one who'd betrayed her husband. "We were idiots." She shrugged, "You play with fire, you get burned."

"Do you think Martin will forgive you? Will you be able to go back home?"

"Not if he finds out I'm here."

"Then we'll make sure he doesn't find out. What did you tell your family?"

"I told them I'd be on the road looking for a job. I'm not even sure what that means, but they bought it. Martin wished me luck and told me not to worry about paying for my phone. He'd keep me on the family plan."

"You miss him." Andor's face was tender and sincere, the face of a tired, aging adjunct professor who'd just been saddled with one more unpaid assignment.

"Yeah, I miss him a lot. We were together twenty-five years. I never thought he'd actually leave."

"Maybe he'll come back, I'm sure he misses you too. Did you bring a sleeping bag?"

Andor had rented an apartment on the second floor of a converted house because it was cheap and the landlord agreed to a short term lease. Sarasota wasn't Cleveland and a visiting professor's salary didn't buy much in the tight Gulf Coast market. Deena was grateful to have a roof over her head, so she didn't complain about the cramped kitchen, the cupboard doors that sagged off their hinges, the bare light bulb in the bathroom, or the cracks in the tile floor. The place was really only two rooms. The first was a large space divided in half to create a kitchen and sitting area. The second was Andor's bedroom. The apartment had come furnished with an old rattan sofa and chair, a chrome dinette set with vinyl seats, and a mattress on a metal frame in the bedroom. Despite its obvious defects, the place was clean and conveniently located near the beautiful Sarasota Bay, not far from upscale condos, restaurants and boutiques.

Deena was desperate for a job so she could move out as soon as possible. She longed for a job as a librarian, but was terrified to apply for any of the positions listed on the American Library Association's website. How would she explain her dismissal from the university? What sort of references could she expect? She felt like a convicted felon, although she'd never been charged with anything worse than running out a parking meter.

As promised, Andor came home late or not at all, occasionally disappearing for days at a time without explanation or apology. Deena suspected he had a new girlfriend, but didn't care enough to ask. When he was home, he was the perfect roommate, always tidy and polite—except now there was a nervous edge to the man, a chronic jumpiness she hadn't seen before. His grooming was as immaculate as ever, but he looked different, haunted or hunted. Deena watched him pace around the apartment, pick up a book, read two pages, then put it down, open a cupboard, take out a dish then walk away. When his phone rang, he stepped out on the balcony and shut the door. Odd, but not her concern. Deena simply shook her head and went back to the serious business of trying to rebuild her life.

Her resume had been stellar, but now it was marred by a huge, glaring hole. Deena rewrote it a dozen different times, but nothing helped. There was no hiding her dismissal. In the end, Deena concocted a lie. She became a divorced housewife who had trained as a librarian, but who had no references because she'd spent twenty years at home raising her family. She could type, had decent computer skills, and would make an excellent secretary or administrative assistant. Deena sent out the new resume along with custom tailored cover letters to twenty different companies. Most of the employers didn't respond at all. It was a buyer's market and she was damaged goods.

When Deena wasn't perusing *Craigslist* or the *Herald Tri-bune*'s online classified ads, she was counting and recounting her money, calculating how much time it would buy. The answer was two months, maybe three if Andor let her stay without paying rent.

Every morning she switched on her phone with a prayer of gratitude that Martin had kept her on their family plan. Did he still consider her family, or was it just too much trouble to notify Verizon that she was no longer entitled to the benefits of being his wife?

Almost no one advertised in the print edition of the clas-sifieds anymore, but Deena noticed a small ad in the *Trib*'s vestigial help wanted column. It wasn't exactly a dream job, but she might have a chance. The small medical supply com-pany had not only placed a print ad in the newspaper, they'd included an actual phone number. Deena picked up her phone and dialed.

A pleasant, grandmotherly sounding woman answered. "Lakeland Medical Supply, may I help you?"

"Hello, my name is Deena Berman and I was calling…"

"Can you hold just a minute, dear? I need to say good-bye to my daughter." Deena waited patiently for several minutes. "Sorry to keep you waiting, but my daughter's buying a new house and needed some advice."

"Of course, that's no problem. As I was saying, I'm calling about the job you have advertised in today's paper."

"Well thank goodness. We need someone as soon as possi-ble. Do you have any experience with computers and keeping track of inventory?"

"I'm good with computers although…"

"Shirley worked here almost twenty years and knew ev-erything, but she had a stroke last week, poor thing. She can't even talk. My son relied on her completely."

"I'm so sorry. That must be difficult for you."

"It is. They say she's never coming back. I'm filling in until he hires someone new, but I'm not cut out for business. So, where have you been working?"

Deena knew her lines. "I'm trained as a librarian, and I'm familiar with Excel, PowerPoint, and Word. I've kept up my skills even though I've been at home raising children for the past eighteen years."

"And now I bet you want to help with their college tuition. You're a good mother. Where did they go to school? My kids graduated from Riverview."

"Oh, they went to school in Ohio. I just moved here a few weeks ago."

"Really? What in the world brought you to Florida in the summer?"

Half an hour later, after regaling Deena with the sad story of her own divorce, and the lack of available men in Sarasota, the woman scheduled a job interview for Thursday afternoon at four o'clock. Deena was optimistic.

If she'd been interviewing for a library position Deena would have worn her gray suit, but it was too dressy for the back office of a small family business. She eventually settled on a Navy skirt with a tailored blouse and low heeled pumps. Surveying herself in the mirror that hung behind the bathroom door, Deena saw a younger version of Alice: competent, sexless, and middle aged. They'd love her.

It was only 2:30 when she got into her Taurus and headed South on Tamiami, the long stretch of road connecting Tampa and Miami. Her phone's GPS told her the drive was only twenty-two minutes, but she was so terrified of getting lost and being late that she arrived a full hour and ten minutes early. She stared at the clock on her dashboard feeling foolish. "Hey, Siri," she finally asked her phone. "Where's the closest coffee shop?"

There was one Starbuck's five miles back and another three miles ahead. She pulled her car out of the parking lot and decided to treat herself to a Venti. Two months ago she wouldn't have thought twice about buying a cup of coffee. Now it was a guilty indulgence. The Sarasota Starbucks looked and smelled just like the Starbucks near the university in Cleveland, and the Starbucks near her home, and the Starbucks off the highway. They all had the same hip hype, the familiar aroma of roasting coffee, the hiss of steaming milk, the mix of wood, chrome, slate and leather. An argument can be made for buying local, but at that moment the national chain felt like home, the one constant left in a life that had come free of its moorings.

Deena took her cup of Komodo Dragon and sat at a small table quietly perusing a local arts and entertainment magazine. She was engrossed in an article about Nik Wallenda's high wire walk across Route 41 on swaying cables when she was startled by a series of loud bangs just outside the window. Everybody in the shop stopped talking and looked up. A gray haired woman at a nearby table walked over to the glass door and peered out. "Whoa," she gasped. "Hope none of you owns a black Taurus." Deena shot up from her seat, throwing her cup in the trash. A group of women in nurse's uniforms also gathered up their things and prepared to leave, but Deena beat them to the door praying that someone else's car had taken the hit.

No such luck. Her Ford Taurus, the car that had made it all the way to Florida without a hitch, was barely recognizable. The back end was a crumpled mess of twisted metal, the trunk pushed into the back seat. The bumper was on the pavement, and the back passenger door was half open and hanging at an odd angle. One of the nurses stopped and shook her head, "Whoa, that's ugly. Good thing no one was sitting in there."

Deena pulled a scrap of paper from her pocket and dialed Lakeland Medical Supply. "I'm afraid that I'm going to have to reschedule our interview. I've just had an accident and my car's not drivable. No, I'm fine, thank you. Could we reschedule for tomorrow or Monday?"

No, they were terribly sorry, but they couldn't. The chatty woman on the phone explained that they'd already interviewed several good candidates and they needed someone with reliable transportation who could start immediately. "Of course, thank you, I understand." Deena clicked off her phone. She understood alright. She absolutely understood.

She walked back into Starbucks and approached the woman who'd first seen the accident. "Excuse me, but did you see who hit my car? Did you get the license plate number?"

"Sorry, it all happened too fast, but I can tell you for sure is it was a truck, black, or maybe dark blue, one of those oversized pickup things. Dinged your car up pretty good, didn't it?"

"Did you see the driver?"

"A guy wearing a baseball cap, that's all I can tell you. Honestly, I couldn't see straight. My heart was going a million miles a minute. I thought for sure it was another drive-by shooting."

The officer who pulled up five minutes later dutifully wrote down everything that Deena told him, then ripped a copy of the report off his pad and handed it to her. "We'll let you know if we find the guy, but don't hold your breath. There's not much to go on here. Do you have insurance?"

"Not collision. The car's eleven years old."

"Too bad." The policeman pulled out his radio, "Where do you want it towed?"

The bus ride home took over an hour. The diesel fumes, the constant stops and starts, and the irrational fear that she'd miss her stop made her head throb. The Taurus was toast, totaled, kaput. If she was lucky the salvage value would cover the cost of the tow. The suitcase and boxes she'd pulled from the mangled trunk were piled on the seat beside her. She watched drivers behind the wheels of their cars going wherever they liked, oblivious of their good fortune, and felt a stab of envy.

In the course of an hour she'd gone from the hope of a job and the prospect of her own apartment to fucked. It wasn't her fault. There was nothing she could have done to prevent it, but she was still fucked. *Fucked, fucked, fucked.* The word repeated itself endlessly inside her head, the anthem of her new life.

The loss of the car was life altering. Tasks as simple as grocery shopping, laundry, or going to the library took effort and planning. The radius of her job search contracted, further reducing her chances of finding employment. It hardly mattered, since she was so tired and weepy that she barely had the energy to scroll through the classified listings. In fact, she'd almost stopped eating. At first, she'd told herself she was cutting back on food to save money, but the truth was she'd lost her appetite. Nothing looked good. Chewing and swallowing were chores. To make matters worse, Andor was clearly becoming annoyed by the shell shocked wraith wandering through his apartment in sweat pants and a dirty T-shirt.

It was three o'clock in the afternoon on a Wednesday, or maybe a Thursday, days didn't matter anymore. Deena was stretched out on the sofa with her eyes closed. A new Margaret Atwood novel lay unopened beside her. It was due back at the library in five days and she'd never get it read if she didn't open her eyes, but the effort seemed beyond her. She was drifting off to sleep when her iPhone began to croak on the bedside table. Suddenly wide awake, Deena fell on the phone praying it was someone calling about a job. Instead, she saw the familiar number of the Alfred Seibel Library. Why would they be calling?

"Hello." Her voice sounded hoarse and throaty like one of the ringtone frogs that lived in her phone.

"Deena, this is Alice Krol. I have some news I thought you should know. I think you'll like what I have to say."

"Yes, what is it?" She swung her legs over the side of the

bed and braced herself for whatever came next.

"The police located pages from four of the stolen books on an antiquarian book site and they've traced them back to a woman named Krystina Pyszka. She owns an art gallery downtown. They arrested her this afternoon. They think she's the woman in the security video."

"Thank you, that is good news."

Krystina Pyszka? Deena flopped forward, her head falling to her knees as she felt herself slide to the floor. Nausea overcame her in waves as her stomach reached its conclusion seconds before her brain had processed the implications of this news. She sprawled beside the bed too dazed to speak, the phone still riveted to her ear. *I'm an idiot. What's the matter with me? How could I be so stupid?*

Oblivious, Alice kept talking, her voice meaningless white noise. "Can you hear me? I said, I never thought you were involved. We've had our differences, but I never imagined you were a book thief for single minute. Frankly, I don't think you'd know which books to steal or where to sell them."

It wasn't easy to sound normal when simply breathing was an effort, but Deena struggled to regain her composure. "I'm not any kind of thief." A sudden thought gave her a spasm of hope. "Does this mean I get my job back?" *My God, does this mean I can go home?*

"I'm afraid that's not my department, but I wanted you to know that you're no longer a suspect."

"Thank you, Alice. I really appreciate you calling. So, how is Archives and Special Collections doing without a director?"

"Oh, we have a director," Alice chirped with joy. "Taylor Smythe was reinstated right after you left. Melanie Johnson from Digital Services is running Humanities now. I don't know who's running her department. It's been quite a game of musical chairs around here."

"You're kidding? They put Melanie Johnson in charge of Humanities?" Outrage flashed its orange banner through

Deena's brain.

"Yes, I'm afraid so. Melanie doesn't know any more about Humanities than you knew about Archives and Rare Books. I don't know how they make these decisions. It was terrible the way they let you go, but you do understand the way things looked."

Deena nodded on her end of the phone and tried to produce some sort of affirmative sound despite her dry mouth and the small tremor in her jaw. *So, Richter had moved people around and smoothed things over as though she'd never existed. Twenty years down the drain.*

"Can you hear me? I think there's something wrong with our connection. I asked if you'd found another position yet?"

"No, not yet." Deena managed to recover her voice. "But thanks for asking."

"Well, good luck, I hope something turns up soon."

Andor got back to the apartment around eight. He checked his mail, grabbed a can of beer from the fridge and was sitting at the kitchen table sorting through a pile of mail when Deena emerged from the bathroom. Her eyes were red and rabbity, but they fixed on Andor with the piercing gaze of an eagle, "Guess who called this afternoon."

"I don't know, your husband?" He continued to study the paper in his hand without looking up.

"Nope, it was Alice Krol from the library. She had some interesting news. It seems that your friend, Krystina Pyszka, is the book thief."

Andor froze. His expression didn't change although Deena saw the paper twitch in his hand. "Who is saying these things? Krystina can be pushy, and I think too full of her herself, but she's not a robber."

"Well, the police think she is. They arrested her this afternoon." Deena watched the color drain from Andor's face. She'd prayed that her gut instinct was wrong, but his expression told her everything.

"What else did Alice tell you? Does she know anything else?" He flipped open his phone and made a show of checking for messages as he spoke. The coward couldn't look her in the eye.

"No, I think that's all they know so far. Of course, she probably wasn't working alone. Someone must have helped her gain access to the security code and the key to the book safe. I bet she'll trade that person's name for a reduced sentence. I expect they'll both be in jail within a couple of days."

"Did Alice say that? Is that what she thinks?" He continued punching at his phone, although his movements looked absurdly random and meaningless. The man was clearly rattled.

"No, that's what I think. Krystina's not the martyr type. I think that she'll betray him. I'm sure that someone will."

Andor stopped fiddling with his phone and looked up, his eyes wide and unfocused. For the first time in ages, Deena felt she had the upper hand.

"Maybe not, some women are loyal and protect their friends. I think Krystina is that kind of woman." He picked up his beer and chugged it down.

"Do you? Is that what you think? Well, I think there's no loyalty among thieves." Deena folded her arms across her chest, her hands balled into fists.

Andor snapped his phone shut and stood up abruptly. "Well, that is interesting news, but it's been a long day. Please excuse me." He disappeared into the bedroom and shut the door.

Deena sank into one of the kitchen chairs and sat listening to drawers being opened and shut, the warped closet door scraping across the floor and the clatter of hangers. It was a small apartment with thin walls. She could hear the zipping sound of Andor closing his suitcase and the small thud as he set it down behind the door. Then, she couldn't hear the words, but there was the muffled sound of Andor's voice on the phone. Finally, she heard the creaking of bedsprings and then nothing but the thump and whir of the kitchen fan rotating slowly above her head. Deena switched off the light, crawled into her sleeping bag and shut her eyes, but her mind was alert, still listening.

Hours later the bedroom door creaked opened. If she'd drifted off to sleep, the sound brought her back to full wakefulness. She opened her eyes and watched as Andor, backlit by a flickering street light, tiptoed across the floor carrying a suitcase and a tangled pile of clothing. As he passed through the kitchen she watched him gather up his mail and his laptop; then she heard the screen door slam, a car motor turn over, and the crunch of shells that Floridians use instead of gravel on their driveways. She didn't move until the low thrum of the engine faded to silence. The dial on her phone read 2:10. Deena got up, filled a glass with water, and looked out the kitchen window. The moon stared back at her with its blank, unblinking eye. They regarded one another wordlessly until a small cloud passed between them, and then Deena walked over to the door, set the dead bolt in place, and went to sleep.

The next morning Deena woke in a tangle of pillows and sofa cushions. She'd spent the night wrestling with a question of morality and law. Should she take her suspicions to the police and become embroiled in a criminal case that would ultimately point back at her, or plead ignorance and get on with the business of finding a job? After all, she knew nothing for certain. Andor's behavior was incriminating, but he hadn't actually admitted anything and she had no hard evidence to offer. Still, he'd definitely been involved with the woman arrested for stealing the books, and how else could she explain his sudden departure? The clincher was Deena's realization that if she could connect Andor to the crime, so could the police, and if they suspected Andor, they'd suspect her as well. After all, she'd probably been the conduit through which he'd deciphered the code and pilfered the key. Would the police see her as a victim or as one of the guilty parties? Better to go to the police with what she knew than to lay low and wait for a knock at the door.

Deena dialed the library at nine sharp, knowing that Alice would be at her desk. "Alice, this is Deena. I've been thinking about our conversation yesterday and I need to talk with Detective Zelinsky. I might have remembered something. Do you have his number?"

"Really? Odd that you should suddenly remember something now, but I do have his number. Wait a minute while I check my file."

Zelinsky wasn't available when she called, so Deena left her number on his voice mail then wandered into the bedroom to see if Andor had left any clues behind. Better than a clue, he'd left a note stuck into the framed mirror above the dresser. *Dear Deena, I am sorry to leave without saying good-bye, but I didn't want to wake you. Like I said long ago, I'm a rolling rock. Do whatever you want with the things I left in my room. Also, if any mail comes for me, just throw it away. The rent is paid to the end of the month, so stay as long as you want. Please believe me that I am very sorry that I've caused you so much trouble. Best wishes for your future life, Andor*

She looked around the room taking inventory. He'd left a stack of journals, a moth eaten sweater, sweatpants, a pair of tennis shoes and a canvas tote bag. She put the tote bag to one side and was debating whether to schlep the other stuff to Goodwill, or simply throw it in a dumpster when an unfamiliar number showed up on her caller ID.

"Mrs. Berman? This is Detective Zelinsky. I thought I might hear from you."

"You did?" The comment startled her. "Why?"

"Sometimes I get a feeling about what a woman's going to do. You could call it my woman's intuition." Deena waited patiently while Zelinsky finished chuckling at his little joke. "OK, so what have you got for me? I understand you remembered something."

"Yes, I know this doesn't put me in a good light, but I thought you should know something about a man I met in Cleveland."

"Andor Farkas, yes, we know about the two of you."

"Oh." Deena felt suddenly violated. It was worse than the creepy sensation she got when a credit card company asked her to confirm her last three purchases or the name of her favorite restaurant. How did Zelinsky know she'd been seeing Andor, and how much more of her dirty linen had he been pawing through? "Well, I was just going to tell you that he's friends with Krystina Pyszka and that he might know something."

"We're already investigating that connection. Is there anything else?"

"Yes, well I think you should know that he's probably on the run. I don't know where he went, but he moved out of his apartment right after he found out about Krystina being arrested. I just thought you might want to know."

"Thank you, I appreciate you calling to tell me. I didn't know that. Is there anything else?"

"Just that I didn't have anything to do with this. I didn't know anything. I've never stolen anything in my life."

"I believe you Mrs. Berman. We have some new information that I can't share with you right now, but let's just say that I have good reason to believe you're telling the truth."

"You do? Really? Have you told anyone at the library? Do they know I'm innocent?"

"I told them it looks like you were duped by a couple of slick hustlers, that Pyszka woman and a guy who calls himself Reno Cartridge. You know him?"

"I think I met him once at Krystina's gallery. Are you saying Andor wasn't one of the thieves?"

"Oh, he was in on it, alright, but that guy's an amateur. These others now, they're pros."

"I see."

Being duped meant she was stupid, a patsy, an idiot, but she wasn't a thief. Tears of relief pricked Deena's eyes. "Thank you, Officer Zelinsky. Thank you so much." Maybe she'd call Richter and ask for her job back. Maybe she'd go home.

It was crazy, but the first thing she did was email Martin and her children with the good news. The letter to Martin bounced back almost immediately with an automatic response reading, *"I will be cycling across Umbria and Tuscany until August 22nd. If this is an emergency, I can be contacted through Tempo Bello Tours. Otherwise, I'll return your message when I've returned home. Ciao."*

They'd always dreamed about traveling through Italy together, and now Martin was there without her. Wasn't that a kind of adultery? He'd run off with Italy behind her back. They were probably drinking Chianti and making goo goo eyes at each other across the Piazza del Campo at this very moment, while she was surveying Andor's empty room.

Deena carried an armload of men's clothes down to the dumpster, then bought a bottle of cheap wine from a convenience store. She'd call Richter in the morning to see what she could do about putting her life back together. A day later she was stretched out on the couch with an empty wine bottle tipped over beside her and an equally empty tumbler resting on her stomach. The call to Richter had not gone well. Without actually apologizing, he'd indicated some remorse that "things had turned out the way they did." Then he'd lapsed into a monologue about the budget and the need to run a lean ship and how Taylor Smythe had returned to take over Special Collections after the unfortunate incident and they certainly missed her but... Deena had stopped listening. There was no job. She couldn't go home. He'd already given her life to someone else.

Chapter Nine

Now that she was no longer a suspect in the case of the missing books, Deena began sending out professional resumes again. Even if the Alfred Siebel Library wouldn't give her a job, Deena was confident they'd give her a decent reference. They owed her that much. Removing all geographic considerations from her search she applied for jobs across the country. Unfortunately, virtually all libraries and universities were dealing with budget cuts so the pickings were slim. All she could do was wait and pray that something would turn up soon. Without Andor paying half the rent her money wouldn't last long. She tightened her belt and started watching her pennies in earnest.

Although Deena no longer squandered her dwindling resources on restaurant meals, she continued to eat out several times a week. Of course, "eating out" now meant packing a sandwich and fruit in a paper bag and dining *al fresco* on a bench overlooking the bay. A cooling breeze blew in from the water as she finished her tuna sandwich. Bayside Park might not be the Ritz, but it was a pleasant change from Andor's apartment. Deena shook the crumbs from her lap, folded the leftover foil into a neat square, then placed the square inside the bag. Her eyes scanned the park for a trash bin, but all she saw were immaculate green lawns, palm trees, and the beautiful blue water of Sarasota Bay. She tucked the trash inside her purse and stood up. Where did she need to go next? After a moment's hesitation she realized the answer was nowhere and sat back down. Brown pelicans flew in circles overhead fishing the shallow waters between the spit of rocky beach beyond her feet and the high rise condos on the Keys. She watched the birds orbit, swoop and dive, a native species happily soaring over familiar waters. *Must be nice,* she thought as she pulled her phone from her purse and started a game of *Angry Birds.*

"What do you want from me? I'm walking as fast as I can. Maybe you think I should fly. You can wait another minute; it won't kill you."

Deena looked up. A small, elderly woman was approaching slowly, pushing a shopping cart filled with large plastic bags. She seemed to be talking to herself. The city was full of homeless people and Deena realized with a pang, that she might be one of them by the end of the month. The woman was wearing a black cardigan, orthopedic shoes and glasses with owlish black frames. Her white hair was cut short and combed back from a broad, wrinkled face. With luck, she'd push her cart right past the bench where Deena was sitting and continue on toward Dolphin Fountain or Marina Jack. No such luck. The woman lowered herself onto the bench beside Deena who promptly stood up.

"Don't get up. Sit, be comfortable, you won't bother us. We don't mind if she sits here, do we?" The old woman addressed this last question to the sky.

Deena followed the woman's gaze to the upper branches of a nearby tree that was heavy with black birds bobbing their heads and cawing loudly. Their cries had been lost in the ambient sound of the surf, the rustling of palm fronds, and the hoarse chirps of the pelicans, but now Deena heard them clearly. The crows appeared rowdy and excited, flitting from one branch to another. "I'm late with their breakfast and they're giving me hell. Maybe you could help with that big bag. I forgot to bring scissors."

"What sort of help do you need?" Deena was wary, but after twenty years as a reference librarian she had a highly honed instinct to be helpful.

"Normally I don't need help, but with these new bags, it's like breaking into Fort Knox. Maybe you've got some dynamite."

Deena smiled and went to inspect a large sac drooping over the side of the metal cart. It was a twenty-five pound bag of oily sunflower seeds sealed with a double stitched row of heavy twine. Deena pulled the end of the string expecting the bag to rip open. Nothing. She pulled harder until the string burned her fingers. Sitting back down she riffled through the contents of her purse. "I think I have something in here." She pulled out a small metal emery board and waved it triumphantly. "Dynamite!" The emery board easily sawed through the string and Deena opened the sac. "There you go. I hope your birds enjoy their breakfast."

"Would you mind, there's one more thing. Maybe you could scatter some seeds over there beneath that pine tree. I'm all out of breath and I... " Her head snapped skyward and she shouted more loudly than you'd expect from someone too winded to stand up. "Settle down, stop kvetching. This nice lady's going to feed you." She shook her head. "They're like children. They can't wait for anything."

The cawing had indeed become noisier and more persistent. "How do they know what's in the bags? Don't tell me they can read the labels." Deena wasn't sure if the woman was crazy or just an odd character.

"I feed them every day. They followed me all the way from Whole Foods. Believe me, they know what's in the bags."

Whole Foods was a mile away. No wonder the old bird was winded. "What do I do, just pour some seed onto the ground?"

"You could do that, but there's an oatmeal carton. I use that for a scoop. It's in the bag with the peanuts. In fact, give them a couple scoops of peanuts too. They'll love you forever."

Deena tentatively opened one of the smaller bags. It was full of raisins and some sort of small dried berries. A third bag held oatmeal, but no scoop. Inside the fourth bag she found shelled peanuts and an empty *Quaker Oats* box. She filled the box with peanuts and scattered them beneath the tree where the woman pointed.

"That's good, good. Maybe two more scoops, then you can start with the sunflower seeds." The woman nodded approvingly as a dozen crows, a handful of seagulls, and a pair of tall gray birds with red caps began squabbling over the windfall. Deena looked around, grateful that the park was empty. She'd just finished tossing a scoop of raisins onto a mound of nuts and sunflower seeds when she realized she was wrong.

A uniformed policeman was barreling down the wide concrete path in their direction. Deena froze, the incriminating oatmeal box still in her hand. He stopped a few feet from where she was standing, shaking his head. She could see his shoulders rise and fall in a great resigned sigh. The officer was young, probably still in his twenties, tan and well built. Streaks of blonde ran through the cropped regulation haircut visible beneath his cap.

"Mrs. Goetz, you've been warned. We've been patient, we've given you more chances than I count, but this is too much. You're coming with me."

"I'm sitting here on a bench minding my own business. Since when is that against the law in this country?" The old woman spoke softly, almost to herself. She looked down, fiddling with the buttons on her sweater with boney arthritic fingers — although it was eighty degrees and sunny.

"You're feeding the birds again. You're attracting nuisance wildlife, littering, introducing foreign plants, and feeding prohibited species, specifically Sandhill Cranes. All those things are against the law Mrs. Goetz. You know that. It's been explained to you a dozen times."

"So, who's feeding birds? I'm just sitting."

"Come on, I'm taking you in. You can't keep tossing citations like they're grocery receipts." He put his hand beneath her arm and slowly lifted her to her feet, then waited a moment while she found her balance.

"You should arrest that lady." She turned her glassy blue eyes toward Deena. "She's feeding the birds, not me."

Deena wheeled around, tossed the oatmeal box into the shopping cart and grabbed her purse. "I don't even know this lady. I'm sorry, but I have to leave."

The old woman chortled. "See, she doesn't even know me. You're going to arrest me because someone I don't even know is making a mess."

The young police officer hesitated, looked momentarily confused, then squared his jaw and took command. "OK, I'm taking you both in. My cruiser is right over there in the parking lot. Don't make me cuff you." He shepherded them toward his police car and helped Mrs. Goetz inside. Deena stood staring at his car immobilized by shock and confusion until the officer repeated, "You too, lady, get in the car."

Deena slid in beside the old woman and the policeman slammed the door. The back seat was so cramped she found herself scrunched over with her head barely clearing the ceiling. She wriggled over to the far side of the seat, as far from the old woman as she could get. The wire cage separating the back seats from the front seats made her feel like a stray dog that had just been impounded. She'd narrowly escaped being charged with book theft and now she was going to wind up with a record for feeding birds. The young officer was speaking to someone over his radio but most of what he said was police gibberish, so she tuned him out, scrunched down in her seat and stared sullenly out the window. Wire mesh embedded in the glass made her reflection stare back at her from behind bars. Her lips trembled and she could feel tears welling inside her eyes so she opened her purse to look for a tissue.

"Hey, I need to take that." The police officer, who had seemed preoccupied with his radio, pulled over and stopped the car. He jumped out, opened the rear door and snatched her purse. "You'll get this back when you're released." Deena wiped her tears on the shoulder of the crew neck T-shirt she'd bought last fall, back when she was trying to look young and collegiate. As if. At the moment she was wondering how she'd look in an orange jumpsuit.

Mrs. Goetz suddenly leaned forward and shouted through the metal cage, "Wait a minute, stop. What about my shopping cart? We can't just leave it for thieves. There's expensive stuff in there."

The officer turned, a small smirk playing across his face. "So, it *is* your shopping cart, is it? I'd better make a note of that." Mrs. Goetz fell back in her seat, arms folded across her chest, her lips pursed. Deena could see the policeman watching them in his rear view mirror. "Park security is picking up your cart. They'll keep it safe, but you're not getting it back any time soon. We're keeping it as evidence until this thing gets settled."

No one said another word until they arrived at the Sarasota County Jail where they were pulled from the squad car and hustled into Central Processing. The young arresting officer who'd brought them in conferred briefly with an older policeman sitting behind a bulletproof window. Seated on a plastic chair in a secure section of the building, Deena pressed her arms and legs into her body trying to make herself invisible. A tough looking character was ushered in wearing handcuffs and a do-rag, but to Deena's relief, he was immediately hustled into another room. She studied the clock on the wall behind a glass window where a clerk with a dour expression was working on a computer. It wasn't even two o'clock, not that it mattered.

Mrs. Goetz leaned toward Deena and spoke in a low, conspiratorial voice. "I'm sorry, I didn't think he'd really do it.

Normally, Kevin's a cream puff. I don't know what got into him today."

"Kevin? You're on a first name basis?" Deena hissed back through closed teeth.

"We go back two years, maybe three now. I was one of his first cases. He already got a promotion." There was something proud, almost maternal, in her tone.

"Why did you have to drag me into whatever this is between you and Kevin? I'm trying to start a new life here. I need a job and a place to live, not a police record. Who's going to hire a librarian with a record? Why would you do this to me?"

"I said I'm sorry. Probably they'll just give you a citation. It's a first offence. You're a librarian?" A uniformed guard gestured for them to be quiet so Deena just nodded and went back to staring at the clock and to the stream of people called up to the front desk for processing. This was a total waste of time, worse than a bad day at the BMV. She should be browsing through Craigslist for an apartment, or a job, or a family. A wave of homesickness hit her like a tsunami. She closed her eyes and counted to six as she exhaled a long, cleansing breath, but she knew that she was drowning.

"Deena Berman." The officer who had hushed her earlier called her name from a list. As Deena stood up the old woman grabbed her sleeve. "Don't tell them anything if they don't ask. Name, rank and serial number, that's it. Good luck."

The officer assigned to determine the disposition of her case had apparently been trained to give nothing away through a smile, a twitch, or a nod. Robots were more user friendly and socially appropriate. Deena sat down across from the automaton and waited while he sifted through some papers and clicked away at his computer screen. Finally, he began, "Is your name Deena Berman." Deena nodded. "Are you known by any other names or aliases?" Deena shook her head. "Answer me out loud, are you known by any other names or aliases?" By the time they were done, Deena felt as though she'd been interrogated for a murder, so it was a shock when he ended by saying. "You're not being cited today. Officer Fenton only issued a warning, but he brought you in to make sure you and your friend appreciate the gravity of the offense. You can collect your personal belongings from the clerk in the back office. Don't get caught feeding Sandhill Cranes or littering again. Those are second degree misdemeanors."

Deena hurried down a long corridor to a small office where her purse was waiting. What were Sandhill Cranes anyway? She'd have to look them up when she got home.

The next morning was warm and sunny, just like every other morning since she'd arrived in Sarasota. Deena filled the kettle for her morning cup of matcha. She'd carried the tin of finely milled tea powder with her from Cleveland. Her morning matcha ritual was becoming an addiction she could no longer afford. Peering into the tin, she realized that its days were numbered. The little tin had set her back nearly as much as she currently budgeted for a week's groceries. When it was gone, it was gone.

Her eyes scanned the apartment's worn walls and tired furniture as she waited for the water to boil. Although she wasn't a fan of the peeling window sills and cracked ceiling, the place was clean and dry. Eddie, the landlord, was a sullen curmudgeon in his early sixties who ran a computer repair shop out of his kitchen. A tattoo of an American eagle ran down the length of his right arm and his thinning hair was tied back in a pony tail. When Deena went downstairs to tell him she'd be taking over Andor's apartment, she expected him to grunt his assent without fuss or formality. Instead, he pulled out a lease application and stood over her while she filled in the blanks. Now, a week had gone by without a response and Deena was getting nervous.

She stared out the kitchen window at the palm fronds that obscured her view of the telephone wires crisscrossing the street. In Ohio she could name all the trees and flowers. Here, all she could do was discriminate between palm trees and not palm trees. If she was going to live in Florida she'd have to start learning the names of the native plants and animals. She was a librarian for God's sake. She ought to do some research. The kettle began to whistle, so Deena grabbed a mug from the cupboard. It had the head of an extraordinarily ugly alligator on one side and *Florida Gators* printed in orange letters on the other. It was enough to make her matcha curdle. She shoved it back on the shelf and was looking for something less offensive when her doorbell rang.

It had to be Eddie, no one else knew she was here. Deena went out on her narrow balcony and peered down. Whoever was ringing the bell was standing on the front steps directly beneath her so she couldn't make out who it was. "Eddie, is that you? Give me a minute, I'm not dressed."

"That's all right, it's just me. If you're not too busy I thought maybe we could talk." A small figure in a long black cardigan stepped out from under the balcony and looked up at her.

"Mrs. Goetz, what are you doing here?"

"I wanted to see you. I didn't bring any birdseed. See, I'm clean." She held her cardigan open to prove there was nothing hidden inside her sweater.

"Well, I'm sorry, but I don't want to talk. That was a terrible thing you did to me yesterday. I could have been arrested." Deena should have gone back inside the house and shut the door, but for some reason she continued looking down over the wrought iron railing at the old woman on the lawn. There was something about her. It was her voice. She sounded like a demented version of her grandmother.

"I came here to tell you I'm sorry. You know it wasn't so easy finding out where you live. Give me five minutes, two minutes — maybe I can make things up to you."

"I'm sorry, but I don't think so." Deena started to back

away, but the woman was persistent.

"Don't run away so fast. I think maybe I can help."

"Oh, for Heaven's sake, I just want to be left alone. You've caused me enough grief already. I don't know how you found me, but please don't come around again." With that, Deena went inside and closed the door.

The kettle was screaming and her nerves were rattled. How the hell had that old woman found out where she lived? It was creepy having her show up like that. She'd just made herself a cup of matcha in a slightly chipped, but otherwise innocuous, white cup, when the doorbell rang again. Deena stepped back out onto her balcony. "Please I told you to stop pestering me. I have enough problems at the moment."

"Hey, what's your problem?" Eddie stepped out where she could see him. "I'm not pestering you. I just rang your bell."

"Oh my gosh, Eddie, I'm sorry." Deena leaned over the rail so he could see how really sorry she was. "I couldn't see who it was under the balcony. I thought you were this old lady who's been bothering me."

"Well, it's me and it's not a balcony it's a lanai," Eddie called back to her.

"What?"

"It's not a balcony; it's a lanai."

"OK, got it. It's a lanai, like in Hawaii, right?" Deena wasn't going to argue with him. She needed the apartment, at least until she found a job.

"Yeah, that's right. Can I come up? We need to talk." He was holding the application form she'd filled out, but he wasn't sending out "nice to have you as my new neighbor" vibes. In fact, he looked unbalanced and kind of edgy. It occurred to Deena that he might be on some kind of drugs.

"Give me a minute. I'll come down."

Deena slipped on her sandals and ran down the stairs still holding her cup. "I see you've got my application. So we're good? Everything's OK?" She was smiling and chirping at him in the hope that he wouldn't disappoint someone so obviously delighted to be his tenant.

"Not exactly." He waved the application at her. "I'm afraid this isn't gonna work out."

Deena blanched, she desperately needed to stay in his decrepit old house until she could afford something better. "I can pay for next month in advance and I'm sure I'll have a job in a couple of weeks if you're worried about the money."

"That's not it. Something's come up. My daughter and her kid need the place now, so you'll have to move out by the thirtieth." Eddie ran his hand over his forehead and looked up toward the second floor unit. "Do you think a toddler would be safe on that lanai?"

"But that's only..." Deena did a quick calculation, "nine days. Isn't there a law that you have to give tenants at least thirty days notice?"

"First, you're not my tenant. Second, the lease says the renter's supposed to give me a month's notice and not run off in the middle of the night, but I need the place back so who cares? Third, I'm being nice and letting you stay until the end of the month even though I don't know you from Adam."

"Please, I can't find a new place in just nine days. Couldn't your daughter wait just one more month? It would really help me out."

"No, she can't."

"Why not?" Deena cringed at the shrill, whiney tone in her voice. "I'm only asking for a month. Maybe we could share it."

He pulled a pack of Marlboros from his jeans pocket and sat down on one of the filthy plastic chairs that he kept on the front lawn. "You wanna sit?" He indicated a matching chair, equally sticky with dirt and bird droppings. Deena shook her head, no. Eddie nodded. His eyes were bloodshot and his skin looked like used sandpaper. "I'll tell you why; my daughter can't live with the scumbag that's been supporting her anymore so she needs a place to stay. My family's falling apart and they expect me to fix everything because I've got a house and a business, that's why."

He lit the cigarette, inhaled deeply, then exhaled a gray cloud of smoke. "Last night I'm sound asleep when the phone rings. It's two o'clock in the morning and some nurse is telling me my daughter's in the emergency room and I need to come get her. They say she's been beat up pretty bad, but she's OK and they're sending her home. So I say, why are you calling me, call her boyfriend. She hasn't lived with me since she was seventeen. Then the nurse says the jerk boyfriend's the one who put her in the hospital." Eddie took another long drag then stabbed the cigarette out on the arm of the chair. "Hell, he didn't just give her the back of his hand, he beat the crap out of her. That animal beat up my little girl." Eddie looked away so she couldn't see his face. When he turned back his voice was a gravely whisper. "She's got bruises all over, broken ribs, a busted lip and she might lose a tooth, so I need that apartment back. Maybe you could of stayed if that idiot hadn't sent her to the ER, but the way it is, you gotta go. Have your stuff out of there by the end of the month."

"Where is she now?"

"Inside." Eddie tilted his head toward his apartment. "She can stay with me until you leave, but we can't live together. My place is too small and frankly we don't get along that well. Anyway, I'm too old to have a baby underfoot."

The blood had drained from Deena's face. Where in the world was she supposed to go? "OK, I'll be out by the 30th. I'm sorry about your daughter."

"Yeah," Eddie agreed. "You have no idea. I could kill the guy. I could tear his nuts off and shove them up his ass." The American eagle tattooed on Eddie's arm flapped its red, white and blue wings as his biceps flexed with pent up rage while Deena stumbled back up the stairs to the apartment she'd have to vacate in just nine more days.

There was no time to lose. Deena opened her phone and typed in *Craigslist Sarasota,* mentally thanking God for the free Wi-Fi. She scanned the list of available rentals, ignoring the large professionally managed condos and apartment complexes that wanted references and ran credit checks. She had no job, no income, a recent bankruptcy and no savings apart from the money in her dwindling checking account. She closed her eyes, dizzy from scrolling through the tiny listings so fast. The plan had been to get a job first, then an apartment. This was all backwards. She was terrified that she might not qualify for anything but a room at the Salvation Army. She took a last swig of cold matcha and picked up the phone.

By late morning she'd been able to schedule three appointments to view apartments, all far from town and all demanding long, tedious rides on the city bus. She grabbed her purse, her sunglasses and her iPhone and headed downstairs. As she pushed open the screen, she noticed a slip of pink note paper that someone had pushed under the door. Deena picked it up and read, *Dear Deena Berman, I have an idea that might help you. Please call me. What can it hurt? Sincerely, Raisa Goetz.* It was from the homeless, crazy lady. There was a phone number scrawled across the bottom of the note. *As if,* Deena thought to herself as she stuffed the paper into the pocket of her trousers and ran to catch her bus.

It was after five when she finally limped home, exhausted and defeated by the Sarasota real estate market. Her forty-eight year old body had lost all its bounce over the course of the afternoon. She hung onto the railing as she climbed the steps up to her apartment, then fell heavily into the old rattan chair that squealed beneath her weight. Two of the landlords had rejected her outright. A third had allowed her to fill out an application, but had clearly thought he could do better. It was the worst of all possible scenarios. She didn't qualify for housing that she didn't want to live in. There weren't many units for rent and most of those were snapped up by snowbirds who inflated the cost for everyone else. What she really needed was a job, but now there was no time to find work before her ass was thrown out on the curb.

All she needed was a room, a clean bed and a hot shower. That would feel like luxury. Deena's mind wandered back to her house in Shaker Heights, the brick Georgian shaded by honey locusts, maples, and a lone elm miraculously resistant to Dutch elm disease. She pictured the late afternoon sun playing over the hardwood floors, the Tabriz carpet in the living room muffling the sound of the mantel clock ticking over the marble fireplace, the small creaks and groans of an old house settling. It had been lovely in its way, but it had also been oppressive. Why had she needed so much? Why hadn't she listened when her mother quoted some rabbi who'd said, "A man who's happy with what he has is a wealthy man."

Deena got up and found a bottle of ibuprofen in the medicine cabinet, washed the tablets down with a swig of water, then poured herself a glass of Chardonnay from a bottle Andor had left in the fridge. Her head was pounding and the muscles in her neck and shoulders were in spasm. She sipped the wine, made a sour face, then poured the vinegary liquid down the drain before returning to the bathroom where she turned the shower on full blast.

By six o'clock she was in bed listening to Bonnie Raitt through headphones plugged into her iPhone and dividing a sheet of notebook paper into neat columns. Deena gnawed on her pencil, adding up her money for the umpteenth time. How long could she make $1,482.34 last? If she checked into a cheap hotel, how long would she have before she'd exhausted her last dollar? The calculator on her iPhone told her two weeks, maybe a month if she lived on rice and oatmeal.

She checked her email for the tenth time that day. Still no message from mberman18@yahoo.com. Martin was still in Italy and incommunicado, or he didn't care that she was within days of being homeless. She fished through the freezer for a box of burritos and stuck the last one in the microwave with the realization that she could no longer take food for granted. The phone rang and for a wonderful split second she thought it might be Martin, but the caller ID was a number she didn't recognize.

"You called about my apartment." It was a male voice that sounded more New Jersey than Southwestern Florida, a fellow transplant.

"I've called about several units. Could you refresh my memory?" Deena was reaching for her notebook and a pen.

"It's a two bedroom on Prospect, west of trail, great location, really nice. Used to be a guest house."

"A two bedroom west of the trail?" West of trail meant west of Tamiami Trail and only a block or two from the bay — prime property and *mucho dinero.* "How much are you asking?"

"Five hundred plus utilities."

"That's pretty reasonable." In fact, it was incredible. Had her luck suddenly changed?

"It's just for you, right?"

"Yep, just me."

"Well, maybe we can work something out. You wanna see it? I'll be there tomorrow — ten in the morning."

"Sure, I'll be there at ten sharp." Deena wrote down the address. A two bedroom west of trail for five hundred dollars? Was that even possible? She could swing it even if he asked for a security deposit — and if she found work before the end of the month.

Deena woke at four in the morning with a bad case of night terrors. Her heart was pounding and a fragment of a dream about trying to scale a moonscape of endless rocks that glowed green with toxic light followed her into wakefulness. The dream vanished as soon as she switched on the bedside light, but she couldn't quite catch her breath and her skin felt cold and clammy. She turned on the iPhone charging beside her bed and checked her email and Facebook accounts. Messages from her old life appeared like light from distant stars. The Cleveland Orchestra hoped she'd consider subscribing for the upcoming season. Williams Sonoma was having a sale. The North Union Farmers' Market was hosting a benefit for the Hunger Center, and a librarian she used to work with had posted photos of her new grandbaby. Deena "liked" the grandbaby then switched off the screen.

She got out of bed and stood out on the lanai in her nightgown. It must have rained while she was asleep. Water was still dripping off the eaves. The night air was warm and humid, scented with citrus, eucalyptus, and decaying wood with undertones of gasoline and asphalt. Across the street a palm swayed slightly in the breeze blowing off the bay. In the distance, she could just make out a pink neon light blinking on and off downtown. It was an alien landscape but not without its charms. If she was going to survive in this new place, she'd have to forget daffodils, autumn leaves and winter boots, and embrace tropical delights, reimagine her predicament as an adventure, a chance for a fresh start.

The sun was pouring through her bedroom window the next time she woke up. The night terrors were gone and she felt optimistic that the guest house on Prospect might be the one. It was already nine o'clock, but Prospect was only a short walk away. She put on her best slacks, a fresh white blouse, low heeled pumps and the gold stud earrings Martin had given her for their fifteenth anniversary. She licked out the last drop from a container of strawberry yogurt then set out in better spirits than she'd experienced in quite a while.

The walk was a little longer than she'd expected, but the morning was beautiful and she moved at a good clip, first past the tiny bungalows and corner shops that hadn't yet succumbed to gentrification, then across Mound and onto Orange where large houses stood protected behind fences of stucco and wrought iron. Between the houses Deena caught

a glimpse of Sarasota Bay lapping at the back of the manicured yards. She turned at Prospect and began checking the
numbers on the houses she walked past. The address in her
hand couldn't be right. She checked it again and then a third
time before accepting that she'd arrived at her destination,
an enormous Italianate structure set behind an imposing wall
of weathered stone. Deena felt intimidated. The place was
a mansion, but she squared her shoulders, climbed the steps
onto a portico supported by huge Corinthian columns and rang
the bell. Several minutes went by with no answer so she rang
again, checked her watch, then looked around in confusion.

"No one's home. I shoulda told you to come around back.
They only use the place in the winter." A short, stubby man
with oily black hair approached on a paved walk that led to
the backyard. "Follow me, it's in the back. I got it all opened
up for you."

She couldn't gauge his age, probably forty-something, but
he might have been older – or younger. His T-shirt had deep
sweat stains under the armpits. Deena eyed him warily. "Are
you the rental agent?"

"Do I look like a rental agent? It's a sublet. I can't afford
the place anymore so I gotta let it go. It's real nice and cheap
for the neighborhood. You're gonna love it." He turned and
headed back the way he'd come. Deena hesitated a moment,
then followed him around the corner to where a pink stucco
bungalow surrounded by flowering bougainvillea sat at the
rear of a spacious lot. It had its own small porch supported by
white columns, replicas of the ones on the main house, and a
large picture window with a view of the garden. There was
no way in God's green earth this place rented for five hundred
dollars a month. The man was standing on the porch holding
the front door open. "Come on, I've got another lady coming
at eleven. You want to see it or don't you?"

What the hell? Deena thought to herself. *I might as well take
a look.* As soon as she stepped inside, her nose was accosted

by the smell of garbage. The living room was strewn with pizza boxes, beer bottles and dirty clothes. Giant flies buzzed at the windows. A tire and an old bicycle pump were leaning incongruously against a white leather sofa. A flat screen TV sat on the floor. Damaged plaster and loose wires dangled from the wall where it had previously been installed.

"I'll be taking the TV with me, the rest of the stuff stays. Five hundred bucks and it's yours. I can be outa here by tomorrow. You wanna look around?"

Deena took a step backwards toward the door. "No, I'm sorry, I shouldn't have bothered you. It's lovely, but I'm afraid it's out of my price range."

The man bolted to the front door as she turned to leave. He leaned against it blocking her way. His expression was still affable, but a chill ran down Deena's spine. She noticed the doorknob and lock disassembled on the floor by his feet. "Tell you what, I really need to get outta here, so how about four-fifty? Have we got a deal?"

Deena tried to smile pleasantly, "Well, that is a great offer, but there are a couple more places I want to look at first. How about if I give you a call in the morning?"

"Hey, you ain't even seen the place yet. You wanna see the bedroom? It's got a king size bed and its own bathroom."

"No. No thank you. I want to go now." Deena tried to move past him toward the open door. The man didn't move. He just stared at her. She could feel him sizing her up.

"Tell you what, I'm going to need a deposit to hold this place until tomorrow. How much you got on you?"

"I don't want the house. I just want to go. Will you please let me out the door?"

Deena's legs had gone wobbly, and there was a tremor in her voice. She tried smiling again, but her face had frozen. A large hand suddenly reached out and snatched her shoulder bag with such force that she was thrown off balance. She stumbled forward falling against the man's chest. He leered at her as she righted herself and stepped away from him.

He opened her purse and pawed through it, scrambling her lipstick, blush, keys, a pen, a wad of Kleenex. He was playing with her. She held her breath, afraid to move or make a sound. He found her cell phone, examined it and nodded approvingly before sticking it in his pocket. At last he pulled out her wallet and quickly and efficiently relieved it of her debit card and all her cash – about a hundred and fifteen dollars, before handing the purse back to her. "That should hold the house until tomorrow. You just give me a call when you've made up your mind." Then he miraculously stepped aside and let her flee across the lawn and back to the street where she retraced her steps without slowing down or looking back until she reached Andor's apartment where she raced up the steps, locked the door and sat panting at the kitchen table for several minutes before bursting into tears.

Once she'd regained her equilibrium, Deena opened her purse to inventory what she still had and what was missing. Her checkbook, in a zippered compartment, had been overlooked. Her driver's license was still there, her library card, a discount card from the grocery, a health insurance card and a defunct employee ID from Garfield University. Thank God she still had identification. Then Deena was struck with an ugly thought. How much information was on her phone? Could that horrible man find her address? Her bank accounts? He already had her debit card.

She felt a yearning for Martin so strong that it made her double over. Deena blew her nose into a paper napkin. There was no sense sniveling, she had work to do. She didn't know where to start but she knew that she'd better get moving. She picked up her purse and started walking downtown.

Late that afternoon Deena hauled herself back up the stairs, hungry and utterly exhausted. She'd lost an entire day giving statements to the police, the bank, and her wireless company. Martin's name was on everything. She'd have to let him know what had happened and she'd have to buy a new phone, something cheap without any bells or whistles. Deena closed her eyes. How was she going to contact Martin? She didn't have a phone, she didn't have internet, and he wasn't responding anyway. Tomorrow she'd walk to the library and use one of the public computers. At the moment she needed to eat something then collapse.

There was nothing in the refrigerator but yogurt, butter, two grapefruit, and a couple of eggs. Deena grabbed one of the grapefruit, peeled it like an orange, and ate it standing over the sink. If the day had gone as planned she'd have rented an apartment and bought groceries by now. As it was, she was another day closer to being homeless and a hundred and fifteen dollars closer to being penniless. She rinsed off her fingers and sat down on the sofa.

Another day shot with no leads on a new place to stay. Stay calm, she told herself. You'll figure it out. But there were only eight days left, eight fucking days. *Don't panic, there's still time, you're resourceful,* an inner voice tried to calm her. But without her phone she couldn't check apartment listings, she couldn't check her bank account, she couldn't check her email, and she couldn't make calls. Her inner voice was delusional. There was no way she'd find a place before the end of the month. The realization hit her like a body blow and she dissolved into a long, loud, wrenching wail. Even when the crying had subsided into irregular gulps and hiccups and she'd taken a drink of cold water and laid a wet dish towel across her eyes, her skin still prickled with terror.

Chapter Ten

Sarasota's Selby Library calmed her the moment she walked through the heavy glass doors into the soaring atrium. A job, any job, in this beautiful, light filled space humming with programs and activities would have been salvation. Unfortunately, the application she'd emailed weeks ago had bounced back with an impersonal response stating, *Thank you for your interest in the Selby Public Library. Unfortunately, we have no openings at the current time and are not accepting applications. We wish you the best of luck in your search for employment.* Of course there were other libraries, she'd been sending applications all over the country, but none of them could find her without a cell phone or a computer.

"Excuse me, what's the procedure for using one of your computers? I'm going to need one for several hours if that's possible." Deena forced a smile, hoping that she looked and sounded more normal than she felt.

"Do you have a library card?"

"Yes, it's right here." Deena presented her Sarasota County Library card with the humbling realization that it was one of the few documents that still connected her to her old identity.

"Good, just go upstairs and someone will get you started. Card holders can use a computer for an hour. If no one else is waiting, you can use it for two hours."

"Thanks." Deena climbed the curving staircase toward the

second floor. Pausing, she turned and looked over the rail at the large, open space below. Tables and chairs dotted the reception area and a fanciful aquarium arched over the entrance to the children's room. Her librarian's heart yearned to belong to this place, or to any library where she could put her years of experience back to work, but there were so few positions available. As promised, banks of computers were arranged in neat rows in an open loft at the top of the stairs. Within minutes she was staring at emails from four different libraries all politely informing her they weren't hiring or that their positions had been filled. Her heart sank, but there was no time to mope.

The hour went quickly, but she managed to respond to every residential listing within ten miles and under $1,000. The realization that she didn't have enough money to pay for more than one month's rent left her faint. She'd have to lie about her prospects and pray for a landlord who wouldn't do a credit check or demand a security deposit. When Deena stood up, she found her vision was blurred and there was a slight ringing in her ears. She made it as far as the drinking fountain in the lobby, took a long drink then grabbed the wall to keep from fainting. *Breathe*, she told herself. *Keep breathing. You can do this*, but she couldn't. The deep cleansing breath caught in her chest and she knew that if she let it out she'd exhale a piercing howl. Instead, she took one more drink and fled the building.

The sun was at its zenith and the day was already hot and sticky. Sarasota wasn't a big city, so the Verizon store couldn't be too far away. Deena headed south on Pineapple, but paused at Five Points Park to stare at a homeless man sleeping on the grass. Several more people—homeless, indigent, and probably mentally ill—were camped out beside a scattering of bags and boxes. She wasn't like them. She was clean, sane, educated and employable. But were they her future? How long could she remain clean, sane and employable while living on the street?

The Verizon store was a neat little box outfitted with the same red, white and gray decor as every other Verizon in the country. Phones and tablets lined the walls while accessories were displayed in the center of the showroom. A young man with a trendy haircut and a name tag that said Wayne, approached her with a smile. "Welcome to Verizon, what brings you in today?"

"I lost my phone and I need a replacement, but I need something inexpensive. What's your most basic model?" A chorus line of smart phones winked and twinkled at her but she ignored them. She had to pinch pennies.

"That's too bad. Let's look up your account and see what we can do. Do you have insurance?"

"I don't think so." There was no insurance because Lauren had convinced her parents that purchasing a used phone would be cheaper than two years of insurance premiums. Maybe she'd been right, but Deena didn't have time to research used phones, she wouldn't know where to have it delivered, and she needed it NOW. She left with an old fashioned flip phone and a checking account lighter by $54.74.

Did the week pass very fast or very slowly? She couldn't say; time had stopped moving in an orderly progression and had begun jumping in fits and starts. On Tuesday she learned there were no boarding houses in the city. On Wednesday she discovered utility companies demand large security deposits and that few Florida apartments include water in the rent. On Thursday she contacted the Sarasota Housing Authority and was told that if she met criteria she could be added to a two year waiting list for public housing. In the meantime, they could offer her the address of a local shelter. On Friday she canvassed as many neighborhoods on foot as her strength allowed in a desperate search for a "for rent" sign posted in a window. On Saturday she stayed in bed trembling in sheer panic, wrestling with waves of nausea. On Sunday the library was closed cutting off her access to computers, so she spent the day packing up her things.

There wasn't much, just what she'd been able to stuff into her car when she left Cleveland: two suitcases and three boxes full of clothes, sheets, towels, useless kitchen ware, and several pairs of shoes. She phoned Martin twice a day leaving progressively more and more desperate messages on his voice mail. "Pick up, damn you. I'm still your wife. Do you understand I'm practically out on the streets? I didn't do anything to deserve this. Where the hell are you? Pick up the damn phone!" But there was no response.

Monday was her last day in the apartment and she still had nowhere to go. Eddie's daughter would be walking through the front door with her baby and all their things in just a few hours. Deena sat down on one of her boxes and stared at the walls. She'd never appreciated walls before, but now walls were all she wanted—walls and a roof and a door that locked. She could make do without a bed or a chair if the universe would just send her four walls to call her own.

Deena didn't sleep that night. She wandered around the apartment like a ghost haunting the living room, then the bathroom, then the balcony. Every time she closed her eyes she imagined a man with greasy black hair and sweaty armpits leering at her. She went downstairs and sat on Eddie's porch, then came back upstairs and tried to read. By the time the sun peeked over the roofs of the apartment buildings east of Osprey, Deena was sipping her fourth cup of tea and making illegible notes on one sheet of paper after another.

At seven o'clock, Deena showered, dressed, and put the long night behind her. At eight she knocked on Eddie's door. She was dressed in jeans, a cotton shirt and tennis shoes. A sweater, two T-shirts, a second pair of pants, several changes of underwear, a box of crackers, peanut butter, two apples and some toiletries were packed inside the large canvas tote bag Andor had abandoned. Her suitcases and boxes were lined up beside her on the porch. "Here's your key back. I think I left everything in order."

"Yeah, thanks." Eddie looked past her to the street then turned his head in both directions. "Is someone coming to pick you up? How are you going to move that stuff without a car?"

"Actually, I haven't found a place yet. I'll be staying at the Midtown Motel for a few nights so I was hoping you'd let me keep these things in your shed until I get settled."

"How long are we talking about? The shed's already pretty full up with my junk."

"Oh, I'm not sure exactly, but not too long. There are a couple of good possibilities. I'm sure one of them will work out."

Eddie scrutinized her closely. Could he smell her fear? Did he pick up the implication of the canvas bag bulging with clothes and groceries? "Sure, why not? You can leave your stuff in the shed for a week or so. I'll get my key."

Ten minutes later Deena walked away from most of her clothes and personal possessions toward a bus that would take her to a fleabag hotel on the outskirts of town.

When Deena opened the door to room 204 she was pleasantly surprised. The carpet was worn and the window offered an unobstructed view of the parking lot, but the room was air conditioned and clean. The odor of bleach and furniture polish almost cancelled the musty smell of the drapes and carpet. She sat down on the bed and bounced a few times. The mattress was great. A remote on the bedside table turned on a newish flat screen TV. The place wasn't bad, much better than she'd expected for $79 per night. Unfortunately, she couldn't afford to stay long. At $79 a night her money wouldn't last two weeks. The only thing worse than not having a room would be not having food. She had to conserve her cash and she had to find a job, and she had to find it immediately. There was no time to worry about smart career moves. She'd flip burgers, wash dishes, whatever she had to do to get through this.

Deena began by going downstairs and asking the desk clerk if the motel was hiring. It wasn't. Feeling somewhat diminished and embarrassed, she left the reception desk and walked outside. The Midtown Motel wasn't exactly in the middle of anything. It owed its existence to a six lane highway that spit out travelers too tired or too poor to seek lodging in the city. If she could make it across the highway there was a pizza place, a nail salon, a drug store and a bank. Maybe one of them had an opening. When that search proved fruitless she got on a bus and rode to Westfield Mall where she spent the rest of the day pleading with store managers, most of them half her age, for any available job. She'd never worked retail, waited tables or operated a floor polisher. Nonetheless, by the end of the afternoon Deena had two dubious prospects. Victoria's Secret had an opening for an entry level sales associate and Ruby Tuesday was hiring wait staff. She'd left an application with each company and been told that someone from corporate would call if they were interested. It was unlikely she'd hear from anyone. Twenty years as a librarian didn't qualify her for a minimum wage job at the mall.

There was a Publix Grocery not far from the mall so she hiked over there to pick up some provisions. Pushing a cart down the aisle of an air conditioned grocery store felt so normal, so familiar. One of the employees, an older woman in a green smock, smiled cheerily, probably assuming that Deena was still a middle class housewife picking up a few things for her family's dinner. She didn't notice that none of Deena's items required heating or refrigeration.

By the time the bus dropped her off a block from the motel Deena was famished. She hadn't thought to bring a can opener or a fork, but the can of SpaghettiOs had a flip top that made a serviceable scoop. An apple, a slice of processed cheese and a glass of water completed the meal. With dinner finished, Deena took off her clothes and stepped into the tub where she happily soaked off the day's sweat and grime. Refreshed, she put on clean underwear, lay down on the bed, and promptly fell asleep.

When she woke two hours later a bedside clock said it was only 9:30 although it felt like the middle of the night. She peeked through the curtains at the cars in the parking lot. There wasn't much to see, just a man walking a large dog past the building. She double locked her door and lay down again, then got up again, then had a drink of water, then tried running through her yoga routine, but there wasn't enough room and she didn't like sitting on the dirty carpet so she finished off the crackers and peanut butter, brushed her teeth, and watched TV until it was late enough to fall back asleep.

Deena recomputed her finances while finishing off the complimentary breakfast at a table in the motel lobby. Her bill for the night had been higher than she'd figured, $87 including tax. There was no way her dwindling resources could sustain a drain like that. There had to be something else. She swiped two oranges, a container of yogurt, a bagel and a handful of plastic cutlery from the buffet table, stuffed them into her purse, then said goodbye to the Midtown Motel, its flat screen TV, hot water, and free muffins. As she rode the bus downtown to the Selby library, the fleece blanket from the motel bed lay neatly folded at the bottom of her bag.

There was no time for sending out resumes or waiting to be called for interviews; she needed a job by the end of the day. Scrolling through job categories on the computer Deena quickly eliminated most of them. She couldn't hang drywall, service swimming pools, teach ballroom dancing or clean teeth. Customer service looked like a good bet, but she quickly eliminated the best positions since they all involved lengthy hiring processes, almost like applying for work as a librarian. Other jobs were quickly eliminated as scams: *Photogenic ladies wanted for Hollywood style movie. Make big money addressing envelopes at home. Do you have what it takes to sell*

Nutrinosh? What was a telephone entertainment rep? She wasn't sure, but she had a pretty good idea and crossed it off the list. Still, there were a few that seemed worth a try: banquet server, cleaner, cashier. One of those low paying, blue collar jobs might sustain her until a better position came along. Deena shot off email replies to every possible posting and left phone messages for two that had listed phone numbers. Her hour on the computer was quickly exhausted and then there was nothing to do but wait.

She found a copy of *Life After Life* by Kate Atkinson and nestled into an upholstered chair in a quiet corner. Libraries were so comfortable and felt so safe. They were air conditioned with clean bathrooms, drinking fountains, tables and chairs. There was even an electric outlet where she could recharge her phone. Why couldn't she just stay here? There had to be some nook or cranny where she could hide unnoticed overnight.

Casually, as though she were just browsing for another book, Deena began searching the building inch by inch for a place to hide. Students were always able to find a dark corner for a quick nap or a romantic tryst at the old Alfred Seibel Library; but this building had nothing but open space and light. Her best hope were the closed doors that might lead to back offices or storage areas. She discreetly tried one knob after another, but all of them were locked.

"May I help you? Are you looking for something?" One of the librarians, the man from the computer lab, was smiling at her, but his smile said, "Gotcha," not "How can I be of service?"

"Oh," Deena smiled back flustered and embarrassed, removing her hand from the doorknob. "I'm just looking for the ladies' room. Can you tell me where it is?"

The librarian didn't say a word, but he turned and looked in the direction of the large sign reading, "Rest Rooms."

"Thank you, I don't know how I missed that." Deena emitted a weak, apologetic laugh then scurried off to hide in the bathroom where she spent the next hour in a cubicle reading her book with her pants around her ankles. By the time she ventured back into the library it was after one o'clock and time for lunch. She walked over to Whole Foods where she ate her pilfered bagel, yogurt and an orange at one of their outdoor tables. She'd have preferred a plate of curried chicken or sushi with sesame seaweed salad, but she had to make her money last. At least she still had food. What she didn't have was a place to spend the night.

Her eyes wandered up and down the street. There were restaurants, boutiques, a parking garage. None of them seemed likely to provide a safe haven, but she began to stroll up and down the street searching for an alcove where she could safely rest her head. There weren't any. Now she understood why the homeless sheltered in doorways and on the sidewalk in clear view of passersby. There was nowhere else to go. By late afternoon Deena was exhausted and terrified that night would find her still wandering the streets. She went back to Whole Foods and bought a cup of coffee that she laced with as much milk and sugar as she could fit into the cup and sat nursing it as she watched more fortunate people, people just like the woman she'd been only a few months ago, going about their business.

The coffee revived her slightly, but she was hot and sweaty and needed a bathroom so she headed back to the library with its blessed air conditioning and immaculate facilities. Ignoring two teenagers applying make-up in the bathroom mirror, Deena stripped off her shirt, gave herself a quick sponge bath in the sink, then dried off with paper towels from the dispenser. Refreshed, she walked out of the bathroom and found a comfortable seat with a view of the park. What luxury to sit in this beautiful building with every creature comfort close at hand. There had to be a way to book herself into the Selby for a few nights.

She phoned Martin for the umpteenth time, and got a

message saying that his voicemail was full, good-bye. Deena clicked off her phone and began a second, even closer inspection of the library. There were upholstered benches in the public areas and bean bag chairs in the children's room that would make wonderful beds, but they were completely exposed. The bookshelves were set with clear sight lines between them. Even the spaces behind service areas were visible from most angles since the desks were low and situated in the middle of public rooms. On the other hand, she didn't see surveillance cameras hung from the ceiling. There had to be a way. In the end, the only place that proved both private and secure was a toilet cubicle. The bathroom was clean, as public bathrooms go, though it offered nothing but hard surfaces and a cold tile floor. Deena didn't relish spending the night in a bathroom, but it was better than the street.

The library was open until eight o'clock so she had time to eat dinner and to try Martin one more time on the chance that he'd returned home and cleared his voice mail. She walked back to Whole Foods, riffled through her backpack for something to eat, then dialed Martin's number as she picked at canned chili with a plastic fork. Predictably, he didn't answer. He was probably in Rome dining on *osso buco* and *risotto ala Milanaise* at some cozy little trattoria. Damn him.

The sun was still bright in the sky when she finished supper. It was a lovely summer evening. If she were a normal person with a normal life she'd go to the beach with her husband and watch the sun set. Maybe they'd stop somewhere for a glass of wine and a light supper before going home to bed. *Get real. When was the last time she and Martin had gone anywhere to watch a sunset?* Deena's purse and bag had grown heavier over the course of the day and her arms were starting to ache from lugging them around. Theoretically, she could have walked over to the bay and watched the sunset by herself, but she was pooped. Instead, she made her way back to the library where she planned to spend the night huddled in the ladies' room.

Deena read and reread the same few pages of *Life After Life*. The only thing that occupied her mind was whether or not she'd be able to make it through the night without being caught. What was the penalty for hiding in a public building? What was the crime? Trespassing? Loitering? Being a public nuisance? Deena had no idea.

At a quarter to eight a series of bells sounded and a voice over a loudspeaker announced that the library would be closing in fifteen minutes. On cue she stood up, gathered her bags and casually walked toward the ladies' room. The stall furthest from the door was empty and a bit bigger than the others. She stepped inside and locked the door. None of her bags were visible under the door because she'd scoped out the hooks where she could hang them out of sight. She turned off the ringer on her phone. More bells sounded and then the five minute warning. A toilet flushed and a pair of tennis shoes vacated the stall beside her. She could hear water running, a door opening and shutting and then nothing. Deena crouched with her feet on the toilet seat so that no one checking for stragglers would guess that she was there. The digital display on her phone read 8:12. Maybe she'd done it, but it was too soon to tell.

A minute later the door banged open and someone else came in, peed, flushed, fiddled with things in a purse and left. *Nothing to worry about,* she reassured herself, *just an employee making a quick pit stop before going home.* It was 8:20. Deena stepped off the toilet but remained alert, listening. At 8:30 she heard footsteps outside in the corridor, but they simply passed by without slowing down or stopping. It was a good thing no one had come in because the sound of her thumping heart would have given her away, but by the time her phone said 9:00 Deena was starting to breathe easier. In another hour, if no one came, she'd wrap herself in her purloined blanket and try to get some sleep.

A minute later her entire body tensed as new footsteps sounded in the hall. She hopped back onto the toilet seat and held her breath. The outer door banged open and someone walked in and began swinging each of the toilet stall doors open, one after another. Deena could see a pair of men's work shoes as someone hit the door to her cubicle lightly expecting it to open. There was the briefest pause before he hit it again with more force.

"Is someone in there? The library is closed. You have to leave now." It was a male voice, tired and with a pronounced Mexican accent. He rattled the door, but the lock held. Would he give up and go away if she didn't breathe or make a sound? "Please, missus, this isn't a hotel. Don't make me take the door off with my screwdriver. I don't like to do this."

Deena stepped off the toilet, straightened her clothes, and took her bags off their hooks. "Sorry, I'll be out in a minute." She tried to sound normal, an ordinary library patron caught a few minutes past closing. A moment later she emerged to find the custodian in blue coveralls waiting with a set of keys in his hand.

"I'll need to let you out. All the doors are locked."

Deena followed compliantly trying to hold her head up, trying to reinvent a version of reality where she hadn't been caught hiding in a toilet. The janitor unlocked the door and held it open for her. "Good-night missus," he said. "Maybe you can stay at the Salvation Army. It's at tenth and Central. *Buena suerte.*"

"Yes, thank you. Good night," she said, then walked out into the dark. Most of the shops and restaurants were already closed. There were no lights on at Starbucks. Whole Foods had brought its tables and chairs inside. The trees in Five Points Park were lit with myriad twinkle lights that slowly changed color, cycling through the rainbow, but there were no benches where she could sit to watch them, nowhere to gather her thoughts or figure out what to do next, so she just kept walking. In her wildest nightmares she'd never envisioned this night and she had no script for playing it out.

In the distance a reggae band played outside on the patio of one of the upscale restaurants. She drifted in that direction so she could sway and nod with the crowd of strangers gathered on the sidewalk listening for free. Maybe she'd buy a coke so she could sit at one of the tables and devise a plan. It was an older crowd, mostly baby boomers and retirees on holiday. Everyone looked well heeled, rested, affluent — everyone except a man with filthy clothes and unkempt dreadlocks sitting on a sleeping bag spread out beside the building. A paper cup beside him had the word "hungry" scrawled across it. Deena stood back and watched as the happy crowd maneuvered around him, looking past him, avoiding eye contact of any kind. Occasionally someone would drop a few coins or a dollar bill into his cup. They didn't speak to him but he smiled and babbled unintelligibly to them, or to himself, or to unseen ghosts. There was no way to know. With her knees shaking so badly that she could hardly walk, Deena dropped a dollar in his cup then headed north toward 10th Street.

The further north she walked the creepier it got. Shops and restaurants gave way to repair shops, warehouses and empty lots. There wasn't much traffic, but a carload of drunken teenagers sped toward her shouting something through the open windows of their car. As they passed, a glass bottle whizzed past and shattered against the curb just inches from her feet.

As she got closer to 10th Street, Deena could see scores of homeless people making camp in a cemetery. Some huddled in small groups, smoking and talking, others slept on the grass between the graves. One man snored loudly on the sidewalk. Plastic bags hung from nearly every picket of an old wrought iron fence that was probably meant to keep the dead in and the homeless out. Deena could feel their communal eyes follow her as she hurried by. What were they doing there? Why would they sleep in a cemetery when they were within sight of a shelter?

The Salvation Army was a large, modern complex of buildings, not what she'd been expecting. Her first thought was that the shelter might not be too bad. There was a well lit parking lot behind a secure concrete wall. Beyond that, a brick walk led to the entrance of a large modern building. It wasn't the Hilton but it looked clean and safe. However, the minute she stepped through the door she knew she'd been transported to another planet. An area that must have once been the lobby of an office building was strewn with bodies on thin rubber mats. A few were asleep, some were talking, others playing cards or searching through their personal belongings. One group was chattering loudly in a far corner. As she got closer she could hear snippets of their conversation. *In the crapper. He musta OD'd, Ask Jerry, Bad shit, How would I know?*

This was the shelter? Where were the beds? Deena hesitated, not wanting to step over the sleeping or wakefully murmuring forms. A team of employees watched everyone from inside a glass cage in the center of the room. Something was up. Behind the walls of reinforced glass agency personnel were talking feverishly on their phones. Everyone was clearly agitated, waving their arms and shouting orders at each other. One of the men inside the cage caught sight of Deena and came out to greet her. A tag that read John G was clipped to a lanyard he wore around his neck. He smiled and offered his hand as though he were the manager of a boutique hotel. "Good evening, are you looking for a place to stay tonight?"

"Yes, I just lost my apartment and I can't afford a hotel. Can you help me?" Deena hoped that John G would see that she wasn't really a homeless person, that she was an entirely different species from the ragtag tribe she'd passed in the cemetery.

"Have you ever stayed with us before?"

"No, never. In fact, I can't believe that I'm here now."

"The first time is always the hardest." John G looked genuinely sympathetic. "Ordinarily we'd find a place for you, but we're filled to capacity tonight. Also, if you haven't stayed with us before, you have to meet with a social worker before we can check you in. It only takes a few minutes, but he's really busy at the moment. If you come back around five tomorrow you can join us for dinner and we'll have a place for you to sleep. There's a $12.00 charge. Is that a problem?"

"No, but where am I supposed to sleep tonight?"

"I don't know." He turned toward the men who were getting rowdy, demanding something. "Hey, you guys, back to the cafeteria and keep it down. Everything's under control." John G turned back to Deena with an apologetic shrug. "Sorry, we're in the middle of a little crisis here. Can you stay with friends or spend the night at a motel?"

Deena gaped at him, was he crazy? *Would I be here if I had anywhere else to stay?* But before she could think of a civil reply, an argument broke out between two women over a choice bit of real estate beside the door.

"I'm sorry, I have to take care of that." John G was already moving away from her. "It's the same fight every night. Come back tomorrow and I promise we'll do what we can to help you."

An ambulance pulled up to the front of the building as Deena left, slicing the darkness with its flashing lights and keening wail. She felt it pulsing behind her as she walked away from the shelter with its false promise of salvation. Deena had no idea where she was going, but her legs kept moving. As long as she was walking she maintained some dignity. She wasn't a lost soul sleeping in a doorway.

An hour later her arms hurt, her feet hurt, her back hurt. She couldn't walk forever, but there was nowhere to sit, much less stretch out and sleep. Eventually she'd have to stop, lie down, collapse. The Midtown Motel probably had a vacancy. She would have happily squandered another $87 on a bed, but the busses had stopped running and an expensive downtown hotel was out of the question.

This was really happening. She was alone and on the street. Every car that whizzed by made her jump. Every shadow seemed ominous. Her legs began to buckle and she felt herself stagger and weave as she walked, but there was no place to rest so she kept on walking until a vision flashed through her mind. She saw her mother, young, strong and half naked, working the water pump back on the New Moon Commune. "Momma," she said softly, but out loud. "Momma." Her mother didn't reply but she looked at Deena, watching her as she kept on working the pump. Then, without saying a word, her mother turned and looked west toward Sarasota Bay and the beautiful Bayside Park. They'd camped out so many nights when she was a child. She remembered falling asleep on the desert floor beneath a night sky dotted with constellations she couldn't name. *OK Mom*, Deena thought to herself. *We can do this. It's just another night under the stars. We've done this a hundred times. No big deal. Let's go.* Her mother nodded her approval before fading from Deena's consciousness. With a last burst of energy she threw her bags over her shoulder and headed toward the bay where she found a secluded place between some shrubbery and a retainer wall. She spread out her blanket and finally fell asleep.

The next morning Deena woke up wedged between a bush and a block of cement. It was still dark out, but her phone told her it was almost six in the morning. She needed a bathroom, coffee and an outlet for recharging her phone. Gathering up her blanket she stuffed it back into her tote bag and stretched out her aching muscles. She'd survived the night. Maybe she'd get through this after all. The park was still dark and empty. A dog was sniffing at a trash can and a couple birds were pecking at the grass. To the west, the waters of Sarasota Bay rose and fell like a creature breathing quietly in its sleep as a few low clouds reflected the first golden light from the sun rising in the east.

Deena started walking back toward town past Dolphin Fountain, past a small playground, past the million dollar yachts moored in the Marina. Someone was already up and stirring on one of the boats. He looked up, coffee cup in hand, as Deena walked by. She smiled and nodded but the man abruptly turned away ignoring her. It was a small gesture, but it chilled Deena to the bone. She was becoming invisible, an outcast, like the man babbling on the pavement.

Starbucks was already open. Deena stopped to inhale the aroma of roasting coffee before slipping into the bathroom to wash up and change her clothes. The back of her jeans were grass stained and covered with grit. Even after she took them off and gave then a good shake, they still testified to a night sleeping in damp sand. Peeling off her T-shirt, and dirty underwear, she traded them for the one fresh outfit still in her bag. As she pulled up her trousers Deena heard the crackle of paper in the pants pocket. It was the slip of paper the old woman had pushed under the screen door the day after she'd gotten both of them arrested. Deena fished it out and reread it. *Dear Deena Berman, I have an idea that might help you. Please call me. What can it hurt? Sincerely, Raisa Goetz.* Was she desperate enough to call a crazy person? Absolutely. A few minutes later with her face washed, her teeth brushed and her hair combed, Deena felt almost normal. Once she'd had a cup of coffee and something to eat maybe she'd make that call.

"Hello." When Deena heard the old woman's voice she smiled in spite of herself. Something about Raisa Goetz reminded her again of her grandmother.

"Hello, this is Deena Berman. I hope I'm not calling too early." It was barely eight o'clock.

"No, it's never too early. I'm up with the birds. Who did you say you are?"

"Deena Berman. You stopped by to see me, but I wasn't very nice. I'm really sorry, I've been going through a bad time.

You left a note saying you might be able to help me. I'm not sure what you meant by that, but I could really use some help at the moment."

"You're the librarian?"

"Yes." Deena tilted her head, puzzled by the question.

"And you need a job and a place to live?"

"Yes."

"So, you can work for me and live in my house. How's that? Problem solved."

"You have a house?" Deena clapped her hand over her mouth. "That's a very nice offer," she began again. "Why do you need to hire a librarian?"

"I need someone to organize a literary archive."

"Really?" Deena rolled her eyes imagining years of incoherent ramblings scratched onto the backs of envelopes and grocery bags, but she'd catalog old newspapers and dead cats if it kept her off the street. "I worked in Archives and Special Collections at a university library in Cleveland."

"Excellent. Organizing a literary estate is different than normal library work, but you'll learn. I live on Harbor Drive. Do you have a pencil?"

A literary estate? La-de-da. Deena fished a pen out of her bag and jotted down the address.

"Come at noon, we'll talk."

At ten o'clock Deena was in the library checking her email, hoping she'd gotten a response from one of the jobs advertised on line. There were, in fact, three messages from prospective employers. Two invited her to send a resume and the third suggested that she show up for a group interview the following week. All of the jobs paid minimum wage and none of them were full time. She'd have to work all three jobs to make enough money to pay the rent on a decent one bedroom apartment in this town.

Deena typed the address on Harbor Drive into Mapquest and discovered that it was just a few streets from Prospect where she'd almost been mugged. Really? Mrs. Goetz lived in the ritziest part of town? Harbor Drive was the last place she'd expect to find an old woman who talked to birds and had a sketchy relationship with the police. She caught the bus.

Deena had no trouble finding Raisa's house. She'd have recognized it even without the wrought iron address plate from the mounds of sunflower seeds scattered beneath the bushes and along the paved walkway. It was a large Mediterranean style house, the last place she'd have expected Mrs. Goetz to live. Deena rang the bell and waited. She rang the bell again, then she tried knocking loudly just in case the bell was broken. Again, no answer. As she stood on the front steps, furious that she'd let herself get fooled again, she heard a faint voice from somewhere inside the house.

"Mrs. Goetz? It's Deena Berman. Can you let me in?" Again, she heard a muffled voice, but there were no footsteps and no one opened the door. She waited, puzzled, then called out, "I can come back later if this isn't a good time." She didn't want to leave. Mrs. Goetz had a house and she might offer her a job. "Are you all right? Is everything OK in there?"

Deena leaned forward, putting her ear close to the door and heard an emphatic, "No." Wiggling the doorknob confirmed that the door was locked, so she walked back down the steps and peered inside the front window. It looked as though someone had dropped a long, black sweater on the floor in the middle of a disorganized clutter of boxes and piles of debris. When Deena knocked on the window the sweater shifted slightly to the right and Deena could make out an orthopedic shoe. "Mrs. Goetz, I'm going to call 911." The sweater moved again revealing a white hand fluttering fitfully beneath its sleeve. "Hang on, someone will be here in just a few minutes."

An Asian woman, probably in her sixties and wearing a red jogging suit, was checking the mailbox next door. Deena called out to her, "Your neighbor, Mrs. Goetz, is hurt and I can't get in to help her. I was just going to call the police. Do you happen to have a key to her house?"

The neighbor shoved a fistful of envelopes back into her mailbox and hustled across the yard. "I told herx to be careful. I told her, 'What if you fall down?' Lucky for her I know where she hides her key." She pointed to a side door with an old milk chute built into the wall beside it. The woman opened the milk chute, extracted a key and was inside the house within a minute.

"Look at this stuff. What does she need this for? Nothing." The woman was waving her arms as she hurried through the kitchen, indicating the boxes, papers and piles of books that covered virtually every surface. "I tell her get rid of this crap but she doesn't listen. She always tells me 'soon, soon.' For ten years she tells me 'soon.' Don't you? Isn't that what you say?" The Chinese woman helped Deena lift Mrs. Goetz onto a chair as she spoke. "Ai, look at you. You look like *gui po*, the old lady ghost. Sit here while I get you a glass of water." While Deena tried to calm the old woman, the neighbor ran into the kitchen.

"That's the Dowager Empress. She thinks she runs the place. Don't let her boss you around," Mrs. Goetz spoke but her skin was ashen, and judging from her pinched expression, she was in quite a bit of pain.

"What happened? Do you think you broke a bone?" Deena watched with concern as Mrs. Goetz tried to stand, but collapsed back into the chair with a small yelp.

"Don't get up. Stay in that chair." The neighbor came back carrying a glass that she pressed into Mrs. Goetz's hand. "First drink this. OK, now make your fingers like this." The Chinese woman wiggled her fingers for Mrs. Goetz to imitate.

"I'm fine, I'm fine. Don't crowd me. I just need a minute to catch my breath." Mrs. Goetz sipped at her water, looking more shaken than she was willing to admit.

"You're an old lady. What if you broke your hip? What

if no one found you? You might have died right here. How many times do I tell you, get a medical alert button: 'Help, I've fallen and I can't get up.' So now maybe you'll listen to me. It's not good for old people to live alone." The Chinese woman seemed more agitated than Mrs. Goetz.

"It was just a little fall. I slipped on the ice, but I'm fine. Everyone can go home now."

"What ice? You're inside your house. Maybe you hit your head. Do you think she hit her head?"

This last question was directed to Deena who only shook her own head in reply. "I don't know. Do you think we should call an ambulance?"

"No, you shouldn't call an ambulance. I'm fine." Mrs. Goetz attempted to stand up again to prove her point, but only managed to rise a few inches before falling back into the chair. "Damn, I did something to my ankle. Why don't they keep the walks shoveled? What do we pay our taxes for?"

"OK, I'm calling an ambulance now. You want more water?" Mrs. Goetz shook her head and the woman ran back to her own house to make the call.

"I don't want an ambulance. Don't let them take me anywhere." The old woman looked frail and frightened for the first time since Deena had met her.

Deena put a hand on her shoulder. "A doctor needs to check you out after a fall like that. Don't you want someone to look at that ankle?"

"No." Mrs. Goetz began pulling on a loose thread hanging from the arm of her chair and seemed to forget that Deena was standing beside her. For her part, Deena felt awkward and out of place, but didn't see any way to extricate herself until the ambulance arrived. She looked around, surprised that the house didn't look like the home of a crazy person; it just looked like a place in desperate need of a housekeeper. The large living room was furnished with fussy, ornate pieces that seemed utterly out of character for the blunt, unpretentious

Mrs. Goetz.

There was a loud knock at the door and a male voice announced, "Paramedics." Since the door was already open, the knock was a formality. Two good looking men with a gurney, an oxygen tank and a large bag of medical supplies rolled into the room. The woman in the red jogging suit arrived right behind them. "That lady," she said, pointing at Mrs. Goetz. "She fell on her head and maybe she broke her ankle."

"What is this, a Chinese fire drill?" Mrs. Goetz looked pointedly at her neighbor. "I'm fine. Go away. *Gay avek.*" She waved her hands at them as though shooing cats from the house.

"Now we just need to take a quick look at that leg of yours. I hear you hurt it when you fell, is that right?" The younger man, probably Mexican, checked his clipboard, "I see your name is Raisa Goetz. May I call you Raisa?"

"No." Mrs. Goetz glared at the young man.

"All right then, Mrs. Goetz," the young man was unperturbed. "May I take a look at your leg?"

"OK, look already, but you're not taking me anywhere." She seemed to notice the run in the armchair's upholstery for the first time and followed it to the thread wound around her finger with a look of surprise. "Now look what you've made me do," she said to no one in particular.

Nonplussed, the medical technician went on. "I'm sorry, we'll make this as fast as we can." Within minutes they'd completed a cursory examination and recorded the results into a digital file. "I'd recommend that you let us take you in for some x-rays. Your vitals are OK, but we need to know what's going on with that right ankle."

"You should go with these men. You need x-rays, maybe a CAT scan." The Chinese woman patted Raisa's hand, ignoring the old woman's attempts to bat her away. "I have to go home now, but it was nice meeting you. My name is Liling Fitzgerald. Thank you for helping my old friend." She smiled at Deena. "Knock on my door if you need more help. I live right there in that house." She turned back to Mrs. Goetz. "Raisa, you should go to the hospital right now. You had a bad fall. I worry about you."

"I'll go to my own doctor if it doesn't get better. Right now I have a headache and I want to lie down." Mrs. Goetz closed her eyes and laid her head on the back of the chair. Mrs. Fitzgerald bowed slightly to the group and left.

"Is this your granddaughter? Will she be here to take care of you?" The paramedics were packing up their gear, but looked reluctant to leave.

"She's my assistant. Don't worry, we'll be fine."

The other paramedic, a surfer dude from the look of him, shook his head then shrugged. He spoke directly to Deena as if Mrs. Goetz were no longer present. "We can't force her to go, but if she runs a fever, if her leg swells, turns red or feels hot to the touch, you get her into the emergency room right away."

Deena stared at them, confused. Why was he talking to her? "I don't have a car."

"Then call us. We can be here in three minutes." They were out the door as quickly as they'd arrived.

Deena watched them through the window as they drove off in their van. Once they were out of sight, she turned back to Mrs. Goetz. It seemed that she had a job, although not the one she'd been expecting. "I'm no nurse but I can cook and do laundry and keep an eye on you until you feel better."

"Just help me over to the couch. I'm going to rest a while." She studied Deena, her head cocked to one side. "You look like Hell. Take the rest of the day off and get some sleep. The room with blue wallpaper has clean sheets on the bed."

A room with blue wallpaper and a bed with sheets, Deena closed her eyes overcome with gratitude. There's a blessing pious Jews say when they're saved from danger. If she'd remembered the words of that prayer, she'd have said it then

and there. Instead, she helped the old woman to her feet and
supported her weight as she limped over to the sofa. "Mrs.
Goetz, we haven't even talked about the job. You know that,
don't you?"

"Who knows what I know? I'm a little confused." She
laid her head down on one of the round, tasseled pillows that
matched the draperies. "Sleep now, we'll talk later." Then she
closed her eyes and Deena started up the stairs. She'd almost
made it to the landing when Mrs. Goetz called after her, "Wait;
there's a bag of sunflower seeds in the back hall. Maybe you
could throw some under the bushes before you go upstairs."

Chapter Eleven

The room with blue wallpaper was cluttered with open boxes, scattered books and two large suitcases, but it also had a double bed, a large wooden chest and a window looking out on the placid waters of Sarasota Bay. A number of large boats, yachts really, were visible from the window. The bedspread was faded and out of date, but it was first quality, just the sort of spread her grandmother would have purchased. Deena caressed the faded fabric as though it were an old friend. How long would Mrs. Goetz let her stay? It was still early in the afternoon and sun was streaming through the bedroom windows, but Deena took off her shoes, lay down on top of the bedspread, and was asleep before her lashes hit her cheeks.

Two hours later she woke up, disoriented at finding herself in a strange room. She put her shoes back on and went to look out the window. Yes, the bay and the boats were still there. It hadn't been a dream. She found her phone and dialed Lauren.

"Hi Sweetie, do you have a minute? I have some news."

"Sure, what's up?" Deena could hear Lauren chewing something at the other end of the phone.

"I've taken a job with an old woman who wants a librarian to organize her literary estate. Her name's Raisa Goetz and she kind of reminds me of Bubbe. It's a live-in job, so I've moved out of my apartment."

"She needs a live-in librarian? I've never heard of that."

"What are you eating? You're chewing right in my ear."

"Sorry, it's cereal. I didn't have time for lunch. So, what's the deal with being a live-in librarian?"

"I'm not sure. The woman's eccentric, but she has a big house in a ritzy part of town. Frankly, I think she might just want company. It's an odd situation, but I kind of like her and I don't have to pay rent."

"Sounds like a cushy job."

"Too soon to tell, but it'll give me something to do until I find a permanent position. Listen, this is important. Have you heard from Dad yet? I don't know if he isn't getting my messages or if he's still giving me the silent treatment."

"As far as I know, he's still biking around Italy, but he should be back any day now."

"Well, if you hear from him, tell him to call me. Tell him I really need to talk with him."

The sound of pots rattling startled Deena. "I have to run. I think Mrs. Goetz needs me, but I'll call again in a couple days. Love you."

Deena hung up the phone then raced downstairs to find Mrs. Goetz in the kitchen filling a kettle with water.

"Good, you're up. Do you want some coffee? I usually need a second cup about this time." Mrs. Goetz was leaning against the sink with all her weight on her good leg.

"Let me get that for you. I know how to make coffee." Deena took the kettle from the old woman who released it without a murmur. "You need to sit down. Let me help you."

"I'm fine, it's just a twisted ankle. You don't have to fuss."

But Deena could see her wince every time she took a step. "How did you even walk to the kitchen with your ankle like that?"

"It's nothing. During the war people walked on broken legs. You do what you have to do."

"Well, thank God, we're not at war. Why don't we get you back to the couch so you can keep your foot elevated, and we should probably be putting ice on it to keep the swelling down." It turned out that Deena wasn't a bad nurse. She had her patient settled comfortably sipping hot coffee with a makeshift ice pack on her ankle within minutes. If this was her new job, she intended to do it well. "There now, how are you feeling?"

"I'm fine. You don't need to fuss."

Fine seemed to be an overstatement, but at least she'd stopped babbling about snow in Florida. Was the woman demented? Was she capable of making rational decisions? "Mrs. Goetz," Deena probed, "tell me something about yourself. How long have you lived in Sarasota?"

Mrs. Goetz started to answer then stopped, a look of confusion coming over her face. "There's a box of cookies in the kitchen. Would you bring them in here? I need a minute to do the calculations."

"Sure." Deena went to the kitchen and dutifully returned with a fancy assortment of boxed cookies. "So, have you figured out how many years you've been in Florida?"

"Too many. The answer is too many. I should have stayed in California. I don't know what I was thinking."

"Why? What's wrong with Florida?" Deena helped herself to a sugar cookie dipped in chocolate, then pushed the plate toward the petulant old woman stretched out on the sofa.

"There's too many alligators." She took another sip of coffee and examined each of the remaining cookies before choosing a vanilla wafer. "Too many alligators and not enough people. A person could get lonely here."

"I see." Deena did see. She'd been lonely for years without even knowing it. "You must have some friends or relatives in the area."

"Not anymore, they all moved. Some moved back north, some moved to nursing homes, some moved to the cemetery."

"What about Mrs. Fitzgerald? Isn't she a friend?"

"Liling? She's a bossy busybody. Anyway, she's moving.

Didn't you see the sign on her front lawn? That's why I like crows. They don't migrate."

Deena nodded sympathetically. "Why don't you tell me about my new job. You need someone to organize a literary archive, is that right?"

"The first thing you need to do is find everything. I've got papers scattered all over the house. I'm a terrible house-keeper."

That was obvious. There were piles of books, newspapers, files and boxes everywhere. "Maybe we could start by getting the house cleaned up."

"Could you do that?" Raisa lifted her head and looked around her own living room as though she had no idea who all the things belonged to. "I wouldn't know where to start."

"Sure, but you'd have to help me. I won't know what to keep and what to throw away." Deena put her cup down and went over to peek inside one of the boxes. It was filled with more papers. She riffled through the pile and discovered that most had been typed on an old fashioned typewriter. "These are pretty old. Did you write all of this?"

"Most of it. What do you think? Can you get that mess organized?"

"I don't know. I might be able to sort it out for you, create an index or something like that. Do you have a computer?" The task looked daunting. Deena had no idea what all those pages represented and she wasn't sure that Raisa knew either. They might be gibberish or they might be literary gold. What she did know was that she wasn't going to jeopardize her place in the room with blue wallpaper. If she needed to spend the next two months creating a readers' guide to the babbling of a demented old woman, that's what she'd do.

"I don't know anything about computers, but if you need one, buy it. That would make Barry happy."

"Who's Barry?"

"My attorney in California. He tells me I don't spend

enough money. Personally, I don't know why you need a computer. I've always managed with index cards. There's a suitcase full of index cards around here somewhere."

"Is it in the blue bedroom? There are a couple of suitcases in there." Deena sat back down and helped herself to another cookie.

"It's the green suitcase. Bring it down here and I'll get you started." Deena started to get up to fetch the suitcase but Raisa stopped her. "No, not now. Right now I just want to rest. We'll start tomorrow after breakfast. So, you'll take the job?"

"Yes, Mrs. Goetz, it's a deal. I'd be happy to be your personal librarian."

"Good, good. Tell me, can you cook?"

"I can. In fact, I like cooking. Why, are you hungry?"

"Not at the moment, but sometimes I like a home cooked meal. I know it's not in your job description, but maybe you could make me dinner sometime."

"It would be my pleasure." Deena watched a contented smile spread across the old woman's face.

"That would be so nice. You're a very nice person. What did you say your name was?"

When Deena got up the next morning, she began nosing through the boxes to get a sense of the job ahead. A lot of the cartons were filled with junk, a lifetime of accumulated kitchenware, *tchotchkes*, old sweaters, office supplies. Unrelated items were tossed together, high heeled shoes with dinner dishes, cleaning supplies with china figurines. The stuff had been packed in a hurry without any care or planning. An eclectic assortment of old magazines, loose papers and piles of spiral notebooks overflowed their cardboard walls. Deena's preliminary inventory left her perplexed and confused. She closed the box she'd been examining and went upstairs to find her new employer.

"Raisa, what *is* all that stuff in the boxes?"

Raisa's leg was swollen so she lay in bed with her foot elevated on a pillow. "Those boxes are my nemesis. We've been at war for fifteen years, but I thought we'd come to an agreement. They'd stay on their side of the house and I'd stay on mine, but it was like partitioning the Ottoman Empire: no one was happy. Now they've started encroaching on my territory, making demands, especially the papers. That's why I hired you. I needed to call in the cavalry."

"It sounds like a dangerous mission. I hope I'm up to it." Deena put her hand on Raisa's swollen ankle. It was red but not warm. "Are you sure you don't want to go to the hospital?"

"Absolutely not. They'd hold me hostage. I might never get out."

"Well, do you want some more ice, or maybe an aspirin?"

"I don't need anything, I'm fine. Well, maybe you could get me a cup of coffee and half a bagel when you go downstairs, and a smear of cream cheese, no jelly."

"Got it," Deena smiled. She liked the old bird. "So this stuff has been gathering dust for fifteen years? It looks like someone moved in, but never unpacked."

"I guess that's what happened. Fifteen years and I never unpacked. Can you believe it? So, I'm here and I'm not here. I'm not here, but I'm not anywhere else. What can I say? I could never decide whether to stay here or move back to California or maybe back to New York. It's been fifteen years and I'm still deciding. That's another life in those boxes."

"What did you do when you moved here — buy all new stuff?"

"The house came furnished. I inherited everything when my son died. He came out here to make a fortune and he did. He built half the buildings between here and Bradenton. Did you ever hear of the Leonard Goetz Charitable Foundation? That's him. Jeannette, his third wife, bought all this stuff. When they divorced she got the apartment in New York and he got this." She gestured to the house with an expression of disgust. "A year later he had a stroke, fifty years old and gone, just like that." Raisa sighed deeply. "So, now all this stuff is mine."

"I'm sorry about your son. Do you have any other children?"

"No children, no grandchildren, just boxes and birds, and I could live without the boxes."

Deena took Raisa's hand and gave it a quick squeeze. "I understand; where do you want to start? Are you ready to look inside some of those boxes, maybe throw a few things away?"

"I don't want to look. You look for me. Do what you have to do. Keep whatever you want, give away whatever you want — but not the papers. Don't touch those without me. Do we have a deal?"

"Deal," Deena stuck out her hand and they shook on it.

Deena tackled her new job with more energy than she'd had in ages. It gave her a purpose and she enjoyed the company of the old woman who reminded her more and more of her grandmother. Raisa was European born, small and gray like Bubbe, and spoke with the same familiar accent, part Yiddish part Lower East Side. But, unlike Bubbe, Raisa had spent years in Hollywood. Jumbled in with the paraphernalia of daily life, Deena unearthed television scripts, production notes, signed photographs of Dick Van Dyke, Eva Gabor, Andy Griffith, Mary Tyler Moore, plus dozens of others she didn't recognize. There were plaques and awards and memorabilia going back to the fifties.

It also turned out that Raisa was a serious reader. Her boxes revealed not only a prodigious amount of popular fiction and old murder mysteries, but a scholarly collection of books on the Holocaust and the second world war. She wasn't surprised when a copy of *Fatelessness* by Imre Kertesz emerged from a carton otherwise filled with cookbooks and kitchen towels.

Deena opened the small volume and leafed through it briefly before going to find Raisa, who was in her office watching *The Today Show.* "Sorry to disturb you." Deena stood in the doorway with *Fatelessness* in her hand. "I came across this in one of your boxes and I was wondering if you'd read it."

Raisa clicked off the TV. "I don't know why they call it the news. It's the same story every day: some maniac with a gun shooting people."

"I know. It's really scary." Deena walked over to the armchair where Raisa was sitting with her leg raised on a small ottoman, and handed her the book.

"You can have it. I don't want to read it again." She handed it back to Deena.

"No, that's not what I meant. I just wanted to know what you thought about it. You've read a lot about the Holocaust, so I thought you might be able to answer a question that's been bothering me. Is Kertesz saying the Jews had a choice somehow, that they chose their fate?"

"What do you think? One day six million Jews decide to take a trip to a concentration camp? Of course he's not saying that."

"But isn't fatelessness the opposite of fate? Wouldn't fatelessness mean freedom, the ability to choose?" Deena hesitated, she didn't want to give too much away. "I had a friend once, a professor. We used to argue about this a lot."

"*Fatelessness* means what it says, no fate, no plan, no meaning. Some people die in concentration camps. Some die of strokes when they're barely fifty years old. Some keep on living way past their expiration date."

"So, no free will?"

"Just the opposite."

"But the opposite would mean the Jews *did* have a choice."

"The Jews, the Nazis, everyone."

"Even at Auschwitz?"

"Everywhere, every step we take is a choice. We can't

choose what happens, but we choose how we respond. Read Viktor Frankl. He says it better than Kertesz."

"Every step we take?" Deena considered all the steps that had brought her to this moment, starting with the choice to leave her mother and New Moon.

"Look at the Germans. Some followed orders, some fought for the resistance, most looked the other way. It was a choice. God didn't make them throw children into the fire."

Deena sat down on the daybed so she could look Raisa in the eye. "Actually, my grandmother believed it *was* God's will. She thought the Holocaust was God's way of punishing the Jews for straying from the law. The fire next time, that sort of thing."

"What a way to think. With a God like that who needs enemies?"

"She disowned my mother for living a life that offended her idea about how people should behave. Or maybe she disowned her as penance. Sometimes I wonder if she sacrificed her daughter out of survivor's guilt.

"She was a survivor?"

"In a way. She emigrated to American before the war, but all her siblings died in concentration camps." Deena had never said this out loud before but she'd been mulling it over for a while. After a long silence Deena added, "I lived with my grandmother."

Raisa's old, wrinkled face sagged, making her look even older. She seemed to understand everything Deena couldn't say. "What a terrible thing."

Visions of New Moon flashed through Deena's mind. There had been hard times and her mother had made some bad choices. She'd been a rebellious kid, irresponsible and immature but she'd also been idealistic, generous and kind. Deena shook her head. "My mom was a hippie kid back in the seventies and my grandmother couldn't accept the way she lived."

"How sad for both of them. Did they ever make up?"

Deena lowered her voice to a whisper. "No, they never spoke again."

Deena was surprised two days later when her phone rang and it was Martin.

"Deena, where are you? Are you alright?"

She could hear the panic in his voice and it was balm to her soul. He hadn't deliberately abandoned her to the streets. Deena tried to answer but found she'd lost control of the fine motor skills coordinating her lips and tongue and breath. She felt like a Japanese actor whose dubbed-in English was out of sync. "Martin," was what she meant to say, but it came out sounding more like, "Marrrgh," and that was all that she could manage through her trembling lips.

"Hello? Are you there? Are you alright?"

Closing her eyes, Deena sat on the side of the bed and took a long, cleansing breath, then exhaled months of fear and anxiety while Martin waited patiently at the other end of the line. At last she managed, "I'm in Florida and I'm OK now, but the last few weeks have been a living hell. I ran out of money and didn't have anywhere to stay."

"I don't understand. I gave you every penny of our savings and the car and you were getting unemployment. You should have been fine."

Deena spoke slowly and deliberately, trying to maintain control of the complicated mechanism that produced coherent speech. "Look, you have your own problems, and I've caused some of them, but the truth is I never got a penny of unemployment. The library fired me because they thought I was a thief, or an accessory to a robbery, or whatever they thought, so I didn't qualify for compensation, and you know we didn't have much in the bank. Then a truck took out the car, and some bastard stole my iPhone, and you were off riding a bicycle God knows where while I was..." *Calm down*, she told herself. *You're blowing it. Don't tell him everything.* "in big trouble."

"My God, Deena. I'm so sorry. What do you mean they thought you were a thief? That's ridiculous."

"Of course it's ridiculous, but I got conned. That professor used me to steal valuable art books from the library. Originally, the police thought I was in cahoots with him, but they've caught his real accomplice and she's in jail. But it cost me my job."

"You know I'd have helped you if I'd known. What the hell are you doing in Florida?"

There was an awkward pause while Deena calculated an answer. "I'm working for an old woman, a retired writer, who needs a librarian to organize her papers. It doesn't pay much, but it includes room and board, so I have a roof over my head."

"Are you OK? Are you safe?"

"Yeah, I guess I am, at least for the moment." She tried to maintain her cool, but the sound of Martin's voice shredded her composure. "Oh Martin, it's been awful. Please, let me come home. I'm so sorry for hurting you. I promise nothing like that will ever, ever, ever happen again."

"Shhh, shhh," he soothed. "Calm down, you're going to be alright."

"You don't know what I've been through."

"Look, you know I don't have savings, but I could send a little something every month, at least until you find work."

Money? He was going to send money? She didn't want money; she wanted to go home. "Oh, for God's sake Martin, don't be an idiot. Are you listening to me? I'm OK financially, at least for the moment. What I need is *you*. I need to know you'll talk to me, that you'll pick up the phone and answer my emails. You've made mistakes too. I'm not the only sinner here."

"Deena, you had an affair. That's a big deal. I can't just forget about it."

"I had an affair because you stopped talking to me, stopped eating with me, stopped sleeping with me. I got conned by that professor because you'd abandoned me."

"I was depressed."

"And maybe I was depressed too. Did you ever think of that? I've never been so depressed and scared and lonely in my life."

"Well, that makes two of us."

"You've been lonely?" Deena held her breath as Martin continued.

"Of course I've been lonely. Listen, I did a lot of thinking in Italy. Six weeks on a bicycle changes you. Everything looks different to me now. It gave me a whole new perspective. Stuff that used to matter doesn't matter anymore."

"What does that mean?" Deena's heart was pounding so fast she thought it might explode.

"It means I'm not the same man I was before you turned our lives upside down, and that's a good thing. I was practically brain dead and didn't even know it."

"You were depressed, but now, I'll be there to help you. We'll be together and you'll be your old self again."

"God forbid! I don't want to be my old self. I never want to be the old Marty Berman again, not in a million years."

There was no equivocation in his tone. He meant it. "So, what *do* you want to do?" *Please let it include me,* Deena prayed silently to herself.

"I don't know yet, but something different, maybe something with bicycles and being outdoors. You wouldn't recognize me. I've lost weight, I've got a great tan and I feel like a million dollars. The trip was amazing, life changing."

"Well lucky you," Deena muttered between clenched teeth. In a voice that was clearly audible, she asked, "So, how did you pay for that six week vacation? I don't know how much time you had coming, but I know you didn't have any money."

"You'd be surprised, it didn't cost that much. Our old air miles covered the flight, and I mostly camped out or slept in youth hostels. Food was cheap: fruit for breakfast, cheese and bread for lunch, pasta and wine for dinner. Most of the best art is inside the churches and that was all free. You just don't need a lot of money to have a really good time."

"You lost weight on bread and cheese and pasta?"

"Yeah, biking five hours a day burns a lot of calories. Honestly, you wouldn't believe how beautiful it was pedaling past fields and vineyards and through little villages that still look like they did a hundred, two hundred, years ago. It's a whole different culture. People don't just live to make money. They know how to enjoy themselves. They've got their heads screwed on straight."

That sounded like New Moon philosophy. Why did everything make her think of New Moon these days? "Have you talked to Lauren or Elliot since you've gotten back?" She didn't want to listen to any more of his travelogue.

"Elliot's incommunicado until boot camp's over, but I called Lauren and left her a message. Deena, you know I care about you and I'm terribly sorry you've had such a bad time, but I still have a lot of thinking to do. Call if you need anything. I promise to pick up the phone."

That was it? The conversation was over? "What about you?" Deena chimed in before he could hang up. "Is there anything I can do for you? You know, I'd do anything to make this right."

"Not right now. If anything changes, I'll let you know." Then he hung up and Deena sat on the bed listening to her husband's absence until Raisa called her from downstairs.

It only took three days to make a significant dent in the boxes. Sorting, organizing and discarding were familiar tasks and Deena was good at them. Raisa refused to even look at her own things. "Chuck it," was her mantra whenever Deena asked what to do with a coat, a lamp, or an electric mixer. The answer was the same when Deena uncovered a trove of paintings and small watercolors propped up between the back of a sofa and the office wall. "You can't just throw these on the

Purple Heart truck. They're beautiful," Deena had protested. "Why don't we find a place to hang them?"

Raisa had graduated from a horizontal position on the sofa to sitting upright in a sturdy armchair in the spare bedroom she used as an office. She was reading the newspaper and barely glanced up. "If you like something, keep it, otherwise, out it goes. Anything still here at the end of the month is paying rent. These things have been freeloading for years. It's enough already. They need to get on with their lives."

Deena was lining up the canvases along the far wall where she could study them. They were abstract works, sharp geometric shapes in vibrant colors that radiated from the canvas. The more she looked at them, the more she was falling in love. They were elegant, sophisticated and joyful, clearly not the work of an amateur. "Raisa, do you know who painted these? They're absolutely gorgeous."

"Dorothy Kanter, she was one of my aunt's friends. She was a real hot shot back in the fifties and sixties but she's gone now. Most of those were gifts. My aunt had them hanging all over her house."

"You knew the artist? What was she like?"

"A typical Hadassah lady if you didn't know she was an artist. I called her Aunt Dottie. There was a big article about her in the *New York Times* with color photographs. That put her over the moon, but it's all out of fashion now."

"If they featured her in the *Times*, these might be worth something. Are you sure you want to give them away?"

"Absolutely. If you like them, they're yours. Keep them, burn them, do whatever you want. I don't care."

"If I owned some walls I'd take you up on that offer." Deena leaned in for a closer look at one of the canvases. "There's no signature. Didn't she sign her work?"

"They're signed on the back. Dottie thought signatures messed up the image. Everything had to be clean and precise. She was a great housekeeper."

"I see." Deena turned one of the paintings over and found *D. Kanter 1959* painted in neat black letters. "Would it be OK if I took a couple of these to a gallery and had someone look at them?"

"What do I care?" Raisa shrugged. "If they're worth millions, enjoy. Buy yourself a mansion on Long Boat Key."

"I could use a mansion, or at least a little house somewhere." Deena hesitated, deciding whether to go on. "When we first met, I told you that I needed a job and an apartment, but it was worse than that. I really didn't have a place to sleep. You saved my life by letting me live here with you. I had a house of my own two years ago, but we lost it in a bankruptcy. We pretty much lost everything."

"We? You have a husband?" Raisa's eyebrows shot up.

"That's hard to say at the moment. I had one a year ago."

"Don't tell me the banks are repossessing husbands now."

Deena smiled, "No, not exactly, but he seems to have gotten lost in the transaction. Everything went south after they took the house."

"Is he lost for good? Maybe you could find him."

"At the moment, he's trying to find himself and he doesn't want me interfering. It's a long story and not very pretty so let's save it for another day."

Raisa stared into Deena's eyes for an uncomfortably long time as though she was trying to see right through her, but all she said was, "You know, I think I might have some biscotti in the cupboard. Why don't you make a pot of coffee and see if you can find them. I could use a little something about now."

When Deena called The Forrest Gallery a pleasant woman with a cultured voice informed her that an official appraisal of the entire collection for insurance purposes could cost thousands of dollars. "However," she told Deena, "most people don't know whether their art is even worth insuring until they bring it in. If you're free Thursday afternoon Mr. Forrest would be happy to look at a few pieces free of charge. It won't be an official appraisal, just an informal assessment, but that might help you decide what you want to do. Would you be free this Thursday at two o'clock?"

It was silly, but the meeting at the Forrest Gallery seemed to warrant dressing up; yet all Deena had with her were the jeans and T-shirts she'd stuffed into a bag for life on the streets. Maybe the time had come to retrieve a few nice things from Andor's old apartment. She let Raisa know she'd be gone for a while and started hiking toward downtown. It wasn't far, but Deena had worked up a nice sweat and her hair was sticking to the back of her neck by the time she arrived back in her old neighborhood. It had been barely two weeks since she'd left, but once-familiar landmarks seemed to belong to a life already fading from memory. Deena pulled a tissue from her purse and dabbed at the perspiration running down her forehead. Most of the houses looked smaller and shabbier than she remembered but, curiously, when Deena turned up the short walk to her old residence, she found it markedly improved.

She rang the bell to the downstairs unit and waited for Eddie to answer the door. The place was definitely in better shape than when she'd left. Someone had hosed off the chairs, mowed the grass and hacked back the overgrown weeds. A sprinkling of bright plastic toys replaced the beer cans and cigarette butts that had littered the yard. Even the window in the front door had been wiped clean. She rang again, then knocked loudly in case the bell was out of order.

"He's not home. Can I help you?" Deena backed off the porch and looked up at a pale young woman leaning over the second floor lanai.

Deena made a visor of her left hand, shielding her eyes from the glare of the mid-afternoon sun. The woman wasn't much older than Lauren, but she looked worn around the edges. Thin brown hair was pulled back into a short pony tail and her eyes looked hollow and tired. Deena squinted up at her, almost certain the woman was wearing one of the blue yoga shirts that she'd packed away in the shed. The face of a toddler peeked out from between the woman's legs and regarded Deena with interest. "I'm Deena Berman. I used to live in your apartment. Your dad let me leave a few things here in storage and I wanted to pick them up."

"Shit!" The woman clapped a hand over her mouth then shot a quick, guilty glance down at her son. "We didn't think you'd actually come back. At least we figured you'd call first. Wait a minute and I'll come down." She scooped up the child and went back into the house letting the screen door slam behind her. It was almost ten minutes before she emerged in a faded orange T-shirt with a University of Florida alligator flashing its teeth across her chest. Three small silver hoops were threaded through her left eyebrow and another ring pierced her nose. She was balancing a plastic laundry basket filled with Deena's shirts and pants while clutching a stack of mail under one arm. "These are all yours. Sorry, we figured you wouldn't be back and I didn't have any clothes here except for this one outfit." She indicated the orange T-shirt which, on closer inspection, was not only faded but torn at the neck. "Dad told me to look through the stuff in the shed. I wouldn't have done it except I'm afraid to go back to my old apartment. Anyway, I know where Dad keeps the key so you can take whatever you want." She picked up a blue spandex shirt with a white lotus flower printed in the center. "Do you want me to wash this for you?"

"No, that's OK. I'll wash it myself."

"Are you sure? I could have it ready by tomorrow."

"That's OK. There's a washing machine where I'm staying now."

"Well, OK, if you're sure. By the way, I'm Ashley and this is Little Eddie." She beamed at her son who was playing with a toy truck on the sidewalk. "You're Deena Berman, right?"

"That's right."

"Then maybe you'll know what to do with all this." She shifted sideways so Deena could extract the envelopes and papers from under her arm. "I don't think any of it's for you. It's all addressed to Dr. Andor Farkas, but if you know where he is, could you send it to him?"

"I have absolutely no idea where he is." Deena shuffled through the pile. There were the usual advertisements, a Comcast bill, a Hungarian language newspaper, a couple letters from the university and a hand addressed envelope from a Mrs. Andor Farkas in Balatonfured, Hungary. Deena reread the return address a second time, *Mrs. Andor Farkas, Balatonfured, Hungary*, before throwing it into the plastic hamper with the rest of the mail.

"He should have filled out a change of address at the post office. I don't know what to do with this stuff. It just keeps coming." Ashley was clearly annoyed.

"Throw it away or mark it, 'Moved, no forwarding address.' Trust me, he won't be back."

"OK, if you're sure. Can you wait a minute? The key to the shed's in my Dad's kitchen." Ashley began to unlock the door to the bottom unit.

"Hi, hi, hi." Deena felt a small hand pounding on her leg and looked down to see the toddler grinning up at her. He held up his toy truck for Deena to admire.

"Well hello," Deena greeted him. "Is that your truck?"

"My tuck," he agreed. The child was an adorable little boy with large brown eyes set in a joyful face topped with a tangle of dark curls.

Deena couldn't help but grin back at him. "Well, aren't you the lucky boy. Do you know what color your truck is?"

"Wed," was the triumphant response.

"That's right. It's red. Good for you."

"Eddie, don't bother the lady," his mother scolded. "She came here to get her things, not to play with you."

"Oh, that's alright," Deena said. "He's not bothering me.

So, you named this charming little fellow for your father."

"That's what my dad thinks, but he's actually named for Edward Cullen." Deena stared at her, puzzled. "You know, Edward Cullen from *The Twilight Saga*. I was in love with him."

What was it with girls and vampires?

"But at the moment, this is the only man in my life." Ashley put down the laundry hamper and picked up her son, balancing him on one hip. "Wait here. I'll be right back with the key."

When Deena opened her suitcase it was obvious that the contents had been ransacked, but Ashley's embarrassment and her desire to set things right made Deena trust that nothing was actually missing. She pulled out a pair of good trousers, a silk blouse, a decent pair of shoes and an armload of other useful things. Without a car, she couldn't carry more back to Raisa's, but why did she need so many clothes anyway? Deena turned and looked at the young woman in the torn alligator shirt who was waiting to lock up the shed. "Would it be OK if I left the rest of these things here a while longer? It's OK with me if you want to use them. In fact, why don't you just keep most of this stuff. I won't be needing it after all."

It wasn't possible to take all the artwork downtown on a bus, so Deena selected two of the smaller oils, and a few unframed prints, wrapped them in cardboard and newspaper, and set off for the gallery pulsing with hope laced with a modicum of excitement. Remnants of her old self had been evident in the mirror as she'd dressed for the appointment. She'd put on earrings and lipstick and blush. Her hair needed a good cut, but it was clean and neatly combed. *Yes*, she'd thought, *I recognize that woman*. Deena had closed her eyes, momentarily overcome with gratitude and relief to discover that she still existed.

At exactly two o'clock, she pushed through a pair of intricately carved wooden doors into a space of utter calm and tranquility. Thick rugs, muted walls and atmospheric lighting whispered luxury and refinement despite the building's proximity to a busy street. A glass table surrounded by upholstered chairs sat in the center of the room. Oil paintings, mostly semi-abstract landscapes in bright improbable colors lined the walls. Glass sculptures rested on pedestals scattered throughout the space while a huge bronze nude reclined in the front window. Deena stood with her packages wrapped in old newspaper feeling awkward and a bit intimidated by the place.

"Here, let me help you with those." An elderly gentleman stepped forward and took the paintings from Deena's hands. While his chivalry was well intended, he was so small and frail that Deena was embarrassed to let him take them from her. "Now, what may we do for you, young lady? I hope you didn't have to carry these too far in this heat." He put the art work down on a large table in the center of the room.

"Oh no, it was only..." She stopped, not wanting to confess that she'd come on the bus. "I'm Deena Berman. I have a two o'clock appointment with Mr. Forrest."

"And you're right on time. Let's see what you've brought me." He lifted the first painting from the pile and deftly removed its wrappings with small, well manicured fingers. "Very pretty. Let's take a look at the signature."

"It's on the back," Deena informed him.

He turned the canvas around and removed his glasses. "Dorothy Kanter, now that's a blast from the past. California School. I haven't seen one of these in a while. Have you had it long?"

"Actually, they belong to a friend. She knew Dorothy Kanter back in the fifties when they were both living in Los Angeles."

"I see." He nodded noncommittally. "Let's open up the rest of these and take a look." Mr. Forrest gave each of the pieces a close examination, murmuring approval and appreciation, before turning to Deena. "It's a lovely collection. So, what are you thinking? Do you want an appraisal?"

"Not a formal appraisal. I mean, would that make sense? An appraisal could cost more than they're worth."

"Her work doesn't come up that often, but Dorothy Kanter was a respected second tier artist. She had quite a following at one time. My assistant loves tracking these things down. If you leave these with me for a week or so I might be able to find out more about them, and then you can decide what you want to do."

"Perfect." Deena was relieved that she wouldn't have to lug the framed canvases back home on the bus. She'd be free to wander around, do a little window shopping, maybe buy herself a cup of coffee. "Thank you so much for taking the time to look at the work. Actually, there are seven or eight more pieces I didn't bring in today."

"Let Jean do her work. We can talk after she's given us some numbers." Deena wrote her phone number on a slip of paper that Mr. Forrest slipped into a large leather appointment book. As she was about to leave, he stopped her with one more question. "Is Dorothy still with us? She'd be a hundred years old, but it's possible."

"Oh no, she died some time ago."

"Yes, of course. Well, thanks for coming in. Expect a call toward the end of next week."

Deena felt sweat rise up beneath her collar within minutes of stepping outside. It was another Sarasota scorcher, mid-nineties and humid. Cleveland summers weren't this bad, and Santa Fe had never left her sticky and panting like a dog. In fact, there had been something magic about summer in New Mexico. Those months of freedom from school had been warm and sunny punctuated with cooling rain that turned the desert green. Deena's legs continued walking down Palm toward Main, but her mind was two thousand miles and thirty years away remembering New Moon in the summer.

As a kid, August always meant a trip into town for Indian

Market Days. She smiled remembering how everyone would pile into the back of Mr. Rios's pickup truck and head toward Santa Fe's central plaza. They'd spend the day cruising Palace Avenue where scores of native artists sold baskets, pottery and jewelry from make-shift tables and blankets beneath large white awnings. It was a sort of carnival featuring dancers in traditional costumes, storytellers, and food trucks selling sweet corn and fry bread rolled in sugar. She and Paz had been allowed to run loose, wild Indians among the Navajo and Pueblo who had tolerated the over-excited children running from booth to booth, pestering them with questions, touching valuable art with sticky hands.

Paz had been a smart kid. He had to know how everything worked, how everything was made. At the time, she'd been annoyed when he'd make her stop to study the intricate pattern of a basket or the construction of an old adobe building, but there had been a keen intelligence at work. She smiled at the memory of his suntanned face, serious, inquisitive, always alert beneath an unruly head of unwashed hair. Had he made it out of New Mexico or was he still stuck at New Moon? Deena stopped walking, literally brought up short by the mean, dismissive way she always thought of her first home. Paz had never understood her embarrassment or her longing for new clothes, and for a mother who looked more like... God, she'd been hard on her mother.

Deena crossed Palm and continued down Main Street toward groups of retirees finishing late lunches at outside tables or getting an early start on their afternoon cocktails. Small dogs on leashes looped around table legs yapped as she walked by. The street looked different by daylight and from the vantage point of knowing that she had a bed. The brick sidewalk was lined with palm trees and upscale shops that appealed to a wealthy clientele. There was a theater up one street and an opera house down the next. Sarasota was a nice town if you were rich. Deena slowed her pace. It was too hot to hurry and she had nowhere to go. She naturally gravitated toward a bookstore and read the poster in its window: "Bookstore1 welcomes Stephen King August 14th. Free and open to the public."

Deena passed through the glass entry and began exploring the brightly lit interior. It wasn't a large bookstore, nothing like Barnes & Noble, but it seemed to hit all the bases. The shop was clean and orderly without being cold or intimidating.

"Are you looking for something special or just browsing?" An attractive woman of indeterminate age had come up behind her.

"Yes, well no, what I mean is," Deena paused and smiled her most ingratiating smile, "I was wondering if you were hiring. I'm a librarian with twenty years' experience, so I know my way around books and I just love this shop."

"Well, thank you." The woman was petite but had a commanding presence. "Unfortunately, I can't help you. We're fully staffed and I don't expect any openings for quite a while. I assume you've tried the library."

"That's the first place I applied, but they don't have any positions open either. I'd never thought of working in a bookstore until I walked into your shop."

"I really am sorry. If we had a position, I'd be happy to talk with you, but there's nothing available."

"That's OK, I understand." Deena turned toward the door then remembered the large poster she'd seen in the window. "By the way, how were you able to book Stephen King? He hardly ever appears anywhere."

The woman smiled an enigmatic red lipstick smile, "Oh, we have our ways."

"Seriously, my daughter might be his biggest fan. She's read almost everything he's written."

"Well then, I hope she'll come to see him, but tell her to come early. We're expecting quite a crowd."

"Oh, she doesn't live in Sarasota, but she'd love a signed

copy of his new book." Deena left Bookstore1 disappointed that there hadn't been a job, but buoyed by the thought of surprising Lauren with a signed Stephen King. She was definitely starting to feel normal again. Attending a book signing was such a Deena thing to do.

Chapter Twelve

The house, cleared of clutter, revealed the long gone Jeannette's overblown sense of interior design. It turned out that Raisa's books and boxes had provided a sort of camouflage, distracting the eye and drawing attention away from the gilt embroidered fabrics and heavily tasseled drapes. The faux Louis Quinze sofa and chairs, washed with a pale green stain, distressed, then trimmed in gold, looked like refugees from a Bourbon summer palace. The decor would have made her grandmother green with envy. No wonder her mother had run away. New Moon was everything this room wasn't: spontaneous, unconventional, creative, undemanding, spare. Why had she chosen her grandmother's store bought version of reality? The question left her feeling as cold and empty as the fake fireplace beneath the marble mantel.

With the downstairs in order, Deena decided to tackle the mess in the back bedroom. Raisa was napping, so Deena had an hour to work in peace. It was hard to imagine, but at one time Raisa had apparently been a clothes horse. Most of her things dated from the 80s and were completely out of style, but they'd been the height of fashion at the time. Tweed skirts, silk blouses, jackets with improbably large shoulder pads, and cocktail dresses studded with rhinestones — all went into black plastic bags. It was odd thinking of Raisa in rhinestones and high heels. There must have been men in her life, friends, and colleagues. What had become of them? Why was Raisa so alone?

The next box was full of smaller boxes containing costume jewelry, endless strands of fake gold chains, pearl chokers, and bangle bracelets that would be a hit at the resale shop. At the bottom of the box were more papers and notebooks. Deena hauled them out, intending to add them to the pile to be organized and archived later. But a few sheets caught her eye and she stopped to examine them more closely. They were handwritten, not typed or printed. The pages were stiff and slightly yellowed. It was the title page that had caught her attention: *Crows* by Raisa Goetz, September 18, 1960. Then, in small fine print, "for my father." Deena had promised Raisa that she wouldn't read any of her writing until they could look at it together, but the old woman was asleep. Why not? Deena closed the door, sat down on the bed and turned the page.

"Calman, Calman," Tschippe called from the top of a scrawny cypress growing along the edge of Santa Monica Bay. "Leave that squirrel alone, it's disgusting."

"Aww, Ma, Aww Ma," Calman was annoyed, but he flew up and landed on a slender branch not far from his mother. The branch bent under his substantial weight and Calman had to flap his wings to keep his balance. "Honest, Ma, it's good. Try some, you'll like it."

"Chokecherries and wild plums everywhere you look, and you're pecking at dead squirrels. What's become of you?"

"I've become a crow. What do you expect? Look at Tante Feiga down there. She lets her chicks eat anything they want. She's glad to see them fill their stomachs."

Tschippe cocked a critical eye at Faiga and her family ripping into a rodent carcass. "Feiga comes from butchers. Your grandfather was a rabbi."

"That's all in the past. Everything's different now."

"Not everything. Some things are different, some things stay the same."

"Well, suit yourself, but I'm not leaving a perfectly good meal for the maggots." Calman swooped back down onto the road where he joined his cousins pecking at the carrion.

"Feh," Tschippe would starve before she put her own beak anywhere near putrefied roadkill. She took off toward the shore, flying low over anemic mimosa and live oak trees that she regarded with disdain. In Poland there'd been real trees: beech, spruce, chestnut, and old growth oaks. Forests were dark places, home to wolves and bears, unseen things that rustled the leaves and scattered at the sound of footsteps. They had enveloped her people and hidden them in caves and crevices, and in the hollow trunks of trees. She pitied anyone who needed to hide in this open, sunlit place.

As Tschippe began her descent, she noticed her friend Gitel preening herself on a piece of driftwood that had washed ashore. *"Gitel, make room, I'm coming down."* Gitel hopped to the side as Tschippe landed beside her. *"Where have you been? I was getting worried."* Gitel had been with the resistance and had an affinity for putting herself in harm's way.

"Relax, I just flew inland to do a little reconnaissance. It's always good to know where you are and who you might run into."

"So, what did you find? Anyone we know?" Tschippe tipped her head sideways to get a better look at her old friend.

"Maybe, but I need to be sure. If I'm right, it's a miracle."

"So tell me."

"Nope, not another peep out of me until I'm sure; but I will tell you about a great deli with an open dumpster. It's like the grand buffet at the Polonia Palace"

"Since when did you eat at the Polonia Palace?"

"Since never, but I'm telling you, the Grand Hotel couldn't be better than the dumpster behind Canter's Deli."

"Then lead the way." The two birds took off with Gitel heading inland toward the treasure.

Zalman was flitting back and forth from one telephone wire to another. He was a nervous wreck. Flying west had been his idea and so far things seemed to be working out. No one was hungry *and they wouldn't face a killing winter like the ones in Poland during the war. But still, once they were in New York, maybe they should have stayed there. It felt more like home, and there weren't so many predators in the city. When he was younger there had been men to go to for advice: rabbis, hasids, the president of the synagogue. Now, it was all on his head. He didn't even have Belle, his wife, may she live and be well, assuming she was still alive at all. Who could have predicted such a life? Who could have dreamed of such a thing?*

A commotion disturbed his reverie as twenty or thirty crows began screaming at the top of their voices. Zalman looked up to see a red-tailed hawk soaring into the sky with one of Feiga's chicks clutched in its talons. The poor thing was as good as dead, but Zalman assumed command, rousing the terrified flock to bring down the damn Luftwaffe. "Calman," he called out, "follow him. Stay on his right. Go for the eyes. You, Lev, attack from above, don't let him land. Keep him out of the trees." In no time, the flock was in hot pursuit, mobbing the hawk, pecking at him, harassing him until, miraculously, he let go of his prey and the chick fluttered to the ground.

Zalman stepped forward to investigate the damage. It didn't look good. Little Shaina was bleeding badly from her shoulder. "Where's Mendel?" Zalman asked the gathered crowd. "Find Mendel, we need a doctor." Feiga was crying, her voice raspy and strangled by fear. Zalman preened her neck feathers trying to console her. He couldn't bear to see the little ones in pain. Thank God he'd never had to see his own daughter suffer. His little Raisa and her mother had been in Los Angeles visiting family when the Germans invaded, and he'd made sure they'd stayed put.

"Let me through, move aside. Let me take a look." Mendel had been a respected surgeon in Warsaw before he'd been marched out of his hospital by the Nazis. But now, as a crow, there wasn't much in his medical kit beside his well-honed bedside manner. Still, he was consulted whenever a medical crisis arose, and sometimes he surprised them.

"*So, Shaina,*" *the doctor began in his kindest voice. "I hear you've had quite an adventure. It's a good thing you have so many brave friends.*" *Mendel peered closely at the wound, which was bleeding profusely. He took the injured wing in his beak and moved it gently from side to side, pausing when Shaina flinched. "Can you move that wing yourself? Can you open it a bit more? Excellent.*"

He stepped back and addressed Faiga and Zalman who were huddled together waiting for his diagnosis. "It's not broken, but we have to stop the bleeding and do what we can to avoid infection. Have a couple birds fly into town and bring back some napkins from one of the outdoor restaurants."

Zalman sent off two trusted crows to appropriate the supplies while Mendel spoke with Shaina's mother. "I'm going to use salt water as an antiseptic. It's not penicillin, but it's worked before. I just don't want any of that sludge lapping up near the shore. It looks clean, but it's full of garbage."

"Do I just bring some back in my beak? What do you want me to do?" Faiga was ready to fly off at once, but Mendel held her back.

"No, not you; your daughter needs you here. When the others come back with the napkins I'll tell them what to do."

A loud metallic pounding made Deena start. Raisa was awake and wanted something. In the absence of a small silver bell, they'd jerry-rigged a call system that consisted of Raisa banging on a metal pot with a mixing spoon. The sound never failed to shred Deena's nerves, but it kept Raisa from getting up and risking another fall. Deena tucked the story back into the box and hurried off.

She found Raisa sitting on the edge of her bed feeling around the bedside table in a state of palpable irritation. "I can't find my glasses. They've walked off again. Why do they keep doing that?"

Deena dropped to her knees and found Raisa's spectacles on the floor. "Here you go. They didn't get too far. I think we caught them just in time."

"Thank you." Raisa fitted them back on her nose and looked up at Deena. "What have you been up to? Why the big smile?"

"Me? I've just been doing some housekeeping. The downstairs is finished so I started on that back bedroom. You were certainly the fancy dresser in your day."

"I was, wasn't I? It was fun at the time but I don't have the patience for that sort of thing anymore. Anyway, I'd scare the crows if they saw me decked out like Mrs. Astor's pet horse."

"Oh, I doubt that. You know, the weather's beautiful today. It's cooled down a bit and there's a nice breeze off the bay. Are you up for a little walk?"

"Absolutely, I was afraid you were going to keep me a prisoner in here forever." She stood up suddenly, excited by the prospect of an outing, lost her balance and stumbled into a floor lamp. Deena managed to catch Raisa but the lamp crashed to the floor. There was a small popping noise as the bulb exploded beneath the fluted shade. Deena set Raisa back on the bed where she sat humiliated and uncharacteristically quiet.

"Are you OK?"

"I stood up too fast, that's all. Sometimes I get dizzy if I stand up too fast."

"Well then, how about if I help you to stand up very slowly and we go for that walk."

Raisa was more tractable than usual and walked very slowly holding Deena's arm. If they could make it to the bus stop, there was a bench where they could sit and rest before returning home. The yards in this part of town overflowed with a profusion of tropical plants. Deena still couldn't name the flowering shrubs and trees, but they were beginning to look familiar. The two women progressed in silence enjoying the late afternoon stillness. The houses all appeared empty, waiting for their owners to return from work or school or a leisurely lunch downtown. Raisa walked with concentration, gripping Deena's arm and scanning the trees for crows. Deena was becoming fond of Raisa, although she was a bit of a mystery. It was clear that she'd had a very different life somewhere else, sometime else.

"Raisa," Deena began, "tell me about all those beautiful clothes. Did you go to a lot of parties? Did you have a job where you had to dress up a lot?"

"Those clothes are all retired. They're old and out of fashion like their owner."

"Yes, but they must have been something in their day."

Raisa smiled, "Yes, I suppose they were. I'll tell you this; they got around. They didn't miss much."

"So, where did they go? I know you lived in California for quite a while."

"Quite a while. I moved there when I was fifteen, my first year of high school, and that's where I lived until Lenny died and left me his house." They'd reached the bus stop and Deena tried to take Raisa's arm as she lowered herself onto the bench, but Raisa flinched and pulled her arm away. "I'm not an invalid. I know how to sit down."

"Yes, of course. I'm sorry." Deena pulled back. There was a delicate balance between making sure that the old woman was safe and hovering to the point that she'd get fired for annoying her. "But you weren't born in California. Where did you grow up?"

"I was born in Poland, but we moved to Brooklyn when I was six. My mother taught piano and didn't get out much, but her sister and brother-in-law were theater people. There was still a Yiddish theater back then. It's gone now, but it used to be a big thing. Did you ever hear of Molly Picon?"

"No, I'm afraid not."

"Jacob Adler?" Deena shook her head. "Keni Lipstin? David Kessler?"

"I went to school with a David Kessler, but I'm pretty sure

that's not the one you mean."

"Boris and Bessie Thomashefsky?"

"I'm afraid not."

"Michael Tilson Thomas?"

"Yes! I've heard of him. He conducts the San Francisco Symphony."

"He's their grandson. He made Thomas out of Thomashevsky. I guess the name was too big for him. Anyway, after the war, who spoke Yiddish anymore? The Yiddish theater was dead, so my aunt and uncle moved to LA and got work in films. A year later my mother and I moved out to be near them. I was so excited moving to Hollywood. As soon as I graduated high school I got a job at MGM."

"You were in films?"

"Not as an actress, I got work in the back office. I started out as a file clerk, then they let me do a little editing, a little writing - press releases, bios, that sort of thing."

"Did you get to meet any movie stars?"

"I met all the movie stars. I met them before they were stars. You know who I had a crush on? Paul Newman. I would have followed him anywhere. Of course, he was married, but what the hell. He was gorgeous, and he was Jewish. Well, he was half Jewish, but if you asked him, he'd say he was Jewish. I'm telling you, if he wasn't dead, I'd run off with him today." Raisa's face glowed with a smile so mischievous that Deena could imagine Paul Newman taking her up on the offer.

"So, who else did you meet? I bet you knew a lot of actors." Deena was having a wonderful time.

"I did, I met everyone, but I was only at MGM a couple of years. Revue Studios offered me a job and after that it was all television. My God, that was fun. We didn't know what the hell we were doing. We had to invent everything as we went along. At first, all we made were westerns. Everyone was a cowboy. Then it was detective shows and sitcoms. I never did game shows though. Game shows are an entirely different thing." Raisa was talking so fast and with such animation that the years fell away and Deena glimpsed the spirited young woman who had worked on those early programs.

"You ought to write a book. I bet you have a lot of stories to tell."

Raisa suddenly and inexplicably stopped smiling. "No, that's over. I'm done writing. I've written enough. There's too much paper in too many boxes already."

"You were a writer? Is that what you did out in Hollywood?"

"I did everything, but mostly I was a writer. Maybe if my husband hadn't been such a schmuck I would have been a housewife, stayed home ironing socks. Who knows? But he left and I had Lenny to support so I wrote. Writing's a good job if you're a woman with a kid. You can work from home. But that was later. In the beginning it was just fun."

So, yes, she'd been a writer. That explained the boxes full of old scripts, and plot outlines, the minutes from years of production meetings. But those handwritten pages had been different. Deena didn't want to confess to reading the crow story, but it had piqued her curiosity. "Where was your father? Did he move out to California with you?"

"My father died in Europe when I was seven or eight, so it was just me and my mother for a long time. She remarried when I was sixteen, but it was just me and my mother when we moved to Los Angeles.

"Your father died in Europe? Was he killed in the war?"

"He died in a concentration camp. He sent me and my mother to live with my aunt in America while he stayed to sell the business, but he didn't get out in time. Our whole village was rounded up and shipped to Auschwitz. My mother and I were eating strawberries and cream while they starved to death." Raisa sighed and shook her head.

"I'm so sorry."

"We learned later that someone tipped them off and the

whole village ran into the forest and hid for months before the Nazis found them, the whole village. Can you believe it?"

There was a long silence while Deena struggled to find a response. "It must have been awful for you."

"No, my father saved us from awful. I was sad, but I was sad eating strawberries and cream. My father and the rest of them, that was awful."

"Yes, of course, it's hard to imagine. I'm sorry that you lost your dad like that. You know, most of my grandmother's family died in the camps. I was named for her sister." Raisa turned and looked into Deena's eyes and nodded. There were no words. Raising her face to the trees she stared stone faced at something Deena couldn't see, an old memory, or an old crow. Deena stood up and stretched a crick out of her back. "You know, it's almost four o'clock and I could use a cup of coffee. What do you say we head back home?"

That night, after Raisa had gone to sleep, Deena crept into the back bedroom and retrieved the crow story from the box. She crawled into bed and switched on the bedside lamp and began to read.

Tschippe followed Gitel due east as the crow flies past a park, a university, a country club and street after street of mansions to a neighborhood of modest stucco houses with arched windows, oak doors and red tile roofs. Each had a patch of lawn, a few low shrubs and an ornamental tree. To Tschippe, they all looked identical, but Gitel identified her target and landed on a wooden fence behind a small yellow bungalow.

"Wait here," she ordered Tschippe. "This is what I want you to see."

An hour later Tschippe's patience was used up. "What are we waiting for? I thought we were going to the deli. You promised me corned beef and blintzes."

"Trust me. You won't be sorry."

"I'll be sorry if the rats make off with all the good bits before

we get there."

A moment later the back door opened and a girl of sixteen or seventeen emerged wearing sunglasses, blue jeans rolled up to her knees and a shirt tied in a high knot that revealed her midriff. A long red pony tail bounced behind her as she walked. "Look down there and tell me what you see." Gitel was riveted, staring down from her perch.

"I see a girl wearing pants and sunglasses with her pupik exposed for the world to see. Why do girls dress like that?"

"Look closer, tell me if she reminds you of anyone." The two birds followed her as she made her way down South Orange toward La Brea, but she never took off her sunglasses or looked in their direction. They gave up after she pushed open the door to a Rexall Pharmacy and disappeared from view.

Tschippe was annoyed, "Why are we wasting time following a girl? You promised me a good meal."

Gitel was unrepentant. "Trust me, if you saw her you'd know why." The sun was already past its zenith as the birds flew to Canter's Deli to feast on half-eaten pastrami sandwiches, apple strudel and pickled herring from the restaurant's dumpster.

An hour later, as two sated crows picked the last bits off the skeleton of a smoked trout, Tschippe was in a wonderful mood. "My God, I don't think I can fly. We may have to walk home. I haven't had a meal like that since we left New York, but we'd better get back before they send a search party after us."

"I want to take one more look at that girl." Gitel was still intent on her mission. "She might be on her way home by now."

Luck was with them and they caught sight of a figure in rolled up jeans and a knotted shirt carrying two large paper bags. Her sunglasses were pushed up on top of her head and she was smoking a cigarette.

"There, do you see her?" Gitel was excited. "I'll make her look up so you can get a better look." Gitel began cawing loudly and flying in circles above the girl's head.

It worked. Her face tipped upward and she broke into a delighted smile. "Well, hello there," she called up to Gitel. "Shalom aleichem."

"Shalom aleichem?" *Tschippe was startled.* "She's Jewish?"

"Apparently," *Gitel cawed back.* "Give her a good look and tell me who she looks like."

Tschippe positioned herself on a low branch several yards ahead of the girl and scrutinized her pale, freckled face, high cheekbones and wide-set eyes. "You're right, she looks exactly like Zalman's Belle, but she's too young. Belle would be what? Forty-one? Forty-two? This kid's a teen-ager."

"Look at her, Tschippe. Figure it out. Do the math."

Just then, the front door of the house opened and a woman stepped outside. The girl quickly dropped the cigarette and kicked it into the grass. "Raisa, gute du bist heym. Raisa, good, you're home." *She addressed the girl in Yiddish.* "I need you to help me in the kitchen. Did you get everything on the list?"

"My God, that's Belle. That's her." *Tschippe stared dumbfounded at the middle aged woman who was pushing a faded tangle of red hair back behind her ears, oblivious to the proximity of her old friends.*

"Well, that confirms it," *nodded Gitel.* "That's Belle, and the girl must be Zalman's little Raisa. "Baruch Hashem, It's a miracle."

Tschippe felt as though she might simply tip over and fall off her perch. "I can't believe it. Look at her with arms and legs and a face just like in Poland.... Belle," *she called out.* "Belle, it's Tschippe and Gitel." *The woman turned and stared briefly at the squawking crows before she let her daughter into the house and shut the door.*

Gitel and Tschippe were exhausted by the time they returned to the roost that evening, partly from the long flight and partly from arguing over the best way to break the news to Zalman. He had to know, but news like that could kill a crow. They'd have to be careful. An uncommon silence pervaded the small cluster of trees where the flock gathered for the night. They could hear the soft chirring of cypress leaves rustling in the breeze.

"Something's the matter," Tschippe whispered to her friend."

Gitel didn't say a word; she just nodded and flew off. Within minutes she was back with news. "It's Shaina, one of Faiga's chicks. She was taken by a hawk this afternoon."

Tschippe gasped, then let out a short distress call that resembled a sob. Gitel tried to calm her. "Your Calman and the others, they chased it off, but she's lost a lot of blood."

"Where's Faiga? I need to go to her."

"They've made a little nest for Shaina in the tall grass beneath the big oak. You go ahead, I have other work to do."

Shaina was asleep when Tschppe arrived. Faiga was leaning over her chick, making little cooing sounds and preening Shaina as though she were a nestling. A wet paper napkin was draped over the youngster's shoulder, giving her the appearance of a wounded soldier in a field hospital.

"I'm sorry, I've been gone all day. I just heard." Tschippe felt like a traitor, glutting herself while her niece battled for her life. "Is there anything I can do?"

"No, there's nothing." Faiga didn't take her eyes off her daughter. "Mendel's stopped the bleeding and he's using salt water to prevent infection." Faiga turned to Tschippe with indescribable pain in her eyes. "Say a prayer. That's all you can do."

As Tschippe bowed her head, she caught sight of Zalman. He was pacing again. Every time she saw him lately, he was pacing. He tried so hard to look after all of them. Maybe she could finally do something for him. Or would the news finish him off completely? Well, this was no time to talk. Her news would have to wait until morning.

Shaina was already awake and taking small bites of a blackberry from her mother's beak when Tschippe found them early the next day. The salt-soaked napkin was still draped across Shaina's shoulder, but she was standing. Thank God for the resilience of the young. After exchanging a few words with Faiga and giving Shaina a loving peck on her beak, Tschippe flew off to find Zalman. She needed to talk with him alone.

It was always easy to find Zalman at this hour of the morning. He was one of the few birds who still started the day praying Shakarait *with a few other old crows by the water's edge. She stood respectfully apart, waiting until Zalman finished saying* Kaddish *and sent the assembled off with good wishes for the day.*

"Zalman," Tschippe intercepted him before he could fly off. "I need to talk with you. It's very important."

"Is it Shaina?" It was a beautiful September morning. The clear, cloudless blue sky was mirrored in the blue water lapping gently against the shore.

"No, Shaina seems to be getting better. She even managed to eat a little breakfast this morning." Tschippe knew that she was about to change Zalman's life forever, but whether for better or worse remained to be seen.

"Then what is it? Are you alright?"

"I'm fine, Zalman. Let's go for a walk. There's something I need to tell you."

The large crow nodded his head as they hopped back toward the beach. There was a long silence punctuated only by the rhythmic sound of breaking waves while Tschippe struggled to find the right words. "It's a strange and unexpected life we're living. Do you ever think we'd be better off if we'd simply disappeared, just dispersed into the wind forever — or is there some grace in continuing to live, even in these unfamiliar bodies?"

"My, you're in a philosophical mood this morning. But, as long as you've asked, my answer is that as long as we're together I'm glad to be alive. I just thanked the Lord for a new day."

"We're certainly a resilient people. It seems we can adapt to anything. So I'm wondering, what would you do if you could see someone from your past, someone you loved, but they couldn't see you, or rather, when they looked at you, all they'd see is what you've become. You couldn't talk with them, you couldn't touch them, you couldn't explain what happened. Would you still want

to see this person?"

"Why are you asking such a question? Why worry about things that can never happen?" Zalman pretended to be annoyed, but he was clearly unnerved. "Really Tschippe, what's gotten into you?"

"Look at us, anything can happen. The impossible is possible. So, I'm asking, if Belle and Raisa lived just a few miles away, if they were still the people you remember, only a few years older, would you want to see them?"

Zalman's legs buckled under him. He hit the sand like a bird who's flown into a wall. "My God," he croaked. "Are Belle and Raisa really here? Both of them?"

"Yes, both of them. They're alive and well. Gitel found them by accident a few days ago. She didn't want to say anything until she was absolutely sure."

"So you're sure? It's really them?"

Tschippe nodded. "I saw them myself. Raisa's turned into a beauty, the spitting image of her mother."

"Give me a minute, I can hardly breathe. My head's spinning like an electric fan. Of course I want to see them. Can we go today? Can we go now?"

"We can go whenever you're ready, but let me get Gitel. She'll want to go too."

The trio soared south over the same trees and roads and fields that Tschippe and Gitel had passed the day before. But now Tschippe felt as though they were on a journey to the past, or perhaps to a completely reordered future. In a remarkably short time, Gitel landed on a telephone wire facing Belle's bungalow.

"This is it? This is where they live?" Zalman was hopping up and down on the wire. Gitel bobbed her head up and down confirming that this was the place. "So, what do we do now? When do we see them?"

"We wait, that's all we can do. We're crows," said Gitel.

"I can look in the windows. I'm going to fly onto the sill and take a look inside." Zalman couldn't wait another minute to see his wife and daughter. But as he flew from window to window all he saw was the interior of a comfortable house. There was a bookcase full of books, carpeting, a Chagall poster, a knitting basket on the sofa and a pipe on the coffee table. Since when did Belle smoke a pipe? He flew around to the back where another window revealed a tidy kitchen with a Formica table set with three dishes and three glasses. Three? Zalman blinked and counted the dishes again before flying back to Gitel and Tschippe who were waiting for his report.

"You've got the wrong place. This isn't Belle's house," Zalman said as soon as he alit beside them. "The three bears live in this one."

"Three? How do you know? Did you see them?" Tschippe was concerned. How many shocks could an old bird take in one day?

"The table's set for three and there's a man's pipe in the living room."

"Zalman, don't blame her. She was a widow with a young child. Be glad she's made a new life. You've been dead a long time." Tschippe tried to console him.

"That's not how I imagined it. I pictured Belle and Raisa by themselves the way I left them. I'm not thinking straight. It's been years."

Just then an aqua sedan with white tail fins pulled into the drive. The birds flew onto the roof of the house to watch as a woman, a teenage girl and a tall man with a pronounced bald spot the size of a small yarmulke carried several bags into the house.

"That's her, that's my Belle." Zalman forgot his distress in his rapture over seeing his wife. "She's so beautiful. She's hardly changed a bit. My God, just look at her." Zalman flew to the window so he could watch them unload the groceries. The man went into the living room, leaving the two women in the kitchen. Raisa sat at the table while her mother began slicing a large onion. Zalman pecked at the window with his bill and they both turned to look at him. Raisa smiled, amused by the bird, but Belle looked alarmed. She left the stove, came over and pulled the shade. Just like that they were gone. Zalman flew back to his two friends *waiting on the roof.*

"*Have you seen enough? Are you ready to head back?*" *Gitel asked.*

"*No, I'm going to roost here tonight. Maybe they'll come out again. My God, did you see them?*"

"*Come home with us now, you can come back tomorrow,*" *Tschippe coaxed, but Zalman wouldn't budge. He'd found his wife and daughter and he wasn't leaving them again.* "*Think about the flock,*" *she persisted.* "*They need you. What if that hawk comes back?*"

"*Oh, that hawk won't be back for awhile.*" *Gitel puffed up her feathers a bit, looking pleased with herself.*

"*Really? Why's that?*" *Tschippe couldn't imagine what Gitel had been up to.*

"*It seems her nest caught fire late this morning, burned to a crisp.*"

"*But how?*" *Zalman stared at her.* "*How could you — without matches, without fingers....*"

"*Crows are resourceful creatures Zalman. I hear they're attracted to bright, shiny things.*"

"*So?*"

"*So, some crows keep a cache of things in reserve: pieces of glass, buttons, pins, bits of broken mirrors. And if one of those crows happened to drop a mirror into a hawk's nest, and positioned it at just the right angle to catch the sun, how long would it take for a bunch of dry twigs to catch fire?*"

"*Gitel, you're a miracle. Let the flock know. They'll all sleep better, but I'm staying here tonight.*"

Zalman didn't peck at the windows again, but he followed the family from room to room until the sun went down, electric lights were clicked on and the drapes were drawn. He set up a vigil on top of the fence where he watched human shadows moving back and forth behind the curtains.

It was quite late and Zalman had been dozing on and off for some time when a window shade was pulled up and Raisa's face appeared at an upstairs window. A moment later the window was wide open and he could see her sitting by herself, blowing clouds of cigarette smoke out into the night. It was a risk, but Zalman was desperate for a closer look. He sailed toward the window and landed on the sill only inches from where his daughter sat in a pale pink nightgown, her red hair loose around her shoulders. He didn't say a word, terrified he'd frighten her away. Far from being frightened, she seemed delighted by his presence.

"Well, hello there Mr. Bird. Gute farnakht, good evening." *She smiled at him. "I guess you couldn't sleep either."*

Zalman hopped closer. Raisa inhaled her cigarette and exhaled it out the window. "So tell me, what's keeping you awake this evening? Feeling lonesome? Your girlfriend didn't go off to college did she? No, probably not. I guess it's pretty nice being a bird."

"I love you," Zalman cawed. "I've always loved you since the day you were born."

"Really? You don't say?" Raisa laughed, amused by the bird trying to talk. "Well, let me tell you something, you can't trust boys. They may say they're madly in love with you, but you'll be lucky if they send you a postcard once they move away."

"I would never have left you or your mother, never in a million years if the Nazis hadn't found us." Zalman knew she couldn't understand, but maybe she'd feel something, maybe something would get through. "Believe me," he went on, "The only comfort I had was knowing you were safe."

"You'd think, after two years, a girl would mean something to a boy. We told each other everything. We went everywhere together." Raisa leaned forward and let out a little puff of smoke. "Don't tell a soul, but I let him touch my breasts."

If a crow could blush, Zalman would have been a cardinal. His daughter, his beautiful daughter was a young woman with breasts. "It doesn't matter, my darling," he tried to reassure her. "Nothing matters as long as you're alive and well. You can't imagine what we endured, and I'm glad. They herded us onto trains like cattle and we rattled along in the dark, in the cold, without food or water for days. Your Uncle Isaac, may his memory be a blessing, died on that train. Do you remember him? He made you a rocking horse and held you in the saddle and rocked you back and forth while you laughed and laughed."

"My goodness you have a lot to say for yourself." Raisa made a series of four little bird-like whistles. Zalman responded with four short cawing sounds. Raisa repeated the whistles with the same result. *"Wow, you're one smart little bird. Well, I won't bore you with any more of my sad story, but you should know that I got a letter from Helen today. She's at the same college with Jeremy, and she says he's already dating someone else. Well, she can have him. Two years and he never brought me flowers, not once. My next boyfriend will bring me armloads of gardenias and he won't be such a liar."* Raisa looked past Zalman toward the sliver of moon rising in the east. Then she shrugged, and a wry, self mocking expression crossed her face. It was the same expression, the same resigned shrug, her mother used to make. *"Pathetic, isn't it?"*

"No, it's wonderful that there's still such innocence in the world. You have your whole life ahead of you. Thank God you were in America because our hopes were illusions. They took our clothes, our shoes, our dignity. They shot my brother, my sweet Isaac, for no reason. No one was too young, too smart, too beautiful for the fire. We all went up in smoke."

Raisa yawned and crushed her cigarette against the window sill. *"Gute nakht, Mr. Bird. Good night, it was nice talking with you, but I'd better get to bed."*

"No, wait," Zalman hopped forward until he was standing directly in front of his daughter. He could have flown inside her room. He could have hopped onto her shoulder, but he just stood there looking at her, and she stared back at him without moving a muscle, waiting to see what he'd do next.

"You need to hear what happened. We were fed to the furnace where we went up the chimney as cinders and dust, flakes of black ash floating into the sky. No one remembers what happened next, but we must have blown westward out to sea. How long were we

drifting on the wind? Who knows? But gradually, those black flakes began to flutter. They began to grow feathers and rise and fall in rhythm, moving with a purpose. We didn't recognize ourselves. Everything was different, yet we remembered who we were. We flapped our unfamiliar wings and kept on moving west until, at last, we landed in New York. Most of the birds wanted to stay there, but I got restless. Something told me to keep moving west. Do you understand what I'm telling you? Do you understand who I am and how much I love you?"

Raisa put out a finger and very slowly, very cautiously, touched her father on his head. "You're one brave little bird," she said. "But now it's time to go to sleep. Good night, sleep tight." She closed the window and disappeared from view.

But Zalman couldn't sleep. He'd seen his daughter. He'd spoken to her and she'd listened with an open heart. The next morning when Raisa woke up, she pulled back her curtain, astounded to find her window sill covered with mounds of small white flowers.

Chapter Thirteen

The next morning Deena and Raisa were sitting in the dining room finishing their breakfasts beneath Jeannette's oppressive chandelier. While the table had been covered with junk like a booth at a flea market, they'd eaten in the kitchen or at the coffee table. Now they buttered their toast and sipped their coffee at the massive table like an old couple in an English manor house waiting for the butler to offer them grilled tomatoes from a silver tray. It made them quiet and self-conscious as though the furniture was judging them with a critical eye.

Deena was collecting the dirty dishes when her phone pinged with a new text message. She hurriedly dropped the plates and cups into the sink and read, *I need 2 stay with u 4 a while. Please call asap & don't tell Dad!!!*

Deena slipped the phone back into her pocket and returned to the dining room. "Raisa, will you be OK by yourself while I make a phone call?"

When Raisa nodded Deena rushed back to the kitchen and punched Lauren's number into her phone.

"Are you alright? What's happened?"

Lauren's voice sounded strained and whiney. Had she been crying? "I'm OK, but I can't be in Boston anymore."

"Why not? What's the matter?"

Lauren ignored her mother's question. "I'm already on the bus. It left at six last night so I'll be in Sarasota at noon tomorrow. Can you pick me up at the bus station?"

"You're already on the bus? Oh my God, Lauren, you should have called me first. I don't have a car anymore and I don't really have a place for you. I'm living in someone else's house. It's not as though I have my own apartment. Couldn't you have moved in with a friend for a week or two?"

"No," Lauren wailed. "I had to leave the city. I can't be in Boston anymore."

"OK, OK, Sweetheart, calm down we'll figure this out." Deena was leaning against the sink staring out at Raisa's brick patio and trying to think of a solution. Her brain was sparking like a ten thousand watt oven plugged into a 15 amp circuit. "This is so sudden, Lauren. I need time to think. Maybe Mrs. Goetz would let you stay here, but it's really awkward. I just moved in myself. I hardly know her."

"Tell her Mrs. Goetz says it's OK. She can stay as long as she wants."

Deena pivoted around to see Raisa, cup in hand, leaning against the door jamb. She stared, nonplussed for barely a moment before throwing her arms around Raisa's narrow shoulders and giving her a grateful hug while chortling into the phone, "You can stay here. She says it's not a problem. This wonderful woman says she'll take you in." Deena gave Raisa another hug as she continued talking. "I don't have a car, but I'll meet you at the bus station. Do you have much luggage? What time did you say the bus arrives?" When Deena hung up, she stood wobbly and unfocused. Lauren was coming to stay with her. She was already on her way. The room was spinning so fast that she had to grab the counter to keep her balance.

"What happened? Her boyfriend throw her out?" Raisa seemed to assume this was the most likely scenario.

"I don't know. She didn't say." It was appalling how little she knew about her daughter's life in Boston.

"You'd better sit down. I'll get you some vodka. You

can put it in your orange juice." Deena stood immobilized by shock and joy while Raisa hobbled off to retrieve a bottle of *Smirnoff's* from the gilt-edged Louis Quinze buffet.

By eleven o'clock the next morning Deena was already camped out behind the small bus terminal on Porter Road. The station was only seven miles from Raisa's house, but city busses are unpredictable. They stop and start and take odd detours and Deena wasn't going to risk being late. A taxi was scheduled to meet them at 12:15. It was a splurge, but two days on a bus was more than enough for Lauren. The very thought of it made Deena queasy.

She went back inside the terminal to make sure the bus was on schedule. The arrival board read eleven fifty-five, the same as the previous three times she'd checked. She bought a cup of nasty tasting coffee and sat down on a green metal bench with a view of the drive. Two minutes later she stood back up and began pacing around the building, too excited to sit still. There were half a dozen people in the station, all quietly reading their papers or staring at their phones. No one else was bouncing around like a kid with attention deficit disorder. Deena walked out to the road and squinted into the distance.

When the bus finally pulled into the terminal three passengers stepped off, none of whom looked like the daughter she'd last seen fourteen months ago. Deena stared hard and swallowed as her brain recalibrated, trying to reconcile its memories of Lauren with the exhausted young woman with spikey blue hair and smeared mascara walking toward her. Deena lunged at her daughter pulling her into a great bear hug and, miracle of miracles, Lauren didn't jump back or push her away. "It's so good to see you. Is that all you brought? Where's your stuff? Oh, my goodness, Sweetheart, don't cry." Deena tore through her bag looking for tissue. "Whatever happened? What's got you into such a state?"

Lauren just shook her head. "Not now, Mom. I'll tell you

later. Right now I just need to find a bed. I haven't slept in two nights." A few minutes later the taxi driver was lifting Lauren's backpack into the trunk of his cab. Deena radiated joy as they sped toward Harbor Drive where a bed with fresh sheets was waiting for her daughter.

As soon as they arrived Lauren took a hot shower and went to sleep. Deena didn't see her again until she came downstairs for breakfast the following morning. Her hair was still blue, but her face was scrubbed clean of make-up. Even after a long night's sleep, she still looked haggard and edgy. Deena gave her a kiss. "Good morning, Sleeping Beauty."

"Good morning." Lauren gave Deena an unexpected hug. "What's for breakfast? I've been eating out of vending machines since Monday."

"There's pretty much anything you want. Name it and I'll see what I can do." Deena beamed at her daughter.

"Could you make French toast like we used to have on Sunday mornings? I dream about your French toast."

"No problem. Come into the kitchen and keep me company while I cook. How about some orange juice while you're waiting?" Lauren leaned against the stove as Deena cracked two eggs, whipped them with milk and sugar while a pat of butter sizzled in a blue enamel pan.

"My God that smells good. I'm absolutely famished. Is there any jam."

Deena smiled, "Look in the fridge. I think there's jam and marmalade. Mrs. Goetz said to take whatever you want." A minute later Lauren was seated at the dining room table too absorbed in her breakfast to say another word. Watching Lauren eat gave Deena a feeling of victory, as though she'd just won a gold medal for...what? Best recovery by errant mother, moral lapses division? She stopped smiling with the realization that she might not yet be forgiven. Some desperate situation had driven Lauren to her door and once circumstances changed, she might disappear again.

With the last bit of French toast swished through a final dab of jelly and washed down with cold milk, Lauren looked up and assessed the room. "This place looks like the lobby of an expensive hotel. Fancee."

"Shhh," Deena put a finger to her lips. "Mrs. Goetz is upstairs taking a nap and she could come down any minute. We owe her a lot and you'd better be nice to her. Anyway, these really aren't her things. The house was decorated by her ex daughter-in-law."

"Does she live here too?"

"No, it's a sad story. She inherited the house and all this stuff when her son died. It's been fifteen years and she's never really moved in." Deena leaned across the table and spoke in a hushed tone. "It's a terrible thing to lose a child. I guess she never got over it. You should have seen this place when I first got here. It was a mess."

"Are you her cleaning lady? I thought you were hired as some sort of private librarian, that you were organizing her papers."

"I'm doing that too. Raisa's an interesting woman. She was a writer back in the early days of television. You should hear her stories, and she's got boxes of TV memorabilia. We're just giving everything away, but I bet it's worth a fortune."

"It probably is, people throw away a lot of valuable stuff. You wouldn't believe what you can find in people's trash."

"I see, and you know this how?" Something told Deena this was more than a random observation about the economy of waste.

Lauren bit her lip as though she'd already said too much. Deena kept her own face impassive, hoping to hear more. Finally, Lauren sighed and went on. "Have you ever heard of freegans?"

"No, what are they?" Deena had no idea.

"Freegans are people who have withdrawn from the consumer culture. They believe that it doesn't make sense for

some people to have way too much while other people are
starving, so they liberate food and other consumer goods for
the benefit of anyone who needs them."

"I see." Deena spoke very slowly, careful not to say anything that might offend her daughter and send her packing.
"Do you know any freegans personally?"

"There are tons of freegans in Boston. It's a whole movement. It started out being mostly about protesting food waste
by liberating perfectly clean, healthy food from grocery store
dumpsters, but then it kind of expanded to include other stuff.
Capitalist culture sucks the blood out of people. I mean, look
what happened to you and Dad. There's something warped
about spending your life earning more and more money so
you can buy more and more things you don't even need."

"When did you become so passionate about economics?"
Careful Deena, tread softly, she cautioned herself. "It almost
sounds as though you might be a freegan yourself."

"I *was*, but now I don't know what I am. I'm still opposed to
wage slavery and wasteful packaging and exploiting the earth,
but I'm done with the movement. Those people completely
fucked me over. Sorry Mom. They just aren't who I thought
they were. I mean, most of them are OK, but others are nuts
and a few are downright dangerous."

"What happened? Why did you leave Boston in such a
mad rush?" The sound of a metal spoon banging on a metal
pot interrupted their conversation. "Damn, that's Mrs. Goetz.
She needs me for something, but we're not done talking. This
isn't the end of our conversation."

Lauren stood up and began clearing the table. "Would you
thank her for me? Tell her I'm really grateful that she's letting
me stay here."

Raisa was getting around much better lately, but she still
needed help maneuvering the stairs. Deena found her standing in the hallway outside her bedroom banging on the saucepan.
"This is ridiculous. I can't get into my own living room with-

out help. Don't get old, it's humiliating."

Deena took the pot from Raisa and held it in her left hand while offering the exasperated old woman her right arm for support. "You sprained your ankle. It could have happened to anyone. You'll be sprinting up and down these stairs again in no time."

Raisa gave Deena a skeptical look. "Is she up? That kid must have been in some sorry state to sleep like that."

"Two days on a bus will do that to you, plus I think she suffered some sort of trauma. I still don't know why she's here, but she did say to thank you. We're both so grateful for your generosity."

"I'm not generous, I'm lonesome. Well, maybe I'm a little generous," she conceded, followed by a quick, self-deprecating smile. "So, let's take a look at my new boarder." As soon as they reached the bottom step Raisa shook herself free of Deena's grasp and pulled herself up to her full five feet, clearly determined to make a dignified entrance.

Lauren came running from the kitchen holding a wet sponge. "Hello, I'm Lauren. Thank you so much for letting me stay here." She started to put out her hand then pulled it back realizing it was wet and soapy. "Sorry, I was just washing up. I'll be right back."

Raisa lowered herself onto the sofa. "She seems like a nice girl. I like the blue hair."

"She *is* a nice girl, but she's changed. Her hair's the least of it."

"How old is she? Eighteen? Nineteen?"

"She just turned twenty. Honestly, she used to be so clean cut, so…"

"So what? Let her live a little. Don't be such a tight ass. Dye your hair purple."

They were both laughing as Lauren came bounding back into the room. "What's so funny? What did I miss?"

"Mrs. Goetz was just saying that you seemed like a lovely

young lady."

"Really? Well, thank you." Lauren started to throw herself into one of the Louis Quinze chairs then caught herself. "I'm sorry, is it OK if I sit here?" Lauren was on her best behavior.

"Sit, relax. you don't have to ask. Make yourself at home." Lauren took a seat, sitting primly with her knees together as though she were wearing a tea dress and not a pair of skuzzy jeans. "So tell me a little about yourself," Raisa continued. "How was life in Boston?"

Deena echoed, "Yes, how *was* your life in Boston? We'd both like to know."

Lauren met Deena's eye, hesitated a moment then said, "Sure, why not? You may as well know."

"So, tell us. We're listening." Raisa smiled encouragingly.

"When I went back to Boston I wasn't a student anymore so I couldn't stay in my old dormitory, but these new friends, people I met through the theater, told me not to worry. They said I could stay with them and I wouldn't even have to pay rent. They were all sharing a big, old house and I could stay for free. So that sounded great, right?" She turned and looked at her mother who nodded noncommittally.

"Well, the reason it was free was because no one exactly owned it. It was what you call a zombie house. The bank starts to foreclose on a property so the owners move out, but then the bank doesn't want the house because then they'd have to pay taxes and maintain it, and they don't really give a damn about the house or the community. Bottom line, no one claims the property and a perfectly good house sits boarded up and rotting for years while tons of people who need houses are out on the street. That's crazy, right?"

"Why don't they just sell it and get their money out?" Raisa was incredulous.

"I'm not sure," Lauren went on. "I think the houses need so much work that the banks would lose money if they fixed them up enough to sell. Something like that. I don't get it either."

"So, you and your friends moved into an empty house and just lived there without paying rent. That's called squatting. You could have been arrested." It was suddenly clear why Lauren hadn't been willing to share her address these past months. A light went on in Deena's brain. "So that's why Matthew Bacon called you Mimi. You were squatting with a bunch of starving artists like in *Rent*. That's it, isn't it?"

"Yeah, I guess so." Lauren kicked off her shoes obviously feeling much more at home. "Anyway, I move into this house and they give me a room in the basement. It's really small. It used to be a locker room or a pantry, but there's room for a mattress and most of my stuff and I even have these built in shelves so I'm happy."

"What did you do for electricity? Did you have light?" Deena felt a wave of nausea clenching her stomach.

"We had lights for a while, until the electric company figured out no one was paying the utility bill. After that, we used big lantern style flashlights, but we tried not to use them too much because lights would tip off the cops and we didn't want to get busted."

"Um-hmm," Deena's lips were pressed into a hard, tight line so no words could escape.

"I know it sounds bad, but we were actually pretty comfortable most of the time. Some furniture had been left in the house and we rescued a sofa and chairs from someone's trash. I had a part-time job at a coffee shop, but we hardly ever used money because there was so much free stuff around. I mean we couldn't even begin to eat all the good food the grocery stores and restaurants were throwing away."

"Sounds great."

"Mom, you don't have to be sarcastic. It *was* great. It was like stepping right out of the whole capitalist, consumer, mass culture world. It wasn't just that stuff was free. We were free. I mean, if you don't buy into the whole economy of excess and waste you can live on almost nothing. We were free to do whatever we wanted: wander around the city, play music, write poetry. There was one girl who made amazing sculptures out of trash. She'd glue random stuff together: egg cartons, wires, soup cans, aluminum pie plates and turn them into these gorgeous animals. She called them Litter Critters and sold them on the street. People loved them."

Deena couldn't bite her tongue any longer. "So why are you here? What made you leave this utopia?"

"Well," Lauren looked out the window for such a long time that Deena was afraid she wasn't going to tell her story, but she eventually closed her eyes and began. "New people moved in. They were into heavy drugs and the place began to change. There was one guy named Squirrel — that's not his real name, but that's what we called him. He was mostly quiet and didn't bother anyone, especially if he was high. In fact, he could be funny if you caught him in the right mood, and he was smart. He went to Tufts before he got involved with heroin. I liked him, but he had scary friends. His dealer started hanging out at the house and then a couple of his partners, then a whole parade of junkies. They started selling out of the house and we were too afraid to throw them out. They had swastikas and lightning bolts tattooed on their arms, and weird dots and letters tattooed on their faces. Whenever they came over we'd leave the house, or barricade ourselves in our rooms until they left. I would have moved, but Boston's really expensive and I didn't have much money."

"My God Lauren, you should have come home." Lauren opened her eyes and stared at her mother. She didn't say, *what home?* But Deena got the message.

"Anyway, a few days ago I was home alone when Squirrel showed up with two of these druggie friends, so I went down to my room and read for a while. When I went back upstairs the living room was empty except for Squirrel who was passed out on the sofa. His breathing wasn't normal, kind of shallow and ragged. I tried to wake him up, but he was out cold. His skin was clammy, his lips were blue, and I thought, my God, he's OD'd. He's dying right here in front of me."

"Oh Lauren," This was beginning to sound like Deena's worst nightmare.

"I know the dealers are still in the house because I can hear them arguing in one of the upstairs bedrooms. I started screaming, 'Squirrel's dying, he's OD'd,' but they don't move. They hear me, but they're just annoyed like I'm bothering them. They yell back, 'Calm down, he'll sleep it off.' I'm shaking so hard I can hardly walk or talk or think straight. At this point, I'm not sure Squirrel's even breathing, so I dial 911. Then I told the guys upstairs that I called an ambulance. That got their attention. They came charging down the stairs and one of them ripped the phone from my hand and shouted, 'No one's calling anyone. What do you want, a bunch of cops all over the place?' But it was too late. I'd already called. About a minute later there are sirens and flashing lights and those jerks took off running. They still had my phone, but I didn't care. I was just glad they were gone."

"What about the boy? Did they save him?" Raisa was leaning forward on the edge of the sofa.

"Yeah, they did. The EMTs said he'd have been dead in another ten minutes if I hadn't called, so I'm glad I did, even if I can't go back to Boston."

"Why can't you go back to Boston?" Deena felt faint, stunned by the story.

"Because it gets worse. When my housemates got home and I told them what happened they got mad at me because now the authorities knew we were squatting and we'd have to move. Then the police came by and interrogated me, which was awful. I told them what I knew, I gave them descriptions, but I didn't know their names or where they lived. I thought they were going to arrest me."

"Oh my God," Deena looked down at her lap. Her hands

were trembling.

"I'm not done. The next night, one of the dealers, the one who grabbed my phone, was waiting for me when I got home from work. He said that if I told the police any of their names, where they hung out, what they looked like, anything, I was dead meat. I told him I didn't even know their names, but he didn't seem to believe me any more than the cops did. He gave me my phone back, but he said I'd better watch my back; if anyone got arrested they'd be coming after me." Lauren's voice dropped to a whisper. "He said they'd mess me up so bad you wouldn't be able to identify the body. Then he picked up his T-shirt so I could see the gun stuffed in his waistband. As soon as he left, I packed up my stuff and caught the first bus to Sarasota. Now you know everything."

Deena couldn't speak. How had her sweet daughter who'd been protected and loved, who'd eaten her vegetables and practiced her flute, wound up in that hell hole? Deena's lower lip began to quiver uncontrollably. She walked into the kitchen to get a glass of water and regain her composure.

When she returned, Raisa was holding Lauren's hand and talking to her in great earnestness. "You did the right thing calling that ambulance. You saved a boy's life. In Israel they have an award for people who saved Jews during the Holocaust. It says, 'He who saves a single life saves the universe.'"

Lauren didn't say anything, but she was listening.

"But now you have to save another life. You have to save Lauren. Find new friends who do nice things. What do you want with drug addicts and *meshugganers*?"

The water in Deena's glass began to tremble. Her whole body was vibrating. She walked over to Raisa and kissed her on the cheek. "Did you know you're a wonderful woman?"

"I know that my crows need their breakfast." She tried to stand, but collapsed back down into her seat. "Oy, who made this couch so low? Someone, help me up." Lauren and Deena both helped Raisa to her feet. Once she had regained her balance Raisa took Lauren's hand. "Now, you come with me. I want to introduce you to my friends."

Chapter Fourteen

Deena and Raisa were sitting in the dining room after breakfast with the newspaper spread out between them. Raisa was working on the crossword puzzle while Deena finished her second cup of coffee and scanned the headlines. She suddenly put down her cup. "Raisa, listen to this. A drug bust in Boston has led to the arrest of a gang leader and several of his followers. The police took fifty thousand dollars' worth of heroin from a vacant house known to attract junkies and squatters."

Raisa put down her pencil. "You'd better tell Lauren."

"Damn, I hope that's not the same house. How did she ever get mixed up with such people?"

"Don't worry too much, she's safe now. No one knows she's here. Just be grateful she had the good sense to get out." Deena's phone started to croak, interrupting their conversation.

Deena recognized the number. It was the Forrest Gallery. "Mrs. Berman, this is Charles Forrest calling about the paintings you left with us a couple weeks ago. We've located some comparables in our database, mostly west coast auction houses, and I think you're going to like what I have to say. Why don't you stop by some time next week so we can talk, and bring the other paintings with you. I'd like to take a look at those as well."

"I'm not sure how many of the paintings I can bring in. I

don't have a car, but I'd love to hear what you have to say."

Raisa chimed in, "Tell him you'll bring everything. We're getting a car."

"Mr. Forrest, can you hold on just a minute?" Deena muted the phone and turned to Raisa. "When did you decide to get a car?"

"Just now. I'm tired of walking and taking the bus. I always had a car until my eyes got bad. You can be my driver as well as my archivist. I'll give you a raise; how's that?"

Deena grinned and unmuted the phone. "Mr. Forrest, would Thursday of next week be good for you? I'll bring in the entire collection."

The following Thursday Deena was sitting at the wheel of a bright red Toyota Camry with all the bells and whistles. Lauren was in the passenger seat and they were in a jubilant mood. They parked in front of the shop, unloaded several large canvases, and pushed through the gallery's heavy doors. Deena paused just inside the entrance and looked around in surprise. The place was completely transformed. The bold abstracts in primary colors had been replaced by western landscapes painted in muted shades of gray and blue, yellow, pink and purple. These were paintings of scenes she recognized, the flat topped mesas and open desert she remembered from her childhood. A wave of nostalgia washed over her as the images brought back memories long suppressed. The past was stalking her, intruding everywhere she went. Viewing those familiar landscapes with Lauren close beside her felt dangerous, as though the stone wall she'd built around her childhood had dissolved into the thinnest membrane and she might fall through at any moment. Deena turned her head away from the paintings, but there was no escape. A Navajo horsehair bowl loomed directly in her line of vision.

She walked up to the piece and touched it. She knew how it was made, how the clay had been mined, washed, dried, ground and sifted, how the potter had kneaded the clay like bread, rolling it into smooth coils that were shaped and pinched into bowls and urns. The raw pots were dried, burnished and fired, then decorated with strands of horsehair as they emerged from the kiln. Traditional potting was long, hard, labor-intensive work. Maybe the Navajo didn't bother with all that anymore. Maybe they'd started buying their clay from art supply companies like everyone else. Deena read the label and then read it again: *Robert Santana, (1944 -) Kewa Pueblo Pictorial Olla $3,400.* Thirty-four hundred dollars? Incredible. The Kewa Pueblo was just a few miles south of where she grew up. Pots like this had gone begging at the Indian Market when she was a kid. Her mother who was a *bilagaana,* a white woman, couldn't sell at the Indian Market, but her pots were just as good. And they'd sold for a fraction of the price.

"Mom," Lauren touched Deena's arm. "Mom, this man wants to talk with you."

"Oh, I'm sorry. My mind seems to have wandered off for a minute. I was just enjoying your new exhibit."

"Thank you, it opened last week. We call the collection *Vision Quests: Contemporary Native American Art of the Southwest.* It will be here through November; then we've got an extraordinary group of textile artists coming in for the holidays. We haven't decided on our spring show yet, but we have an idea, and that's why I wanted to talk with you. Come over here and take a seat. Just put those paintings over here." He pointed to a space along one wall.

Deena's heart began to flutter. Their spring show? This was starting to sound like very good news indeed. Once they were all seated at the large center table, he called to his assistant. "Jean, would you mind bringing us some coffee."

Deena's excitement rose as Mr. Forrest began to court them as though they were important customers. What was going on here?

"Well, I have some good news and some better news. Which would you like first?"

"The good news," Lauren broke in as she helped herself to one of the cookies that had arrived with the coffee.

"Well, the good news is that Dorothy Kanter has been enjoying a bit of a resurgence lately. It seems she may be the only female member of the California Hard Edge School. Two of her pieces sold between ten and twenty thousand dollars in Santa Monica last year. Of course they were bigger than these paintings." He indicated the artwork stacked against the wall. "Unless you have larger canvases at home." He paused and looked at Deena hopefully. She shook her head *no* so he went on. "In any case, your work certainly has value. However, what intrigues us is the depth of your collection. How many pieces do you have all together?"

"There are six paintings, three drawings and ten or twelve small prints. I brought you everything we could safely fit in the car."

"Well, I'd like to see the rest. As I said, mid-century modern is really hot right now and Sarasota has always epitomized the style. Have you ever heard of Paul Rudolph? No? Well, he's a major figure in mid-century modern architecture. There are examples of his work all over the city."

Deena nodded intently, although she'd never heard of Paul Rudolph.

"We'd like to make mid-century modern the theme of our spring show and to include Dorothy Kanter as one of our featured artists. Wait, before you say anything, let me explain how this works." Deena leaned forward in her seat, listening intently. "You would give us your Kanter pieces on consignment, then Jean would do a thorough appraisal at our expense and determine a fair value. We'd feature your pieces in the spring show and, if they sell, you'd get fifty percent of the purchase price. Only two or three paintings would actually be put on display but all your pieces would be in the catalog. How does that sound?"

"It sounds wonderful. Can you tell me what you think

they're worth?"

"We haven't had a chance to look at the new work you brought in, and I know you still have a few pieces at home, so I can't give you a hard number, but perhaps a hundred thousand all together. I expect they'll do very well. I wouldn't be making you this offer if I didn't."

"Well yes, of course, that would be wonderful. I wouldn't have any idea how to sell these things on my own."

Mr. Forrest looked at her amused. "You couldn't sell them on your own, at least not for the prices we can command. Let's just say the medium is the message. The simple fact that they'll be included in one of our shows and hung in our gallery makes them more valuable."

"Then, thank you again. A setting like this really does show artwork off to its best advantage." Deena stood up and surveyed the gallery. "For example, I was admiring that Navajo pot over there. When I was a little girl I lived outside Santa Fe and my mother made pieces very similar to that one, but they weren't that impressive on a card table at a flea market." She pointed toward the large ceramic bowl by Robert Santana. "That bowl is gorgeous, but it would have sold for almost nothing when I was a kid."

"Your mother was Navajo?"

"No," Deena smiled. *Why was she telling them this, talking about things she'd always kept a secret?* But she couldn't stop herself, a dam had cracked and stories were seeping through. "She was Jewish, but she met a Navajo woman named Harri Shonto at the Indian Market one summer. Harri had grown up in northern Arizona, in an area where they still made traditional pottery, and my mother absolutely fell in love with her work. She begged Harri to take her on as a student but Harri refused. I mean my mom was just a hippie ..." Deena stopped herself. She was saying too much. "Well, she wasn't Navajo and Harri probably thought she wasn't serious, but my mother kept after her for a full year. Anyway, Harri and my mother eventually became good friends and my mother learned to make traditional pottery, except that she absolutely wasn't allowed to use traditional Navajo designs. Harri would have killed her if she'd done that."

Lauren was staring at Deena, dumbstruck. "I never knew Grandma made pottery. In fact, I don't know much of anything about her."

"Lauren, we'll talk later. Right now I want to find out how to get our paintings into Mr. Forrest's spring show."

Mr. Forrest beamed, "Excellent. There's a contract to sign and then that's about it. We'll insure the pieces while they're with us. If you give Jean your address, we'll send our van to pick up the remaining pieces. Any other questions?"

Deena didn't have any more questions, but Lauren certainly did. She could hardly wait until they were out the door to begin interrogating her mother. "Grandma studied pottery with a Navajo artist? How come you never told us that? She sounds fantastic. Why didn't you talk about her? Why didn't you show us photos?"

Deena stopped walking and turned away from her daughter pretending to examine a display of summer dresses in a shop window. She felt as though she were on the rim of a precipice, and the wrong word would send her over the edge. Unable to face Lauren, she continued studying the bright, shapeless florals. "I have some photos of my mother. I told you about them. They're in storage now, but you can see them whenever you want. There's no big secret."

"But those are baby pictures and old school photographs. Aren't there any pictures of Grandma after you were born?" Lauren paused, struck by a sudden thought. "Did she have a wedding album? Are there pictures of her and Grandpa at their wedding?"

"I think they eloped. They probably got married by a Justice of the Peace and never had a real wedding." Deena wasn't sure how long she could keep this up. She wasn't even sure why she was continuing to lie. "I think they didn't want to spend money on a big wedding because..." She couldn't finish the sentence. She sputtered and stammered and spit but couldn't produce another coherent word. The lies would no longer come out of her mouth. Deena closed her eyes, took a deep breath and deliberately stepped off the precipice. "Lauren, nothing I just said was true. Let's find a place to talk. There's a lot I have to tell you."

Lauren followed Deena across the street and down the block to the same Starbucks where she'd found refuge after sleeping in the park. She'd felt absolutely naked and exposed that morning, but it turned out there were still more layers to uncover. What if she peeled away all the lies and there was nothing at her core? A wave of nausea roiled Deena's gut but she swallowed hard and didn't turn back. There was an empty table in the corner and they sat down without ordering.

"Lauren, I haven't been open with you about your grandmother or about me for that matter. Your grandmother never married my father, and she wasn't a teacher. In fact, she never went to college. She was an artist and a hippy and a lesbian. She ran away from home and got pregnant by a guy she hardly knew the summer after graduating from high school. Basically, when I was born, she was just a kid, younger than you, living in New Mexico in a sort of commune."

Lauren pushed a strand of blue hair off her forehead. "Why did she run away from home?"

"She and Bubbe were like oil and water. Bubbe was very judgemental and your grandmother was a free spirit. For example, as much as Bubbe loved you, she would have hated your blue hair, and she'd probably have found some Jewish law prohibiting blue hair. So then, God would be on her side and there'd be no way to change her mind."

"She wasn't that inflexible."

Deena shook her head. "You're wrong. She *was* that inflexible and my mother made her crazy. At the beginning,

Bubbe didn't know my mother was a lesbian; but she knew her daughter was jumping into the whole hippy thing head first: sex, drugs and rock and roll. This was back in 1968. Parents were disowning their kids for growing their hair too long. I can't imagine what went on under that roof. There must have been fireworks every night. Anyway, as soon as your grandmother finished high school she threw some things into a backpack and left for San Francisco. She hitchhiked out there all by herself. Can you imagine?"

"No." Deena and Lauren looked at one another, each trying to picture a sheltered girl from a religious family climbing into the cab of a stranger's truck and heading west.

"Once she got to San Francisco she met a guy named Dante. They spent a lot of time together, had a little summer fling, but at the end of August he kissed her good-bye and went back to his real life. Grandma was pregnant by then but she never told him, at least that's what she told me."

Lauren was transfixed. "Well, that's more than you told me." Deena watched as her daughter's inner landscape shifted, as she struggled to reinvent her sense of self. This wasn't the legacy Deena had intended to pass on.

"Lauren, I don't even know if Dante was his real name." Deena thought a moment, then remembered a nugget of information she could offer up. "He had dark curly hair and went to Berkley and played the guitar. That's everything I know about him."

"So, what did Grandma do?"

"She called her mother and said she wanted to come home. Bubbe said great, come home. I'll take care of everything. All you have to do is study hard, dress modestly, and behave like a good orthodox Jewish girl. We'll tell people you're divorced. It wasn't a terrible offer, but my mother balked. She didn't have a clue where she'd live or how she'd support herself and a baby, but she turned Bubbe down cold." Deena shook her head. "Probably, not a smart move, but she was an impulsive kid."

"Wow, she was a wild child. You think I'm a free spirit, but I'm not that brave. I'd probably have come home."

Deena reached across the table and took Lauren's hand. "A couple of days later, she went to a big outdoor concert in Golden Gate Park and happened to sit next to a young woman who was nursing a baby. They started talking about babies and how hard it is to raise a kid on your own. The woman's name was Casey, and it turned out that she was living by herself in an old house outside Santa Fe. She said that if my mother wanted to hitchhike back to New Mexico with her, she could have a room in her house and they could help each other out. A big guy with a beard overheard them and he said, 'Hey, I have a van. I'll drive you both to New Mexico if I can stay too.' So they all got into his van and drove off. It sounds crazy, it was crazy, but that's the story."

"That's insane." Lauren was smiling now. She was loving this improbable tale. Deena had always imagined she'd be horrified, traumatized to learn the truth about her grandmother, but she only seemed amused.

"The guy's name was Buddha. He was a musician who spent a lot of time on the road, but he always came back to Santa Fe. Casey and my mom eventually fell in love and became partners and the three of them lived together for years. The place was just an old farmhouse on a couple of acres Casey had inherited when her parents were killed in a car accident, but they called it New Moon Commune. That's where I was born."

"New Moon Commune, I like that. I can't believe you never told me all this before."

"I've never told anyone before, not even your father."

"Why? I don't understand. Is it because Grandma was a lesbian?"

"No, that isn't it, although being gay was a much bigger deal at the time. Do you want to hear more? Maybe you'll understand then."

"Sure, I'm listening."

"Originally, New Moon was just a normal, middle class house, but by the time I was born it had regressed back into the nineteenth century. We used a hand pump for water. There were no electric lights, no working toilets, no refrigerator."

"I can't picture you living like that."

"I know, but that's how I grew up. My name wasn't Deena then. They called me Harmony. Bubbe named me Deena after I moved back to Cleveland, but I was Harmony all the time I lived in New Mexico. When I was little I was happy enough, but once I started school and saw how the other kids lived, I hated everything about New Moon. I hated my mother, I hated Casey, I hated Buddha, I hated the house. The only people I didn't hate were Paz and Mr. and Mrs. Rios, a Mexican couple who lived on the property just behind us. They were sort of the neighborhood grownups. I don't know what my life would have been like without them."

"Who was Paz?"

"He was Casey's son, and he was sort of like my brother."

"And you've never told us about him?" Lauren shook her head in disbelief. "Where are all these people? What happened to Grandma? Is she really dead?"

"I honestly don't know. I was fourteen years old when I left." Deena's throat went dry and she began to cough. She coughed until her eyes teared, but she couldn't stop. Lauren jumped up and came back with a cup of coffee. Deena took a sip and felt her throat relax. She took another sip and wiped her eyes before going on. "Here's what happened. Bubbe flew out to visit us a couple of times when I was little. Can you imagine Bubbe on a hippie commune? Well, it didn't take her long to figure out what was up with my mom and Casey and the whole hippie drug scene. It disgusted her so much that she tried to have my mother declared unfit so she could get legal custody of me. She lost the case, but there was always bad blood between your grandmother and Bubbe after that, and she never visited again. I didn't even remember what she looked like, but she sent me school clothes every August and a new coat every winter. I called her my fairy grandmother and imagined that she lived in a beautiful house that had been ripped right out of a department store catalog, which was my idea of heaven at the time. I'd write back telling her how miserable I was and how I wished I could live in a normal house. To be honest, New Moon had improved a lot by then. My mom and Casey were both working and the utilities had been turned back on, but then Buddha died of a drug overdose and ..."

"My God, that's awful. Was it heroine?"

Deena nodded, "Yeah, that's what they told us. He must have gotten involved with it on the road because New Mooners pretty much stuck to pot."

Lauren reached across the table and took Deena's hand. "Were you close to him?"

"I'd grown up with him my whole life. He wasn't exactly a father figure, but yeah, we were close and I was totally devastated when he died. Devastated and scared.

"Maybe I told Bubbe what had happened. I don't really remember, but that winter a Chanukah present arrived all done up in blue paper and silver ribbons. When I opened the box I found a new coat with a one-way ticket to Cleveland and two hundred dollar bills stuffed inside the pocket.

"I'd never been on an airplane and I hadn't seen Bubbe since I was four years old, but this was my chance. I filled my gym bag full of clothes and carried it onto the school bus. Then, as soon as I got to school, I called a taxi from the payphone in the parking lot and told the driver to take me to the Albuquerque Airport. It was that simple. Bubbe picked me up in Cleveland and an hour later I had my own room with a four poster bed with a floral spread and matching curtains."

"But what about your mother? Didn't she come after you?"

"Bubbe called her right away and told her where I was, figuring if she held me hostage my mom would leave Casey and come back to Cleveland. Instead, my mother told her where to shove it. Bubbe just turned purple and hung up. My mother called right back and told me to get my ass on the next plane home and that if Bubbe didn't pay for the ticket she'd call the cops and have her arrested for kidnapping."

"Go Grandma."

"But I wouldn't leave. I told her I was never going back, that I hated New Moon, that all I wanted was a chance to live a normal life with normal people. I might have called them a bunch of freaks."

"Whoa, you said *that* to your mother? That was harsh."

"Yeah. Two thousand miles can make you pretty brave. Anyway, I must have knocked the wind out of her because there was this long silence. Casey took the phone and tried talking with me but I wouldn't listen to her either. Finally, my mom came back on the line and asked if I understood what I was doing and I said that I did, absolutely, one hundred percent." Deena looked away from Lauren. "Then my mother said, 'OK, live your own life. Who the hell am I to tell you what to do?' Then she said, 'Good-bye Harmony. Call if you ever change your mind.' We hung up, and no one ever called me Harmony again." Deena's voice had become softer and softer as she told the story, until she wasn't sure if she'd even uttered the last sentence out loud or if it was just a thought reverberating inside her head.

"She never called again? She just let you go? My God, you were only fourteen."

"She didn't call me again, but she called my grandmother. There was a terrible, screaming argument on the phone that night. Bubbe still wanted my mother to move back to Cleveland and gave her an ultimatum, but it didn't matter; my mother refused to leave Casey and New Moon. She chose them over me and I guess I've always hated her for that. I'd run away, but I've always felt as though she'd abandoned *me*. Anyway, at the end of that call Bubbe yanked the phone from the wall and threw it across the floor, ripped the collar of her blouse with both hands and cried, 'Your mother's dead. I no longer have a daughter.' I can still see the buttons popping and bouncing on the carpet."

"You poor thing."

"Grandma called the rabbi and we sat Shiva. Friends paid condolence calls. It was worse than if she'd really died. It felt as though we'd killed her. It was awful."

"Does Dad know about any of this?"

Deena shook her head. "It's taken thirty-four years Lauren. I'm forty-eight years old and you're the first person I've ever told."

"Are you all right?" Lauren stood up and moved around the table so she could put her arms around her mother's neck. "I can't believe you held this in so long. Why didn't you tell anyone? Why was it such a big secret?"

"I know sitting Shiva was just symbolic, but it really felt as though I'd really murdered my own mother. I was ashamed. I guess that's it. I was ashamed of New Moon, ashamed of how Buddha died, ashamed of myself and ashamed that my mother had abandoned me."

"What were their names? You've never told me their names."

"You know your grandmother's legal name, Leah Marcus, but people in Santa Fe used to call her Rain. Casey's last name was DaSilva, Paz and Casey DaSilva. I can't tell you Buddha's real name. He was always just Buddha like my father was just Dante. I wonder what's become of them. It's been such a long time."

"I'm going to tell Dad and Elliot what you just told me. They deserve to know. Leah Marcus is Elliot's grandmother too."

"Sure, tell everyone. I'm done with secrets.... No, don't

tell your father. Let me do that. I need to tell him myself."

Two days had passed since Deena's confession to her daughter. She hadn't quite recovered although Lauren hadn't mentioned it again. She was sitting in the living room, chewing on
her thumbnail and staring out the window at late afternoon
shadows playing along the side of the neighbor's garage when
Lauren breezed in carrying a weather beaten guitar case. Her
cheeriness was jarring.

"You won't believe what I found." She gave Deena a quick
hug, then plopped down beside her on the sofa.

Deena responded with a weak smile. "I'm guessing it's a
guitar."

Lauren reached into the case. "Bingo!" She pulled out the
instrument with a flourish and held it out for Deena to admire.
"A Fender Stratocaster in mint condition. Even used ones sell
for five hundred dollars. Guess how much this one cost?"

"I have no idea." It looked like a nice instrument, shiny
with lots of metal doodads.

"Twenty-five dollars. They wanted thirty, but I showed
them where some of the strings were broken, so they let me
have it for twenty-five. Is that unbelievable? I bought new
strings for ten bucks and the guy at the music shop put them
on for free."

"Does it work?" Deena knew nothing about guitars. Everyone at New Moon had played with more or less skill, but
she'd obstinately refused to learn even the basic chords Buddha tried to teach her.

"You bet it works, but it really needs an amp. The music
store sells this exact same guitar for six hundred dollars. Once
I get it cleaned up this thing's going to be amazing."

"I don't remember you having an interest in guitars. Do
you even know how to play?"

"No, but I've fooled around with a friend's, and he thought
I was a natural. Honestly, he'd die if he saw this. All he has

is a cheapo no-name instrument that Santa brought him when he was twelve. This one's the real deal. Anyway, I figure if my grandfather played maybe it's in my blood, maybe I should give it a shot."

So Lauren was using what she'd learned. The guitar was a way to reclaim lost history. "Your grandmother was musical too. She had a remarkable singing voice. Those music genes skipped me, but you seem to have inherited her talent. I'm sorry you never knew her."

"Well, I'm going to know her. Not everything I discovered today came in a bag." Lauren looked up with a triumphant grin.

Deena froze, gaping at her daughter. "Lauren, what do you mean? What have you done?"

"How hard do you think it is to find someone on the internet? Actually, I couldn't find Grandma, but Paz DaSilva came right up. I had his phone number in about two minutes. You could have called him anytime. He's right where you left him."

"Lauren, you had no right. I never thought you'd contact them."

"You were wondering what had become of everyone, so I found out. Mom, don't look so upset. I haven't called them yet."

Deena felt hot. Her cheeks were burning, and tears like molten lava overflowed her eyes. She wasn't red with anger, she was overcome with shame, shame and a paralyzing fear that a vengeful god or goddess was about to mete out whatever punishment twenty-first century deities reserved for unnatural daughters whose sins felt mythic and who had no way to escape.

"Oh, Mom, please don't cry. I promise, I won't call. Wait a minute; I'll get you a tissue." Lauren ran off to the bathroom while Deena stared out the window, making no effort to wipe away the tears running down her cheeks.

Lauren handed Deena a wad of balled up toilet paper. "Wow, I didn't think you'd have a meltdown. It's OK, nothing's happened. I just found Paz on the internet. Do you want to know what I found out?

"Paz still lives at New Moon?"

"He does. He's an architect now. Do you want to see his website?"

Deena blotted her face and wiped her nose. "Sure, I'd love to know what he's been doing all these years."

Lauren pulled out her cell phone and brought up a photo of an adobe mound emerging from the desert. A door, two large windows and a chimney made it resemble a hobbit house, but Deena recognized the basic shape of a hogan. Without anyone telling her, she knew that the door faced east to meet the rising sun, following Navajo tradition. In large letters at the top of the page were the words "DaSilva Sustainable Structures – Traditional Solutions for Twenty-First Century Living." *So Paz had become an architect with his own business, and he'd done it without ever leaving New Moon. How had he managed that?*

Lauren clicked off the phone. "Sustainable architecture sounds pretty cool."

"It does. He was always really smart. I wish I'd kept in touch with him."

Lauren leaned into her mother so their foreheads were nearly touching and whispered, "You know, it's not too late. I bet he'd love to talk with you. Maybe it's time to go back."

The past year had been like living through an earthquake that wouldn't stop. All the walls she'd built began to crumble, and every time a piece fell away, New Moon became more visible through the chinks, until she couldn't pretend not to see it anymore.

"Maybe, but not yet. I need to get my life together first." Deena felt a headache coming on and she was suddenly so tired that she could barely pull herself out of the chair. "Lauren, I need to lie down for a while. Don't bother waking me for supper."

"OK, and don't worry about the crows. I'll help Raisa with the seeds."

A loud, twangy tone rang from Lauren's phone. It faded out then chimed a second time. Deena listened as it sounded again. "What is that? What's that noise?"

"It's a tuning app. I'm going to rock this thing."

Deena looked at her blue-haired daughter sitting cross legged on the sofa with the guitar across her knees, and something inside her whispered, *New Moon rising.*

Chapter Fifteen

A white van that read *Charles Forrest Gallery* in an elegant calligraphic font pulled into their drive early the next morning. Deena had been expecting a burly guy with muscles, but it was Mr. Forrest's Jean of all trades who rang the bell. With remarkable speed and efficiency Jean wrapped and labeled each work of art, had Deena sign a contract and an itemized invoice, then carried everything out to the van.

She was gone before Raisa could dress and hobble downstairs to supervise the proceedings. "They're gone already? I wanted to show them a Russian tea set and Jeannette's Lladro collection."

"The Forrest Gallery doesn't deal in stuff like that. They're strictly fine arts. Maybe we could find an auction house to take those other things."

"Forget about it, just donate them to some charity. Is the gallery giving you money for those paintings?"

"Raisa, I told you, they're going to put them up for sale this spring. Assuming they sell, we get half the purchase price."

"Not we, you. It's all yours. I hired you to organize my stuff and get rid of it. If you can sell them, the money's yours."

Deena had been secretly counting on the money, but she didn't want to take advantage of Raisa, especially since she sometimes seemed a little foggy. "When you gave me the artwork, I don't think you realized it was valuable. Mr. Forrest hasn't put a dollar amount on the collection yet, but it might be worth a hundred thousand dollars. If you want them back I'll certainly understand. They're your paintings."

"I have enough money. I have too much money, too much everything. At my age, you want less not more. I have bankers, brokers, advisers, trust funds, annuities, the whole *megillah*. When I die my attorney will come from Los Angeles to see that I'm buried, that the house and furnishings are sold, and that my photographs are burned. In the end, whatever he doesn't steal and the government doesn't take will be doled out to charity. I'm just trying to tidy things up before I go, maybe save some of the old scripts and papers in case someone wants them."

"I'm sure someone will want them. They're an important historical archive. You helped shape American culture."

"Oh no, you're not blaming me for that mess." It was time for the crows' morning meal and they were beginning to congregate, cawing noisily outside the window. Raisa waved at them and raised a finger to let them know she'd be out in just a minute. "Can you set up an endowment to feed crows? I'd like to do that, seriously. I'm calling Barry, my guy in Los Angeles, and asking him." She walked over to the window and knocked on the glass. "Keep it down, I said I'd be out in a minute."

Deena could hear Martin's shock and disappointment over the phone. "That's quite a story. So basically, you're a hippy chick. You're telling me we lived together for twenty years and I never knew you at all."

"You knew me, you just didn't know everything. I want to start over with a clean slate, no secrets, no lies." Deena knew she was being optimistic. Martin would probably want to do his starting over with someone else.

"Honesty's a good place to start." Martin took a gulp of something. Deena could hear ice-cubes clinking in a glass. "I guess, if we're being honest, I'm no saint myself. I fell apart, just when you needed my support. Maybe I'm partly to blame for what happened. Which reminds me, your professor friend was just apprehended somewhere in Nevada. It made a nice little story in the Metro section of yesterday's *Plain Dealer*."

"Was I mentioned? Did they use my name?" She'd never be able to go home again if her name had made the papers.

"Nope, you got lucky. They just mentioned a Krystina somebody and Reno Cartridge. Reno Cartridge? Who comes up with a name like that? Deena could hear Martin chuckle, at least she thought he was laughing. "And I thought our big problem was being too dull and predictable. Wrong again, it turns out you're not boring."

"What I am is a coward. I want to go back to New Moon, but I still can't face my mother. I'm terrified that she won't even talk to me, or she'll say, 'Go back to your *normal* life and leave me alone.'"

"I probably don't get a vote, but I think you should go. Maybe you'd finally get your head screwed on straight. If you wait, who says she'll even be alive?"

"I'd like to see Paz again. He's an architect now. Why don't you go with me? I bet you'd like him and I could really use some moral support." *Please*, Deena was praying silently. *Please, go with me.*

"Sorry Sweetheart, you're going to have to take that journey by yourself."

Had he just called her Sweetheart? "The thought terrifies me, Martin. I still don't have the courage, but I think about it. I've changed a lot this past year."

"I'm not the same person either, but I'm still your friend, and I'm telling you, you need to go to Santa Fe."

Raisa was getting stronger and becoming more insistent that they move on from cleaning closets and emptying boxes to the main task of organizing her papers. The plan was to sort the scripts, memos, journals and diaries into binders with a cross-index that would allow researchers to locate material by name, date, or subject matter. Eventually, she'd scan everything into a computer and create an electronic archive in addition to the physical files. However, at the moment Deena didn't have so much as a three ring notebook or a set of colored markers, so she began by making a list of supplies.

Money was never an issue with Raisa. She'd glanced at Deena's list and simply handed her a credit card. "Get whatever you need. Let's get this show on the road."

"Are you sure? We won't need anything high end, but computers are expensive."

"Whatever you need. I don't know from computers, that's your department."

So Deena commandeered Lauren for a shopping trip, and they took off for one of the big box stores. It was fun filling her cart with everything she could possibly want without regard to cost. They stopped for frozen yogurt on the way home and returned in a celebratory mood. As they pulled into the drive Lauren pointed to a sheet of paper fluttering on Raisa's front door. Tradesmen frequently papered the neighborhood with circulars advertising new gutters or asphalt repair so neither of them thought much about it. They entered through the back door, showed off their purchases and were making plans for dinner when Lauren remembered the paper and went outside to bring it in. Deena was checking the cupboard for spaghetti sauce when Lauren returned, carrying a paper with a large target printed on it. RAT BITCH were printed in large black letters across the center of the bull's eye.

Lauren was shaking. "How did they find me? How could they know I'm here?"

Deena turned off the stove, snuck a furtive peek out the window in case someone was lurking in the bushes, then pulled out her phone and dialed 911.

Dispatch transferred her to a police officer who took down all the relevant information, but didn't offer much in the way of comfort. "So, no one actually saw this guy put the note on your door and you don't know his name. Yeah, I agree, it may well be someone associated with a Boston drug gang, but we can't pick him up without more to go on. Even if we caught the guy, the most he'd be guilty of at this point is trespassing, maybe a menacing charge. We'll contact Boston law enforcement, see if they're looking for anyone that matches your description. In the meantime, be careful. Off the record, this might be a good time to take a little vacation, get out of town for a while. You got people you could visit?"

Deena hung up the phone and turned to Lauren. "Pack up your things, we're leaving right now."

"I'll be ready in two minutes." Lauren disappeared up the stairs just as Raisa hobbled in from the living room.

"What's the commotion? Is everything alright?"

Deena looked at Raisa's small, determined body, her thick, owlish glasses and wrinkled face and her heart sank. What horror had she brought to this poor woman's door? Raisa had opened her home to two lost souls and this was the thanks she got. Deena put her hands on Raisa's shoulders. "We've just had a bit of a shock. The man who threatened Lauren in Boston, the man she's been hiding from, found her here. I just talked to the police and they think that we should leave, that it's too dangerous to stay here now."

"Is this true? We really have to leave?" Raisa, confused and dumbfounded, turned to Deena for guidance. "Where would we go?"

Deena tried to focus, but she was dazed herself, concussed by the sudden turn of events. She spoke slowly, aware of what her words would set in motion. "The police are right. We can't risk being here if that man comes back." Raisa blinked at Deena, too stunned to speak. Deena took her hand and led her to the couch. "Raisa, just sit tight while I gather up a few of your things. We'll be fine. We can spend the night at a hotel while we figure this out. My God, I can't believe this is happening."

As Deena hurried toward the stairs, Raisa called after her, "Don't forget the suitcase with my papers. I want those with me."

Within an incredibly short period of time, a matter of minutes, they were clambering into the car. The trunk was filled with whatever clothes they'd swept from their drawers, plus assorted coats, shoes, phones, chargers, Lauren's new guitar and Raisa's files. Lauren sat in the back while Raisa and Deena sat up front. Without any discussion, Deena drove toward the highway and turned onto Route 75 North, toward Tampa.

It was only seven thirty but twilight had already settled over the odd, foreign-looking fields dotted with spiky palmetto fronds, and live oaks draped with silver chains of Spanish moss. The seasons were changing and the days were getting shorter but the trees remained green and the air was hot and muggy. Back in Shaker Heights the leaves would be turning red along Horseshoe Lake, and there'd be a bracing chill in the air. She'd be washing up after supper, maybe settling down with a good book, not fleeing a homicidal maniac. As she drove through the foreign landscape into a future that felt alien and surreal, a familiar rumble in her stomach told her it was time for supper.

Deena broke the long silence that had descended on the car. "There's an exit coming up ahead with a bunch of fast food places. Let's stop for dinner and figure out a plan." She maneuvered into the exit lane and headed toward the bright lights that meant food, gas, rest rooms and a chance to catch their breath.

They all felt better after eating, but no one stood up to leave. Deena was dealing with the queasy realization that she was homeless again, but this time with her daughter and an old woman in her care. Lauren was the first to broach the obvious question. "So, where do we go now?"

"Raisa, this isn't fair, but you're the only one with money. Could you pay for a hotel? We could all share one room."

Deena was humiliated. They'd run the woman out of her own home and now they were asking her to pay for the trouble.

"My credit card is good anywhere; just find a hotel." Raisa had clearly had enough for one day.

Deena pointed out the window toward a Holiday Inn down the street. "Let's spend the night there, then decide where to go in the morning. I can't think straight at the moment."

Raisa had a sick headache and wanted to go to sleep as soon as they'd checked into the hotel. Deena helped her prepare for bed, turned off the light, then went downstairs to sit in the lobby with Lauren, who was happily distracted by a big screen TV.

Could they stay with Martin? *Don't be stupid,* she told herself. Even if he wanted to take them in, he lived in a small one bedroom apartment. Maybe they could rent a house or condo for a month, but where? It would have to be somewhere no one would ever think of looking, and it would have to be cheap, but it would also have to be safe, and comfortable enough for an elderly woman. The fried chicken she'd had for dinner was upsetting her stomach and her whole body ached. Maybe things would look better in the morning. Deena went back to her room and slipped into bed where she mentally drove from one city to another until Raisa's snoring finally lulled her into unconsciousness.

The smell of coffee, toast and maple syrup welcomed Deena as she entered the breakfast room just off the lobby. Although it was only a little after seven in the morning, the place was humming with hungry travelers piling their plates with mountains of complimentary eggs, bacon, and biscuits. There were pastries wrapped in cellophane, envelopes of instant oatmeal, a machine that made hot waffles and another that dispensed unlimited quantities of orange juice, milk and coffee. She peeked beneath two metal covers on the steam table and found grits and sausage gravy, proof they were still in the South. She helped Raisa into a chair at an empty table.

Although Raisa's leg was much better, she'd lost some of her confidence and continued to lean on Deena for assistance.

"What would you like? The waffles smell good." Deena was gathering up the paper plates and empty cups left by the previous occupants, while blotting up a small pool of milk with a dirty napkin.

"Just a cup of coffee, I'm not hungry." Raisa watched Deena clearing the table. "When did you become a waitress? I thought you worked for me."

"It's every woman for herself around here; they don't seem to have any servers." Deena tossed the trash into a bin. "Why don't you have some toast? You should put something in your stomach; this could be a long day."

"How long? I don't even know where we're going. This is very confusing for me."

"Oh Raisa, don't worry. I promise to look after you. We're just off on a little adventure, that's all. Deena squeezed Raisa's hand. "Let me get you some coffee, and then we'll talk. I have a wonderful idea for a trip."

"Who's going to feed my crows? I didn't even say good-bye to my birds."

"They'll be fine. Your crows can fend for themselves for a few days." *Would it be just a few days?* Deena had no idea how long they'd be hiding out. "For now, let me grab something for your breakfast before these vultures pick the buffet clean."

By the time Deena returned with two cups of coffee and a plate of English muffins, Lauren was sitting at the table wolfing down waffles swimming in artificial maple syrup. "Mom, what are you so happy about? You're grinning from ear to ear."

"Am I? I didn't know I was grinning, but I do have some good news."

"Did they arrest the guy who was threatening me? Can we go home?" Now Lauren was smiling.

"No, but I made a phone call early this morning. I talked

to Paz and he's invited us to stay with him at New Moon."

"That's fantastic! What did Paz say? What's he like?"

"He's wonderful. He said he'd always hoped I'd call one day. My mom's still there in the old house, but he's built a separate house for his family. He's married and has grown kids and a new grandbaby. He says I won't recognize the place."

"Did you talk to your mom?"

Deena shook her head. "No, not yet. That's not a conversation for the phone."

"Where are we going?" Raisa looked lost. She'd been searching for something in her purse and hadn't followed the conversation.

"Santa Fe." Deena and Lauren spoke simultaneously, grinning at one another.

"Why New Mexico? That's a long drive." Raisa appeared to have some reservations. She took a sip of coffee. "You'd better tell me about Santa Fe. All I know is Georgia O'Keefe painted flowers there."

Lauren had finished her waffles and was opening a small container of yoghurt. "I've never been there either, but Mom lived there as a kid. We're going to stay with her family."

Raisa was suddenly all attention. She gave Deena a quizzical look. "We're staying with your mother?"

"Yes," Deena took a bite of her muffin trying to sound nonchalant. "I called last night. They say they can't wait to see us."

"The mother you haven't seen since you were a little girl?" There was no fooling Raisa. She clearly understood what this meant to Deena.

"Yes, that mother." Deena stared back at Raisa.

Raisa, didn't miss a beat. "Good, let's go. I want to meet this woman."

"Santa Fe's supposed to be really beautiful. Come on, Mom. Tell us what it's like," Lauren begged.

"Oh my God," Deena began. "I can't believe this is happening." Then she sat down, took another sip of coffee then began resurrecting memories she'd suppressed for thirty years. She told them about the Sangre de Cristo Mountains and the winding roads with breathtaking views at every turn, the fiestas and the Indian Market, the old Spanish style buildings along the plaza, Mexican food and Indian art. By the time they were done with breakfast Deena's heart had softened, or maybe her backbone had stiffened. In any case, she gathered her things, got into the car, and allowed it to carry her, mile after mile, back to people and places she hadn't seen since childhood.

Without Raisa they might have made the 1700 mile trip in two grueling days, but as it was, it took four days to drive through Alabama, Mississippi, Louisiana and Texas before finally crossing the border into New Mexico. It was three in the afternoon and they still had another two hours ahead of them. Lauren was texting Paz to let him know they'd arrive in time for supper. She'd communicated with Paz every day of the trip, sometimes twice a day with updates on their progress, and he quizzed her on what they liked to eat, what toiletries they needed, and whether they'd brought enough warm clothes. Deena kept her eyes on the road while they talked, pretending she wasn't there. She'd watched the landscape change from palm trees, palmettos and parched grass to deciduous forests and lush green fields and now, over the past few hours, she'd watched the fields and forests give way to the high desert she remembered from her youth. Deena briefly closed her eyes, trying to quiet her heart that pounded faster and faster with each passing mile.

Lauren clicked off the phone. "They're so excited to see you, Mom. Paz keeps asking me questions. He'd really like to talk with you."

Deena opened her eyes and exhaled a cleansing breath, or maybe it was just a sigh. "I told you, I'll talk to everyone when we get there. This is a big deal for me. Why can't you understand that?"

"OK, sorry."

A few minutes later they exited the highway onto Route 3 and everyone became silent as they gazed at the endless plain rolling to the horizon, every bit of it glowing with small yellow shrubs that seemed to radiate their own light. In the distance, a majestic butte towered purple against a cloudless sky. Buttes and mesas, land formations that had been part of Deena's earliest conception of the earth, were foreign to Raisa and her daughter. Raisa kept muttering, "and I thought I'd seen everything," while Lauren murmured "wow" or "awesome" over and over again.

Deena had forgotten that chamisa bloomed in September. There was so much she'd forgotten, and even more she'd refused to remember. As the car began its ascent into the Sangre de Cristo Mountains, the temperature that had hovered around ninety degrees since they'd left Sarasota, began to drop. She rolled down her window and inhaled the woody, feral scent of the chamisa flowers carried by the breeze. Other odors rose up from the ground, the scent of dry grass and the mineral smell of sandstone and shale. Her vision blurred as she was overcome with homesickness for these rocks, these plants, this stretch of sky.

She imagined her mother, Paz, Casey and Buddha waiting just a few miles up the mountain. What would they look like after thirty years? Paz would be a middle-aged man. Her mother would be in her sixties. Buddha ... was ... gone. When they asked why she'd left and why she'd never called, what would she say? And what would they think of the mess she'd made of her life? If they gloated at her crawling back in defeat after all these years she would turn to sand and simply blow away.

But what would her mother say when Deena asked why she'd never come to Cleveland, why she hadn't fought to keep her daughter? Her mother had a lot of failings, but she wasn't a coward. So why, after those first hysterical phone calls, had she simply given up and disappeared? *Because she never gave a damn about me*, was what Deena had always told herself. She'd imagined her mother hanging up the phone after the last time they spoke, lighting a joint and going back to her pinch pots with a shrug. The teenage Deena had told herself, *I was right to leave, right to pretend that she was dead*; but the grown Deena, the Deena who was now a mother, wasn't sure. What had really happened? Deena rolled up the window, hoping that she'd know the answer before dinner.

Once they turned off Route 3 onto Rio Claro, Deena braced herself for a bumpy ride on an old dirt road pitted with ruts, but to her surprise, unbroken blacktop stretched ahead of them for miles. What else had changed in thirty years? The answer became evident as they passed large houses with land-scaped yards where Deena remembered open fields and small cabins surrounded by wild grass. She stared open mouthed at the modern, suburban houses the way Raisa and Lauren gaped at buttes and mesas. When she finally brought the car to a stop in front of a low adobe structure with solar panels on the roof, she had no idea where she was. A sheepdog ran to the car followed by a tall, thin man with a neatly trimmed beard and a small round woman with short, dark hair.

"Harmony!" The man swung the door open and extended his hand to help Deena from the car. She emerged hesitant and confused, blinded by the sun. The dog was sniffing her shoes and she bent down to pat its head. Nothing looked the same, not the friendly, over-exuberant man, not the house, not the buildings that had cropped up in the distance. Finally, her gaze fell on a walnut tree standing in front of a grove of pines that ran from the far side of the yard to the back of the house.

"That's where we built our tree houses, isn't it?"

"That's right. My kids built their tree houses there too, and I expect the grandkids will be building tree houses there before long, but how the hell are you? My God, it's been a long time."

"A very long time," Deena agreed, standing stiffly, her body hugging the side of the car. "In fact, I feel really awkward showing up like this after so many years. You really didn't need to do this."

"Of course we did. You're family."

"Oh, I think the statute of limitations must have run out on that a long time ago."

"There's no statute of limitations on family." Paz held out his arms and the next thing Deena knew she was wrapped in a giant bear hug and sobbing against his shoulder. When she finally managed to catch her breath and wipe her eyes she saw Lauren, Raisa, the small dark haired woman and the dog gathered around her in a protective circle.

"It's alright, I'm OK." She managed a little reassuring smile. "Does anyone have a tissue?"

"We have lots of tissues and good hot coffee in the house. Please, come inside. I'm sure you're all tired from such a long drive." The small woman was surprisingly forceful, herding the group toward the door.

"Where's my mom? I thought she'd be here."

"Your mom's at our house cooking dinner. She wasn't quite ready to see you yet. This is very emotional for her, having you come back."

"Yeah, for me too," Deena wiped her eyes on her sleeve. "Where is your house? Where do you two live?"

"We built just over there." Paz pointed to one of the buildings in the distance. It was an odd circular structure with a chimney sticking up from the center. Deena recognized it from the photo on Paz's website.

"It looks like a wigwam." Raisa squinted into the distance trying to get a better view.

"Not a wigwam," Paz corrected her. "It's a modern hogan, modeled after traditional Navajo structures that embody the sustainable building practices we're trying to relearn."

"I told you he's an architect who designs green houses. A lot of his houses are completely off the grid." Lauren was clearly awestruck.

"Greenhouses like for tomatoes?" Raisa was skeptical.

"No, a different kind of green house. We can talk about it later. Now, you should rest and have something to eat." The small woman led them into the house. "I baked sopaipillas with honey for you just like my mother used to make. Do you remember my mother's sopaipillas?"

"Your mother?" Deena looked around the living room, but couldn't get her bearings. The old house had been gutted and rebuilt into something utterly unfamiliar, only the smell of hot sugar and cinnamon brought back fond memories.

"You don't recognize me?" The woman's eyes twinkled mischievously. "I thought for sure you would say, 'Sophie you haven't changed a bit.'"

Paz put his arm around the woman and turned to Deena apologetically. "I'm sorry, I should have introduced you. Sophie's my wife. She was Sophie Rios when you lived here, but since she was only nine years old when you left you probably don't remember her. She's changed a good bit — and a good bit for the better don't you think? And this is Cooper." Paz stroked his dog along his muzzle. "He sort of runs things around here."

Sophie's smile was warm and welcoming. "Please sit down, all of you, and tell me how you like your coffee."

Once they'd been revived by caffeine and small fried pastries, Deena was full of questions. "The house looks fantastic, but I'd never recognize it. The place I remember was a mess; it wouldn't have qualified for an occupancy permit much less a spread in *Architectural Digest*. What happened?"

"A lot happened, but not all at once. Things just sort of evolved. We were all depressed and out of whack after Buddha died and you took off, but then my mom got a good job with the county and your mom started selling her pottery in trendy shops. I left for college, and Sophie turned into a beauty." Paz winked at his wife. "I don't know why, but after you left everything started to change; maybe losing you was the wakeup call we all needed."

"Now you sound like my husband." Deena gave him a wry smile. "But still, how did you create all this?" Deena's gesture encompassed everything, the room where they were sitting and the cluster of small houses visible through the window.

"Oh, I built most of this myself with grants from the University of New Mexico and the Mount Blanca Foundation. It's a demonstration project to teach best practices in sustainable architecture. Your mom let us use New Moon as a model for ways to retrofit existing houses. We get groups coming through here several times a month. I was the architect, but Sophie manages the project. I'd love to show you around."

"He'll talk your ears off. Let's get you settled for now and save the tour for tomorrow. I thought Lauren could stay with us in the hogan and Harmony and Mrs. Goetz could stay here at New Moon. How does that sound?"

"New Moon like *Rosh Chodesh*?" Raisa butted in. "That's a Jewish holiday. It's a nice name for a house."

"Really? It's a Jewish holiday?" Paz leaned forward with his mouth open slightly and his eyebrows raised. It was an expression Deena recognized. He really was Paz.

Deena nodded, "It's not a big holiday, but it's special for women, like an extra Sabbath where they get the day off. The sisterhood at our synagogue runs *Rosh Chodesh* programs with new agey stuff like Jewish chanting and yoga."

"Jewish yoga?" Paz looked amused.

"Yeah, it's a thing." Deena assured him.

Sophie stood up and began gathering empty cups and plates. "So, we're agreed, Deena and Raisa stay here and Lauren comes with me."

So far, New Moon had been a revelation. Deena had expected changes but not this utter transformation. The exterior of the frame house had been covered with adobe while the front window had grown into a glass wall that flooded the room with light. The old wood floors had been bleached and polished, and the fireplace had been refaced with sandstone that ran to the ceiling. The furniture was an assortment of brightly painted vintage pieces and creatively repurposed junk that somehow meshed beautifully with the large clay pots that had to be her mother's handiwork. A large Navajo rug tied everything together to create a space that was both comfortable and chic. Deena had never seen anything like it outside the covers of a magazine and yet there was nothing pretentious about any of it: quite the opposite, everything looked worn and used and utterly at home.

Once Sophie, Paz and Cooper had left with Lauren, and Raisa had settled down for a nap, Deena finally had a moment to herself. She wandered into the living room feeling awkward and embarrassed. For years she'd imagined her mother and Casey living marginal lives in an old dilapidated house. As her eyes swept over the room she noticed a group of framed photographs on the mantel, one was of herself at age seven sitting on a pony at the Indian Market and another of her eighth grade graduation. It seemed that part of her had never left.

"Knock, knock," Paz let himself and his dog in through the unlocked door. "I just came back to see if you needed anything."

"No, we're fine thank you."

"And to see if you had time to talk."

"I don't have a thing to do until dinner."

"OK then, have a seat. Can I get you a drink? I'm pretty sure your mom keeps beer in the fridge." There was nothing Paz said that put Deena on high alert; it had to be his tone.

"No thanks, how's Sophie managing all her guests?"

"My wife's a trooper, nothing fazes her. If a busload of refugees landed on our doorstep she'd make soup and put them all up for the night without batting an eyelash."

"I remember Sophie as a little girl with long black braids, and now she has three grown children. I feel like Rip Van Winkle waking up from a long nap."

"We have two boys and a girl. Our daughter gave us our first grandbaby last March." He took one of the framed photographs off the mantel and handed it to Deena. "This is the whole crew. They'll all be here tomorrow for Sunday supper. I hope you like Mexican."

"What a good looking family. Your mom must be ecstatic."

"She *was* ecstatic. That's what I came over to tell you. My mother died five years ago from pancreatic cancer. We all still miss her, especially your mom. At least she got to see the kids grow up."

Deena didn't say anything for a long time as she remembered Casey decorating their disaster of a house with mason jars of purple yarrow and yellow arnica. She'd been the gentle, quiet mother, the one more apt to kiss a bruised knee or prepare a hot meal. "She was a good soul. I'm sorry that I never got to tell her how much she meant to me. I was expecting to find her in the workshop with my mother. To be honest, I was expecting them to look pretty much the way they did when I left, maybe a couple wrinkles and a silver hair or two."

"Yeah, I know what you mean. I've always thought of you as a snotty teenager with her nose in a book. I should have guessed you'd become a librarian."

"Snotty? Is that how you remember me?" Deena winced. "How does my mother look? It's been so long I'm afraid I won't recognize her."

"She's OK now, but after you left she went into a bad depression. She just shut down and practically stopped talking. Sophie's mom came over almost every day and sat with her for hours.

"Then why didn't she write or call me on the phone?"

"What are you talking about?" Paz was indignant.

"No, what are *you* talking about? I'm telling you she never wrote or phoned."

"Are you kidding? She called every day for months, but you never answered. You wouldn't even pick up the phone. It broke her heart."

"That bitch!" Deena stood up suddenly, startling the dog lying at her feet. "That wasn't me; that was my grandmother. I never saw those letters and I wasn't allowed to touch the phone without permission — one of Bubbe's rules. She never told me anything."

"You could have written."

"No, I couldn't because ... I know this sounds weird, but I couldn't write to her because she was dead. We sat Shiva for her."

"What?"

"We sat Shiva for her. It's a Jewish ritual for when someone dies."

"I know what sitting Shiva means, I just can't believe you would do a thing like that. You have no idea how much you hurt her. First Buddha died then you ran off. She was devastated."

Tears pricked Deena's eyes. "I didn't know. I thought she didn't give a damn about me. I thought she never even called."

"Well, it seems you and your mom have a lot to talk about. They're expecting us at the hogan in twenty minutes. Are you going to be OK?"

Deena nodded yes, but in truth she wasn't sure.

Chapter Sixteen

Paz entered first, opening the door to a large well lit room. Deena followed, helping Raisa across the threshold, keeping her eyes down, concentrating all her energy on the old woman. She knew she'd eventually have to look up and face her mother, but fussing with Raisa, getting her seated, straightening her sweater and smoothing her hair, delayed the inevitable a few more seconds.

"Welcome home, Harmony." Deena immediately recognized the voice and looked up to see a small woman with short, gray hair wearing painter's overalls and a blue shirt. Despite the wrinkles and drooping eyelids creased with lines, there was no mistaking her mother, who was gaping at Raisa, transfixed by the old woman with a queer expression on her face. After a long, uncomfortable pause her mother said, "Mom?" It was a question, not a greeting.

"Oh no, no. This is a friend of mine." Deena rushed to correct the mistake. "This is Raisa Goetz. Bubbe died years ago."

Her mother turned away to fuss with something on the stove. "That's what I thought, but nobody told me anything, so I wasn't sure. Your friend looks a lot like Bubbe."

"Yeah, I've noticed that too." Deena stood stiffly beside Raisa's chair feeling awkward and embarrassed.

"Who do I look like? I bet she was good looking." Raisa

wasn't going to be talked about as though she were an inanimate object or someone not in command of her faculties.

"Oh, she was a beauty all right, a real charmer."

Deena winced at the sarcasm in her mother's voice. "Raisa, I'm sorry, I should have introduced you. This is my mother, Rain."

"It's Leah Marcus now. I haven't been Rain for a long time. How do you do." Leah Marcus lifted a wooden spoon from the pot and raised it in Raisa's direction as a sort of casual salute.

"Wow, everything's changed around here. Why did you go back to your old name?"

"Do you know what Leah means in Hebrew?"

Deena shook her head.

"It means weary. I went back to the name my mother gave me, Weary Marcus. What do you call yourself these days?"

"Deena."

"Deena? OK, so is that what we call you?"

"No, call me Harmony. I'd like to be Harmony again."

For the first time, both women smiled. They were shy, close-lipped smiles with just a hint of a crinkle around the eyes. A faint light became visible through the layers of dark ice.

"Well, Harmony, my granddaughter tells me you've had quite a journey. I bet you could use some supper."

"Absolutely. I'm famished, and whatever you have in those pots smells wonderful." Now that Deena was no longer staring at Raisa or the floor she able to look around and take in her surroundings. Like her mother's house, the hogan was sparsely furnished with colorful, eccentric furniture. She guessed that the same person, probably Sophie, had decorated both. But here, a large circular room was constructed around a central stove with a ventilation pipe that extended through the ceiling. The ceiling itself was constructed of exposed timbers radiating from the center, an homage to a traditional Navajo dwelling, despite the fact that this was clearly a modern home.

Lauren was standing at the stove stirring a large pot. She spooned a bit of thick stew into a cup. "Grandma, taste this and tell me if it's ready."

"What are you making? It smells wonderful." Deena inhaled the spices wafting from the pot.

"Casey's three bean chili. I make it every year when the nights start to get cold."

"I remember her chili. She always served it over hot cornbread. Did you make cornbread too?"

In response, her mother pulled a pan of golden cornbread from the oven and set it on the stove. "Lauren, there's a salad in the refrigerator. Put it on the table and let's sit down to eat."

Moments later three generations of Marcus women sat down at the same table and shared a meal for the first time in a generation.

In Santa Fe September days begin cool then climb into warm, sunny afternoons. Deena stretched and looked out the window. She must have slept in because the sun was already high in the branches of the old walnut tree. It was so odd, lying in bed and looking out at the same tree that had greeted her every morning of her childhood. A whole lifetime had passed, but the tree looked just the way Deena remembered it. It was one of the few things on the property that Paz hadn't transformed. It stood behind the house as green and eco-friendly as ever.

By the time Deena dressed and ventured into the living room, Lauren and Raisa were already in the yard listening to Paz give an animated lecture. Deena poured herself a cup of coffee and carried it outside to hear his talk on sustainable architecture.

"Take a look at the windows. They're all constructed of specially insulated glass and set at a 50 degree angle to receive the sun's rays in winter and deflect them away in the summer." Paz paused to smile at Deena and wave her over. "I'm sure Harmony remembers when this house was a leaky sieve like most traditional frame houses with single pane windows. We cut energy consumption in half by wrapping the house with straw bale insulation then adding an adobe skin. Of course, this house is a retrofit. It will never be as efficient as the new hogans we're building with a type of reflective fiberglass insulation that holds the heat from the sun during the day and radiates it back into the house at night. Hogan design naturally creates thermal mass, and when we combined that with reflective insulation and solar panels we virtually eliminated the need for fossil fuels. Now let's go back inside so I can show you how the waterless toilet works."

Deena sipped her coffee and grinned as they trooped back into the house to admire the toilet. Everyone was relaxed, talking, giggling and teasing one another like old friends. As the tension of the last few days disappeared from her throat and back and neck, Deena became aware of how much stress she'd been carrying and how good it felt to finally let it go.

"Where's my mother?" Deena asked Paz when the tour was over. "I haven't seen her this morning."

"Probably in her pottery shed, but I wouldn't go in there. She doesn't like to be disturbed when she's working, especially when she's getting ready for a big show. If you want company, Sophie's going to the farmers' market. You can catch her if you hurry."

Deena lowered her voice because Raisa and Lauren were still within earshot. "Thanks, but I don't want to leave Raisa alone. She's a trooper, but she must be completely disoriented. We've turned her whole life upside down."

"We'll keep an eye on Raisa for you. She'll be fine."

Deena looked over at Raisa who was sitting at the table doing a crossword puzzle. "Raisa, would you mind if I went into town with Sophie for a couple of hours?"

"Why should I mind? Go ahead, do what you want."

"OK, we're just going shopping. I promise to be back before lunch."

"Take your time. What's a six letter word meaning magpie?"

"Corvid," Paz responded without a moment's hesitation.

"Right," Raisa filled in the letters and looked up. "That reminds me, if you're shopping anyway, bring me a bag of sunflower seeds for the crows."

"What crows, Raisa? I haven't seen any crows around here."

"Trust me," Raisa was undeterred. "There are always crows."

Deena and Sophie returned from the market with baskets of peppers, squash, apples, onions, tomatillos, corn, cilantro, goat cheese and mozzarella. Deena surveyed the colorful produce overflowing onto the kitchen counter with dismay. There was no way the hogan's small kitchen could accommodate such bounty, but Sophie reassured her. "Don't worry, it will be gone by tomorrow night. I make a fiesta whenever my kids come and they eat like wild animals. Do you like to cook?"

"I used to, when I had my own kitchen. If you show me what to do, I'd be happy to help."

"Give me an hour to get organized and then we'll put you to work."

"OK, I want to check on Raisa anyway. She'll be happy to get her birdseed. When she's at home she feeds crows twice a day."

"Well, we have plenty of crows in Santa Fe and they're always hungry. Raisa can make a fiesta for the birds while we're cooking dinner for the human people."

Deena smiled, "I'll be back in an hour." She hurried to the house smiling at Sophie's use of the term, *human people*. Raisa would like that, with its implication that she, conversely, was feeding the bird people.

Deena found her mother, Raisa, and Lauren engrossed in a spirited game of Five Card Stud at the dining room table. Judging from the pile of unshelled almonds heaped up in front of Raisa, she was making a killing. Lauren picked a card, glanced at it without twitching a muscle, then threw two nuts into the pot.

Raisa took a card, grinned widely, then raised the stakes by throwing in three nuts.

Deena's mother regarded Raisa through squinty eyes, "You're bluffing. I'm not buying it this time. I'll see your three nuts and raise you two." She tossed five almonds into the center.

"I'm out." Lauren put her cards on the table then turned to her grandmother, "Be careful, Grandma, she's sneaky."

"Don't worry about me. I've dealt with some tough hombres in my time."

Raisa picked a final card and added six nuts to the pot. "What do you say to that?"

"I say, let's see what you've got." Deena's mother tossed in her last six nuts, then spread out her hand to reveal three queens and a pair of deuces. "A full house," she leaned back in her chair grinning broadly.

Raisa hesitated, dithering with her cards and rearranging them in her hand.

"Come on, show us what you've got," Lauren insisted.

Raisa fussed with her cards a few more moments before laying the ten, nine, eight, seven and six of diamonds on the table. "I think they call this a flush, is that right?" she asked disingenuously as she gathered in her winnings.

"Shit! You got me again." Deena's mother pretended to be miffed, but the grin hadn't faded from her face.

"Sorry, you're all busted for illegal gambling and I'm impounding your nuts as evidence." Deena walked over to the table and began sweeping everyone's nuts into one big pile. "Actually, Sophie needs these for a Mexican wedding cake.

It's a surprise for her kids."

"Well, I guess this is a day full of surprises. Guess who called me this morning?" Deena's mother looked at her with raised eyebrows, waiting for her daughter's response.

"I don't know. Who called?"

"My grandson. It seems that my grandson, whom I have never met, would like to come by and pay me a visit."

"Elliot?"

Her mother nodded. "He'll be flying in tomorrow morning, so tell Sophie to put down another plate."

"Elliot's coming here? Tomorrow? My God, I can't believe it. I haven't heard a word from him since the end of May."

Now Lauren was beaming. "He's got one week of leave between boot camp and his permanent posting, and he's going to spend it here with us. He wants to meet Grandma and see where you grew up. I can't believe you never told us about this place." Lauren snapped a rubber band around the deck of cards and stood up. "Can I help with the cooking?"

"Does he know I'm here? I mean, does he want to see me too?"

Lauren put her arm around Deena's waist and gave her a hug. "Of course he wants to see you. You're his mother."

Deena looked at her own mother who stared back, stoic and silent, before turning away to clear a handful of dirty cups from the table. Deena gave Lauren a peck on the cheek then followed her mother into the kitchen. "Mom?" Her mother was standing at the sink rinsing the cups and adding them to a stack of dirty breakfast dishes.

"What?" her mother didn't turn around.

"We haven't really talked yet and there's a lot to say. Do you have a minute?"

"I'll wash you dry. Towels are in the drawer under the breadbox." She waited while Deena found a clean towel and came to stand beside her at the sink. "So talk."

There was something surreal about finding herself back

at New Moon standing beside her mother, looking out at the same trees, the same distant mountains she remembered from her childhood. "I'm really sorry about Casey."

Her mother handed Deena a soapy plate without saying anything.

"I was hoping she'd be here because there were things I wanted to say to her. I wanted to tell her that she meant a lot to me, that I loved her." Her mother still didn't say anything so Deena went on. "When I left here I was just an angry kid. I thought New Moon was the worst place in the world and that you were all horrible people. I'm sorry, but that's the truth. I mean none of you were exactly normal, and for the longest time normal was the only thing I wanted, the only thing I dreamed about. I'd hear other kids complaining because they couldn't watch TV until their homework was finished and I'd think, 'You spoiled brats, you don't know how lucky you are. We don't even own a TV and my mom doesn't care if I've finished my homework or not.' Or they'd be bitching because their moms made them go to bed at ten o'clock on school nights and I'd be thinking, 'I have two moms and neither one knows where I am half the time.'"

"We always knew where you were."

"Trust me, you didn't."

"Well, we wanted you to grow up free and independent, to make your own decisions, choose your own life the way we did. So, I guess we got what we wanted. Although we always figured you'd want to stay in touch, call on Mother's Day, send a birthday card or something." She turned and looked Deena in the eye. "Have you ever heard of someone being sick with grief? Well, I was sick with grief for a long time after you left."

Her mother's hair was gray and her cheeks were pleated with deep wrinkles from years in the desert. Deena studied her, wiping her own eyes with the damp dish towel. This was too painful. She wanted to stuff the towel in her mouth to stifle the sob that was rising in her throat. "I'm sorry."

"Yeah, well I'm sorry too. If Casey and Buddha were here, they'd be sorry. We'd be one sorry bunch of bananas."

When she could talk again, Deena said, "I've been thinking about what happened, trying to get some perspective. Maybe we just weren't a good match. You and Casey were free spirits, artistic types like Lauren. I'm more like Bubbe. I wanted everything that you were trying to escape."

Her mother handed Deena a plate. "So, how'd that work out for you?"

"Please Mom, I'm trying to be honest. When I left, it was probably just normal teenage angst and rebellion. I was upset about Buddha and maybe I wanted your attention. I'd have probably been home in a month if Bubbe hadn't convinced me that New Moon was Sodom and Gomorrah, that I'd end up like Buddha if I went back. You and Casey smoked a little weed, but she thought you were dangerous addicts and I was so angry and confused that I sort of believed her. She offered me everything I'd ever dreamed about, security and comfort, college and a room of my own as long as I stayed in Cleveland and lived by her rules."

"Yeah, she made me the same deal, but I said no."

"Well I didn't. It wasn't your fault, but Buddha's dying scared me. Besides, I wanted all the stuff that Bubbe offered. At fourteen I'd have sold my soul for a color TV and a pair of Doc Martens."

"You let your soul go cheap. It was worth a whole lot more than that. So tell me, if your grandmother was so holy, why didn't she teach you to honor your mother? I believe that's still one of the top ten."

"Mom, Bubbe wasn't evil, she was just judgmental and inflexible. Raisa says some survivors reject God, others become religious fanatics. Bubbe became a fanatic. In her mind, she sacrificed her only daughter because she thought that's what God wanted her to do."

"Bullshit!" A saucer went flying and crashed against the

kitchen wall. Deena swiveled toward the door, afraid the noise would bring the others running, but no one came. They must have gone outside.

"Anyway, once she finally realized you were never coming home, she just gave up. She pretended you were dead and we sat Shiva for you. She grieved, and put your things away. She wouldn't even let me say your name."

"How could she stop you? You were fourteen when you left, but then you were fifteen, then thirty then forty. Don't tell me she wouldn't let you say my name. Don't tell me that she wouldn't let you call. If you're so intent on being honest, how about admitting that you didn't want a lesbian for a mother? Casey and I embarrassed you. You were just like Bubbe, ashamed of the people who loved you most."

"No, that's not true. That's not it. I loved you and Casey. I loved you both."

"Well, that's a news flash. Too bad Casey never got the memo. She died thinking she was the reason that you left."

"Oh my God, no. That wasn't it, I just..." Deena saw her mother staring at her, arms crossed, eyebrows raised in disbelief, and she couldn't finish the sentence. "You're right. I should have called, especially after Bubbe died, but by that time I sort of believed the lies we'd told. It was easier to just keep on living the story we'd invented. It was a shitty thing to do and now I know it, and I'm saying that I'm sorry. I'm begging your forgiveness."

"Thirty years, Harmony, thirty years. You graduated from high school, then college, you got married, you had two children, my grandchildren, and I missed all of it. No one even had the decency to call me when my mother died."

Deena collapsed into one of the ladder back chairs and put her head on the table. When she looked up her cheeks were streaked with tears. "I was just a kid when I left. You were the adult. Why didn't you come and get me? Why didn't you storm into the house and force me to come home? That's what

I would do if Lauren left. That's what mothers do. Maybe I never called because I figured that you didn't give a damn about me." Deena's could feel her neck and cheeks flush with emotion. She sat terrified, waiting for her mother's reply.

Leah had begun sweeping up the broken dish, but she paused to stare at Deena. "Hold on there, Missy. First, I wrote and I called for months, but my letters all came back unopened, marked refused. Second, you said you hated me, that you didn't want anything to do with me or with New Moon. You said we were freaks. Do you remember that?"

"I was fourteen years old."

"Whatever, it hurt like hell, but I wanted you to have the life you wanted because I did love you. I didn't want to be like Bubbe and force my daughter to live a life she hated. Call me stupid, but I honestly thought you'd be grateful, that you'd wake up one morning and say, 'Gee, thanks Mom, you're the greatest. I really appreciate the way you let me be my own person and make my own choices.'" She tipped the dustpan into the trash. "Instead, you disappeared for thirty years."

"Maybe you should have been more like Bubbe. Your mother fought for you. She fought for years to bring you back to Cleveland."

Leah slammed the lid down on the trash can and faced her daughter. "She didn't want *me* back in Cleveland. She wanted some Kosher daughter she could take shopping and show off at the synagogue. She would never have let me live my life or accepted me for who I am. Do you see Casey sitting at her table? Do you see her letting us share a bed?" Leah pounded her chest percussively as she enumerated her mother's sins. "She didn't love *me.* She didn't accept *me.* She couldn't even see *me.*"

"I'm sorry, Mom. I'm really sorry."

"And she got exactly what she wanted. She got you, the good Jewish daughter of her dreams." Leah turned back to the sink and turned the water on full blast. The sound of the water couldn't conceal the fact that she was crying.

Deena went to her mother wanting to touch her. Her hands hovered above her mother's shoulders like birds afraid to land. "We've caused each other a lot of pain, but I'm back now."

Her mother turned off the faucet and turned toward Deena wiping her soapy hands on her overalls. "Are you? For how long? Just how long are you planning to stay?"

"I don't know, but I promise I won't disappear again. I see you and I know who you are and I want you back in my life. Will you take me back? Can I be your daughter again?"

Leah reached out and brushed a stray lock of hair off Deena's forehead. "You know, we're still not normal."

"I know. No one's normal, we just are who we are."

"You've got that straight. OK, Harmony, welcome home."

Chapter Seventeen

A cacophony of noisy crows woke Deena the next morning. It didn't matter. She was too excited to sleep anyway. Elliot would be arriving in just a few hours. She got out of bed to take a closer look and found the trees full of hopping, nodding, flitting, preening crows. There had to be hundreds of birds weighing down the branches of the trees and pecking at the ground. Deena pulled on a pair of jeans and a T-shirt and went to see if Raisa was awake. She found the small woman, dressed in her customary black pants and cardigan, already standing outside shouting at the trees.

"Do you think I'm made of seeds? Do I look like a sunflower? How am I supposed to feed all of you?" As Deena approached, she smiled and pointed at the crows. "They must have seen me coming." Deena noticed a burlap bag at Raisa's feet. Apparently the birds had already gone through half the sack.

Deena scanned the trees and surrounding fields. The entire landscape was alive with crows. "Raisa, you can't feed all those birds."

"Well, I can't send them home hungry. Buy four more bags. Charge them to my account."

Deena's mother poked her head out the side door. "Come on in. The girls are making pancakes. Those birds are something, aren't they?"

"Yeah, they sure are. Is this normal?" Deena had her arm around Raisa's shoulders, helping her back inside.

"No, those are some odd birds," her mother answered. "They usually don't gather like that until November."

Deena helped Raisa to the table, then sat down beside her. Lauren slid two pancakes, hot from the griddle, onto Deena's plate and two more onto Raisa's. "Go ahead and eat. We're already finished."

Deena put a bite of pancake on her fork, stared at it a moment then put it down. "This looks great but my stomach's all butterflies about seeing Elliot again."

Raisa dug into her breakfast with the appetite of someone half her age and twice her size. "Your sweet daughter helped me feed the crows this morning." Raisa informed Deena between bites. "I couldn't carry those big bags by myself."

"It is strange having them roost right behind the house like that and so early in the season." Leah was standing at the sink looking out at the crows as she spoke. "I wonder what brought them here this early in September."

"They probably came to see me. Crows follow me around." Raisa took a sip of coffee, beaming at the human people perched around the kitchen. The ladies met each other's eyes with amused, indulgent grins, but no one said a word to contradict her.

Lauren was the first to spot Elliot as they drove through the arrivals lane at the airport. She started waving and pointing and directing Paz to pull over to the curb in front of baggage claims where a tall, clean-shaven young man was sitting on a duffle bag and talking on his phone. Paz hadn't even brought the car to a complete stop when Lauren threw open her door and made a wild dash toward her brother. As soon as he saw her, Elliot stood up and braced himself for a collision as Lauren threw herself into his arms.

He gave her a brotherly peck on the cheek and picked up

his duffle bag while still talking on the phone. "You should see this, your daughter has blue hair. Yeah, she looks like a Smurf. Seriously, it's sky blue. Hey, Smurfette, Dad wants to say hello." He handed the phone to Lauren then turned to Deena who was standing quietly by the curb. How odd to feel shy in front of your own son, but he'd been so angry when he'd left, and then the months of silence. But it only took two steps for him to reach her, two seconds spent trembling like a stray cat hoping to be fed, before he bent over and kissed her on the cheek. "Hi Mom, how've you been?"

"Fine, I'm fine," she said as she wrapped her arms around her son. "Have you grown another inch? I'd swear you're taller than when you left."

"No, but I've gained a couple pounds. Everyone told me I'd lose weight at boot camp, but I put on five pounds."

He looked wonderful. If he'd gained weight it was all muscle. Deena looked up at him brimming with pride and relief. "Well I'm glad they fed you. How bad was it? I've always heard boot camp is brutal."

"Let's just say it's challenging, but I learned a lot. I'm not sorry I did it."

Paz popped the trunk, Elliot threw his bag inside, and they started back to New Moon. Paz looked at Elliot through his rear view mirror. "Hello, young man. I'm Paz, an old friend of your mother's."

"Thanks for picking me up. Lauren told me about you. You're the architect."

"I am, and I have two sons a little older than you and a married daughter. They'll all be visiting tonight. Everyone wants to meet you. My wife's planning quite a fiesta. I hope you packed a big appetite in that bag."

"Oh, I never go anywhere without it." Elliot sounded happy and relaxed.

Paz, for his part, was ebullient. "It'll be quite something having everyone together, an historic occasion. You know your mother and I grew up together."

"That's what I hear." There was the faintest hint of sarcasm
in his voice. Deena blanched, afraid he'd berate her for all the
years she'd kept this world a secret, but he didn't say another
word.

As they pulled onto the highway Paz asked, "Have you ever
been out this way? Do you know this part of the country?"

"I've never been to Santa Fe, but I was camping in Arizona
just this spring."

"You're going to love it. It's the Wild West out here. I bet
you didn't know your mother was a cowgirl." He turned to
Deena who was sitting beside him in the passenger seat. "Do
you remember when Yazi showed up with that herd of sheep
and he thought we should all become shepherds?"

"Yes, oh my God," Deena started to giggle. "Only everyone
at New Moon was vegetarian and we wound up making them
all into pets, an entire herd of smelly sheep."

The rest of the ride was filled with stories and laughter. By
the time they arrived back at New Moon, everyone was in the
mood for a fiesta.

Cars began arriving just before sunset. Deena stood watching the parade through New Moon's large front window. First,
an old Volvo parked in front of the hogan and Deena saw Sophie race out to greet a young couple with a baby. Next a
white car drove up with two good looking young men, and
then a red car arrived with an elderly couple and a young
woman wearing a traditional Mexican costume with a wide,
flouncy skirt.

Sophie had instructed Deena to come over as soon as she
was ready, but Deena hesitated, momentarily overcome by her
old shyness. She wanted another minute by herself to reflect
on the miracle of being reunited with her family, and to steel
herself against all the noise and commotion of a party. There
was only one person she wanted to talk to at that moment.

She pulled out her phone and dialed Martin's number.

"Hi, I just wanted to thank you for buying Elliot's ticket. He told me it was your graduation gift for completing boot camp."

"How does he look? He sounded great when I talked to him earlier."

Martin sounded pretty great himself. Deena wondered how he looked after all these months. "I'll ask Paz to take some photos so you can see for yourself. He's changed, Martin; he's not a kid anymore. It happened so fast. He's beautiful. Both our kids are beautiful. They turned out better than we could have hoped."

"You're right. Raising those kids was one thing we didn't mess up. Is Elliot behaving himself? I told him to get off his high horse and start treating you with more respect."

"He's been perfect. Thank you for that, Martin. I can't tell you how emotional the last few days have been, but in a good way. There's something magical about being here with my mother and both my children. It feels right, like everything fits together. My mother looks a little like Bubbe now that her hair's turned gray. Her partner, Casey, died a few years ago and I think that aged her. It's really painful to lose your lover."

"I know." Neither of them said anything, but Deena could hear Martin breathing. There was something so intimate, so comforting, in her husband's regular intake and release of breath. If she closed her eyes she could almost imagine she was lying beside him in their old bed.

"Are you figuring things out? Do you know what you want yet?" Deena was whispering although there was no one else in the room."

"Maybe, but you'll laugh if I tell you."

"Tell me."

"Bicycles. Ever since my trip to Italy, bicycles are the only things that interest me."

He was right, Deena wanted to laugh, but a joyful laugh, not a laugh of scorn or derision. "Seriously, bicycles? Well, I guess we're all returning to our childhoods. You were a serious biker back in college when I met you."

"I should have stuck with it. Where did I get the idea that grownups don't ride bikes? That was so wrong. I've met geezers, I mean really old people, who are serious bikers. It keeps them alive."

"Well, live your dream. There's nothing stopping you. I'm glad you found something you love."

"I wish I could do it full time. If I didn't have to push pills for a living, I'd make bikes my life."

"Are you thinking Tour de France?"

"No, I was thinking more along the lines of a small bike shop."

"Well then, for heaven's sake, what's stopping you? It's not like you want to play pro football or become an astronaut. There's no reason you can't open a bike shop."

"Really? For one, opening a bike shop takes money, not a fortune but a lot more than I've got at the moment. Don't get me wrong, there's nothing wrong with being a pharmacist. I'm lucky to have a good job, but you asked me what I wanted. That's the dream."

"Martin, listen to me." Deena knew just what she wanted to say. "It's possible that I might come into a small windfall this spring. It probably won't be enough to open a bike shop, but whatever it is, I'll split it with you. You gave me all our savings, so it's the least I can do. I owe you that much."

"Seriously? What did you do, buy a lottery ticket?"

"No, the woman I work for gave me some paintings and told me to do whatever I wanted with them, so I took them to a gallery in Sarasota and it turns out they're valuable. The gallery's going to feature them in a show this spring. If they sell, they might bring a nice little bundle."

"That would be sweet, but I'm still working. You're going

to need that money to get back on your feet. Anyway, who knows if they'll even sell. A bike shop's just a fantasy."

"Well, I want your dreams to come true. Being back here with my mom and the kids feels like my dream at the moment, so I'm not kidding: if those paintings bring some money, half of it's yours." Deena looked back out the window. Cars were piling up beside the hogan and the sun was just a red line on the horizon. "It's getting late and I've got a fiesta to attend, but it was good talking with you and thanks for making things right between me and Elliot. You're a wonderful man."

"Enjoy the party. Give Elliot and the Smurf a kiss from their Dad."

"Will do. Good-night, Martin." Deena hesitated a moment then added, "I love you."

In response Martin paused, sighed deeply, and finally said, "I know."

Sophie had outdone herself even though the party included only immediate family, the fugitives from Sarasota and a handful of neighbors. The girls had strung paper lanterns around the outdoor patio and picked wild flowers to decorate the tables. Deena wished she'd packed a skirt or a dressy blouse, but since no one had imagined attending a fiesta when they'd fled the house on Harbor Drive, a red T-shirt with dark jeans and fresh lipstick was the best that she could do.

The big surprise was the trio of musicians setting up in front of the greywater recycling tank that had been artfully camouflaged beneath a pair of colorful serapes. People were milling about, filling their glasses and sampling the salsa and guacamole before Deena arrived; but the party didn't really start rolling until the elderly couple dressed as rancheros pulled out a guitar and a trumpet and their granddaughter began to sing.

There were enough tables and chairs for everyone, but no one sat down. Everyone wanted to dance and everyone

danced with everyone. Handsome *muchachos* danced with
pretty young *señoritas*. A middle aged woman danced with her
mother. Old men danced with their wives, sons danced with
their fathers and women danced with each other. A grandmother danced with grandchildren she'd only just met. Babies
were danced to sleep, and one old woman, swaying to the music in a young man's arms, smiled beatifically at all assembled.

"Leah, get up there and show them what you've got." Paz
had been dancing with Deena's mother, but now he was nudg-
ing her toward the musicians. "Go ahead, do 'Bobby McGee.'
No one sings it like you do."

"No, I don't think so. You're thinking of someone named
Rain. She used to sing a little, but not me, not anymore."

"Come on, Grandma. Mom told me you could sing. I want
to hear you sing." Lauren had gotten into the act, trying to
coax her grandmother toward the makeshift stage.

Someone, maybe Mr. Rios, called out, "Sing it, Rain."

Another voice demanded, "Yeah, let's hear it, Rain."

"It's been too long, I'm not sure I even remember the
words. I haven't sung in front of anyone in years."

A chant went up, "Rain, Rain, Rain."

"Come on, everyone knows 'Bobby McGee.' I'll sing it with
you. Is that a deal?" Lauren took her grandmother's hand
and led her to where the rancheros were playing. The vocal-
ist stepped aside and, even before Lauren could ask if they
knew the song, they'd broken into the intro. Lauren and her
grandmother came in right on cue, wrapped their arms around
each other's waists and sang their hearts out. They sang about
freedom being another word for having nothing left to lose,
and about how having nothing made you free. At the turn,
they faced each other and Lauren began to harmonize and
sing backup as though they'd been singing together all their
lives. Having nothing was freedom and freedom felt great and
that, they agreed, was good enough for them — for them and
Bobby McGee. Rain looked thirty years younger, as though all

the weariness had finally fallen from her shoulders. The audience applauded, whistled and stamped their approval while Deena's heart expanded with a joy she'd long forgotten.

Hours later, when the babies had been put to bed and the young people had withdrawn to whisper and flirt in the shadows, a faint crescent moon smiled benignly at the dispersing guests, the last star blinked on, and the Milky Way spread a protective canopy over the Sangre de Cristo Mountains. Empty bottles floated in tubs of melted ice, a trumpet settled back into the blue velvet lining of its case. Headlight beams flashed on in the yard, then turned to illuminate the road back home.

Deena helped Sophie and Paz carry bowls and platters and heaps of dirty dishes back to the kitchen. Something inside her hummed as she juggled the dirty crockery and wiped down the tables. She carried a last load into the kitchen and dumped it on the counter beside Sophie who was standing at the sink. "That was a wonderful party. I can't remember the last time I danced like that."

"You were really moving and your mother was amazing. It was a beautiful thing, seeing her singing again. We've missed the old Rain. I should thank you for coming and giving us an excuse for a party. I bet you didn't know Paz could dance." She performed a sassy little hip swaying move and Paz responded by grabbing her around the waist and executing a rather professional inside turn. Sophie pulled away, swatting him with a dish towel. "That's enough, now. Get back to work. Dance with the dishes." To Deena she said, "He had two left feet when we first danced, but he was a fast learner."

"I was a natural. All I needed was the right woman to teach me the moves." He and Sophie exchanged a look so sweet and intimate that Deena turned away. She was happy that Paz had made a good life for himself, and he'd done it right here at New Moon. For the first time since she was fourteen years old, Deena wondered why she'd ever left.

Chapter Eighteen

A week passed without any indication they'd outstayed their welcome. Apparently, despite all the changes at New Moon, the old open door policy was still in effect. It was remarkable being with her children and old friends, telling jokes and sharing stories. Deena knew she couldn't stay at New Moon forever, but there was nowhere else she wanted to be and nowhere else she had to go, so she continued drinking Margaritas, watching sunsets in the desert and waiting for a sign.

Lauren, for her part, had no plans to leave. She spent hours sitting on the front steps plucking her guitar, practicing the chords her grandmother taught her and singing softly to herself. She was clearly smitten with the place and maybe a little smitten with Carlo, Paz's oldest son. According to Carlo the university in Albuquerque was remarkably affordable if she'd just establish residency. He'd even offered to show her around and help her with the paperwork. Deena wasn't surprised when she found Lauren browsing *Craigslist Santa Fe* on her laptop.

Someone had resurrected an ancient cowboy hat and stuck it on Raisa's head to protect her from the sun and she refused to take it off. Whenever Deena looked out the back window she'd see Raisa, a diminutive figure in a large hat, talking to the crows roosting in the tall pines.

Most young sailors would have spent their last precious

days on leave sleeping late and partying 'til dawn, but not Elliot. He was fascinated by the engineering that took New Moon off the grid and spent hours with Paz studying sustainable construction and helping to install solar panels on a new community building. In a few days he'd be at the Navy's Great Lakes School in Illinois, training to be a cryptographic technician, whatever that was. It sounded like something with computers and secret codes and Deena was consoled by the image of her son sitting in a lab designing software or soldering wires somewhere safe and far from danger. If that wasn't right, she didn't want to know.

Paz had added a daily run to the hardware store for sunflower seeds to his morning chores, so it was still early when he delivered a burlap sack to Raisa on her second Friday at New Moon. The ladies were in the kitchen deciding whether to drive up to Bandelier to see the ancient cliff dwellings or into town for the arts festival. Their time at New Moon had been like a vacation. Deena felt younger and more energetic than she had in years. The future was still a mystery, but it now seemed alive with possibilities.

"Oh good, you're back. The crows were beginning to complain about the service around here." Deena teased Paz as he joined them in the kitchen.

He helped himself to half a bagel. "Do you want the seeds in back of the house or in the garage?"

Raisa immediately pushed herself up from her chair. "Take the bag out back. I'm sure the birds appreciate you driving into town to buy them breakfast."

"Well, you tell the crows it was my pleasure, but I won't be able to join them this morning. I have to get back to my office."

"Lauren, will you help me scatter the seeds?" Raisa reached out for Lauren's hand.

"I'll go too." Deena took Raisa's other hand.

"Me too." Elliot surprised Deena by joining them. He

wasn't usually interested in the crows.

The little group proceeded out the door and around to the back where scores of crows continued to roost in the high pines. It was a fine day, cloudless and sunny with just a hint of autumn in the air. Elliot opened the bag and scattered a handful of seeds on the ground. By the time he'd emptied half the bag a small river of seeds snaked beneath the trees. Within minutes a flock of hungry birds was hopping about, squawking, squabbling and putting on quite an amusing show for their human audience.

The moment was sweet, too sweet to last. Deena felt her skin go cold and the fine hairs on the back of her arms stand up. She intuited disaster before her eyes or ears knew what was happening. Maybe she'd glimpsed a shadow at the corner of her vision. Maybe she'd heard a subliminal footstep, a cracked twig. Maybe she'd smelled something feral, something foul, coming from an unseen source. Her rational mind tried to imagine away the danger, to reassure itself that Paz had returned or that Sophie was stopping by, but logic and reason failed her. The man who followed the shadow into their yard was short and stocky. He was wearing a black leather vest over a white T-shirt. Swastikas were tattooed on his arms and a constellation of dots were tattooed beneath one eye. He wasn't a big guy, but the gun he pointed at them looked enormous. They all saw him at the same moment and simultaneously drew in their breath. For a moment the silence was so absolute that even the birds seemed to stop quarreling and tilt their heads to listen. There was a click as the man cocked the hammer and swung the gun toward Lauren.

"NO!" Raisa let out a scream that shattered the daylight, echoed off the mountains and reverberated through the trees. In that same instant a hundred crows took flight, blacking out the sun and blinding Deena with an eclipse of black feathers as a gunshot rang through New Moon. Deena put her arms over her head and hunkered against the ground in terror.

A moment passed and then another and another, but there were no more shots, just the fluttering and cawing of birds winging off toward the Sangre de Cristo Mountains to the west. As the birds dispersed and Deena's wits returned, she lifted her head and opened her eyes, frightened that she might see Lauren or one of the others bleeding, wounded or worse. The first thing she saw was Raisa in her black cardigan standing frozen in the spot where she'd been standing when the shot was fired, her arms still raised in alarm. Gradually, she lowered them like a bird folding its wings, then her head pivoted and her mouth gaped open. Deena followed her gaze to where Elliot lay sprawled, face down on the grass. Her heart stopped and she doubled over, nearly passing out until her eyes focused and she saw that her son was lying on top of the intruder, pinning him to the ground. Deena watched, astounded, as her mother picked up the pistol that lay on the ground just beyond the gunman's reach. She moved quickly, without a moment's hesitation. *Had her mother ever touched a gun before?* Her mother leveled the revolver at the man's head without saying a word as Elliot stood up, pulled the guy to his feet and took the gun from his grandmother.

"Harmony, we need some rope." Her mother kept her eyes focused on the man as she spoke. "There's a roll of clothes line in the garage above the trash cans. Go get it and call 911."

Deena ran to the garage where she found Lauren crouched on the floor talking on her phone. "Lauren, call 911."

Lauren clicked off the phone and put it in her pocket. "The police are on their way. Is he still here?" She was visibly shaken; even her hair looked a paler shade of blue.

"Your brother has him. I'm getting rope so they can tie him up, but don't move. Stay right where you are." Deena grabbed the rope and ran back to where Elliot and her mother were waiting. She watched in awe as Elliot secured his prisoner. Had Elliot learned to tie knots like that in Eagle Scouts or boot camp?

Deena put her arm around Raisa who was shell shocked and trembling. "You saved us," Deena crooned into her ear, "you and your crows. Everyone's alright."

It was a relief when four patrol cars with sirens wailing pulled up in front of New Moon. Moments later she and Raisa, safely inside the house, watched as two officers led the tattooed man, his hands cuffed behind his back, out to a patrol car and drove away.

"This is too much excitement for an old lady. I'm going to lie down." Raisa excused herself and hobbled down the hall toward the bedroom.

Lauren peered tentatively into the living room. "Is he gone? Did the police take him away?"

Deena nodded. "Yes, thank God, he's gone. Are you alright?"

"I'm not injured, but I'm not exactly alright. I've never been so scared in my life."

"How did he find us? How could he have known we were here?" Deena slumped into a chair, her knees too wobbly to support her weight.

Elliot walked in behind a policeman with graying hair and deep bags under a pair of tired eyes. Elliot was saying, "We learned how to disarm a shooter in basic training, but you don't expect to practice that maneuver at your grandma's house."

"You'll make a good soldier. You probably saved these people's lives." The policeman patted Elliot on the shoulder. "Now, anybody else want to tell me what happened?"

Lauren looked wary. "I'd rather not tell you. I think this all started because I talked to the police."

"Either you make a statement now or we'll take you in for questioning — unless you don't want to press charges. We could just let him go." He raised his eyebrows. "Your decision."

Lauren's eyes darted to Elliot who nodded at her, encouraging her to tell her story. She sat on the sofa beside Deena and took her hand. "It started when I moved into this vacant house in Boston..."

The officer took detailed notes as she told her story. When she finished, he closed his notebook and said, "You're one lucky lady. Those guys don't mess around."

Lauren, pale and chastened, was still holding Deena's hand. "What I can't figure out is how he found us here. No one could have tipped him off. None of my friends know this place exists."

"Do you have a smart phone?"

"Sure," Lauren answered.

"Well, that's how he found you. I'll bet any money there's tracker software on that phone. It's a kind of spyware. We see it all the time."

"He always knew where I was?"

"Probably, at least he always knew where your phone was. Those things use GPS and they're very accurate. It's a lot harder to hide than it used to be."

"My God, we drove halfway across the country for nothing. He knew where we were the whole time."

The policeman was looking at Lauren and shaking his head. "Get a new phone and stay away from creeps. This could have been ugly. Eight years ago I got called out on a situation like this, only there was no young hero around that day. Believe me, you never want to walk into a thing like that. Eighteen years and I still have nightmares."

Sophie walked in without knocking. "What's happening? I saw the police cars and came right over." Everyone started talking at once, retelling the story and thanking God that Elliot had been there to save them.

"Martin, we're all fine, and you can thank Elliot for that. He was amazing. We were all terrified, screaming and running in circles. There were crows flying everywhere. It was chaos, but Elliot stayed focused and took the guy down. That boy is a miracle. I don't know where he gets that kind of courage. I'm in awe of him. It's the truth; I'm in awe of my own son."

"*Your* own son? Maybe he gets it from me. He's my son too." Martin was beaming; Deena could hear it in his voice.

"It's weird, but I just realized that if you hadn't paid for Elliot's trip down here a lot of people might have died. It's strange how things work out. Do you believe in fate?"

"Not really, but it sure feels like someone finally cut us a break. The last couple of years have been nothing but unintended consequences, one after another."

"Yeah, I never expected to be back at New Moon, but here I am."

"How's that working out for you?"

"It's wonderful. I've spent my whole life running away from this place, and it turns out that it's probably where I belong. We all love it here. Lauren wants to enroll at the university in Albuquerque, and I'm going to look for a job at a bookstore. This feels like home."

"That's great, I'd really like to see Lauren back in school. Tell her I'll help with her tuition."

"If she establishes residency she won't need much help. I'll be living at New Moon rent free, plus I'll be working so money shouldn't be a problem. We're going to be OK."

"Yes, I think we are. Would your mother mind if I stopped by for a couple days before Elliot goes back to Illinois? I don't want to intrude, but I was taking some time off for Rosh Hashanah anyway, and well, I want to see my kids. The thought that I almost lost all of you..." Martin's voice trailed off.

"Of course you can visit, but you'll have to come right away if you want to see Elliot. He's leaving on Thursday."

"Expect me sometime tomorrow. I'll send my flight information as soon as I've got a reservation."

"OK, see you tomorrow then. I think you'll love this place,

Martin. I think you'll absolutely fall in love."

The next morning Deena and Lauren were doing yoga together while they waited for Martin to arrive. They stretched
out on the lawn behind the house while Leah and Raisa were
inside baking apple cakes with honey. That night a new moon
would signal the beginning of Rosh Hashanah, the first day
of the Jewish new year. All the New Mooners, despite their
varying religious persuasions, would share a holiday meal of
challah, matzo ball soup, chili rellenos , enchiladas, sopaipillas, apple cake and honey. They'd ask one another for forgiveness, ask God to inscribe their names in The Book of Life, and
cast crusts of bread carrying their sins into the Santa Fe River.

Lauren recited the *Modeh Ani*, the morning blessing, as
she and Deena flowed through the sun salutation followed by
seven *asanas* to free the flow of energy through their bodies.
They recited the *Shema* in Hebrew and sang *Oseh Shalom*, a
Jewish prayer for peace, and ended by chanting the *Sat Nam*
mantra.

Deena was stiffer than she'd been when she left Cleveland and she couldn't hold the poses very long, but she felt
more grounded, more present, than she had in Heidi's studio.
Maybe it was because they were outside on the warm grass
behind her mother's house where crows were cawing in the
trees, or maybe it was because her daughter sat beside her
and no secrets stood between them. Maybe it was because
she was Harmony again, the weight of Deena lifted from her
shoulders.

The sun warmed her face and electrified her hair. Every
atom of her being felt alive as she sat in a modified lotus position intoning *Saaaaat Naaaam, Saaaat Naaaam*. It was the
way Heidi had always concluded their yoga sessions. As she
continued to chant she could hear Heidi's voice in her inner
ear, *Sat means truth and Nam means name. When we chant Sat
Nam we are saying, I know your true name. I recognize the di-*

vinity within you. Know your true name. Recognize the divinity within you.

Saaaat Naaam, Saaaat Naaaam, Saaaat, Naaaam. Harmony's third eye popped open and stared agape with wonder, even as her two physical eyes remained closed, and she continued chanting *Saaat Naaam, Saaat Naaaam, Oseh Shalom, Oseh Shalom* beside her daughter.

- The End -

The Author

Patricia Averbach, a Cleveland native, is the former director of the Chautauqua Writers' Center in Chautauqua, New York. Her first novel, *Painting Bridges* (Bottom Dog Press, 2013) was described by Michelle Ross, critic for the *Cleveland Plain Dealer*, as an intelligent, introspective and moving novel. Her poetry chapbook, *Missing Persons* (Ward Wood Publishing, 2013) received the London based Lumen/Camden prize in 2013. It was listed by *Times of London Literary Supplement* (November 14, 2014) as one of the best short collections of the year.

Previous work includes a memoir about her very early career as Anzia Yezierska's sixteen year old literary assistant
and an article about the Jewish community in a virtual world
called *Second Life*. Her work has appeared in *Lilith Magazine,*
Margie, The Muse, and *The Blue Angel Review.*